Barbara Vine is the pen-name of Ruth Rendell, the bestselling crime novelist. She has written many novels, including *The Lake of Darkness*, *The Killing Doll*, *The Tree of Hands*, *Live Flesh*, *Heartstones*, *The Veiled One* and *Harm Done*. As Barbara Vine she is the author of *A Dark-Adapted Eye*, which received huge critical acclaim and won the Mystery Writers of America's Edgar Allan Poe Award; *A Fatal Inversion*, winner of the 1987 Crime Writers' Association Gold Dagger Award; *The House of Stairs*, winner of the Angel Award for Fiction; *Gallowglass*; *King Solomon's Carpet*, winner of the 1991 Crime Writers' Association Gold Dagger Award; *Asta's Book*, shortlisted for the 1993 *Sunday Express* Book of the Year Award; *The Brimstone Wedding*; *The Chimney Sweeper's Boy*; *Grasshopper*; and *The Blood Doctor*. All of these titles are published by Penguin. *Gallowglass*, *A Dark-Adapted Eye* and *A Fatal Inversion* have all been the basis of successful BBC television series.

Ruth Rendell is a Fellow of the Royal Society of Literature. In 1991 she was awarded the Crime Writers' Association Diamond Dagger for a lifetime's achievement in crime writing. In 1997 she was created a life peer and took the title Baroness Rendell of Babergh.

BARBARA VINE

The Blood Doctor

PENGUIN BOOKS

PENGUIN BOOKS

Published by the Penguin Group
Penguin Books Ltd, 80 Strand, London WC2R ORL, England
Penguin Putnam Inc., 375 Hudson Street, New York, New York 10014, USA
Penguin Books Australia Ltd, 250 Camberwell Road,
Camberwell, Victoria 3124, Australia
Penguin Books Canada Ltd, 10 Alcorn Avenue, Toronto, Ontario, Canada M4V 3B2
Penguin Books India (P) Ltd, 11 Community Centre,
Panchsheel Park, New Delhi – 110 017, India
Penguin Books (NZ) Ltd, Cnr Rosedale and Airborne Roads,
Albany, Auckland, New Zealand
Penguin Books (South Africa) (Pty) Ltd, 24 Sturdee Avenue,
Rosebank 2196, South Africa

Penguin Books Ltd, Registered Offices: 80 Strand, London WC2R ORL, England

www.penguin.com

First published by Viking 2002
Published in Penguin Books 2003

1

Copyright © Kingsmarkham Enterprises Ltd, 2002
All rights reserved

The moral right of the author has been asserted

Set in 10.5/12.5 pt Monotype Bembo
Typeset by Rowland Phototypesetting Ltd,
Bury St Edmunds, Suffolk
Printed in England by Clays Ltd, St Ives plc

Except in the United States of America, this book is sold subject
to the condition that it shall not, by way of trade or otherwise, be lent,
re-sold, hired out, or otherwise circulated without the publisher's
prior consent in any form of binding or cover other than that in
which it is published and without a similar condition including this
condition being imposed on the subsequent purchaser

To Richard and Patricia, Lord and Lady Acton,
with love and gratitude

Henderson Family Tree

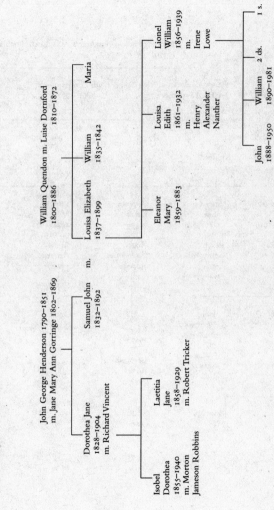

Nanther Family Tree

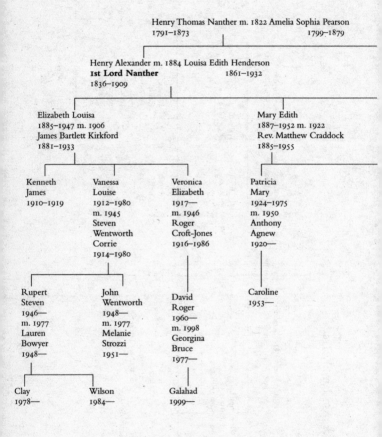

Henry Thomas Nanther m. 1822 Amelia Sophia Pearson
1791–1873   1799–1879

Henry Alexander m. 1884 Louisa Edith Henderson
1st Lord Nanther   1861–1932
1836–1909

Elizabeth Louisa   Mary Edith
1885–1947 m. 1906   1887–1952 m. 1922
James Bartlett Kirkford   Rev. Matthew Craddock
1881–1933   1885–1955

Kenneth   Vanessa   Veronica   Patricia
James   Louise   Elizabeth   Mary
1910–1919   1912–1980   1917–   1924–1975
               m. 1945   m. 1946   m. 1950
               Steven   Roger   Anthony
               Wentworth   Croft-Jones   Agnew
               Corrie   1916–1986   1920–
               1914–1980

Rupert   John   David   Caroline
Steven   Wentworth   Roger   1953–
1946–   1948–   1960–
m. 1977   m. 1977   m. 1998
Lauren   Melanie   Georgina
Bowyer   Strozzi   Bruce
1948–   1951–   1977–

Clay   Wilson   Galahad
1978–   1984–   1999–

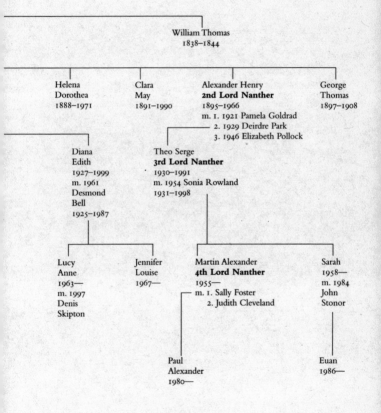

William Thomas
1838–1844

Helena
Dorothea
1888–1971

Clara
May
1891–1990

Alexander Henry
2nd Lord Nanther
1895–1966
m. 1. 1921 Pamela Goldrad
2. 1929 Deirdre Park
3. 1946 Elizabeth Pollock

George
Thomas
1897–1908

Diana
Edith
1927–1999
m. 1961
Desmond
Bell
1925–1987

Theo Serge
3rd Lord Nanther
1930–1991
m. 1954 Sonia Rowland
1931–1998

Lucy
Anne
1963—
m. 1997
Denis
Skipton

Jennifer
Louise
1967—

Martin Alexander
4th Lord Nanther
1955—
m. 1. Sally Foster
2. Judith Cleveland

Sarah
1958—
m. 1984
John
Stonor

Paul
Alexander
1980—

Euan
1986—

Blood is going to be its theme. I've made that decision long before I shall even begin writing the book. Blood in its metaphysical sense as the conductor of an inherited title, and blood as the transmitter of hereditary disease. Genes we'd say now, but not in the nineteenth century when Henry Nanther was born and grew up and achieved a kind of greatness, not then. It was blood then. Good blood, bad blood, blue blood, it's in the blood, in cold blood, blood and thunder, blood thicker than water, blood money, blood relations, flesh and blood, written in blood – the list of phrases is endless. How many of them am I going to find apply to my great-grandfather?

I'm not sure if I'd have liked him, and up till now it's been essential for me to like, or at least admire and respect, the subject of the biographies I write. Perhaps, this time, it's only going to be necessary for me to be interested in him. And that won't be difficult. It's only because I found out that he'd kept a mistress for nine years and, when his fiancée died, married her sister (giving her, incidentally, the same engagement ring) that I decided to write his life at all.

Of course I knew, we all knew, he'd been an eminent medical man, the acknowledged expert of his day on diseases of the blood and Physician-in-Ordinary to Queen Victoria. I knew that for his services Victoria had given him the peerage I've inherited, and that he took his seat in the House of Lords in 1896. I knew he'd had six children, one of whom was my father's father, and died in 1909. But although he was distinguished in his day, an acquaintance of Darwin and mentioned as a friend in letters from, among others, T. H. Huxley and Sir Joseph Bazalgette, although he was the first doctor of medicine ever to receive a peerage – the great surgeon Joseph Lister got one a year later – as a biography candidate I was only keeping him in the back of my mind. In the front of my mind I had Lorenzo da Ponte, Mozart's librettist. Now there was an interesting history: unfrocked priest, political dissident, philanderer, store-keeper, distiller and professor of music at Columbia University. I could have got trips to Italy out of it and maybe Vienna, but reluctantly I had to give him up. I don't have enough musical knowledge. Then the letter came from my sister.

Our mother died last year. Sarah has had the job – it's always the women who get it, says my wife – of sorting out and disposing of or keeping her personal possessions. Among them was a letter from our great-aunt Clara to our grand-father. Sarah thought it would interest me. She even wrote, 'If you've given up the Marriage of Figaro man, why not Great-grandfather?' I've never seen any of Clara's letters before – why would I? – but I've a feeling she wrote a lot. My mother probably once had Sarah's task of sorting through her father-in-law's possessions when he came home from Venice to die, found the letter and simply neglected to throw it away.

It makes me feel a bit uneasy, disquieted and at the same time slightly excited, to notice the way Clara, his fourth and youngest daughter, refers to her father not as 'Father' or 'Dad' or 'Papa' but as 'Henry Nanther'. Odd, isn't it? Here is this maiden lady, to use my own father's expression for her, half-educated, who lived a quiet life in London, who never worked for her living and died at the age of ninety-nine, writing to her brother of their father as if he were some acquaintance she didn't much like. Her letter is dated early in 1966 and must have been sent to Venice. This is what she said:

You always speak of Henry Nanther as if he were some sort of pillar of society and high morality and all that sort of thing. In contrast to you, as you put it. I know you disliked him as much as the rest of us did with the exception of poor George. You will say that if he was a more or less absent father and a remote rather awful figure in the household, that was normal when we were children. But did you know he kept a mistress in a house in Primrose Hill for years and years? I am sure you did not know he was *engaged* to Mother's sister Eleanor, who was killed in the train. We had all heard the story of the train, but neither Mother nor Henry Nanther ever said he was engaged to her first, and then took up with Mother when she was dead. They kept *that* dark for reasons of their own, or reasons of *his* own. Henry Nanther did other monstrous, quite appalling things, but I don't feel like telling you about them in a letter. If you are interested you can ask me when you come home in August and we will have a good long talk. But, dear old Alex, you may not like what you hear . . .

Did they ever have that talk and did my grandfather learn what the monstrous things were? If he did he either didn't pass them on to my father or my father didn't pass them on to me. Before he could come home, he was dead. He died in June. But that letter was what fixed me. Sarah was right. I've been amassing Henry Nanther memorabilia ever since. Fortunately, he obviously wanted his 'life' to be written, and left behind him all the diaries, letters and works of his own he calculated would furnish suitable material. It's apparent, though, that he took care it included nothing that

3

might show him in any light but that which shines on paragons. And of course there's not a sheet of paper, a photograph or a diary note among the lot to give a clue as to what Clara meant.

No one is at home but me. The house is empty, as it always is on weekdays at this time. Jude is at the publishing house in Fulham where she works and Lorraine, who cleans for us, left an hour ago. I am sitting in my study in Alma Square, working at what used to be our dining table: a large heavy mahogany affair, six feet long by three feet six wide, its surface marred by greyish blotches and black rings where Jude and I have put down hot plates, under the mistaken impression that the other one had put down the felt underlay before laying the table. Like most people we know, we have given up dinner parties, so I have 'commandeered' (Lorraine's word) the dining table and brought it in here.

Desks are never big enough. Desks are for chief executives in offices who have secretaries. On the dining table, as well as the computer and printer, are: the *Shorter Oxford Dictionary* and *Roget's Thesaurus*, a stack of (fairly useless) printouts from medical Web sites on the Internet, several mountain ranges of photocopied extracts from medical books, medical books themselves, Bulloch and Fildes' *A Treasury of Human Inheritance*, Henry's notebook, three box files of his correspondence, three books from the London Library, which, incidentally, I see are due back today, and a rather sketchy family tree, created by me and full of gaps. My own line, which begins with my grandfather Alexander and ends, for the time being, with my son Paul, is there in accurate detail. My grandfather's small brother George, who died aged eleven, is there, and so are his four sisters, Elizabeth, Mary, Helena and Clara, but I don't yet know the names of

4

husbands, children and no doubt grandchildren, and I must hunt for them in the records.

As well as all this are the fifty-two leather-bound diaries, in various colours, designs and sizes, Henry kept from his twenty-first year until a year before his death, his own books, photograph albums and some loose photographs. Letters about him and letters which mention him are on the table too.

He was obsessed with blood. Why? He wrote books about it but he wrote private memoranda too; curious essays that, presumably, no one else ever read in his lifetime. These are contained in a notebook with a cover of black watered silk. One of them – I have it here, it's the top one in the red box file but like all of them, undated – starts:

I have often asked myself why it should be red and I have asked others. Among the answers given to me has been, 'Because God made it so.' If I had never seen it but knew of its existence, its presence and function in the human body, I would have expected it to be brown, a light yellowish-brown. But it is red, the pure scarlet of the poppies that grow in the cornfields and which I remember from my boyhood. One of my children asked me, as children will, what might be my favourite colour. I had no hesitation in replying to her: red. I cannot recollect that I paused to cogitate, to give any consideration to the matter, though I had never previously thought about it. The word 'red' sprang naturally to my lips and, as I uttered it, I knew I was speaking perfect truth. Red is my favourite colour. No one knows why blood is red, although its composition is of course known and pigment of this colour is present in it. To me a splash of blood is beautiful and I profoundly lack understanding of those who flinch or even faint at the sight of it.

Not in any way incriminating, though, is it?

A royal doctor who happened to be given a barony would hardly be a suitable subject for a biography unless he was otherwise interesting. He made one important discovery in his own field and thus contributed to the sum of medical knowledge, but he seems to have cured no one; I doubt if he even alleviated pain *or would have wished to do so*. Is that where the interest lies? Perhaps, rather, what fascinates is not only this obsession with blood but the mysteries and anomalies the biographer comes upon in every decade of Henry Nanther's life.

I make myself a cheese sandwich and eat a tomato with it. If I intend to have a look at the house in Hamilton Terrace and call in at the London Library on my way, I haven't much time. The House sits at 2.30 and I remember as I'm finishing my sandwich that I have the third starred question to ask.

This house that Jude and I live in, though far from an ancestral home, was my father's and my grandfather's but never Henry's. His was a huge stucco mansion on the other side of Abbey Road, next door but two or three to the much prettier house of Joseph Bazalgette who built London's drains and river embankments and not far from Lawrence Alma Tadema's studio. It's a mild pleasant sort of day, though so early in the year. I come down into Hamilton Terrace by way of Circus Road and pause on the other side of the street to take a look at Ainsworth House, the name he gave it. Having at one time been divided into flats, it has returned to its single owner-occupier status, the owner-occupier being a multi-millionaire property developer called Barry Dreadnought. Since buying it for three million, he has had the front garden paved with two square boxes

6

inserted as flowerbeds and two enormous white urns each containing one of those spiky red palms. A covered way with plain glass sides and a stained-glass peaked roof runs from the gates to the front door.

I have never been inside. I wrote to Dreadnought last year asking if I could have a look at the room I calculate was Henry's study but he didn't answer, even though my letter was written on House of Lords paper. Will we still be able to use the headed paper after they've abolished us? I suppose not. I've never thought of that before and it slightly depresses me. If they won't let us keep club rights and computers they're certainly not going to let us have our paper.

The two sash windows on the second floor on the left indicate Henry's study. Or so I've guessed. There's something about the house – there was long before Dreadnought came – that troubles me, something unpleasant, I don't know what it is. Of course it's ugly, the worst kind of Victorian, but it's not that which makes me uneasy. I suppose it's that I sense there was suffering and misery within those walls while Henry and his family inhabited it, though I've no real reason to think there was, only a suspicion. As far as I know, Henry was happily married and, in spite of what Clara says, a good father by Victorian standards. I suppose I'm seeking inspiration when I come here to look at Ainsworth House, as I do every so often. Seeking perhaps answers to questions I, as Henry's biographer, ought to be able to answer but can't yet. Just the same, I wouldn't live in that house for all its owner's cash.

A woman stares at me out of Henry's study window. It's the dark unhappy face of one of those domestic slaves who look after other people's children and send money home for the care of their own. But no, I'm imagining that. Why should she be any different from Lorraine? The millionaire shouldn't be condemned out of hand just because he didn't answer my letter.

I take the Jubilee Line from St John's Wood and get off at Green Park, which isn't far from St James's Square where the London Library is. The rest of the way is on foot, through the park and over the bridge, and though I've walked this way a thousand times, I always stop for a second on the bridge to look at the view of Whitehall and Horse Guards and the Foreign Office: water and trees and majestic buildings, and the pelicans on their island. At this time of the year the great influx of tourists hasn't yet begun. It's an ordinary walk to the Palace of Westminster, not a battle through dawdling crowds with cameras as it sometimes is. Outside the Peers' Entrance, Richard Coeur de Lion sits on his horse, his sword arm and sword upraised. I always give him a glance and wonder what it was like to go on a crusade, when the rabble of peasant soldiers of Christ thought it quite permissible, indeed praiseworthy, to kill infidel women and their babies and roast them for dinner. The doorkeeper says, 'Good morning, my Lord,' though it is twenty-five past two, but, as peers should know when they've been here five minutes, it's morning in the House of Lords until prayers have been said.

I hang my raincoat on the peg that says 'Lord Nanther', which is next door but two to the Duke of Norfolk's, go up the staircase to the Principal Floor and in the Printed Paper Office I pick up an order paper, and there is my starred question: 'What, in the opinion of Her Majesty's Government, is the likelihood of the Jubilee Line extension being completed in time to offer public access to the Millennium Dome by 1 January 2000?'

Not being fond of bishops, I stay out of the Chamber

until after prayers. It's always a bishop that says them – there are twenty-four in here and two archbishops, and each does a week-long stint – but these days few of them use the fluting tone associated with the High Church of my father's youth. I go into the Chamber as part of the great influx from the Peers' Lobby and take my usual seat in the third row from the front of the cross-benches on the spiritual side. Not strictly the cross-benches at all, they are in the middle, parallel to the clerks' table and the throne, but an extension of the government area behind their bit of the front bench where the privy counsellors sit. Lord Callaghan and Lord Healey are often seated there but not today. My grandfather sat on the cross-benches on the rare occasions he attended, describing himself as independent and Bohemian. My father and Henry were staunchly right-wing, both of them diehard Conservatives.

When I first entered this chamber at the age of eleven and sat on the steps of the throne as my father's heir (the Hon. Martin Nanther) I thought the place very ugly, its Gothic ridiculous, its colours crude, especially the king-fisher-blue carpet and blood-red leather benches. The gilding of the throne, almost too dazzling to look at, reminded me of a stage set in the Aladdin pantomime I'd seen at Christmas. Thirty-five years ago Gothic was still unfashionable, taken for granted as being in bad taste. I was particularly scornful of the stained-glass windows, uncompromisingly red, green, blue and yellow. But I was still young enough to like the carved figures of lion and unicorn which serve as finials on the posts at the bar. Now I feel differently, if I don't quite go along with whoever it was the other day that described the Palace of Westminster as the most beautiful building in London. It *is* beautiful and I shall miss it when I'm gone. I shall miss giving the unicorn a pat on his polished head when I pass through the gate in the brass barrier we call 'the bar', bow in the general direction of the throne and the Cloth of Estate (non-existent, spiritual, a space only, marking the position which the Queen, if present, would occupy) and make my way up the steps to my place. The Chamber is full, for today is the first day of the second reading of the House of Lords Bill. First reading is, of course, a mere formality, so the second reading is very important and feelings will run high. Quite a lot of hereditary peers acknowledge that their day is done, that a man or woman – there are a few women hereditaries – should not have a right to make the country's laws just because an ancestor helped the king in war or an ancestress slept with him. It's not this which most of them will dispute, but the uncertainty surrounding what kind of a House will come after them, the brutal talk about 'getting rid of them' and the loss of their privileges to eat and drink and smoke in the House and use its library – in other words, their club rights.

But questions first. There's one about Railtrack and one about nuclear weapons and then comes mine. The Clerk of the Parliaments gets up and says, 'The Lord Nanther,' and I say, 'My Lords, I beg leave to ask the question standing in my name on the order paper,' but I don't ask it because it's printed for all to read on the Orders of the Day.

The minister says there's no question but that the Jubilee Line will be completed. I'm obliged to ask a supplementary question and this is something that makes a lot of peers sweat, lest the minister pre-empts them and they're left with an enquiry that's already been answered. Also you may write down your possible supplementaries as a mnemonic but not read them aloud. When I first came in, I got into a muddle over this and Conservatives began chanting, 'Reading, reading!' I resolved never to ask another starred question but of course I did, and then another, and now it doesn't worry me much. Very soon it won't worry me at all but by then I shall have been banished.

I get up and ask if the minister is aware that almost the only access to the Millennium Dome will be by tube and bus, and if the opening of the Jubilee Line is delayed attempts will be made to reach the Dome by car, an awkward situation since there is virtually no car parking provided. But I abstain from savagery because, although I don't take their whip, I'm sympathetic to the Government and almost always vote with them. The minister (an urbane man, shaken by nothing) repeats his earlier reply and adds that the tube will be finished and serving Greenwich North station not just by 31 December but by October. Now it's open to the rest of the House to ask questions and peers do so, diverging wildly of course from the subject and belabouring the minister with queries as to why the Northern Line is so bad and getting worse, whether the Dome is to be a permanent or temporary structure and when is the Government going to do something about restricting the number of cars in the capital? Every starred question and its supplementaries gets seven and a half minutes to ensure we're done in half an hour, so we soon pass on to the last one which is about e-mail.

The public gallery is full today, so are the press seats and the places below the bar where peers' guests sit on the temporal side and their spouses sit on the spiritual side, so-called because the bishops sit there as well as the Government. Reforming the House of Lords is a hot potato, as the *Sunday Times* said yesterday. I drift off into thoughts about Henry. He was in this House as a Conservative, but it seems he put in few appearances. He made a maiden speech on the subject, appropriately enough, of the contribution of good drainage to health, and seldom spoke in here again. Too busy with his blood quest, no doubt. The armorial bearings, produced for him by the College of Arms, show (I'm not getting the heraldic terms right) castellated turrets in two quarterings, red hearts in two, the motto *Deus et Ego* or God and I, which Jude says is very bad Latin.

Questions are over and the Government chief whip is on his feet telling the House that while the debate today and tomorrow is not time-limited it would be best for everyone if back benchers restricted the time they spoke to seven minutes in view of the long list of speakers. Reasonable and fair man as he is, he repeats that he can only offer guidance, but he points out that it would be in everyone's interests if speeches were not unduly extended into the small hours.

'The time at which the House adjourns tonight and tomorrow night,' he says, 'is entirely in your Lordships' hands.'

Earl Ferrers, who looks everyone's idea of a general commanding an army, gets up and asks why the chief whip is always asking for restraint. Some noble lords are going to be restrained for the rest of their lives so why should they be restrained on the Bill that is perforce to restrain them?

And so it has begun. Lady Jay, the Lord Privy Seal, opens it with the words, 'My Lords, I beg to move that this Bill be now read a second time,' and one after another, from all benches, they put their cases. Peers come and go, leaving quickly and entering slowly, always pausing to give a court bow to the Cloth of Estate. I go out for tea when the debate adjourns, and when I come back again it is a quarter past five and Baroness Young is saying from the Conservative benches that this is one of the saddest days of her political life. The Bill, she says, means the end of the House of Lords and the end of hundreds of years of history. It won't lead to a chamber with democratic legitimacy, for life peers are just as undemocratic as hereditary peers.

She goes on for a long time in this gloomy way and when she's finished I'd like to get up and say that if there's no democracy in this House, and there can't be in her view since it's composed exclusively of lifers and hereditaries, the best solution would be to abolish it altogether and we'll all go home. But I can't speak since I haven't put my name down on the list. When I look round again I see that Jude has come into the Chamber and taken her place below the bar. She's had her hair done and is wearing a very elegant black trouser suit. It's only a couple of years since women started wearing trousers in here and an even shorter time since the wives of peers did. Trousers are not a good idea on overweight women but, come to that, they're not a good idea on overweight men, only they don't have a choice about it. I smile at Jude and she raises her eyebrows and smiles at me and I mouth, 'Dinner?' and she mouths, 'Yes.'

Lord Trefgarne is speaking now, pointing out, very much to the dismay of those who haven't counted, that nearly two hundred lords have their names down to speak in the two days' debate. He says that he has no intention of confining his speech to seven minutes and goes on to ask if the Government realize what a tough battle they have to face. It is six o'clock. I get up and leave, pausing to let Jude precede me out of the Chamber and into the Peers' Lobby. We head for the Peers' Guest Room and a drink.

'It's not as if you won't all keep your titles,' says Jude, over her large glass of Chardonnay. 'You'll still be called "my Lord" or "your Grace" or whatever and your heirs will still inherit.' I'm touched by Jude's attempt to reassure, especially as this comes from the woman who is known as Lady Nanther and 'my Lady' only in here, and otherwise spurns her title and insists on being known as Judith Cleveland. 'I can't see what all the fuss is about. Half of them never come in here.'

I ask her what she thinks Henry would have said about it. She takes a keen interest in Henry and likes discussing him, even though Paxton Osborne, where she's a senior editor, won't be publishing the *Life*.

'They've tried to reform the House of Lords before, haven't they?' she asks. 'I mean, in the nineteenth century and again in 1911? He wouldn't have been surprised at the idea.'

'He died in nineteen-oh-nine,' I say. 'He came in here very little but he valued the peerage. Isn't that why he was so desperate for an heir? All those girls born, one after another, four of them before the son finally came.'

The shadow I've sworn I'll never provoke again passes across her face and I want to bite my tongue or cover up my mouth. But I've done it again and now it's too late. She doesn't say anything about it, she seldom does these days, she doesn't need to because the pain is there in the tiny wince and the attempt at a smile. It's only about five seconds before she's talking again, telling me of a letter about Henry she's come across in the biography of a musician they've just had come in. She's even brought me a photocopy of it and as I take it from her I feel a thrill of excitement go through me. It's just possible I'm going to begin discovering some of the thoughts that went through Henry's head.

2

The letter from the musician's mother has joined the others in Correspondence One on the table. 'One' because it was written when Henry was still fairly young and practising at St Bartholomew's Hospital. The mother had taken her son, who was to grow up a world-renowned violinist, to Henry expecting a diagnosis of haemophilia on the grounds of his frequent nosebleeds. Here she is writing jubilantly to her cousin of the result of the consultation:

Dr Nanther is a most charming, courteous and *very handsome* man. He had little to say to Caleb, no doubt understanding that a child of seven, however talented, is without judgement or self-knowledge, but was very gracious to me. In the course of our conversation I told him, as I was bound to do, though with great fear in my heart, of my husband's uncle who had the *Bluterkrankheit* or what we would call Haemophilia and died from a haemorrhage at the age of fifteen. Imagine my joy, dearest Christina, when Dr Nanther, explaining with great patience, told me that a boy could inherit that disease only through his mother, never through his father, that, in his judgement, what Caleb suffered was a mere *Epistaxis* or a chronic bent towards nosebleeds and that he would grow out of it . . .

Grow out of it, we know from this biography, he did and lived to be nearly eighty. More emerges from this letter about Henry than about the child. He apparently had a highly developed bedside manner. His photographs had already told me he was good looking but not, of course, that he was courteous and gracious. To the mother, very likely a young and pretty woman, he behaved charmingly, while he took no notice of the child.

Henry Nanther was born at Godby near Huddersfield on 19 February 1836, elder son of Henry Thomas Nanther, a woollen manufacturer and active Wesleyan. His mother was Amelia Sophia, daughter of William Pearson.

That is *Dictionary of National Biography* stuff. Plain un-adorned facts. Though his entry states that Henry was the eldest son it naturally makes no comment on the fact that his parents had been married for fourteen years before he was born. These days you come across plenty of couples married for many years before having children but that is the result of careful planning, the woman wishing to succeed in her career, the establishment of a suitable home for a family, and so on. No family planning existed in Henry Thomas and Amelia Sophia's day. So what happened? Did she have miscarriages – and this is something I know plenty about – or give birth to stillborn babies? Did conception for some reason never happen? Women who worry about their failure to conceive are less likely to conceive than those who are carefree. So Jude was told by her doctor, as if it was conception she had trouble with. It seems unlikely that Amelia didn't worry, given the times she lived in and the fact that the woman was inevitably blamed in cases of failure to produce children.

At last a child came along. By that time Amelia would have been over her anxiety, for she was past her mid thirties and may have given up the idea of becoming a mother. The baby, to be baptized Henry Alexander, was born at the family home, Godby Hall, a handsome healthy child.

Within two years of his birth another son came along, but this one was different. With very little evidence to go on, it's hard to know precisely what was wrong with William Thomas Nanther, but, given that his mother was in her late thirties at the time of his birth, it sounds as if he was a Down's Syndrome child. This would be a likely explanation for his being described in Amelia's letters to her sister Mary as 'strange', 'backward' and 'different-looking'. In one letter she writes, 'Billy looks not at all like either Mr Nanther or me. The village people call him a changeling, which hurts my feelings when I hear it, though I try not to attend to the opinions of ignorant folk.'

Henry Thomas Nanther was the owner of a woollen mill and most of the able-bodied population of Godby worked in it. Rows of back-to-back cottages had been built climbing the hillsides to accommodate the families who had moved there for the sake of certain employment. The Nanthers lived in a big house, built in the Georgian style, a little outside the village; a white stucco building, not particularly suitable for the Yorkshire climate, to the front of which Henry Thomas had added a monstrous portico with a domed roof, supported by eight disproportionately fat columns with Corinthian capitals. It's still there, or the exterior is, and the interior hasn't been much altered.

To their credit, Henry Thomas and Amelia kept Billy at home rather than committing him to some kind of institution. No doubt they were aware of just how dreadful such a place would have been, comparable, I imagine, in awfulness to the children's homes and homes for the mentally ill which still exist in Eastern Europe. Or worse. Henry Thomas was wealthy and, if he and his wife were never quite accepted by the local gentry, they were respected. He was a deeply religious man, assiduous in carrying out his

duties as a Methodist lay preacher, and determined to practise what he preached. Perhaps he genuinely believed it
would have been wrong to lay the burden of his second son
on other shoulders. Of course there was a children's nurse
at Godby Hall and a nursery maid as well as the usual staff
of servants. Billy, according to his mother, was good, sweet
and affectionate. Down's children often are. If it was
Down's. It's equally possible his incapacity was due to a
difficult birth during which his brain was damaged by being
temporarily deprived of oxygen. We don't know and now
never shall.

In his elder brother's second year at the day school he
attended at Longfield, three miles away, Billy fell ill. As we
know from the fate of several of the Brontë sisters whose
home, in Haworth, wasn't far away, tuberculosis was rife in
the hills and valleys of Yorkshire in the 1830s and 40s. That
it was contagious was not known at the time or, rather, it
was assumed that infections came from 'miasma', a kind of
noxious vapour that rose from standing water and sewage.
Why Billy caught tuberculosis and not his brother or his
parents is a mystery. Why, after all, did Emily, Anne and
Maria succumb to it while Charlotte and their father
remained free of infection?

By this time – Billy was five – his mother had become
more attached to him than to his elder brother. And this in
spite of what she had earlier written to her sister about his
strangeness and retardation. His illness drove her to the edge
of insanity. The letters she wrote to Mary are rambling or
wild and full of threats to end her own life, 'if the Lord takes
my Billy'. Her husband, perhaps because of his business and
commitments at the mill, seems to have been less involved.
What was Henry's attitude? We don't know. He was at
school in a village to which he was taken by pony and trap

each morning and fetched home each afternoon. Amelia writes that she had been in the habit of driving him herself, at least for the morning trip, but that this ceased with Billy's illness. Did Henry mind? He must have done. Those drives constituted perhaps the only times he was alone with his mother. Now he had been deprived of this pleasure by the illness of a brother he had always, according to a worried letter from Amelia to Mary, treated with some amount of contempt.

A progressive doctor who attended Billy told his parents that a dry climate at a high altitude would improve his health and recommended Switzerland or the Bavarian Alps. In 1843, in Yorkshire, that was like telling parents today that they ought to take their sick child to the Antarctic or the top of the Himalayas. But no, even that's not a parallel. Today's parents wouldn't find going to Nepal or the far south nearly as preposterous as Henry Thomas and Amelia found the idea of the Continent. Neither had ever been out of England and neither had any intention of going. Instead, Amelia took Billy to the Lake District. If anything, he grew worse and they returned within a fortnight for Amelia to write to Mary that he had spat blood on three mornings in succession.

Appallingly risky as it seems to us today, the two little boys shared a bedroom. It was called the night nursery and Amelia often mentions it in her letters.

I went into the night nursery at first light this morning [she writes], and found both boys asleep, but for the third time this week there was blood on Billy's pillow, quite an excessive amount. I felt so sick at the sight after I had hoped and prayed there would be none this time, that I thought I should faint. If only Billy would call me or nurse when he coughs and the dreadful blood comes!

But he is so good and – oh, imagine it! – would not want to trouble us.

How much of this coughing did Henry hear and how much blood-spitting did he see? Most of it, surely. Remember that he disliked and despised his brother and felt it was he who occupied the prime place in their mother's affections. Did he know what coughing up blood meant? Probably. There's no reason to suppose Amelia was discreet about demonstrations of grief. No doubt Henry witnessed this nausea and these near-faintings. He was seven, the age of reason. His brother coughed up blood and his mother reacted as if the world was coming to an end; therefore the blood indicated Billy was very seriously ill and might die. Isn't it likely that he too looked for blood on his brother's pillow and when he saw it rejoiced in what it meant?

I'm wondering – and perhaps I shall always just wonder – if this equating of the evidence on Billy's pillow with the removal of a rival and with a happier future was the beginning of Henry's passion for blood.

Jude and I went home after dinner. The House sat till ten past three this morning, finally adjourning after Lord Vivian had given statistics about the number of peers who attend the House daily, and Lord Falconer had asserted that changes under the Act would make the place more independent. They're going on with the debate today. Easter is coming, the House will rise tomorrow until 12 April, and soon after we shall be at committee stage. Jude has taken two days off and we are going up to Yorkshire to take a look at Henry's birthplace by invitation of the owner.

Jude is nearly eight years younger than I am, which puts her still very much on the right side of forty. Those few years are precious to her because they mean she still has a chance of a baby. Unlike Amelia Nanther, Jude has no trouble conceiving. It's carrying a child beyond two or three months that seems impossible for her. I've a son from my first marriage, Paul my heir, who in his turn has sat on the steps of the throne. If a child comes I'll be happy for Jude's sake. I'd like to see her joy and I do sometimes imagine the things she'd say and the plans she'd make and her face lit up with happiness. But I don't long for a child in the way she does, and in my heart I don't believe there'll ever be one. Jude conceived three years ago but miscarried at eight weeks, conceived again and lost the baby at three months. She's recently been trying a new treatment but it isn't working or hasn't worked yet, I can tell by her face. She's sitting opposite me in the train, on the side where they have single seats with a table in between, and although she appears perfectly healthy and not pale or unwell, she has that set look about the mouth and misery in her eyes that indicate her period has come.

There's a kind of parallel there with the way women behaved in the 1840s, menstruation being the forbidden subject. Presumably, Amelia had some form of words in which to tell Henry Thomas she'd be 'unwell' for the coming five or six days, but her diffidence came from prudishness and female delicacy. Jude doesn't tell me because she can't bear to mention it, she can't use the word, any of those words that mean another month's gone by and by the time one more has passed she'll be thirty-seven. I think she believes I secretly mind but hide my disappointment for her sake. No amount of assuring her of my indifference helps. When we were first together and then when we were first married I'd see the box of Tampax lying about in the bathroom or the cardboard tube floating in the lavatory pan, but now she hides the evidence as if she really is living in some past time. The only sign of her period is in her unhappy eyes.

No one is looking at us and I don't much care if they are, so I take her hand and lift it to my lips and kiss it. Jude has beautiful hands, long and slim, the joints not at all obvious, the nails almond-shaped and always unpainted. Kissing hands is an erotic thing for us – she kisses mine too – and sometimes it's just a loving thing with a meaning of I'm here and all will be well. But will it? If all being well means a baby, I think it's more likely to be all being ill.

We take a taxi at Huddersfield station, a rather magnificent Victorian building, and it gets us to Godby in twenty minutes. Rather to my relief – though from the messages and fervent apologies he left behind him not to his – the owner of Godby Hall, a computer tycoon named Brett, has been called away to Bradford for an urgent meeting. His wife, as the au pair who comes to the door tells us, is visiting her sick mother in Scarborough and has taken the baby with her. That, at any rate, pleases me. One of my missions in life is to hide babies from Jude, though I don't really know whether the sight of one upsets her or if it's just that I think it must.

Godby Hall is in serious need of painting outside, its white walls and columns streaked with blackish greenish trails where water has spilt down it from the gutters. In Henry Thomas's day, I suppose it was blackened with soot from factory chimneys. Indoors it's anaemic-looking, everything painted white, pale rugs lying about on pale wood-block floors, and it looks cold, though it doesn't feel it with the central heating going full blast. The au pair, who's German and speaks perfect but heavily accented English, takes us up to the second floor where the day and night nurseries were. I marvel, not for the first time, at the way the Victorians and pre-Victorians placed their children as far away from their own quarters as possible.

I start wishing Jude hadn't come, it was she who insisted on coming, though there's nothing in this room to show it was once a night nursery. It's the au pair's own room now, one end lopped off to make an en-suite bathroom, but, apart from being rather untidy, it's as bleak as the rest of the house. The unmade bed has a pink and white duvet bunched up and flung across one end of it. There's a built-in clothes cupboard and a built-in dressing table the au pair calls a vanitory, its top laden with cosmetics of all kinds, jars and bottles and tubes. I try to imagine where the two beds were and what else might have been in this room. Toys? Books? The equivalent of the 'vanitory', a washstand perhaps, would have held a great many medicaments for poor Billy. Were candles in use upstairs at Godby Hall or did they use colza lamps in which coleseed oil was burned? Downstairs, probably, but up here it would have been candles. And now I remember that Amelia refers in one of her letters to lighting the candle when she goes to attend to Billy in the night.

Jude is looking out of one of the sash windows and I join her. We admire the view of green hills and dark woodland and in the foreground the village of Godby, cleaned of smoke deposits and spotless in the icy March sunshine. The wind is so strong that even from this distance we can see the weathervane on the church tower furiously spinning round. The houses that were built for the mill workers look from here as if each one of them has been radically converted into a dwelling for the young upwardly mobile, smartened with Sandtex and brightly re-roofed, a green strip of lawn with shrubs running between their backs. I imagine Henry kneeling up here on a window seat or ottoman, looking at the familiar view and then, perhaps, creeping back to relish the sight of blood splashes on his brother's pillow.

'The younger one, Billy, he died, didn't he?' It's Jude asking and she looks sadly at the corner where I've suggested his bed might have been. 'How old was he when he died?'

'He was six.'

The au pair looks suitably aghast and asks why he wasn't given antibiotics. To do her justice, she probably knows nothing of any of this and supposes Billy died twenty or thirty years ago.

'This was a hundred and fifty years ago, more than a hundred and fifty,' I tell her. 'There wasn't a cure for tuberculosis. He coughed and his lungs bled, he got thinner and weaker and in the winter of eighteen forty-four he died.'

'There were two boys, I think?' The au pair has picked up a bottle of something off the 'vanitory' and is spraying the inside of her wrist with whatever is inside it. 'What happened to the other one?'

'He grew up and became the Queen's doctor – not this queen, her great-great-grandmother – and had six children and was made a lord.'

'Why didn't he get tuberculosis?'

'I don't know.'

'If everyone in the nineteenth century who was exposed to it caught it,' says Jude, 'there wouldn't have been any people left in England.'

This is an exaggeration but I know what she means. The au pair asks if any of Henry's children died.

'One of them did. His second son.' I'm nervous of talking about all these children in front of Jude, those that lived and those that died young, but she seems quite tranquil and the sadness has gone out of her eyes. 'His name was George and he died in nineteen hundred and eight, just a year before his father. But his father was seventy-two and he was eleven.'

The au pair is persistent. 'Was that tuberculosis too?'

'Perhaps, but I don't think so,' I say. 'It sounds more likely to have been leukaemia, but it's only guesswork on my part.' I suddenly feel nauseated by it all, the room and the knowledge that the boys slept here, and Billy suffered here and died here, and I suggest we go outside and have a look round the garden.

It's too cold to stay outdoors for long. Besides, everything has changed utterly in a century and a half, which is only what I'd expect. There's a big oak that was probably a young tree when Henry was small, he may even have climbed it, but otherwise all the trees and shrubs are replacements, and second and third replacements, for the ones that were there in his day. We come indoors again and into Amelia's drawing room, which she must have crowded with knick-knacks and antimacassars and wax fruit under glass domes and *gros point* cushions, but has recently been furnished by someone who prefers the stark look. The au pair says Mrs Brett has told her to give us a drink and offer us lunch but we're both so eager to turn this down that we come out with a, 'Oh, no, thank you very much,' in unison and call for a taxi on Jude's mobile.

We get lunch in Huddersfield very late, at nearly half-past two, and decide not to do as we'd planned and stay the night at a hotel in York but to go home on the next available train. We're going to France for Easter so it'll be nice to have a few days at home first. Jude takes my hand and says she supposes I've noticed she's got her period. Like her, I count the days and become, for her sake, only for her sake, more and more strung up and alternately hopeful and despairing as the crucial day approaches. Maybe it's fortunate for both of us that she's absolutely regular, almost to the hour. Yet even if it hadn't come, how many weeks this time would she have carried a child?

'You thought it upset me,' she says, 'all that talk about the children and children dying, but it didn't, not really. It was all so long ago.'

'A lost world where they order things differently?'

'Something like that,' she says as we get into the train.

Henry's elder son Alexander, the one who didn't die, was my grandfather. I remember him well and visiting him in Venice. And now, back in my study at the scarred dining table, I think about the two dead boys: Billy, who succumbed to tuberculosis in 1844, and George, who died of some incurable illness in 1908. How did Henry feel when his younger son died? He was an old man, the boy more like a grandson surely than a son. Clara implies that George was fond of his father, at any rate that he didn't dislike him as the rest of them did, but this may only be a case of the Youngest Child Syndrome, according to which even unaffectionate parents lavish love on the last to come into the family. Henry wrote many learned works on diseases and deficiencies of the blood but, perhaps naturally, never refers among the cases he mentions to his son's condition. He kept a diary of a sort, that is he kept a bald record of what he had done, read, written and where he had been each day, but there is very little in the entries about his feelings, nothing at all in the later ones. His peculiar writings on blood, the notebook essays, are an almost metaphysical jotting down of his innermost responses to aspects of blood and disease and pain. They remind me in a way of Sir Thomas Browne and *Religio Medici*.

I haven't been able to identify any of the cases he mentions or people he refers to. His children are cited but as 'one of my daughters' or 'my elder son', seldom by name. Even in the notebook with the black watered-silk cover his brother never appears. He seems to have forgotten he ever had a brother and once or twice refers to himself as his parents' only child.

That he hoped to be the subject of a biography is clear from the orderly way in which he kept every significant (in his view) letter he received and often made copies of his own letters to other people. Very little that is personal can be found in any of them; that, no doubt, is the way he wanted it. Everything he calculated would be of help in the writing of that biography he kept and packed into three large wooden chests. These he left to his elder son Alexander, his only surviving son, my grandfather, making clear in his will what they contained. Probably he thought a *Life of Henry Nanther* would be written within a few years of his death. Scientists often think differently from the rest of us as to what constitutes a good biography; a dry as dust account of the subject's work and a few bald details as to dates of birth, marriage and death, suits them best. That this was Henry's opinion soon emerges from an examination of those chests' contents. They include a published copy of each one of his learned tomes, as well as papers from other haematologists, some of them very old, which he presumably believed contributed to his own findings.

Alexander was not quite fifteen when his father died. He was at Harrow. The chests remained in Ainsworth House where his mother continued to live with her daughters, or with three of her daughters, the eldest, Elizabeth, having married in 1906. The house was also Alexander's but Lady Nanther had a life interest and there she stayed until

Alexander sold it and bought Alma Villa where I'm sitting now and writing this.

The Great War came while Alexander was at Oxford. A bright boy, he had gone up at seventeen, but a year later he enlisted and within days was in France. Wounded in the first battle of the Somme and again at Mons, he returned again and again to his regiment, miraculously escaping death a dozen times, and came out of the army in 1918 as Major the Lord Nanther and with the Military Cross. He was twenty-three.

A few years later he sold Ainsworth House. His mother moved to Alma Square and the chests went with her. Though never an intellectual, Alexander had worked reasonably hard at school. Now he was utterly changed. Were the things he saw in France responsible? The dreadful sights have been so well-documented, particularly recently, that there's no need for me to go into them here. Whatever it was that changed him, it was plain to see, plain at any rate for his mother and sisters to see, that Alexander had no intention of returning to the university or pursuing a career or even of taking a job. His father had left him a modest amount of money which, invested, brought in an income rather more than adequate to live on. He went off to live on it in the South of France.

Alexander's lines, as his parents' contemporaries used to say, lay in pleasant places. Fate smiled on him. In Mentone he met an American heiress, the only daughter of a pastrami millionaire. The story goes that it was Wrenbury Goldrad who first described pastrami as the New York Jew's answer to ham. He was only too delighted for his daughter to ally herself with an English lord and winner of a distinguished decoration, and Alexander Nanther and Pamela Goldrad were married in Cannes. They had a villa on Cap Ferrat and became well-known as a fashionable host and hostess, long before such people as Somerset Maugham and various deposed crowned heads of Europe discovered the place.

She must have been a nice woman, Pamela Nanther. I would have liked for her to have been my grandmother, but she wasn't. She divorced Alexander in 1929 round about the time of the New York market crash. By careful management she and her father were unaffected by the fall and she was able, though under no obligation, to settle a large sum of money on the husband she had divorced for continual flagrant infidelity and desertion. In the divorce court she said she still loved him and wished him well. These statements caused more shock and horror than any of the revelations about Alexander's other women.

He married one of them, Deirdre Park, and married her just in time. My father was born three months later, in the spring of 1930, the Hon. Theo Serge Nanther. None of your dreary Victorian names for Alexander and Deirdre. They came back to England and lived in this house for a while, presumably because Henry's widow, my great-grandmother Edith, was dying. After her death there was nothing to keep them in England and they set up house, with the heir, for some unknown reason in Geneva. The chests of Henry's papers and the rest of the furniture from Ainsworth House remained in Alma Villa, watched over by my great-aunts Helena and Clara. Mary, two years Helena's senior, had married a clergyman with a parish in Fulham, the Revd Matthew Craddock, in 1922.

Alexander and Deirdre came back to England a few months before the Second World War started and three years later my father began attending St Paul's School. When he was fourteen his mother ran off with an American serviceman. Hoist with his own petard, Alexander divorced her, married for the third time and he and his new wife departed for Venice. There they lived for the next twenty years on the third floor of a dirty old palazzo on what would have been a back street if it hadn't been a canal. I stayed there with my parents for a week in 1965. In the following year my father became Lord Nanther when Alexander died of lung cancer. I remember being fascinated, as a boy of ten, by the amount he smoked. I calculated that in order to get through eighty cigarettes a day at five an hour, which is good going, he would have had to start at 8 a.m. and have the last one at midnight. I admired his relentlessness enormously and vowed to do the same myself.

Meanwhile Helena and Clara lived on in Alma Villa, two old ladies who'd missed the chance of marriage because the men who might have married them had been killed in the 1914 war. Occasionally, on a Sunday, I and my sister Sarah and our parents would drop in on them while out for our afternoon walk and they'd give us tea, chocolate cake, Maryland cookies, meringues and no bread and butter. My father was a solicitor, comfortably off but not rich, and we lived in a big flat in Maida Vale. I was grown up before I had any idea that Alma Villa belonged to him, had been left to him by *his* father and would most likely one day be mine. It was just a house full of old people's clutter where my great-aunts lived and where one got a better tea than anywhere else.

My parents, my sister and I moved into the house ourselves when Helena died and Clara asked if my father would mind if she left and went into sheltered housing. She lived on for a considerable number of years and died when she was just a few months short of her hundredth birthday. Her nephew, my father, died soon afterwards. By this time, my mother had bought herself a small house in Derbyshire close to Sarah; and Sally and I and our son were living at Alma Villa – with the three chests of documents, copies of learned works and diaries.

Sally despised 'family' while being careful to ensure everyone addressed her on envelopes as the Hon. Mrs Martin Nanther. What she would have been like if I had inherited the title while she was still with me I'd rather not imagine. Long before my father died she had left. She was a committed member of CND, went briefly to prison for cutting the wire on the perimeter of a Suffolk missile base, and in the mid-eighties departed to live on Greenham Common and never came back. I haven't seen her since 1989 but I understand from what I hear about her that in whatever commune or collective she happens to find herself she insists, despite our divorce, on being called Lady Nanther.

At some point after my great-grandmother Edith died (she was never called Louisa, and was always known by her second name), the three chests had found their way up into the attics. No one had ever drawn my attention to them, for in most people's eyes they had lost their importance. No biographer had suggested writing Henry's life, but I knew the chests were there and if I ever thought about them it was only to wonder how anyone ever succeeded in carrying them up fifty-six stairs. I even thought they might have been drawn up to the attic window on a pulley from outside. Perhaps they were. Five years ago I lifted the lid of one of them and saw the sombre dark-green and navy-blue bindings of several of Henry's works, *Diseases of the Blood*, *Haemorrhagic Disposition in Families*, *Epistaxis and Haemorrhagic Diathesis*. We had copies of these works downstairs along with several others and at that time I had read none of them. Quite naturally, it had never occurred to me to read them, believing they'd be beyond my comprehension as, when the time came, they almost were.

I'm running down the stone staircase at St John's Wood tube station carrying a briefcase weighed down with my great-grandmother's photograph album: the one I believe is particularly relevant. It's for passing the time while I'm in the House but not in the Chamber. The down escalator at this station has been out of use for months and no doubt will be for months to come. It's something to do with the extension of the Jubilee Line which I asked my question about on Monday. Waiting on the platform, I think how good it will be when the line goes all the way through to Westminster. I'll be able to go to the House without changing. And then I tell myself what a fool I am. I shan't be *there* when the line goes through, they'll have got rid of me.

Today the House rises for Easter and I'm only going in because I want a couple of books from the library but I may as well go into the Chamber and collect the expenses to which I'm entitled once I pass the bar. The debate isn't very interesting and I've nothing to contribute, so I sit there in front of Lord Weatherill, Convenor of the Cross-bench Peers and former Speaker of the House of Commons, and behind Lord Annan and listen for half an hour. The television cameras move from right to left and left to right with their slow steady rhythm, come to the left again and linger on the minister while she's speaking. Cameras are always on us while we're in here but you're only conscious of them for about five minutes on your first day. After that you take them for granted.

When I've done my duty I leave the Chamber and go to the library, encountering outside the Bishops' Bar a very old Conservative hereditary, well-known for voting against women being admitted to the House in 1957. He tells me, sure he's being very risqué, laughing so much at his own wit that he can hardly get the words out, that since the rise of feminism women no longer menstruate, they 'femstruate'. I can't bring myself to join in his laughter or even produce a smile. Jude has come into my mind and I'm suddenly filled with love and pity for her. The old anti-feminist tells me I've no sense of humour. I shake my head, collect my books and sit at one of the tables. The smell of the place reminds me of my grandfather Alexander. Peers come in here to smoke and read the papers as much as to work or study something. Visitors aren't allowed but when they find out about all the smoking that goes on in these rooms they're amazed it's permitted in a library. Doesn't it damage the books? they ask. I don't know whether it does or not and I don't mind the smell, though I broke that vow I made in Venice to follow in Alexander's footsteps and I suppose I've had no more than a couple of cigarettes in my whole life.

Great-grandmother Edith, whose elder son he was, recorded a good deal of her life in photographs. Sepia ones up to about 1920 and black and white after that. The first photograph made in a camera was as early as 1826 but amateur photography really became possible in the 1880s with the introduction of roll-film cameras. Henry and Edith were married in 1884 and it appears that she first began taking photographs five years later, using the newly introduced Eastman Kodak box camera with its handy roll of negative paper. One of her first photographs was of her third child Helena at the age of three months in her christening robe. Did she buy the camera here? It seems unlikely. Her cousin Isobel Vincent had married an American in 1886 and gone to live in Chicago, so perhaps the Kodak was a present from her.

That picture is in another album. The one I've brought with me contains interior shots of Ainsworth House. A favoured hobby of Edwardians was taking photographs of the insides of their houses, over-furnished rooms kept in immaculate condition by housemaids, and these are mostly of that kind. But several of them are roomscapes with figures and the one I'm looking at is of all Edith's children clustered together on a sofa in the drawing room. It's a big squashy sort of sofa, covered in velvet or plush, and the children have been arranged in a human pyramid in the middle of it.

The two eldest girls, Elizabeth and Mary, aged in their late teens, lean over the back, smiling down at their younger sisters Helena and Clara who, though sitting quite far apart, are leaning the upper part of their bodies close together with their arms round each other's necks. Between them, so that their shoulders and arms and faces make an arch above his head, sits Alexander, grinning artificially. He seems to be about ten and is obviously not enjoying this at all. All the girls have long curls and hair ribbons and wear versions suitable to their ages of pinafores over dark or striped dresses. Alexander is in a Norfolk jacket and bow tie. In front of him, on a low stool, sits George, the youngest child, the sick child. He is in a sailor suit which does nothing to make him look healthier or more robust. He leans against his brother's knees, one arm along the sofa, the other bent into his lap, his legs tucked under him, and he is smiling a gentle, rather sad smile. There they all are, the six children, preserved for ever (or for as long as the album lasts) by their mother's Kodak.

I turn the page and there it is, Edith's photograph I knew was in the album but which I haven't looked at for years. It's of Henry in his study, seated at his desk but looking at the camera, and, in front of him, on the desk, is his celebrated work, *Epistaxis and Haemorrhagic Diathesis*. Possibly it has just been published and this copy has been sent or given to him. Possibly it is to record the arrival in the house of this book that Edith has taken the photograph. If this is so the date of this photograph will be sometime in 1896, and there will have been other events for Lord and Lady Nanther to celebrate, for it was in that year that Henry received his peerage and his younger son was born. He looks pleased with himself, a still handsome man of sixty who has just published another book. It's hard to tell from the front but it seems he has all his hair, though it has become quite white. He seems proud, self-satisfied, but pleasant enough; and in the curve of his mouth and his interested eyes are hints of the famous charm. There is absolutely nothing in this picture to give a clue as to why his youngest daughter referred to him baldly as 'Henry Nanther'.

After we moved into Alma Villa with our parents, Sarah and I found the trunks in one of the attics. No one else ever went up there. We only opened one of them. Inside we found things which weren't of much interest to young people: diaries, bundles of papers and letters, brown, faded photographs and photographs in thick albums with cracked, padded leather covers and brass clasps, certificates and diplomas in manila envelopes and books of which we had copies downstairs. Disappointed, we got no further than the top few layers. Almost three decades went by before Sarah sent me Clara's letter and I investigated the trunks again.

3

A Labour life peer, whose name I can't remember, has come up behind me and is looking over my shoulder. He asks who the 'old boy' is and I tell him it's my great-grandfather. So of course he quotes the famous phrase Henry is known for, maybe the only clever thing he ever said in the House.

'Control circumstances and do not allow them to control you.'

Apparently Thomas à Kempis said it first and Henry was only quoting him in his maiden speech. But everyone has forgotten that if they ever knew it. More malicious members aren't above reminding me of another notorious statement of Henry's: *What is the answer*, Hansard quotes him as asking, *that is the question*. The life peer asks me if I've heard about the ancient hereditary peer the opposition 'bussed' in to vote on a motion in last week's debate.

'He was in the loo,' he says, 'the one by the Bishops' Bar, and he heard this ringing and clattering. So he comes tearing out, asking everyone what that frightful noise is. Of course it was the division bell. He'd never heard it before, he hadn't been in for forty years.'

I laugh because it's funny, though it's also a mite embarrassing, and the life peer ambles off. Because I am plainly not an aristocrat, people forget that I inherited my title and don't seem to think twice about using expressions like 'getting rid of the hereditaries' in my presence. The accurate description of what they're aiming at is removing hereditary peers' right to sit in the House and vote but even that hasn't a gracious sound. I must try not to be so sensitive, though in the past I've never found that possible. 'Control circumstances and do not allow them to control you.' The truth is that you can only do so up to a point. Did Henry ever discover that? I wonder. There's nothing I can do to control the circumstances that are going to turf me out of here, and we're all victims of circumstance in the end.

I turn the page in the album and here is another photograph. It's not dated but this is the last picture ever taken of Henry. He is in that same room where in 1896 he was sitting and looking smug, but this time his two sons are with him, the healthy and the sick. The younger boy seems eight or nine, so that is the length of time which has passed. The room itself has changed. It is less crowded with furniture and bric-a-brac. Lighter coloured curtains hang at the window. But the change in the room is nothing to the change in Henry. He is an old and broken man. A metamorphosis has taken place in regard to his skin and his hands and his now thin hair, so that it looks as if a carapace of some creased-up, roughened and worn material has been spread across his face and neck and hands, entirely hiding what nine years before remained of his youth. Alexander sits beside him looking cheerful and unconcerned. George, who must by this time have been no more than two years from death, leans against his father's shoulder and Henry has his arm round him. I can't read the look on Henry's face. Sad? Bitter? Desperately tired? Perhaps all those things. I shall perhaps know when I have found out everything I can about him.

Big white letters come up on the red background of the television monitor: House Up. I put the album back into the briefcase and go down the corridor towards the Prince's Chamber, the stairs, the cloakroom and the outdoors. A newish life peer, a woman of maybe fifty, a QC and chair-man of some august body, with a fine head of blonde hair and legs nearly as good as Jude's, comes out of the door that leads to the Barry Room and walks towards the blue carpet. Behind her a couple of active old hereditaries are talking and one says to the other, 'Who's the new girl?'

I'm reminded of something and I go back into the library to look it up. You can look up anything in here or someone else will do it for you. And here it is, part of the speech Earl Ferrers made in opposition to the bill that would, and eventually did, allow women to become members of this House.

'Frankly,' he said, 'I find women in politics highly dis-tasteful. In general, they are organizing, they are pushing and they are commanding. Some of them do not even know where loyalty to their country lies. I disagree with those who say that women in your Lordships' House would cheer up our benches. If one looks at a cross-section of women already in Parliament I do not feel that one could say that they are an exciting example of the attractiveness of the opposite sex. I believe that there are certain duties and certain responsibilities which nature and custom have decreed men are more fitted to take on; and some responsi-bilities which nature and custom have decreed women should take on. It is generally accepted that the man should bear the major responsibility in life. It is generally accepted, for better or worse, that a man's judgement is generally more logical and less tempestuous than that of a woman. Why then should we encourage women to eat their way, like acid into metal, into positions of trust and responsibility which previously men have held?

'If we allow women into this House where will this emancipation end? Shall we in a few years' time be referring to "the noble and learned Lady, the Lady Chancellor"? I find that a horrifying thought. But why should we not? Shall we follow the rather vulgar example set by Americans of having female ambassadors? Will our judges, for whom we have so rich and well-deserved respect, be drawn from the serried ranks of the ladies? If that is so, I would offer to the most reverend Primate the humble and respectful advice that he had better take care lest he find himself out of a job . . .'

That speech was made not in Henry's time but in 1957 and Ferrers was only twenty-eight when he made it. I put the photocopy from Hansard into my pocket for Jude to see and retrace my steps along Pugin's gold and crimson corridors and across the bright blue carpet.

It's a strange mad old place and I don't want to leave it.

The school Henry went to was Huddersfield College. He left at the age of fifteen for his father's woollen mill in Godby, where he spent two years learning various processes. Why? According to a letter from his mother to his aunt Mary, his father was appalled by Henry's ambition to become a doctor of medicine. His only surviving son must go into the business. There follow two pages in which Amelia gives vent to her grief at the death of Billy, a sorrow that seems as intense as it was immediately after his death. If only he had lived, she writes, he might have learned the factory processes and one day taken over, leaving Henry to do as he chose. Perhaps it was too painful to confront, but she ignores the fact that Billy, suffering as he did from some kind of mental incapacity, could never have developed business acumen.

Nor, apparently, could Henry. At any rate, in 1853, when he was seventeen, he was apprenticed to a surgeon in

Manchester and entered the Owens College in Quay Street. This seems to have been one of the first medical schools in the country. His father had relented and made him a fairly generous allowance. Possibly, he saw there was a future in medicine. It was no longer the rather disreputable trade, a 'leech', a 'barber surgeon', which it had been in the first decades of the century when he was young. At the Owens College and at the Manchester Royal School of Medicine Henry gained medals in chemistry, materia medica, operative surgery, physiology and anatomy, and in 1856 he carried off gold medals in anatomy, physiology and chemistry at the first MB London examination.

Marcus Grady, the Professor of Materia Medica at Manchester Royal School, wrote a glowing letter to his father. It was carefully preserved, firstly I'm sure by Amelia, then by Henry, between sheets of tissue paper in one of the trunks.

When it fell to my lot to announce the prize list last Thursday, I did something I have certainly never done before in such an assembly. In the midst of the applause I congratulated your son. Unorthodox though my conduct was, I could not help myself, I was so struck by the substance of his exercises, their scholarly style, and evidence of a truly awesome command of their subject.

Easy to see why Henry kept it. In the following year he became a member of the Royal College of Surgeons and licentiate of the Society of Apothecaries in London. Very evidently, he had known what he wanted and had answered a genuine calling. While at Manchester Royal School he began to keep a diary and apparently made the first real friend of his life. This was a young Scotsman, Richard Fox Hamilton, one year older than himself, the youngest son of a cousin of Lachlan Algernon Hamilton, Lord Hamilton of

Luloch. Henry notes all this in his diary, including Hamilton's full name and details of his cousin's peerage. Entries in those early days were much fuller, and even though they could hardly be described as emotional, at least they were less unemotional than they later became.

Henry writes in the diary of his parents and their pleasure at his success, of an increase his father has made in his allowance and, in the summer of 1859, of taking Hamilton home with him to Yorkshire to meet his father and mother and enjoy a walking holiday on the moors. It seems that Amelia took such a fancy to Richard Hamilton that Henry describes him as regarded by her as a substitute for her lost son Billy. Henry had himself apparently never been considered as a replacement.

The first post he had was as house physician at St Bartholomew's Hospital, London, and while there he contributed two articles to the *British Medical Journal*, 'Haemorrhagic Disease' and 'Cases of Epistaxis'. These were his first publications. I found yellowed copies of the journal in one of the trunks under a bundle of letters from Richard Hamilton. Before taking up a post at the Great Northern Hospital, he went abroad for the first time in his life. This was to spend a year studying at the University of Vienna, recognized as a world leader among medical schools. No doubt this was financed by his father who would have been much mollified by Henry's obvious brilliance at his medical studies. At Vienna he showed an aptitude for languages, learning to speak fluent German within three months.

His mother kept every letter he sent to her and his father. Henry made copies too.

I find in myself [he wrote] an unexpected aptitude for learning foreign languages. I had not attempted it before, with the exception of Latin which is hardly to be thought of as a spoken language. Here I have made the acquaintance of a Swiss gentleman who vows to teach me his own peculiar tongue within the remainder of my stay. The language in question is Romansch or Rhaeto-Romanic, derived from the Vulgar Latin – therefore not entirely unfamiliar to me – and spoken in southern parts of Switzerland.

While at Vienna he indulged two of his favourite interests, walking and train travel. From the train to Salzburg he had a 'glorious view' of the monastery at Melk, which he describes in a letter home as 'one of the most beautiful edifices this world has to offer'. He enjoyed a walking tour in the Austrian Tyrol and later made a trip to Lake Thun in Switzerland, taking with him his Baedeker, the famous travel guide first published some thirty years before. Whether he had an opportunity to use his newly acquired Romansch he doesn't say. But these holidays established for him a lifelong fondness for Central Europe, its mountains and lakes.

If he also wrote to Hamilton the correspondence has been lost. In his absence his friend had become assistant physician at University College Hospital and the two men shared a set of rooms they took in Great Titchfield Street. Henry was back at Barts, lecturing on anatomy when he was only thirty-two. While there he wrote his first book: *Diseases of the Blood*. For many years it was regarded as the definitive authority on haemophilia and used by generations of medical students. Henry was made a Fellow of the Royal College of Physicians.

That same year he and Hamilton went together on a walking tour in Austria, staying at a pension outside Innsbruck. Both wrote home and Hamilton also wrote to

Henry's mother, no doubt appreciating the fondness she had for him. Henry's friendship with Hamilton was genuine and deep but there may have been some element of admiration on Henry's part for the Scotsman's aristocratic relations. Several times in his letters to his parents he reminds them that Hamilton was related to Lord Hamilton of Luloch. He seems to have enjoyed hob-nobbing with the great. An occasional visitor to Great Titchfield Street was Richard's sister Caroline, a few years younger than he, who was living as a companion to her aunt not far away in a gloomy house in Percy Street. Henry, in a burst of frankness unusual for him at any time, describes Caroline Hamilton in the diary as 'a handsome young lady'. She is mentioned several times and he was evidently very attracted by her. He mentions her 'elegant manners' and her modesty, her affection for her brother and concern for her aunt, who was some kind of invalid. Was he in love with her? Perhaps. In a curious way he seems to have been a little in love with both brother and sister. He writes about them in more affectionate and more admiring terms than of any other characters who appear in the diary at that stage of his life. I have to add the caution here that about those who appear in later years he writes in no terms at all. Their presence, as for instance dining companions or acquaintances he called on, is merely noted.

He went from strength to strength in his profession, holding several offices, as lecturer in comparative anatomy in St Mary's Hospital Medical School, consulting physician at the London Fever Hospital and physician to the Western General Dispensary. Somehow he found time to write another book, even longer than the first, and to revisit his beloved Alps. In 1872 he accepted a professorship of pathological anatomy at University College London, and at the same time set up in private practice in Wimpole Street.

Richard Hamilton had become consulting physician at Edinburgh Royal Infirmary and left for that city in 1869. His aunt had died the year before and Caroline had returned to the parental home. How Henry felt about this double departure from his life of the only two friends he had is recorded nowhere in the diary. He writes only, 'Hamilton has departed for Edinburgh. I drove with him to the King's Cross station this morning and saw him off on the train to the north.' Trains were to play a significant part in Henry's life and a disastrous one. But if the two tragedies, the first involving his best friend, the second the woman he was engaged to, put him off travelling by rail himself, there's no hint of it in his writings. Though train journeys were among his pleasures, he owed his life – and I my existence – to his avoiding one of them.

By the time of her brother's departure for Edinburgh, Caroline had been absent from the diary for a year. Had Henry asked her to marry him and been refused? This is the merest speculation. I've no reason to believe it. She never appears in the diary again, but he corresponded regularly with Hamilton and many of the letters he received from him were carefully dated and packed in one of the trunks.

Hamilton writes of his work, of his family, of the Miss Susannah Murray he had become engaged to, but whom he never married, and occasionally of Caroline. A letter of autumn 1874 describes her wedding to a doctor in Aberdeen. Hamilton was best man. No mention of this is made in the diary, in which by then the entries are growing shorter and more repressive. Henry does, however, record visits to Scotland in 1876 and 1879, commenting in the first

44

entry at unusual length on the pleasures of train travel. He stayed at Hamilton's parents' home, he and Richard went on a tour of the Trossachs, and one glorious evening dined at Luloch Castle near Dundee with Lord and Lady Hamilton. Another time the two men spent a fortnight at Godby Hall with Henry's mother, still apparently doting on Hamilton, and his now ailing father.

If he couldn't replace him, Henry had found a seemingly adequate substitute for Hamilton in Barnabus Couch, another physician he appears to have met while both were working at the Western General Dispensary. Letters from Couch and copies of letters Henry wrote to Couch, were carefully preserved in the trunk. But whereas Hamilton is often referred to as 'my friend Hamilton' or 'RH' and even once as 'dear old Hamilton', Couch gets only his bare surname. The same applies to Lewis Fetter, another medical man Henry knew and occasionally corresponded with.

The composition of Queen Victoria's Medical Household seems extravagant today. Three Physicians-in-Ordinary and three Surgeons-in-Ordinary were in attendance and all were both consultants to the Queen and her general practitioners, while the senior physician was styled Head of the Medical Department and the senior surgeon Sergeant Surgeon.

Ranked below them were the Physicians and Surgeons Extraordinary. If they did well and found favour with the Queen they were promoted to in-Ordinary while those among the in-Ordinary who became unfit for the task through age or ill-health reverted to Extraordinary. Besides these, the great medical army included obstetricians, ear and eye specialists and apothecaries. These last were more like general practitioners than dispensers of drugs. Some of them, Apothecaries to the Household, took care of the health of everyone outside the royal family, while Apothecaries to the Person attended the Queen and any members of the family who might be staying with her. Some of these people were at Windsor, some at Balmoral and others at Osborne. Henry's position among them was, from the first, peculiar.

The Queen appointed him Physician Extraordinary in 1879. Most of her other doctors were in permanent residence but Henry, though sometimes staying a few days at Windsor and several times travelling with her to the Isle of Wight, retained his professorship and his London home. Though he began on the lowest rung of the royal medical ladder, he enjoyed a special position. He was the Queen's consultant on haemophilia.

He had been in attendance only a year when he was promoted Physician-in-Ordinary to her youngest son the Prince Leopold who suffered from this disease, the blood disorder in which Henry specialized. The second essay in the notebook is about its occurrence in the royal family and Henry writes with unusual frankness. Perhaps, needless to say, none of this found its way into any letter or memoir of his or into his published works.

Since the end of the last century it has at least been adumbrated that haemophilia manifests itself in males but is carried by females. The Queen must know that it is she who carries the disease, she and she alone, and that it must have passed to her via the Reuss-Ebersdorffs, from which family her own mother came. She is well-known, of course, for her refusal to face facts and a genius at pretending that things which are so, are not so. When she mentions HRH's disease she insists it is 'not in the family' and his must be an isolated case. I would not take it upon myself to tell her she is a conductor and responsible for the occurrence of the disease in this one of her sons and very probably in her grandson

46

Frederick William of Hesse (known as Frittie) who died eight years ago at the age of two after falling out of a window. She is fortunate that in her own case, it occurred in this son alone of the four and, as far as can be seen up until now, only one of her five daughters, but more of that later.

Telling her would do no good, I suppose, even if I could bring myself to do it. It would in any case be useless as the damage is done and in the present state of our knowledge cannot be undone. What the future will bring as regards further enlightenment no one knows, though I pray God I may be His instrument in discovering more about the disease and some kind of alleviation of its awful symptoms, if not a cure.

It is unlikely that the Princess Beatrice will ever marry, will ever be allowed to marry, she is so much the apple of the Queen's eye, but if she does I await with a dread I am astonished to find in myself, the birth of sons to her. For some reason, I cannot tell what, perhaps an intuition deriving from my own experience, I see in the Princess's smooth young face and handsome figure a forewarning, some kind of premonition, that she is a conductor of haemophilia like her sister Alice, Grand Duchess of Hesse.

The Queen made Prince Leopold Duke of Albany in 1881, though he still lived at Court and had no residence of his own. But if Henry believed he was unable to alleviate the symptoms of haemophilia, Queen Victoria appears to have thought otherwise. In a letter to her eldest daughter, the Princess Frederick of Prussia (later Crown Princess, later Empress), she claimed to have been 'much struck by the improvement in dear Leo's health since Dr Nanther began his attendance upon him'. So struck was she that in 1883 she conferred a knighthood upon Henry and he was able to have engraved on his brass plate in Wimpole Street, Sir Henry Nanther, KCB, followed by his string of degrees.

It was said that it was this improvement in the Duke of Albany's health that persuaded the Queen to allow him to marry, something she had in the past been set against. Princess Helene, known also as Helen or Helena, of Waldeck-Pyrmont was his choice and they were married in April 1882. The bride seems to have been devoted to her semi-invalid husband. In her journal Queen Victoria wrote that at the wedding he was 'lame and shaky'. It's hard from this distance in time to see what Henry did to make the Queen believe Leopold was in better health. Early in 1883, at Windsor where his wife had given birth to his first child, the Princess Alice of Albany, Leopold sprained his leg. A serious hazard for haemophiliacs is bleeding into the joints as the result of external damage. Perhaps Henry was able to alleviate the pain and reassure the Queen. But how did he so win her confidence and affection that she knighted him that same year?

His famous charm perhaps. I see him as the prince of the bedside mannerists. He was tall, he was very handsome, no doubt he could be a courtier. And there was another factor in the mystifying business of his rise to eminence. John Brown died that spring and the Queen was distraught. Deeply mourning her Highland servant, she may have turned for comfort to Henry. Her recovery is usually accounted for by her conversion to spiritualism, but suppose that, though she was 'grievously crushed and brought low', as she wrote to the Princess Frederick, it was Henry who went some way to replacing the lost men in her life?

A little under a year later, but not before a son was on the way, Leopold died in Cannes from a haemorrhage of the brain, his death the result of what would have been a minor injury in anyone else. Far from this tragedy turning Queen Victoria away from Henry, it seems to have consolidated her faith in him and she appointed him among her personal physicians, giving him the title of Physician Royal, though he was accountable first to Sir William Jenner and then to Sir James Reid, one after the other the Queen's Senior Physician-in-Ordinary. He was exceptional too in that he never lived at any of the royal residences but was summoned when needed.

In a letter to Couch he describes a train journey he took to Osborne in 1883.

The journey to the Isle of Wight was accomplished in about three hours. I find rail travel a most enjoyable experience, as you know. The speed and ease with which these great steam-powered horses of iron gallop through the countryside never ceases to amaze me, and gratify me also at the advance of science and the accomplishments of industry. I went up to the engine where I was invited to watch the stoking of the furnace – I am not sure here if I am using the correct terms but you will know – and was engrossed by the sight of the coal being cast in by shovel, an endless process achieved by a half-naked man, bathed from forehead to waist in perspiration. We crossed the Solent in HM's yacht. The strait is narrow enough but the water was choppy, the craft tossed about and I confess I experienced severe nausea. All was well, of course, when we came to land and I had my first sight of this beautiful and verdant island . . .

Jude is home before me. It's her turn to cook and she's in the kitchen doing something with chicken breasts and mushrooms. I bring her a glass of wine and one for myself. She looks younger and happier than she has for a week. Hope has returned. Her cycle has begun again, this is another new beginning, and she's off on her regimen of folic acid, ginseng, echinacea, the gynaecologist's medication and the rest of it. When I think like this I stop laughing because I hate hope. I don't think it should count among the virtues, it's not in the same league as charity and faith. Whoever it was said that hope deferred makes the heart sick, is my hero.

Jude turns the gas down under the pan and sits down with her wine. She hasn't drunk any of it and she says that perhaps she shouldn't drink it. Somewhere or other she's read that alcohol provokes miscarriages. That makes me angry, though I don't think I show my anger. I see her spoiling her life for the sake of a dream child I don't believe she'll ever have. I tell her gently that a couple of glasses of red wine is recommended by doctors but she shakes her head.

'If I drink wine,' she says, 'and I never do manage to – well, you know' – it's always 'well, you know' these days – 'I'll look back and think if only I hadn't been so weak maybe I'd have . . .'

'You must do whatever you think best,' I tell her, and then she starts talking about some new manuscript she's reading. Not that she doesn't want to talk about conception and babies but that she's afraid of boring me, of making me impatient. I think – I'm almost certain – the existence of my son Paul weighs heavily on her. She likes him, she always makes him welcome when he comes here, but he's an ever-present reminder to her that *I don't need any more children*. If I never have another it won't make me unhappy, it won't be the end of the title, for what that's worth, and I'll never repine. This is what she intuits and she intuits right, though I put up some sort of a show. But a difficulty lies here too. If I seem to yearn as much as she does and no child ever comes she's going to feel she's let me down, she's disappointed me as well as herself.

She asks about my Henry research and I pass her a sheaf

of handwritten papers of his I've had blown up to readable size. She leafs through them, stops about halfway in and reads part of a lecture Henry gave to some august body, as much because she's intrigued by what he writes as I am.

These diseases are carried by the blood. Of that we must be certain. But what is it in the blood that affects some people with haemophilia and others with purpura? A substance, of course, that is passed by way of the blood from a parent to its offspring. It is very hard to see, therefore, how a *father's* blood can enter and affect the foetus in the *mother's* uterus, when what he has contributed to conception is semen or seed. But it must be so. All blood looks the same but it is not the same. Medical men have been attempting to transfuse blood from one human being to another or from one animal to another since 1665. Pepys mentions such an experiment, using dogs, in his diary. In France Jean-Baptiste Denis transfused lamb's blood into patients until a fatality occurred and he was arrested. Since then very little progress has been made, though James Blundell recorded successful tranfusions five years ago. Mostly, what occurs when red blood cells from one individual are mixed with serum from another is clumping of the red cells or in some cases *bursting* of the cells. Will we ever know why?

'Yes, we will,' Jude says. 'We do. When did this Blundell record successful transfusions? Once you know that you can date this paper to five years later.'

I said I'd check and Jude lays down the paper, saying dinner's probably ready by now and would I like to drink her wine? While we're eating we talk about this amazing novel she's publishing by a man from what we're now supposed to call 'the Asian subcontinent' and which she thinks is a front runner for the Booker Prize. It's about marriage in India and the five big events in it are weddings.

This leads her to ask me if I've yet done any research into Henry's marriage, when it happened and why.

I ask her who can tell why anyone gets married and she says she knows why she did. We smile at each other across the chicken and mushrooms and I say that of course one knows oneself but can others ever know?

'You told me he was keen on Caroline Hamilton.'

'It looks like it, but she married someone else.'

'And there was that woman Sargent painted,' she says. 'We've got the picture on the kitchen calendar.'

'He didn't marry her, either. She married someone called Caspar Raven.'

'And Henry?'

'He married Louisa Edith Henderson, always called Edith, who was my great-grandmother. He was Sir Henry by then, a distinguished and famous physician. It was eighteen eighty-four and Henry was forty-eight.'

'How old was she?'

I tell her Edith was born in 1861 so she must have been twenty-three. Quite a gap, says Jude, but not unusual in the nineteenth century, and she wonders what he did for sex all those years. She's heard London was full of prostitutes, so did he use them? Or did he visit brothels?

'He kept a woman in a house in Primrose Hill.'

'How do you know?'

'Through that letter from Clara and then the woman's granddaughter. I'm planning to meet the granddaughter in a couple of weeks' time. At the moment I don't know any more than that her name was Jemima Ashworth, though she was known as Jimmy. She lived in a little house in Chalcot Road which he bought for her or more likely rented for her.'

Jude asks if Henry left any indication of Jimmy Ashworth's existence in his diary or letters, and I tell her about the pentagrams.

'I'm not sure if I know what pentagrams are.'

'Sort of stars, asterisks. You take a pen or pencil and draw a diagonal going upwards, then another going downwards to make an angle of forty-five degrees, another up to cut halfway across the first one, then across, down and up, until you've made a five-pointed star.' I show her on the sheet of paper we keep for shopping lists pinned to a cork board. 'Henry has pentagrams in his diary more or less twice a week for nine years, starting in autumn 1874.' Immediately there comes into my mind the memory of hearing about women doing this to mark the days their periods are due or actually taking place and I feel the blood mount into my face. Jude doesn't seem to notice. It suddenly occurs to me that the date the first of those pentagrams appears coincides with Caroline Hamilton's marriage in Aberdeen. Is it only coincidence or something more deliberate? Is Henry saying, 'I can't have her, that's all over, so I may as well forget morality and get myself a mistress'?

We've carried the dishes into the kitchen and it's my turn to clear up. With a dishwasher there's not much clearing up necessary, especially if you're lazy and put the saucepans in as I do. Jude's looking at the calendar and has turned its pages back to February and there is Mrs Caspar Raven. Underneath the reproduced portrait is the legend saying Sargent painted it in 1894. She'd have been thirty-four or thirty-five by then and she's a stunningly beautiful woman of the same type as Jude (a fact I point out to her) but of course not as slim as Jude is. Olivia Raven is fashionably plump with large full breasts and rounded arms and soft snowy shoulders, dressed in oyster-coloured satin, low-cut and with a collar of pearls at her white throat. Her waist is tiny, a narrow column, encircled by a lilac sash. Her hair is Jude's, chestnut going on black, copious and wavy, piled up with a stray curly tress pendent over one shoulder. Sargent has done wonderful things with her luminous skin and her moist red lips. She looks wealthy, spoilt, cosseted and, not surprisingly, loved.

'She could do with losing a couple of stone,' says Jude, 'but I suppose they liked women like that. She *is* lovely. Why didn't Henry marry her?'

'Who knows?' I say. 'She had a lot of money as well as looks. He wasn't rich by the Bathos' standards – her father was Sir John Batho – but he was good looking and a knight and a physician to the royal family.'

'Have you got a photograph of him when he was young?'

'There's his wedding photograph. Is forty-eight young?'

Jude grins and says it'll do. 'What did Jimmy Ashworth look like?'

I've no idea. Will this granddaughter of hers know? At the moment I know practically nothing about this side of Henry's life. The granddaughter isn't called Ashworth but Kimball, Mrs Laura Kimball, so she may be Jimmy's son's daughter or her daughter's daughter, and that son or daughter may have been born pre-Henry or post-Henry. In a fortnight's time I hope to find out, while being rather afraid Mrs Kimball may by now be a very old lady indeed. The handwriting on her letter was shaky and spidery. Her daughter I spoke to on the phone said Mother was wonderful for her age, which I heard as a warning of what to expect.

I go into my study and fetch Henry's diary and his wedding photograph, this last never framed but still in its pristine cover of embossed cream-coloured card, threaded through with white satin ribbon and with a silver curlicue design on its corners. It wasn't in one of the chests but among Great-aunt Clara's possessions that came to my father when she died. Jude and I sit down on the sofa and I show her the diary with its pentagrams and together we look at the photograph. The date is October 1884. They were married in Bloomsbury, Edith's parents lived in Bloomsbury, in Keppel Street, a pleasant enough district but still a far cry from Grosvenor Square where Sir John Batho's home was.

Henry looks very handsome in his morning coat, tall and thin, clean-shaven then. The moustache came later. His hair is plentiful and still dark, though there may be grey which doesn't show in the photograph. Jude says his face reminds her of the first President Bush and I can see what she means. If I didn't know how old he was I'd guess him to be ten years younger, but I expect they touched up photographs in those days just as they do now. His bride is overdressed in quantities of white satin embroidered with pearls and her veil is held in place on an elaborate structure of blonde curls by a pearl tiara. She carries what I suppose is a Prayer Book bound in white velvet with a long ribbon marker hanging down against her crinoline and a spray of white roses somehow fastened to it. Her mouth is full-lipped, her nose retroussé, her chin rather too small but she has fine eyes, large and dark.

Henry and Edith, my great-grandparents. Blood-obsessed Henry, the haematologist, and his bride less than half his age. After the pictures are taken, after he has changed into whatever travelling costume middle-aged men wore in 1884 (I shall have to find out) and she into her 'going away' dress with bonnet and gloves, they are off to Rome and Naples on their honeymoon. The same destinations, incidentally, as he had planned for his honeymoon with Edith's dead sister. Presumably, in those pre-winter sports days, Austria and Switzerland would have been too cold in February.

'What happened to Jimmy Ashworth?' Jude wants to know.

'Discarded,' I say. 'Sadly, that's what happened to kept women. It's very unlikely Edith ever knew of her existence.'

'I'm getting to dislike Henry.'

I smile and say that though he may have been charming, he wasn't a likeable man. But he was nicer once, before the events of 1879. These were both terrible and wonderful. We've all heard stories of people who've missed a flight by getting to the airport two minutes late and an hour later the plane's crashed, with no survivors. Something like that had happened to Henry when he was in Scotland with Hamilton for hogmanay five years before he was married.

4

No one shall be a member of the House of Lords, says the Bill, by virtue of a hereditary peerage. The holder of such a peerage shall not be disqualified by virtue of that peerage from voting at elections to the House of Commons, or being elected as a member of that House. When the Bill becomes an Act it shall come into force at the end of the Session of Parliament at which it is passed and it's to be called the House of Lords Act, 1999. And that's all, a very simple Bill. Getting it through, though, will be far from simple.

Some peers, and not necessarily those with peerages dating back many hundreds of years, see themselves as having a God-given right to rule. Not that they can do much ruling in there, not that any of us can. With the Government having such a huge majority in the Commons almost anything we decide on can be overturned. What we *can* do is delay and revise. No doubt, it's fine to be a life peer. As yet it's the media alone, muttering and growling about appointees and prime minister's cronies, who feebly question their right to be where they are. That may change when the militant hereditaries sharpen their weapons. It's still something to be a hereditary whose ancestor was a pal of Charles I or married to a mistress of Charles II, but it's all so long ago everyone's forgotten how it came about in the first place. We, the hereditaries whose peerages have come to us through great-grandfathers and grandfathers being ambassadors, colonial governors, field marshals, admirals, cabinet ministers and, as in my case, a royal doctor, we are the ones who fall between two stools, our peerages neither hallowed by time nor redeemed by the knowledge that we were personally chosen.

I say all this to Paul over lunch in the Peers' Guest Dining Room. I wouldn't have dreamt of holding forth on the subject if he hadn't asked me. He seems not to like what he's heard, a reaction I've often noticed in him when he's been insistent about getting information. It's as if he expects the narrator to improve unpalatable facts for his sake. Someone – was it T. S. Eliot? – said that human beings can't stand too much reality. Paul can't and, as always, I wonder if it's because Sally and I split up when he was only six and if that was the first reality he taught himself not to face.

'I shall never call myself Lord Nanther,' he says.

I tell him with a facetiousness he brings out in me that he may change his mind about that, he's got a long time to wait as I'm only forty-four.

'Titles will go,' he says. 'That'll be the logical next step. You'll get what happens in Europe where lots of people are counts or whatever but everyone else has forgotten it and only snobs call them by their titles.'

'You may be right.'

'Yes, well, I'm right in two senses. *I'm* right when I say you shouldn't have a voice in here just because your great-grandfather wrote out a few prescriptions for a royal highness and *it's* right that this year will see an end to it.'

'You have a harsh way of putting it.'

Paul smiles rather grimly. He has a harsh way of putting most things, he enjoys reproof, even mild reproof, and seems to flourish on it. He loves being told off. I dare say

I'm quite wrong in saying his skin is as thick as a rhinoceros's, psychologists would tell me that's only a carapace over his sensitivity, to which I'd reply that he could fool me. Paul is nearly nineteen and clever, a student at the University of Bristol, and with his armoured outside, quick grasp, it seems to me, of everything he turns his mind to and readiness for the fray, he'll make an ideal politician one day. By then, to get into the House of Commons, he won't even have to renounce a peerage.

I order coffee and ask him how his mother is. All right, he says, or so he supposes. Sally has been living for the past year in a self-supporting community in the Outer Hebrides and Paul says he never writes letters, only e-mails, which, he says, puts her outside his remit. No one, anyway, could expect him to travel to a remote Scottish island in April even if he could afford the train fare. We asked him to Alma Villa for the Easter holiday, it is after all his home, but he prefers staying in a friend's flat in Ladbroke Grove, something I understand perfectly.

'Can I have pudding?' he says, like a little boy.

It moves me, just as it does on the rare, the very rare, occasions when he calls me dad. I want to hug him the way I did before Sally left and took him away, but that of course is out of the question now and for ever. The sweet trolley comes round and he has profiteroles in chocolate sauce. Paul is taller than I am and much better looking. I notice the other diners, peers and their wives and women peers and husbands, stealing glances at him. There's a former prime minister sitting at a table under the portrait of Henry VII. He's spotted Paul, recognized him and favoured him with a wave and a nod. Thank God Paul smiles back and dips his head. I suspect it's ironic but no one else does.

The time is approaching a quarter past two and things are

speeding up because the House sits at two-thirty. Everything is run with exquisite precision in here, the organization superb and nothing neglected or forgotten; coffee served in plenty of time for peers to drink it, pay their bills – or pay them tomorrow or next week – and amble off towards the Peers' Lobby and the Chamber. No rush, no urgency and no unpunctuality. Maria has passed our table, given me the smile that indicates nothing could be further from her thoughts than expecting me to pay before next week, and Farouk has removed Paul's plate. We get up.

Last time I brought Paul in here he was sixteen, shyer and less confident than he is now. The doorkeepers called him 'the Honourable Paul Nanther', gave him the book to sign and showed him to the steps of the throne, where peers' eldest sons sit by right.

In one way I'd like Paul to come into the Chamber. I'd be proud of him sitting on that step, which is really a padded seat, his back against that towering structure, such a bright gold it hurts the eyes to look at it for long, beneath that spiritual oddity the Cloth of Estate and below the hallowed chair where only the reigning monarch may be seated. After half an hour, after question time, I'd catch his eye and we'd go out together. On the other hand, I'd be afraid he might do something, misbehave himself in some way. Not shout, not make some inflammatory statement so that he had to be bundled out, but put his head in his hands or favour the House with that look he's bestowing on me now as we walk down the corridor towards the Prince's Chamber, supercilious, critical, slightly incredulous. It tells me he's rejecting the steps of the throne this time. It's very likely his last chance but he won't care about that.

'I'd better go, Dad,' he says, and of course my heart goes out to him. I want him to stay. That I've got an appointment at four with two people I really want to see alone weighs nothing with me. I ask him if he's sure he doesn't want to come into the Chamber.

'Not much point, is there?' he says in a sulky way. 'I soon shan't be able to,' he complains, as if I'm personally responsible for the reform bill.

I walk downstairs with him and outside the Peers' Entrance renew our invitation to come and stay at Alma Villa whenever he likes. Thanks, he says, but he's fine where he is and spoils a perfectly reasonable form of refusal by adding that he doesn't suppose Jude and I want anyone else around. I've noticed that lately he's begun talking about us as if we were still on our honeymoon or a couple of teenage lovers who've just moved in together. The last I see of him he's standing in front of the lavishly robed statue of George V on the far side of the street, giving it I suppose one of his incredulous looks. But he has his back to me and I can't see his face.

I call in at the Printed Paper office, pick up yesterday's Hansard and go into the Chamber during the first starred question, seating myself behind Lord Quirk and in front of Lord Northbourne. I'm not very interested in the question so I discreetly read the record of yesterday's proceedings. You may read in here so long as it's not a book or a newspaper, which are severely frowned on and may be confiscated. Hansard is all right. In 1877 a Treasury grant had been made to the Hansard firm enabling them to employ four reporters and report more fully than had been the case when the volumes were mostly compiled from newspaper reports. Henry was introduced in 1896 but it wasn't for another thirteen years that Hansard became the Official Report and its text 'full'. By then Henry was dead. Still, the relevant 'Parliamentary Debates' are quite adequate to show me the few times he spoke after his maiden speech. I look up and picture him somewhere on the spiritual side when the Tories were in power, proud of himself perhaps but a little uneasy too because the peers on either side of him are of ancient lineage and his peerage is of first creation. Is it only the English or only *Europeans* who rate blood (genes now, Henry, DNA) more highly than achievement?

When I'd decided to write Henry's biography I advertised in *The Times*, the *Spectator*, the *Author* and a good many other places, for descendants of people who'd known him, who possessed letters from him or letters and documents in which he was mentioned. The advertisement I put in *The Times* is still going and may still, I'm hoping, summon up further information. Of course I've had dozens of responses. It's been largely a matter of sifting through them for what's useful and what isn't. Among the people who replied were the two women who are coming in this afternoon. They didn't sound likely readers of *The Times* but the younger one explained she was told about it by her son.

I'll have to go back into the Chamber sometime, but not yet. The Salisbury Room beckons and I make my way quietly down there and sink into one of the slippery leather chairs. These chairs, especially the low black ones, seem designed to keep an occupant from falling asleep, their backs being too short for comfort and their seats too long. A bearded Lord Salisbury, or a bust of him, looks through me towards the river and St Thomas's Hospital, and that reminds me that no one's allowed to die in the House. It's supposed to be something to do with the Queen's coroner having to preside at the inquest on anyone dying in a royal palace and that being too difficult or too expensive or, as my son might say, whatever. Anyone who does die is carted off by ambulance to St Thomas's and pronounced dead on arrival.

I read my Hansard and then I read my *Guardian* as devotedly as if I sat on the Government benches. The *Guardian* reminds its readers of the Salisbury Convention – appropriate for this room – which postulates that any intention a political party presents in its manifesto shall be taken as the will of the people if that party is voted into government. Somehow, I don't think that rule is going to cut much ice with the opposition when it comes to the sitting and voting rights of hereditary peers, though the Government plainly set out that it intended to abolish their parliamentary right.

I think back over the records of my forebears. Henry did his bare duty, made a maiden speech, came in sometimes, occasionally spoke, and Alexander seldom attended. Of course he was only fourteen when he inherited but, though living in England for a while after coming out of the army in 1918, he seems to have shown his face in here only once before he went off to the South of France, and only a couple of times in the thirties. He must have found it trying, not being permitted to smoke in the Chamber. My father was dutiful. It's an advantage to be a lawyer in Parliament and he made an eloquent maiden speech presenting the humane case for the abolition of the death penalty. Afterwards he came in regularly once a week, though he never said any more, apart from occasionally intervening with a supplementary at question time. I've attended regularly, but I doubt if I've contributed anything memorable or that my absence, after the Bill becomes the Act, will be much noticed.

Back to the Chamber for half an hour during which I strive to attend to a series of amendments I don't much like and will vote against if any of them are brought to a division.

I'm struggling not to fall asleep. Sleeping is all right for the over-sixties but frowned upon if you're younger. If you happen to be seated behind a minister and you sink into a doze a doorkeeper will come and politely wake you up, reminding you that as soon as the minister gets up to speak you too will appear on television, open-mouthed and snoring.

At five to four I go downstairs to sit on the throne-like chair to the right of the fireplace and await the coming of Mrs Kimball and Mrs Forsythe, the two women who replied to my ad. I've a picture of what they'll be like in my mind, Mrs Kimball small and round and white-haired, her daughter the same shape but with brown permed hair, both of them dressed by Marks and Spencer and both shy and overawed by this place. By my age I ought to know better than to do this because I'm always wrong. This time I'm more wrong than usual. The revolving doors swing open in a confident manner, the way they do when Lord Cranborne or Lady Blatch walk through, and in come two tall thin gaunt women with aggressive expressions, each clutching a brief-case. There must be a minimum of sixteen years between them and more like twenty-three, seeing they are mother and daughter, but they look much the same age, sisters perhaps.

We shake hands. Mrs Kimball is probably eighty but she's as upright as a girl of eighteen and her hair is dyed a savage black which makes a curious contrast with her pale wrinkled face and the dark-red lipstick she wears. Her daughter is a little less wrinkled and her hair is dyed a rich shade of chestnut. Both wear raincoats, long, dark and belted, over afternoon dresses of flowered silk, one wine red and white, the other various shades of green and white. The doorkeeper takes their coats and I ask him if he wants to put their briefcases through the X-ray machine but he says, 'Not as the ladies are your guests, my Lord,' which leaves me with mixed feelings. Along with my gratitude for the courtesy and consideration of the staff in this place, goes a kind of shameful hope that the doorkeeper doesn't think Mrs Kimball and Mrs Forsythe are related to me.

They are more unbending than they looked at first. And shyer. The vast cloakroom with pegs labelled for such august figures as the Duke of Edinburgh and the Prince of Wales overwhelms most people and Laura and Janet (which they ask me to call them) are no exceptions. Janet Forsythe wants to know if 'Prince Philip' ever comes in and I have to tell her I've never seen him except at State Openings when he accompanies the Queen. Does he use the peg then, she wants to know, but that's something I can't answer. We go up the great staircase, another awesome experience for newcomers, and I point out the armorial bearings on the walls, painted there by a family of artists who hand this function down from father to son.

Their rather gaunt faces, regular features and olive skin remind me of someone but I can't think who. Probably a photograph I've seen or something on television. We're bombarded with images these days. It's at this point, as we cross the Prince's Chamber and I have to tell them to keep their voices down and walk quickly across the blue carpet, that Laura, stepping on to the red carpet once more, tells me she's got her grandmother's marriage certificate to show me. She's so insistent I see it at once that we all sit down on one of the red-leather benches opposite the painting of the Chamber in former times when a lot of peers wore silk hats. For a moment, no more than a couple of seconds, I wonder if she's going to give me proof that Henry married

Jimmy Ashworth in a secret ceremony, thus making his marriage to Edith Henderson bigamous and his descendants' claims to sit in this House fraudulent. But the certificate is not world-shaking at all. It merely shows that Jemima Ann Ashworth, aged twenty-eight, daughter of George Edward Ashworth of Somers Town, was married to Leonard William Dawson, aged thirty-three, porter, of Lisson Grove, Marylebone, at the Church of St Mary-le-bone, on 30 October 1883.

'My mother was Mary Dawson. She was born the following year,' says Laura.

And where was Henry? Transferring his affections from Eleanor to Edith, I suppose. Without the diary, which is in Alma Villa, I can't recall when the pentagrams stop, though I know it's sometime in 1883. Laura asks if I'd like to 'copy down' the details on the marriage certificate but I tell her I can do better than that and I take it round the corner to the nearest photocopier while the two of them stand behind me and watch the process. Then we go into the Peers' Guest Dining Room.

It's intimidating, no doubt about it, and even more so when, as today, Baroness Thatcher is in there, presiding over a tea table of attentive men. Laura and Janet stare as if they'd hitherto doubted she had a real existence. A table for the three of us is secured and I order a pot of Indian tea with sandwiches, teacakes and pastries. According to the screen up on the wall, we're still on amendment 32, a controversial one I don't like, and its mover is on his feet. Laura asks if I'd like her to tell me everything she knows about her grandmother's romance (her word) with Dr Nanther and, just as I enthusiastically agree, the white letters DIVISION come up on the screen with the on and off flashing picture of a red bell and the division bells start to clatter.

Like the hereditary who hadn't been in for forty years but with more justification, Janet wants to know what that awful noise is. Is it a fire? I do my best to explain, tell them I'll be back in five minutes, and as I get up the tea and sandwiches come.

Laura recovers her equilibrium, says she'll be mother and not to worry, I'm to be just as long as I like. We used to have six minutes to get into the lobbies but, after pressure was exerted by government peers, the time was extended to eight minutes. That's ample for me, I'm against the amendment, so I go through the Not Content lobby where I don't even have to give my name, for I'm recognized before I reach the clerk who's crossing us off. The Labour whip at the door grins as I go by and whispers, 'More to come,' which doesn't affect me as I don't take the Labour Party whip, though I suddenly find myself thinking of doing so for my remaining time in here. Back in the dining room, where a great exodus has taken place, it seems I'm the first to get back. Laura and Janet are contentedly eating cucumber sandwiches and already look much better-tempered.

'Was everything all right?' Janet asks.

Uncertain of what she means, I nod and smile and ask Laura to start on Jimmy Ashworth's history. She produces something else from the envelope that contains the marriage certificate. It's one of those postcards that were popular with the Victorians and Edwardians and which were the forerunners of World War Two pin-ups and today's newspaper pictures of models. Famous Beauties of the Day, they could be called. I remember seeing one of Lily Langtry. Jimmy Ashworth (the name under the photograph is Jemima 'Jimmy' Ashworth) isn't at all like Mrs Langtry, but quite a lot like Olivia Batho and thus, I suppose, Jude. It's a perfectly proper photograph, though the satin gown she wears is cut rather low, exposing a formidable cleavage into which ropes of pearls disappear. She's also wearing elbow-length white gloves and a corsage of lush flowers of the lily and stephanotis type. She has more pearls in her elaborately dressed dark hair and bracelets *over* the gloves.

'She has a very sweet expression, don't you think?' Laura asks.

I agree, I can't very well do anything else, but if I'd been honest I'd have said the sweetness is tempered by calculation and by something else. Not greed, not the 'hardness' one might expect, but – and I see it rather to my own dismay – despair. 'Desperation' might be the better word, it's not quite as profound as despair. Jimmy Ashworth is very young in this picture, a good way off twenty-eight, and life isn't holding out great promise for her, no matter that she's got her photograph into the Famous Beauties series. I ask Laura how my great-grandfather met her and in her reply I detect that the whitewashing of all concerned has begun.

I can understand people putting the best possible construction, for the ears of outsiders, on the behaviour of their husbands or wives or children or even parents. It's natural not to want to be closely associated with cheating or lying or even with failure and thriftlessness. But a grandmother? Does it really matter how one's grandmother behaved? Is it of any account, at the end of the twentieth century, that one's grandmother in the nineteenth was less chaste than she might have been? That she was a gold digger? A kept woman? Some people would be proud of it, seeing it as an interesting feature of their ancestry. Not Laura Kimball, who begins by telling me Henry was taken to Jimmy's 'apartments'· by a friend who introduced them. Could

Henry have seen the Famous Beauties postcard? This was some time in 1874 when Jimmy was nineteen. I ask where the apartments were but Laura doesn't know. All this, she explains, was told her by her own mother, whom I at once suspect of doing a good deal of doctoring of the facts on her own account. What very likely happened was that the friend had originally 'kept' Jimmy, had possibly taken her off the streets, and when he grew tired of her – or planned to marry? – passed her on to Henry.

Henry was 'madly in love' with Jimmy and, of course, she with him. 'They were made for each other,' says Laura. 'Dr Nanther desperately wanted to marry her, he proposed over and over, but she always said no.'

I asked why this was, considering they were in love.

'Dr Nanther's father was against it. He absolutely forbade his son to have anything to do with my grandmother. That was why they had to meet in secret. That was why he took that little house in the back of beyond – well, it was then – so that it wouldn't get back to his father.'

I nod sympathetically. There is no point at all in telling her that by 1874 Henry was thirty-eight years old, hadn't received an allowance from his father for more than a decade and, most significantly, the old mill-owner who was bedbound and paralysed through stroke two years before, had died in 1873. Henry's reason for not marrying Jimmy Ashworth was that men of his standing didn't marry women in her position in the 1870s. In their eyes there were three sexes in the world, men, good women and fallen women. The good woman in his life was Olivia Batho, she was up on a pedestal, while Jimmy, if she'd ever been on one, had fallen off it long ago.

If she thought she could get away with it, Laura would probably try to persuade me that relations between Jimmy

69

and Henry were entirely chaste, a matter of Henry occasionally coming to tea with the great love of his life but never laying a finger on her. Perhaps she knows that would be too much even for me to swallow. She gives me a searching look as she admits she has no photograph of her grandmother with my great-grandfather. Henry, of course, took good care none was taken. In those days photography was a long and involved process, very different from today, and easily avoided. She tells me about the jewellery Henry gave Jimmy, some of which is in her possession. Would I like to see a photograph of her daughter wearing 'a beautiful star brooch of real diamonds'? I say I would, though I doubt the diamonds. A man who gave his first fiancée's engagement ring to his second wouldn't give diamonds to a mistress.

'They fixed up a marriage for him with a Miss Eleanor Henderson,' Laura says. 'He was heartbroken and many an evening him and my grandmother spent desperately thinking of ways to get him out of it, but they'd tied him up too tightly for that.' I ask her who 'they' were and she says Henry's father and Mr Henderson, who were 'business associates'. 'His engagement to this Eleanor was announced in the August and him and Jimmy were forced to part.'

That last bit sounds pretty accurate. As far as I can recall, the pentagrams come to an end at about that time. Janet chips in now to remind me that Jimmy got married two months later. Leonard Dawson, she says, had been her faithful swain for more years than she'd known Henry, but obliged to worship from afar.

'They'd call him a stalker these days,' says Laura, 'always hanging around her, following her about, standing on the street where she lived, gazing up at her windows.' Alarmingly, she sings a couple of appropriate lines from *My Fair*

Lady in a cracked soprano. 'Well, when Dr Nanther – he was Sir Henry by then – when he had to give her up and she had to give him up, she naturally turned to Len. I suppose you could say she took him on the rebound.'

'What happened to the house?'

'The house?'

'In Chalcot Road, Primrose Hill. What happened to it?'

'It was hers, wasn't it? Her and Len stayed there, they started their married life there, my mother was born there. Then they sold it and moved to King's Cross.'

Relief is what I feel. I don't know why I should, why I should care. Perhaps it's because there's something gloomy about having to set Henry down as a complete out and out bastard, without as far as I could see a redeeming feature. But here, now, was one. When he left her he gave her the house. More probably he continued to pay the rent of it. Did he give her the husband as well? Maybe. Leonard Dawson is described as a porter on the marriage certificate. Is that a railway porter or a *hospital* porter? A house, a husband and a lump sum? Five hundred pounds? Henry wasn't quite as black as I've been painting him.

'You could say she pipped Dr Nanther - that is, Sir Henry, I should say – to the post. He didn't get married to that Eleanor till eighteen eighty-four. She'd have been your great-grandma.'

I let it pass. Pointless to engage in long explanations. Eleanor *might* have been my great-grandmother if she hadn't met a horrible death and if Henry had married her, but she did and he didn't. He married her sister. I say nothing to Laura and Janet about this. A waiter comes with the tray of pastries and they help themselves. The screen clears and gives the result of the division: Contents, 66, Not Contents, 82. So we defeated the amendment. Laura begins to talk about her mother, born in 1884, the idyllic childhood she had gambolling on Primrose Hill, being taken for walks by her nurse in Regent's Park.

All this time I've been asking myself who they remind me of but I still haven't come up with the answer. Laura hasn't told me *when* in 1884 her mother was born and I'm not going to ask. I can easily find out for myself from the records. Len Dawson and his wife, it appears, had five more children, all happy, successful and well off, according to Laura. Janet says they were a long-lived family and she's proud to tell me her mother's aunt Elizabeth, Jimmy's daughter born in 1891 (the same year, incidentally, as Clara Nanther) lived on till well into the nineteen eighties.

Tea is over and we walk back the way we came. I ask if I may borrow the Famous Beauties postcard as an illustration for my biography when the time comes and Laura grudgingly agrees. 'You wouldn't want the postcard yet, would you?' Janet asks.

'Probably not for two or three years,' I tell her, and then wonder if that's a tactful thing to say to someone who can't have been born later than 1923.

Janet evidently feels the same. She says quickly that the picture will be quite safe with her and she'll see that I get it when the time comes. She also tells me about a genealogical table she's made, which shows how philoprogenitive Mary Dawson was. Twelve children were born to her between 1903 and 1918.

'They all grew up healthy and all had children,' Laura says proudly.

We approach the Prince's Chamber and Janet wants to know what that woman's doing sitting on a chair in front of the fireplace. I explain that she's a Labour whip and that she's there to make sure her 'flock' vote, and to catch back benchers if they try to escape and go home. Neither of them believes me, though it's true.

'Why do they have to stay?' Laura asks.

'They have to vote and make sure the Government wins.'

'Couldn't they get out some other way?'

'They often do,' I say, and Laura and Janet are still wondering if I'm having them on when I take my raincoat off its peg and accompany them out into the street. I'm going home too and as I'm seeing them into Westminster tube station, thanking them and saying goodbye, Laura says, 'Thank you very much for tea, my Lord,' which embarrasses me and I think I go red in the face.

On my way home I ask the cab driver to drop me off in Primrose Hill. There's something magical about the place, especially after dark. The green hill and the green slopes rise up, crossed by sandy paths like a countryside, and you feel you've come to the edge of London, there can be nothing beyond but fields and woods. Then, as soon as you're over the summit, you see the long terrace of big Victorian houses, the shops and restaurants all lit with golden light, and the narrow streets running back into the hinterland. And, almost immediately, you find yourself in a little urban island, the heart of it the prettiest part, for it is here that Chalcot Road runs into Chalcot Square, where on its eastern side Sylvia Plath lived and died. The houses are all irregular, all Victorian or earlier, painted pink and purple and yellow and brown, overhung by big trees, with a little green garden in the centre. There is no more charming square in all London. Alma stands no comparison with it.

The curtains are undrawn, and behind the windows chandeliers glisten and flowers in vases shimmer, their colours bleached by the many and varied lights, their leaves shining. I walk up Chalcot Road, wide and straight. It bisects this area, dividing it almost evenly down the centre. A little way along there's a pub called the Princess of Wales, but it was named for Alexandra, wife of Edward VII, not Diana. This persuades me that it and these houses would have been put up in the sixties during the nineteenth century, for Edward married Alexandra in 1863, but I shall have to check.

It's not a beautiful street. It's too wide and the houses were built in long dull terraces, all much the same. One of them would have been occupied by Jimmy and later by Jimmy and Len Dawson, but I've no way of knowing which. The Dawsons seem to have moved away after a couple of years and gone to live in the less salubrious district of King's Cross. Why? Surely because Henry was unwilling to pay the rent for more than two years.

I retrace my steps, back to Rothwell Street, the main road and the hill. It's a fine night, mild and clear enough to walk home. I take one of the paths, then St Edmund's Terrace and I'm in St John's Wood. While I walk I'm thinking about the illusions people like to keep about a respectable family past, and about pentagrams in a diary, and then, suddenly, I know who Laura Kimball and her daughter remind me of.

My father. Those long rather gaunt faces – they used to call it 'lantern-jawed' – are my father's face, and maybe Alexander's too if I remember rightly. The looks of the women Nanther men marry don't seem to affect the off-spring – not until my father married my mother, that is. All Nanther children got from their mothers till then was fair hair and sometimes blue eyes. If Laura and Janet resemble my father, they must also look like Henry. *Ergo*, they are not Len Dawson's descendants but Henry's, just as I am?

5

This morning I went to the Family Records Centre in Islington where the records are kept to add to the rather pathetic family tree I've made. There I carefully noted that of Henry's daughters the first, Elizabeth, married James Kirkford in 1906 but the second, Mary, waited another sixteen years before marrying Matthew Craddock. Elizabeth had a son, Kenneth, and two daughters, while Mary had two daughters, Patricia and Diana. Finding out all this takes quite a long time and I still had to track down Jimmy Ashworth and her family. I knew enough about her to make this easy. Her daughter Mary was born in February 1884, four months after her mother's marriage to Leonard Dawson. A child born in wedlock is presumed to be her mother's husband's (*Quem nuptiae demonstrant pater est*), which was no doubt why Henry was anxious to get Jimmy and Len married as soon as possible. But Mary was *his* daughter, I'm certain.

I wanted to talk to Jude about all this last night. I found a photograph of Henry, taken when he was about the age Janet is now, and the resemblance was even more striking than I'd thought. The shape of the forehead, the rather high-bridged nose, the straight eyebrows, the long upper lip, they were all there. Henry's, my father's, Laura's, Janet's. Could you see it in me? I scrutinized my face in the mirror. But, no, I look more like my mother. It's a strange feeling you get when you discover some unexpected offshoot of your family, exciting and slightly distasteful. I told myself

I was as bad as Laura, trying to whitewash a forebear I'd never known and probably wouldn't have liked. But it wasn't quite that which disturbed me, rather the feeling that I shared my genetic inheritance with strangers, almost alien people. It was a kind of sick joke. I'd disliked what the doorkeeper said when he'd politely implied that any guests of mine must be beyond reproach and suggested that Laura and Janet were my relations. But they *were*, all the time they *were*.

For half an hour I'd come closer to liking Henry. For his generosity, his determination to look after the woman he was deserting. Since then my feelings had once more taken an about turn. What had it been like for Jimmy Ashworth, obliged by the man whose child she was carrying to marry a man provided for her, someone she cared nothing for and who was not that child's father? And for Len Dawson? Could anything be more humiliating? Sally and I had often got on badly, especially towards the end of our marriage, but I can remember the tenderness I felt for her when she was pregnant with Paul, the pride I took in the changes her body underwent and in walking down the street with her holding my arm. My child. None of that for Len Dawson. Could they ever have discussed it? Talked about the coming baby and its paternity? I imagine rather Dawson saying, perhaps on the eve of his wedding, 'We're never going to say another word about it,' and even, 'Sir Henry's fixed up things comfortable for us, we're grateful and we've no cause to mention it again.'

I'd like to know more about Jimmy Ashworth, not just her parentage, the date of her marriage and that she was twenty-eight when she married Len Dawson. Both her parents were alive at the time of the marriage, and living in Somers Town, not all that far away. Of their circumstances

I know nothing. Did Jimmy on leaving school, at a no doubt very early age, work long ill-paid hours in a sweatshop somewhere? Was she in danger of losing her sight or poisoning herself with white lead? And was this why she went on the streets, after the fashion of many poor Victorian girls? If she did. I don't know who her first 'protector' was or even if it was he who introduced her to Henry. I'd like to know if she loved him. I'm sure he didn't love her. Then there's the baby, conceived after nine years. It may be, of course, that others were conceived and Jimmy aborted them. Does that mean she wanted this baby? That she even thought Henry might marry her if she was pregnant with his child? I shall never know. Henry left nothing to go on except a five-pointed star signifying he'd paid a visit to his mistress that day.

I can't repeat any of this to Jude. I'm not going too far when I say anyone's baby would do for her. Someone else's eggs and someone else's sperm, if you like, other people's blood, DNA, it wouldn't matter. She asked me after the second miscarriage if I'd find a surrogate mother to have my child for her. I hated saying no, I always hate saying no to her, but I had to. If I'm indifferent to the possibility of a child, I positively hate the idea of having one with someone else. Len Dawson was involved in a sort of surrogacy and I don't suppose he liked the idea any more than I did. So instead of telling her about this, I content myself with recounting the story of the Tay Bridge disaster, but first I said a few things about Laura and Janet and our tea party. Instead of mentioning the resemblance between them and my father I said that Jude looks a bit like the Famous Beauty Jimmy Ashworth.

'And therefore Olivia Batho,' she said.

'And Olivia Batho.'

'Why on earth didn't Henry marry her?' she wants to know, and then she asks the same question about Caroline Hamilton and did Caroline look like the other two. I don't know the answers to these questions, and unless I come across more letters, I never shall. So I leave the subject of Jimmy and her descendants, go back some few years into the eighteen seventies and show Jude the photocopied extracts from *The Times* of 30 December 1879. The typeface is very small and the text hasn't come out very well. She says it's too hard to read, she'll need a magnifying glass, and why don't I just tell her the story of Henry and the ill-fated train? She'd like that much better and she takes my hand and kisses it. Our thing. Our special thing, I think, as I kiss her thin very smooth fingers.

'Henry's father was far from disapproving of any marriage he might have made,' I tell her. 'He died in 1873. His mother still lived at Godby Hall. She had two nurses, paid for by Henry. He was dutiful and correct if not particularly affectionate. She was eighty and senile. I suppose we'd call what she had Alzheimer's. In a letter to Couch written ten years later he writes that she no longer knew who he was, she'd an almost total memory loss. Couch was some sort of specialist in geriatrics and Henry describes his mother's condition to him.'

'This was all ten years later?'

'That's right. Before she became senile Henry had been in the habit of going to Godby for Christmas. Presumably he thought there was no longer any point in going once she no longer recognized him. Anyway, in that year, 1879, he was invited by Richard Hamilton to Hamilton's parents' home in Newport-on-Tay in Fife. It was a little place then. I believe it's quite a big town now.'

After Christmas Richard and Henry were to join a

houseparty at Luloch Castle. I imagine that the prospect of this had a good deal to do with Henry's enthusiasm. It would have meant far more to him than a quiet Christmas with an elderly couple in a Scottish village. He was a snob, though a strangely intermittent one. In order to reach Dundee from the Kingdom of Fife it's necessary to cross the Firth of Tay and at one time this could be done only by ferry. The first railway bridge to span the firth was begun in 1871 and completed seven years later. It was opened on 1 June 1878 and after nineteen months, collapsed into the waters of the firth, taking a train and its passengers with it.

Jude wants to know why. 'It took seven years to build and in the first bad storm it fell down?'

'It was all finished and painted by February 1878. Some general inspected it, I don't know who he was or why he was chosen. They coupled six locomotives together, each one weighing seventy-three tons, and drove them over the bridge at forty miles an hour. I'm quoting now from the report of the inquiry into the disaster, "The behaviour of the bridge under these tests appears to have been satisfactory, there having been only a moderate deflection in the girders, a small degree of tremor, and no indication of looseness in the cross-bracing." On the fifth of March the general said he saw no reason why the bridge shouldn't be used for passenger traffic but that, "it would not be desirable that trains should run over the bridge at a high rate of speed". Twenty-five miles an hour was what he recommended. It was the longest bridge in the world at the time, two miles long, taken in eighty-five spans of iron and concrete, the middle part a hundred and thirty feet above the high water mark.'

'So what happened?'

I tell her we have to go back to Henry. Since 23 December

he'd been staying with the Hamiltons in Newport. He and Richard had decided to take the train from Edinburgh, not an express but a train which stopped at numerous small stations and, having crossed the bridge, was due to reach Dundee at 7.15 in the evening. It was Sunday 28 December, and during the day a great storm had come up with a gale-force wind and driving sleet. Still, the two men saw no reason to postpone their journey. The arrangements were that they would be met by Lord Hamilton's carriage at the Tay Bridge station.

About an hour before they were due to leave the house where the Hamilton parents lived a telegram was delivered to Henry. It was from the housekeeper at Godby Hall and it told him his mother was sinking fast and he should come as soon as he could if he wanted to see her alive. We don't know what Henry thought about this. He was looking forward to his visit to Luloch Castle and he seems to have preferred the company of Richard Hamilton above all other. His mother wouldn't know him and, in any case, would very likely be dead before he reached Yorkshire.

'Did he go?'

'To Godby? He tried to. He gave up the idea of Luloch Castle.'

'I bet he only gave it up because the others had seen the telegram,' says Jude. 'If he'd been alone and no one had seen the telegraph boy he'd have screwed it up and pretended it had never come. I know him.'

'He'd have screwed up the order of release if he had. Once on that train and he'd have been a dead man.'

'And you'd not be here,' she says, taking my hand. 'I'm glad he got the telegram.'

I say that so am I, and maybe he wasn't quite as callous as she thinks. No doubt, he'd loved his mother and he knew

80

his duty. The two men went to the station together, Henry to catch a southbound train and Richard to go north. In the event, of course, Henry's train never came. He waited, the train failed to come, no doubt he enquired what was wrong, and was told telegraphic communication between the Fife side and Dundee had ceased, the equipment also having been damaged by the storm. What became of him for the hours and a few days after that isn't known. Presumably, he could have gone back to the Hamiltons' house and stayed there. Perhaps he waited on the station in the hope another train would come. Certainly he would have attempted to find out what had happened to the train crossing the Tay Bridge. He may have stayed up all night, for remember his great friendship for Richard Hamilton, even perhaps his love for Hamilton. He'd have been very anxious, he wouldn't have been able to rest, but he may eventually have found himself somewhere to spend the hours before morning. During that night his mother died.

'How do you know all this?' Jude wants to know. 'I'll never believe Henry put it in his diary.'

'It's the subject of a very long letter Caroline Hamilton Seaton wrote to her cousin in Leuchars.'

Meanwhile, Richard Hamilton had boarded the train among about ninety other people. The storm was, if anything, worse. There's no reason to think the driver of the train exceeded the prescribed twenty-five miles an hour. Since no one lived to relate what happened there are no eye-witness accounts of how it felt to be in that train, the severity of the storm or whether passengers were afraid. Jude, the publisher, tells me at this point she's just remembered that the novelist A. J. Cronin wrote an account of it through a passenger's eyes in a novel called *Hatter's Castle*, published in 1931.

'But he can't have really known,' she says.

No one can really know. A man called Lawson of Windsor Place, Dundee (this is according to *The Times* of 29 December 1879) went out with a friend just after seven on the evening of the disaster. The two men talked about the fury of the gale which was blowing from the south-west and wondered if, on such a night, the Edinburgh train would venture on to the bridge. They followed with their eyes the line of lights along the lower spans and into the high girders and were transfixed by a sudden tremendous flash. This flash, like a shower of fire, descended into the water, a falling mass of flame, and the lights along the span went down with it.

An eye-witness – I don't know his name but he had a great sense of drama – said, 'I was seated by my fireside last night, listening to the clamour of the storm without, when a blast of wind more furious than before caught the chimneys of a house opposite and brought them down to the ground with a crash that startled every one of us to our feet. Stepping over to the casement, I gazed out upon the street and just then a blaze of moonlight lighted up the broad expanse of the Tay down below, and the long white sinuous line of the bridge came into view . . . I instinctively took out my watch. It was exactly seven o'clock. "The Edinburgh train will be due immediately," I exclaimed to my wife. "Come and let us see if it will attempt to cross on such a night."

'So saying we turned down the gas in the parlour, and with many expressions of thankfulness that no friends of ours, so far as we knew, had to cross the river at that time, prepared to await the appearance of the expected train. The light by this time had become most fitful, masses of cloud were scouring across the expanse of the heavens, at times totally obscuring the light of the full moon. "There she comes," cried one of my children, and at that moment the slowly moving lights of the Edinburgh train could be seen rounding the curve at Wormit. Then it passed the signal box at the south side, and entered on the long straight line of that portion of the bridge. Once on the bridge it seemed to move with great swiftness along, and when the engine entered the tunnel-like cloisters of the great girders, my little girl exactly described the effect of the lights as seen through lattice work when she exclaimed, "Look, Papa. Isn't that like lightning?"

'All this takes some time to write, but to the eye it seemed almost simultaneous with the entrance of the train upon the bridge, a comet like a burst of fiery sparks rang out, as if forcibly ejected into the darkness from the engine. In a long visible trail the streak of fire was seen till quenched in the stormy water below. Then there was absolute darkness on the bridge . . .'

'In consequence of this,' says *The Times*, 'loud appeals were made from the Esplanade to the signalman.' He said that the train was signalled to him from the southern side at nine minutes past seven and at fourteen minutes past it entered the bridge. From his box he had watched for the train but had seen nothing. He tried to telegraph to the signalman on the south side of the bridge but between 7.14 and 7.17 'the means of communication had been interrupted'. The news spread, as such news does, and a crowd gathered at Tay Bridge station. Tickets had been sold for the southbound train but it remained at a standstill in the station.

'That was Henry's train?' asks Jude.

'That was the train he'd have taken.'

It's clear that no one knew what to do next. The violence

of the gale was so great that at first no one dared set foot on the bridge. Then two men attempted it. They were a railway superintendent and the stationmaster at Tay Bridge. They clung on to the rails, cutting their hands, it must have been appalling. Imagine the wind and the wet sleet driving in their faces as they hung on to the slippery ironwork. They got far enough to see that the middle part of the bridge had disappeared and the high girders were gone. But first they saw clouds of spray coming from the pipe that ran along the bridge and carried the water supply for Newport and they knew it had broken when the bridge went down.

The moon was bright but frequently covered by clouds tearing across its face and it was impossible to see the extent of the destruction. They made their way back to Dundee and 'confirmed the worst fears of the crowds'. Quite a lot of people still believed that though the bridge had gone down the train had not and was waiting unscathed in Fife. They clung to this hope until mail bags from the train were picked up at Broughty Ferry on the other side. The gale was still blowing fiercely. At ten o'clock the ferry steamer *The Dundee* came in but brought no news from Newport. The Provost of Dundee with railway officials boarded the steamer at Craig Pier and it set off again, making considerable headway as the storm began to die. When the vessel approached the ruins of the bridge they saw that the whole stretch of the high girders, 3,000 feet in length, had been swept away.

One ghastly result of the watchers' horror and the fluctuating moonlight was that they fancied they saw human beings clinging to the piers, an illusion brought about by the strange shapes the ironwork took when portions of it were torn away. Thirteen huge girders had been wrenched off by the force of the wind, yet no sound had been heard in the town of this enormous mass of iron falling. The roar of the storm had deadened all other noises. They soon saw that it would have been hazardous to approach nearer to the ruined bridge. The harbourmaster took the helm and they pulled away into the darkness, peering down at the water but seeing nothing of the girders nor the train.

First of all they thought there had been three hundred passengers aboard. Estimates of the numbers killed in disasters are always greater than they turn out to be and the total was finally fixed at ninety. Diving operations began next morning. The only body to be recovered, that of an elderly woman, was washed ashore at about the same time.

Jude says, 'So was Henry in the thick of it? Did he go out with one of the boats? Did he see those people or what they thought were people clinging to the wrecked bridge?'

'I don't know. Caroline Hamilton didn't know.'

'So they never found Richard Hamilton?'

'Not his body, no. His luggage, a small suitcase with his initials on it, was washed up at Broughty Ferry with a box of table knives and forks, a package of two pounds of tea and a bunch of temperance pledge cards from the Catholic Society for the Suppression of Drunkenness, among a lot of other things. *The Times* says that two gentlemen – it doesn't name them – had intended to board the train but changed their minds. Henry must have been one of them.

'Caroline mentions Henry quite a lot. I don't know how she knew what his feelings were but the most likely explanation is that he wrote her a condolence letter when he'd found out Richard was dead. Or perhaps wrote to Richard's parents. Nothing was known of the fate of the train until next day. Henry may not have known the whole of it until he saw a newspaper in Huddersfield.'

'His first thought would have been,' Jude says, 'there but

85

for the grace of God. He'd have been shocked by the narrow squeak he'd had.'

Well, maybe. But he'd been deeply attached to Richard Hamilton and now he'd lost the sister and the brother. Jude wants to know why I believe it was grief he felt rather than relief it wasn't him and I tell her because his character changed. Losing Richard Hamilton changed him for the worse.

Perhaps Hamilton kept him in check. He must have known about Jimmy Ashworth. An apparently chaste and celibate man himself, a Scots Presbyterian, he may have urged Henry to give up Jimmy and marry. Victorians seemed to think preaching to one's friends about their conduct perfectly acceptable behaviour, so perhaps Hamilton preached at Henry and up to a point was successful. He could justifiably have said, 'You're past forty now and it's time you became respectable and settled down.' Henry had already met the Batho family by the end of 1879 and Hamilton may have suggested Olivia as a suitable bride.

I've a photograph of Richard Hamilton. He's wearing a gown and mortar board, sitting in an armchair with one elbow resting on a bamboo table on which stands a potted palm. He might be Olivia Batho's brother or Jimmy Ashworth's. A very handsome man, he has their white luminous skin, dark eyes and hair, regular features. His mouth is well-formed and full for a man. Like them, he was Henry's type. His was the appearance he was most attracted to, both for love and friendship. Yet after the disaster, Hamilton is never again mentioned in the diary. The entries become briefer and colder. His name never occurs in any of Henry's subsequent letters. Richard Hamilton, dead under the waters of the Tay, passed from his life, superficially as if he had never been. This photograph, in its parchment folder, found in one of the trunks, is the sole memento of him, apart from his letters.

Henry never mentions his dreams in the diary or the notebook. But it's common for a once loved and now lost person to make an appearance in dreams, promising to come back or denying that he or she has ever been away. So as I put all these papers back into the appropriate files and boxes I ask myself if Henry ever dreamed of Hamilton, of Hamilton as he was or as he might be metamorphosed into a woman or even of the two of them eventually sharing a home, two ageing medical bachelors. But more likely he pictured the storm raging outside the window, the bridge splitting and collapsing and the train breaking and falling in flames to its fate under the waters of the firth.

6

Jude says shrewdly that I may find some big sins when I learn more about Henry's private life. The worst I'm likely to come across, I tell her, is another Jimmy Ashworth turning up after his marriage to Edith Henderson. A petty sin, a grubby one. I go downstairs and cut Mrs Caspar Raven's picture out of the Sargent calendar. Jude and I look at it together, admiring the way Sargent could paint flesh, giving it that pearly luminosity, and Jude says Goya did the same thing in *The Naked Maja*. Taking my second long look at Olivia Batho Raven, trying to find a trace of resemblance to her grandson, Stanley Farrow, I see something spoilt and fretful in her face along with the imperiousness. And I think of some French count or other whose mistress threw her glove into the lion's den, challenging him to pick it up. This awful feat he performed, whereupon the King of France said, according to Leigh Hunt, 'No love but vanity asks love a task like this.'

Mrs Raven was the kind of woman who threw her glove through the bars of the cage and took away her favours if men didn't brave the lion to rescue it. But her husband was the kind of man who'd throw *her* to the lion if she spoke to him like that. And, remembering what Lord Farrow told me, as I take the calendar page into my study and put it into Henry File 1, I ask myself what sort of a life she must have led Caspar and he her. But what sort of life does any husband lead a wife and wife a husband?

★

I've never read about this or heard anyone say it, but I do wonder how many men in my peculiar position feel the way I do. It's been growing for some time now, the feeling, to put it bluntly, that I'm wanted only as a sperm provider. Although it's never been voiced, it's there, real in my mind, and I'm pretty sure real and urgent in Jude's. Her ardour, if that's the word, happens to be strongest on those vital days in the middle of the month, on each one of those days. There's no longer any spontaneity, but a calculated and I think *simulated* urgency. If I instigate our lovemaking there's something unreal about her ardent response. I never get a 'no' or even a hesitation. Sometimes I feel like a fertility machine, to be switched on as often as possible. If I were eighteen I think this might be acceptable, but I'm not and it isn't. And there are times now when if I don't actually say no, I hesitate. A fear is taking root that I'll become impotent.

And that makes it all the more strange that I have an erotic dream. I haven't had one for years. If this were a matter for joking one might say I haven't needed to with my passionate – if that's the right word – bed companion. But I have one tonight, in the small hours. It's about Olivia Batho and, strangely enough, her sister Constance, and Jimmy Ashworth. I'm Henry, I think, very correct in frock coat and silk hat, and they're taking part in one of those *tableaux vivants* that were the Victorian equivalent of shows in strip clubs. They're the Three Graces, naked and all looking like each other and like Jude. I wake up and turn and reach for Jude. She's deeply asleep *and she doesn't want me*. In sleep her contrived passion has gone away somewhere and her unconscious mind rules, the part of her that demonstrates what she really wants – or doesn't want. She even murmurs crossly, 'No, no,' but I'm just as insistent with my urgent, 'Yes, yes,' and she gives way with a pettish, still half asleep, 'Oh, all right.' This must be the first time for a year I've really wanted sex, really wanted, that is, what lovemaking should be, a free and spontaneous impulse. Only it's not that for her and when it's all over, which happens much more quickly than it should, I'm afraid – and I'm ashamed of myself later – I'm exultant that I got my way for once.

One thing's for sure. I'm pretty certain it won't happen like that again.

Henry wrote his first book in 1869 when he was thirty-three. He called his book *Diseases of the Blood* and subtitled it *Haemophilia in Europe and America*. At that time medical opinion was that haemophilia had only recently become known. This was true, but it isn't to say that haemophilia wasn't happening. As far as is known men have been 'bleeders' and women carriers since the beginning of time. *Diseases of the Blood* was probably instrumental in moving the Royal College of Physicians to recognize haemophilia by name, which it did in the mid-eighteen seventies.

Haemophilia is a condition characterized by a chronic liability to immoderate haemorrhage. Certain clotting factors are absent from the blood of sufferers or are in low supply. The haemophilia gene is carried by females on one of their X chromosomes and that's why, today, the disease is called an X-linked condition. A carrier has one X chromosome with a normal gene and one X with a defective gene. Therefore there's a 50 per cent chance of each of her male children having haemophilia and a 50 per cent chance she'll pass on the defective gene to her female children, which means each of her daughters has a 50 per cent chance of also being a carrier. Boys born to a haemophilic father and a non-carrier mother won't have the disease because, in order to be male at all they must have his Y chromosome, but all daughters born to haemophilic men will be carriers because in order to be female they must have his X chromosome. Most female carriers have no health problems related to the gene they carry but others suffer excessive menstrual bleeding, and copious bleeding after surgery or dental work and in childbirth.

Some of this was known in the later decades of the nineteenth century but nothing, of course, about genes or chromosomes. Nor was the cause of haemophilia known, so there was no effective treatment. What Henry did was describe all the cases documented or hinted at in medical and non-medical literature during the centuries of ignorance. He mentions Judaism's *Tractate Jebamoth* in which the story is told of the four sisters living in Zipporah. The first had her baby son circumcised; the clotting factor being absent in his blood, he bled to death. Infant sons of the second and third sisters met the same fate. When the fourth sister had a son she went for advice to the Rabbi Simon ben Gamaliel and he ordered that her son was not to be circumcised. Since Gamaliel lived in the second century AD, Henry claimed that this was the oldest known reference to the disease. He writes next of Maimonides' ruling that a boy was not to be circumcised if his two brothers by the same mother but by different fathers had died after the operation, though Henry of course knew by then that the condition of their fathers could make no difference.

He treats in the book of other isolated recorded examples, quoting the *Al-tasrif* of Alsaharavius, the greatest surgical writer of the Moorish period. There Alsaharavius writes of a village in Spain where men who were wounded suffered an uncontrollable haemorrhage. Boys whose gums were rubbed too harshly had also been known to bleed to death.

In 1539 Alexander Benedictus described the case of a barber who haemorrhaged to death when he accidentally cut his nose with a pair of scissors. Another was that of a rare instance of the boy who at birth bled from the umbilicus. Henry comes to the nineteenth century and refers to Dr John C. Otto, a physician of Philadelphia and his *An Account of a Haemorrhagic Disposition Existing in Certain Families*, published in 1803. He lays before the reader 'Nasse's Law', the assertion of Christian Friedrich Nasse, Professor of Medicine at Bonn, that males alone are the subject of haemophilia and females alone the transmitters, but adds the discovery he may have made himself but was probably made by some other, that the daughters of a male haemophiliac are *always* carriers. These principles inform *Diseases of the Blood*, a tome eight hundred pages long, packed with pedigrees, engraved maps of Swiss Cantons and New England counties, genealogical tables in which subjects are marked in black rings and carriers in white squares, and, of course, a learned, detailed, meticulous text that Henry evidently saw no reason to make accessible, still less interesting, to the layman. It is as dry as dust. I don't know how I managed to grind my way through it. Difficult though it was, the medical profession liked it and it started Henry on the road to fame.

It's unlikely that Queen Victoria read it. If she had, and understood what she read, if she had read there that life expectancy for a haemophiliac was *eight years*, would she have made its author Physician-in-Ordinary to her haemophiliac son? By the eighteen seventies the theory of haemophilia and its inheritance was well-known and thoroughly documented in publications of Elsaesser, Davis, Coates, Rieken, Hughes, Wachsmuth and many others. The late Prince Albert, always fascinated by anything scientific, and with German as his native tongue, would have been acquainted with some of them and would surely have passed information on to the Queen. Leopold's haemophilia was known to his parents but the truth is that Queen Victoria didn't want to know. Least of all did she want to believe that it was through her agency that the disease was passed. We can be sure she didn't read Henry's book, nor probably its successor, *Haemorrhagic Disposition in Families*, and equally certain Henry never passed on to her the current medical opinion, that marriage should be banned for the sisters of haemophiliacs. Taking that advice to heart would have prohibited the dynastic alliances made by at least three of Prince Leopold's sisters.

Henry himself must have had something of the courtier about him to find his way into Victoria's favour. We know he was handsome from his photographs, that he had a beautiful voice, 'low, rich and mellifluous', from a letter Olivia Batho's sister Constance wrote to her friend Lucy Rice. Henry was learned, with probably a charming bedside manner, and can we doubt that he had the assurance and confidence which come from excelling at the job one is good at and most wants to do? Did he perhaps tell the Queen what we now know to be true but which he himself believed *not* to be the case, that haemophilia may occur at random, no one knows why? An irony if he did. It was not until well into this century the discovery was made that the disease may begin through spontaneous mutation.

Whatever Henry said or did, the fact was that he was appointed physician to the Prince, at that time nineteen years old. Leopold had been the most unruly of Victoria's children. Boys with haemophilia are often daredevils, playing the sort of games most dangerous to them, just as their mothers are over-protective. The kind of minor injuries which all children encounter, bruised knees, small cuts and grazes, resulted in Leopold's case in prolonged blood loss. Almost worse were the internal bleeding and bleeding into the joints and from the gums.

He was also, some say, the nicest of the Queen's four sons and the most intellectual and he insisted on being allowed to go up to Oxford. That Henry was sometimes in attendance on him there is mentioned in the Queen's letters to her eldest daughter, the Crown Princess Frederick. In 1881 Leopold was made Duke of Albany and eventually decided to marry, in spite of his mother's terrors and warnings. Perhaps Henry was able to calm her fears. Many years later, while on holiday with his own family in the Lake District, he wrote the following to Barnabus Couch, a propos of his attendance on the haemophilic son of Princess Beatrice of Battenberg:

I very well remember Her Majesty the Queen's distress when HRH the Duke of Albany proposed to marry. She had determined HRH was far too great an invalid to consider matrimony. Her opinion was that he should remain quietly at Court, pursuing if he wished to do so his scholarly interests. Even she, with her fervid imagination, could not conceive of a haemophiliac subject injuring himself with writing and reading materials, though in fact HRH did once cause a violent and protracted bleed through piercing the roof of his mouth with a steel pen! Then, when he proposed to the Princess Helene and was accepted, there came first shock and grief but this was swiftly followed by assertions on HM's part that she, and none but she, had arranged the alliance and nothing could be more proper. I was anxious not to tell her falsehoods but there was one question I avoided. Fortunately, she did not ask it. I could not tell her the truth, that any daughters HRH might beget would inevitably be conductors of haemophilia.

It was extraordinary how coarse HM could be. She told me without a blush and with not the least diffidence that she doubted if the Prince was capable of fatherhood. There, of course, she was wrong, for the Duchess of Albany had produced a daughter – certainly a conductor – and was soon to produce a son when her husband met his untimely death. As HM and I discussed Prince Leopold's future, making reference principally to the various treatments (the application of ice, cauterization, rest) I had in mind for his incurable condition – she believed, if you please, that he would 'grow out of it' – she turned suddenly upon me and remarked that it was time *I* considered matrimony myself. I must be approaching forty, she said, flattering me greatly by lopping some five years off my age. She then astonished me more than I can say by quoting Shakespeare! She looked at me and declared I must not take such 'graces to the grave and leave the world no copy'. You, my dear Couch, are the only man (or, come to that, woman) to whom I have related these extraordinary events. As you know, I did marry three years later, though my decision and my choice of wife had little to do with Her Majesty's counsel.

That is the single reference in letter or diary that Henry makes to his wife with the exception of noting at the appropriate time in the diary, 'E. delivered of a daughter' or later on, 'E. delivered of a son.' Of course that means very little. Henry was a Victorian and, like most Victorian men out of the upper middle class, kept his domestic life distinct from his professional life, even to the extent of regarding his diaries as the repository of professional engagements and his letters as purely man-to-man confidences. None of that indicates that he married Edith Henderson for any reason but personal choice, because, in fact, he was in love with her.

★

But, at the time of Prince Leopold's marriage to Princess Helene of Waldeck-Pyrmont, Henry was in love with Olivia Florence Charlotte Batho, or he was giving a very good imitation of being so. She also is never mentioned by name in the diaries or letters but her father and mother are, along with their London house and their country home, Grassingham Hall in Norfolk. He seems to have met the Bathos some time before but the first diary entry is in March 1882. Henry notes, 'Dined with Sir John Batho in Grosvenor Square.' There is something else on that page of the diary, for the same day: a pentagram, indicating an afternoon with Jimmy Ashworth.

Henry dines with the Bathos again in April and again in May, two days before taking a two-week walking holiday in Switzerland, and one week after his return goes riding in Hyde Park with 'Lady Batho and her daughters'. There is nothing, anywhere, to tell us how he met the Bathos, still less how he felt about them. But in the early October of that same year he 'went down to Norfolk for the shooting' and, although he doesn't say where he's staying, the entry ends with the words, 'Grassingham Hall very fine'. In September he had given a dinner party at his rooms in Wimpole Street, having apparently nipped back from Chalcot Road, for there's a five-pointed star on this page too. The dinner party is the first ever recorded in the diaries, and he lists the guests in strict alphabetical order: Mr and Mrs Annerley, Sir John and Lady Batho and – there it is again – 'their daughters', Dr Barnabus Couch and Dr and Mrs Vickersley. Who were the Annerleys and the Vickersleys? They occasionally have a place in the diaries, but without a clue as to their identity. Henry had very correctly invited an equal number of men and women. Who sat where? No record of that exists either. The one significant fact to emerge is that, by Victorian standards, Henry was seeing a lot of Olivia.

In October, Constance Batho writes to her friend Helen Milner,

Dr Nanther called this morning, his excuse being that he had come to enquire after Mama's health, but Mama, as he as a doctor must know, has only a common or garden cold and has not even taken to her bed. His real reason was to see Olivia – who was not at home, if you please! So he is to return tomorrow, simply of course to see Mama, whose health concerns him, and to bring her some remedy for an inflamed throat.

Dr Nanther is very handsome, very proper, very clever and very *old*. Well, very old to our 'young eyes', Mama says. He must be forty-five. And Olivia is just twenty-two. The bother of it is that she has begun fretting about *getting old* and *missing her chances*. She has been out four years, you see, and no one she likes has offered for her. She does like the Doctor, was quite put out when she came home and heard that he had called but she had missed him. Mama and Papa would like them to make a match of it. Mama, being old herself, calls Dr Nanther a young man 'in the prime of life'. Her only objection to him, as far as I can see, is that he lives in chambers above his consulting rooms in the unfashionable (in Mama's eyes) neighbourhood of Wimpole Street.

But he was considering a move. An entry in the diary at the beginning of December, underneath a rather large carefully executed pentagram, notes that he has been to look at a house which is for sale in Green Street, Mayfair. This would probably have suited Lady Batho's taste but Henry doesn't buy it and in the following February is viewing another in Park Lane. Could he have afforded the upkeep of a house

97

in Mayfair? True, the Godby woollen mill has come to him by inheritance, but it had long since ceased to do well. Long before his father's death a manager had been put in to run it and it had declined pathetically under this man's management, causing among other things by the depression which followed, great distress and poverty among the mill hands. Henry would be hard put to find a buyer for the house and it would have fetched very little. In fact, he kept it and eventually it became the Nanther family's country home. It was my father who sold Godby Hall for a pittance in 1970.

So Henry had inadequate funds to think of setting up house in this desirable area. All that would change if he married Olivia Batho, who would bring with her the personal fortune of thirty thousand pounds, a vast sum in the 1880s. I am indebted (as they say in acknowledgements) to Stanley Farrow for most of what I know about the Batho family. My great-grandfather, as usual, tells his posterity so little and not a word of any of it appears in the diaries. Because it never touched his heart? Because he simply didn't care enough? Or had Olivia never meant much to him and had disappeared altogether from his consciousness when he met the Hendersons?

Stanley Farrow came over to me in the Peers' Guest Room where I was having a drink with a couple of other cross-benchers, and lent towards me rather diffidently, one hand on the red-leather back of the spare chair at my table. I thought he wanted the chair, the bar was very crowded, and I said, 'Yes, of course,' which rather puzzled him as well it might have.

Light dawned. 'I don't want the chair. I only wanted to say I've seen your ad in *The Times* and I think I can give you some info. Well, it may be all nonsense, of course.'

'You do want the chair,' I said and I held out my hand. 'Martin Nanther. Sit down.'

'Stanley Farrow.'

I shifted a little way along from the others who had embarked on a discussion about European Monetary Policy. 'You're a newish life peer,' I said. 'You came in last July. I was in the Chamber at your introduction. You're Lord Farrow of Hampstead.'

'Hammersmith. But you're right about the rest of it. Can I buy you a drink?'

'I've got a drink,' I said, 'but I'll buy one for you,' and I ordered the gin and tonic he asked for. 'What sort of info?'

Stanley Farrow is a little old man, in his seventies, white-haired, with a sharp elfin face, very upright as small men often are. 'It was my wife who actually saw your ad. She said I ought to speak to you. Does the name Caspar Raven mean anything to you?'

'He was the man Olivia Batho married.'

'Well, actually,' said Farrow, as if apologizing, 'they were my grandparents.'

It's hard to find anywhere in the House of Lords where you can be alone with someone. Meetings will be taking place round the clock in every committee room. Interview rooms are tiny and claustrophobic and viewers crowd the Television Room. The library is full of smokers. Few peers have an office to themselves and are lucky to have a fourth or sixth share in one. It was particularly busy on 20 January, because earlier in the afternoon Baroness Jay, the Leader of the House, had made a statement on the White Paper the Government were publishing that day about Lords Reform, the first positive intimation (after the announcement in the Queen's Speech) that reform was definitely to happen.

I decide to take Stanley – we are soon on first-name terms – into the Royal Gallery. This is a vast and very grand hall with a towering ceiling, all ornamented in red and blue and gold, the floor cold marble, set about with darkly polished tables and leather chairs and sofas. It's always cold in the Royal Gallery, the place being virtually unheatable, but at least it's quiet and nearly deserted. The few who were in there that day were entirely uninterested in us and what we were saying. Stanley produced photographs from his briefcase and laid them on the table.

'Her daughter was my mother,' he said. 'Olivia got married in 1888 and Mummy was born in ninety-one.'

One of the photographs was of Olivia in a simple Pre-Raphaelitish white gown, her dark hair loose, a sweet smile on her face. I'd like to use it in my biography, maybe on the page facing the one where Jimmy Ashworth will be, but all I could think of at that moment was that it might have been a photograph of Jude. For some reason the resemblance is far greater here than in the Sargent portrait. The poignancy comes from what Olivia's doing; she's holding her baby in her arms. I made a mental note that this is one Jude must never see – well, unless the impossible happens, she must never see it.

'Your mother must be dead now, of course?'

'She died fifteen years ago. I owe the fact that I've got all this stuff, these pictures and bits of jewellery and some letters' – I pricked up my ears at that – 'to my wife. Men aren't much interested in genealogies, family history, that sort of thing, do you think? John Singer Sargent painted my grandmother and Vi – that's my wife – saw it somewhere or a reproduction of it. When Mummy died she kept all this stuff, she said Olivia had been famous and you never knew who might want to know about her.'

'Thoughtful woman,' I said. 'Someone does. Who are the letters from?'

'Her sister Constance mainly. A couple from her husband – my grandfather, that is. I'm afraid that if you were hoping for any from Lord Nanther you're in for a disappointment.'

'Tell me something,' I said. 'If there are no letters from him and no photographs of them together' – I'd made sure there weren't, not at least among those on the table – 'how do you know my great-grandfather was – well, keen on her?'

He's a man who can't keep his wife out of any conversation for long. It seems she dines with him at least once a week in here. 'My mother told Vi. Vi was deeply devoted to Mummy, they were the closest of friends, for which of course I'll always be eternally grateful. You see, my poor mother had a most unhappy childhood, she and her brother and sister all did, she never really got over it, she was always talking about it – to me, and just before she died to Vi – on the grounds that talking about something rids you of the burden of it. Only it never seemed to do that for her.'

I was mystified. What could there be that was so unfortunate about being the daughter, or come to that the son, of the prosperous Caspar Raven of Raven's Bank and his wife Olivia? Poor old Farrow's eyes were suddenly very bright, as if full of unshed tears. But surely not. I saw him then, and I was right, as the devoted son of a possessive mother who, when the mother grew old and perhaps senile, married a wife to be a mother substitute when the time came. The tears were held back but the voice faltered a little.

'I see you don't know,' he said. 'Olivia had a lover, they'd call him a boyfriend these days. She ran away from her husband and deserted her three children. She went off with a man whose name I can't remember – Vi would know. My grandfather obtained a divorce, very difficult in those days but not so hard since the divorce law was passed a few years before, and of course there was no question of Olivia having the children. They had a sad time of it.'

'When was that?'

'In eighteen ninety-six. My mother was five, her sister was seven but the little boy was only two. My grandfather, Caspar that is, had a very savage temper, though it really only came out after his wife left him. Before that he worshipped the ground she trod on, Mummy said, would have done anything for her. He took it out on the children later and, as I said, they had a sad time of it.'

I asked him what happened to Olivia. Did she marry the man? Instead of answering, he asked me if I was 'familiar with the works of Oscar Wilde'. Pretty well, I said.

'He's supposed to have based his Lady Windermere on my grandmother, only my grandmother *did* run away with her man and Lady Windermere didn't. As to what happened to her, she didn't marry the man, I don't know what he was called, but moved in with another one and another. This was in France, somewhere in the south of France. My grandfather knew, he told his children all about it, in the most savage way. Olivia came back here just before the Great War. My mother was grown up by then and she sometimes visited her, unbeknownst to her father of course. When Olivia died in nineteen twenty-four they found she had a heart defect you only get if you've contracted syphilis at some time or other.'

While I resolved to check up on *Lady Windermere's Fan* because I'm not sure the dates tally, he was picking up the photographs and putting them back in his briefcase. 'Look, I'm going home now. It's only Hammersmith. Why don't you come back with me and talk to my wife?'

7

Often ahead of his time with his discoveries, Henry had postulated in the early spring of 1882, in a paper he gave to the Royal Society, that two factors contribute to the clotting of blood. Calcium was one of them and what he called 'thromboplastase' the other. He was wrong but he was heading in the right direction. Twenty years were to pass before the four factors and two products theory came into being and many more before medical science understood that the factors concerned in the activation of prothrombin by thromboplastin were twelve in number, all finally to be designated by roman numerals.

None of this is the interesting stuff of biography but it will have to go in so that readers understand how Henry strove to be a pioneer in his field. The dull with the exciting, the rough with the smooth. He seems to have worked hard, to have put his whole heart and soul into his studies and his practical work, but to have known too that change and rest were essential for him. His walking holidays were a high point of his year. The trip abroad he took in the last week of April 1882 began in Chur, Cùera in Romansch, the oldest town in Switzerland, now a ski resort, in the south-east corner of the country. This may have been familiar territory to him, recalling his time at the University of Vienna when he first grew to love the Alps.

From Chur he seems to have set off to walk the mountain paths of the Hinterrein. There was no Richard Hamilton to accompany him and no Hamilton to write to now. Did he miss Hamilton, his companion on so many walking tours in the past? He must have, perhaps bitterly. From a village high up in the mountains, where he boarded at the home of the Schiele family, he wrote to that other medical friend he seems to have become acquainted with at Barts, Lewis Fetter:

My dear Fetter,

This is as remote a place as I was led to believe it would be, a mere scattering of houses on the south-eastern meadow slopes of the Graubünden. Very beautiful if one's tastes tend to the picturesque. Communication between these houses and the outside world must be established over broken and dangerous tracts of land. No driving roads exist. Fortunately, as you know, I have always been a walker and am undeterred by the prospect of covering several miles on foot. As it happened, I was obliged to make a journey of six hours to reach here from Versam, a distance I calculate as no less than twenty miles. You may believe me when I say I was heartily glad to reach the quaint and picturesque house inhabited by the good Schieles, to find a meal of roast meat, potatoes and a kind of fruit porridge awaiting me, its consumption followed by rest in a comfortable bed in a clean and airy room.

The snows are gone except from the highest peaks and the alpine meadows bursting into glorious bloom. This village is much exposed to the weather, but sunshine and a dry atmosphere render it a healthy place. Except, according to V and G, as you know, in one respect. Still, all that is in the past now. Presently, the population consists of about a hundred and fifty persons, healthy and sturdy people for the most part. Pleurisy, pneumonia and arthritis deformans are, however, common. Scurvy and purpura are unknown and phthisis rare . . .

The rest of the letter is concerned with compliments to Fetter's family, enquiries after his own health and assurances that he, Henry, will be 'back in Wimpole Street by the twelfth of May'. He heads his letter Safiental, Graubünden. Who are or were V and G? Friends Henry and Fetter had in common? Or could they be authorities on public health at the time? Could V be the Dr Vickersley who was one of the guests at Henry's dinner party the following September?

If Henry also wrote to Olivia Batho or Jimmy Ashworth, his letters haven't turned up but, knowing his character as I'm starting to, I'm inclined to think he didn't write to either of them. Henry was a disciple of the Byron School and would have agreed that 'man's love is of man's life a thing apart'.

I didn't go home to Hammersmith with Stanley Farrow that evening. I was taking Jude out to dinner. I stopped on the way home and bought red roses, for no reason except that she likes them. Stanley eventually renewed his invitation. He seems to take his role and function as a working peer for the Government lightly as some of them do, coming in for questions and disappearing before the ordeal of staying behind to vote, and often not coming in at all. Of course he may have been there on the few days I wasn't. It was well into February before we encountered each other again. I was having a cup of tea in the Bishops' Bar, when he came over to me, said Vi was 'dying' to meet me and would I like to bring my wife for dinner? I made such a mess of refusing that he must have been left with the impression my marriage was unhappy and that Jude and I led completely separate lives. In the end I said I'd come on my own, but for a drink, not dinner.

The day I went I'd received in a parcel the letters Henry

wrote to Barnabus Couch. It rather shocked me, that their possessor risked sending them by post, even though by recorded delivery. The sender, a Mrs Deborah Couch, widow of Henry's friend's great-grandson, was not to know that Henry made copies of every letter he ever wrote. After her husband's death, she'd found the letters neatly packed, wrapped in sheets of newspaper (*The Times*, of a date some time in August 1906) when she was turning out the attics of the old rectory where they'd lived. They were a dozen among hundreds. Couch had had a voluminous correspondence and apparently kept every letter he'd received, instructing his unmarried daughter, according to Mrs Couch, just prior to his death, to 'preserve them all or, by God, I'll come back and haunt you'. It's a strange thing but I've often noticed how upset otherwise quite rational people can be by this threat.

I went into the House at about four, met Stanley and left again at five-thirty for his home in Queen Caroline Grove. Lady Farrow was very much what I had previously expected Laura Kimball to be, round, white-haired, maternal – perhaps I had her in mind? She helped Stanley out of his overcoat and would have helped me out of mine if I'd let her. We went into a living room whose decoration and furnishings spoke eloquently of the late Mrs Farrow. She, obviously, had been the first possessor of the limed-oak sideboard and dining table, the 'fireside' chairs, the table lamps on which attenuated marble maidens, naked but frigidly chaste, held up parchment shades on out-stretched arms. Her invisible presence was palpable. I was reminded of something a well-intentioned friend said to my mother after my father died. 'He hasn't gone, Sonia. He's here in this room with you.' Mrs Farrow was here in this room with her son and daughter-in-law. Particularly her daughter-in-law. It was soon clear that Lady Farrow's mental processes, her heart and soul if you like, were occupied not only by her mother-in-law but by that mother-in-law's mother too, the pair of them curiously mingled, intertwined with each other, so as almost to form one matriarchal entity.

Stanley fetched sherry. It hadn't been offered but simply appeared, that least acceptable sherry (to me) which is as pale as Sauvignon and which you expect to be dry but when you take your first sip gives you a shock because it's sickly sweet. I tried not to show surprise. Photographs were produced along with the twiglets. A biographer, proceeding as I do, soliciting contributions from all possible sources, soon becomes inundated with photographs. But I'm not complaining. It helps very much to have a picture in your mind of the people you're writing about, even more to have those faces on the working surface before you. I was presented once more with Olivia in the kind of gown classical statues wear, holding her infant daughter. The ones I hadn't previously seen were of Olivia at her wedding, Olivia with her sons, Olivia with that same daughter five years on, the year of the Sargent portrait.

'What was her name?' I asked.

That opened the floodgates. 'Violet,' said Lady Farrow. 'Violet – the same as mine. Sweetly pretty, don't you think? And she was such a lovely woman. It was through her that Stanley and I met, I was her closest friend, so it seemed *meant* that we should come together.'

So they had been married only fifteen years, these two. Stanley never became an orphan, for his mother dying provided him with a mother to take her place. A wife who, by a stroke of luck and coincidence, shared her christian name.

She seemed to read my thoughts. 'Oh, I wasn't *christened* Violet. I was *christened* Jean. Jean Smith. But Stanley liked to think of me having his mother's name and now it seems as if I've always had it. I'm much more Violet, as you might say, than Jean. The second Violet Farrow, I always say.'

Stanley seemed to approve. He smiled complacently. Lady Farrow picked up a photograph, sighed and put it down again. 'She had a tragic life. First that dreadful deprived childhood, then a lonely youth. Caspar wouldn't let her see her mother, you know. He was such a cruel man, so unforgiving. After all, what did he want? He had his children, he had his place in society. Everyone respected *him*. But she was condemned to utter loneliness . . .'

'Excuse me a moment,' I said. 'But which one are we talking about, Olivia or Violet?'

Lady Farrow put one finger to her forehead as if pinpointing a pain there. 'Violet. Yes, Violet. My *friend*. I tend to confuse them – can you understand that? Mother and daughter, both so unhappy, both victims of a man's cruelty.'

'Don't upset yourself, darling.' Stanley laid a hand over hers. 'Let me give you some more sherry.'

'Thank you. I will. She was only five, you know, when her mother fled. I say "fled" because, of course, Caspar drove her to the brink. And it was only necessary for someone just that little bit kinder to come along and pull her into the abyss . . .' Lady Farrow continued in this way while I wondered how to stem the flow and pin her down to what I really wanted.

At last I said, 'Lady Farrow, all this is most interesting.'

'Violet. Call me Violet.'

'Violet, all this is most interesting but it's Olivia whose early life I'd really like to hear about.' I decided to flatter her. 'You're unique in knowing first hand' – more like third hand, really – 'what that life was like. What she felt, what sort of a person she was.'

Luckily for me, Violet Farrow née Jean Smith wasn't offended. She smiled reminiscently, shaking her head to mitigate the smile. The lights in the room were bright enough but she reached out and pressed the switch between the feet of a malachite lady holding up a lampshade with a green Greek key border. 'There, that's better. Now I can see you properly.' Words always calculated to cause unease in their hearer. 'Olivia was mistreated from the start. Some said there was a clash of temperaments but what they really meant was Caspar was a bully and Olivia wasn't accustomed to bullying. Quite naturally in such a beautiful *sheltered* girl, she was used to having her own way. They say, marry in haste, repent at leisure and poor Olivia had married in haste.'

And Stanley and Violet the Second had certainly married at leisure, very likely taking twenty years or so to make up their minds – or get maternal permission. 'Why in haste?' I said.

'There was nothing like that,' said Lady Farrow, looking affronted. I nearly laughed. I'd never imagined there was, not among the upper class in 1888. It was a different matter for Jimmy Ashworth and Len Dawson. 'Violet said Olivia wanted to be married. She was twenty-seven, you see. That was quite old to be still single. Caspar was the first man who had asked her who she felt she could stand, apart, that is, from your great-grandfather – it was your great-grandfather, wasn't it? – that she felt she could bear near her. She told me Henry Nanther was the great love of her life.'

'You mean Mrs Farrow told you?'

'That's right. Didn't I say? *Her* mother told her she was deeply in love with Henry Nanther. It was a terrible disappointment when nothing came of it. He jilted her, you know. I'm sorry to have to tell you that about your great-grandfather, I really hope it doesn't offend you. I'm sure he was a very great man and a good doctor and all that, but he jilted my – Olivia, that is.'

Stanley intervened. 'They were never actually engaged, dear.'

'That's not what *she* said. She said there was an understanding between them. Her father and mother knew all about it and approved. Henry Nanther was looking for a house for them, he looked at several houses in Mayfair.' That was true. And suddenly verisimilitude was given to what she was saying. It wasn't all imagination and memory distorted by time. 'Olivia wanted to live in Park Lane. You can't imagine it today, can you, anyone thinking they could live in Park Lane? She'd have been near her family, you see. They were in Grosvenor Square. Violet liked to think they lived where the American Embassy now is but I don't know if that's true.'

I picked up a photograph of Olivia, her parents and her sister Constance, taken against the background of a sort of summer house, presumably in the Grosvenor Square garden. Did they have a private garden? Or was this the garden of the square itself?

'What happened?' I asked.

'Nothing,' she said with a sort of dismal triumph. 'Nothing at all. He simply dropped out of the Bathos' lives. It was the summer of eighty-three. Poor Olivia held the dates in her memory. June the fourteenth, it was a Thursday, he was invited to dine in Grosvenor Square, and he cancelled in the afternoon. No phones then, of course – well, they were just coming in. Henry Nanther, *Doctor* Nanther, I should say, I don't mean to be offensive, and by then he was Sir Henry, anyway, he sent a message by hand that he couldn't come, he was indisposed. That's what he wrote. Olivia said that afterwards she could never see that word "indisposed" or hear anyone say it without experiencing the most dreadful pain.'

'But she can't have known then, Vi,' said Stanley. 'She can't have had any idea he was going to let her down.'

'She had a premonition that all wasn't well. And she was right. She never heard another word from him. "Indisposed," she kept saying. "*Indisposed*. He was indisposed to seeing *me*."'

I had given up asking Lady Farrow how she could possibly know such things, how a mother would tell a daughter such things. What I wanted most at that moment was to be home with the diary open in front of me to check if there was a pentagram on the entry for 14 June 1883.

'Her father wanted to bring an action for breach of promise, you know. They did that then. They put notices in the papers warning other parents to be wary of men who might behave badly to their daughters.'

'But Sir John Batho didn't?' I said.

'Olivia stopped him. Her pride wouldn't let her agree to that. "She sat,"' said Lady Farrow surprisingly, '"like patience on a monument, smiling at grief." That was how Violet put it. Pretty, isn't it? She was very gifted, she wrote lovely poetry. If you'd like any of the photographs for your book, I'm sure you're very welcome.'

'Be our guest,' said Stanley.

'On the understanding we get them all back intact, of course. And Stanley has photostatted all the letters for you.'

At least I wasn't offered samples of the poetry. I was out in the hall when the two of them dived back into the living room and began a whispered colloquy. Lady Farrow came out, fetched my coat and insisted on helping me into it.

'Oh, by the way, I hope you didn't take that seriously, what Stanley said about Olivia contracting a – well, a *contagious* disease. Of course that wasn't what he meant, was it, dear?'

Stanley, hovering behind her, said, 'Certainly not, dear. Certainly not.' He astonished me by screwing up his eye in a histrionic wink.

'He was thinking of someone else.'

It was only when I was walking down the street towards the tube station that I remembered 'contagious' was the Victorians' euphemism for what we'd now call a sexually transmitted disease, and what less mealy-mouthed people, and indeed Stanley himself, called syphilis.

How much of that could I believe? Not all, certainly. Jude was out at a launch party for one of her authors when I got home. I went into the study, put the two photographs I'd borrowed with the rest, and found the diary for 1883, a green leather one, octavo size. Henry wrote in a typical Victorian hand, sloping, spidery, conventional, the upper loops tall, the lower loops deep. For Thursday 14 June he had written only: 'Audience with HM 11 a.m. Feeling unwell, I cancelled my evening engagement.' No mention of what or where the evening engagement was, not a word about the Bathos. And no pentagram either. The next one of those occurs on Monday 18 June. At that time, February, I didn't know about Mary Dawson, I hadn't met Laura Kimball, but I do now. Sitting where I sat two months ago, in the light of my new knowledge, I'm looking at May, the month Jimmy conceived her daughter Mary Dawson, and there are three pentagrams that month, one on the 13th (the day after Henry returned from the Lakes), one on the 17th and one on the 29th. Since Mary was born on 21 February

1884, it seems likely conception took place on 13 or 17 May. Of course, there isn't and can never be any way of absolutely fixing this. I think fleetingly of Jude who would so love to make such calculations for herself.

Two very different women, I'm sure, Mary Dawson and Violet Raven. What happened to Violet is clear enough, marriage to a man below her father's station, a happy enough life probably in a villa in then suburban Hammersmith. One child, Stanley, to whom she was a devoted and possessive mother. What would Olivia have thought of her grandson following in the footsteps of 'the great love of her life' and entering the House of Lords? I've checked him out in Dod and discovered he was for many years Leader of Hammersmith Council. As for Mary Dawson, all I know is that she was Laura Kimball's mother. And, of course, my half great-aunt. I'm curious, so when I write to Laura asking for the postcard of Jimmy Ashworth I'll also ask for information about Mary, though I fear it will only evoke more white-washing.

And now I'm back again to the question of why. What is the answer? That is the question, as Henry said in his maiden speech. Why did Henry, apparently so keen on Olivia, Henry who had begun looking for a house in which to begin married life, Henry who dined regularly with the Bathos, went riding with Lady Batho and her daughters, stayed at Grassingham Hall (according to the diary) on three separate occasions, why did he coldly and callously drop her? Not jilt her perhaps, for 'jilt' implies an engagement, but led her to believe he wanted to marry her and, without warning, threw her over. Suddenly it occurs to me that Jimmy Ashworth's pregnancy could be the reason. The objection to that is that if Mary wasn't conceived until the middle of May, in those days long before testing, Jimmy couldn't have known she was pregnant by 14 June. And conception was impossible before that because Henry was in the Lake District from the last week of April until 12 May. Could Jimmy have known it if Mary was conceived on 13 May? Just about, if she had a regular cycle. But why would the discovery of Jimmy's pregnancy make Henry drop Olivia? It's very unlikely Jimmy was proposing to blackmail him. The consequences of such an attempt would be ultimately worse for her than for him. It's out of the question Henry was considering marrying her – or is it? I'm asking myself if he'd come to want a child, an heir, as early as 1883. Men of his standing and position had been known to marry their mistresses. Sometimes. Very occasionally.

She seems to have been the type he preferred, dark-haired, white-skinned, dark-eyed, voluptuous, soft-featured with a short nose and full lips. But Olivia also belonged to that type. And Olivia had a fortune of thirty thousand pounds. There's a powerful argument against the pregnancy being responsible for Henry's dropping Olivia. He *didn't* marry Jimmy. And there's no question but that she would have accepted if he'd asked her. A gentleman for a husband, a father for her coming child. She'd have jumped at the chance, she'd have been in seventh heaven.

So, why?

8

Back to the House of Lords Bill today. There is much talk, and more gossip, about the so-called Weatherill Amendment, an amendment to the Bill put down by Lord Weatherill, Convenor of the Cross-bench Peers. It was he who led the cross-bench negotiating team, the other members being the Earl of Carnarvon and Lord Marsh, which produced the idea of 10 per cent of the 750 hereditary peers remaining. And he put down the crucial cross-bench amendment which bears his name along with Marsh, Carnarvon and Viscount Tenby. This provides for ninety-two hereditary peers being retained in the House during the interim period between the general banishment of hereditaries and the second stage.

How will the ninety-two be chosen? By the 'hereds' in the different parties or by all members of a party? Lord Shepherd asked that back in March but I don't remember that he got an answer. It was also he who suggested for the first time in this House, I believe, that the smooth passage of the Bill would depend on the way Lords behaved themselves.

I am in the Chamber from the start today because I intend to speak and it's not considered good manners here to come in, just say a few words and rush off again. Lord Dinevor, a hereditary peer, took the oath before business began, reminding me of my own entry to this House eight years ago. Though the process has been curtailed, life peers are still introduced with pomp and ceremony, each having a supporter to precede him and another to follow him, the three wearing scarlet robes. All that happens when a hereditary's father dies is that he comes quietly in wearing a lounge suit. Holding the New Testament, he mutters a few words before shaking hands with the Lord Chancellor.

I took the oath on a day when two life peers had already been introduced and ministers and whips, banished to the back to make room for the procession, were scurrying on to the front benches. I doubt if anyone would have noticed I'd come in at all if it hadn't been in Hansard next day: 'Lord Nanther sat first in Parliament after the death of his father and took the Oath.' I must check up on what Hansard said when Henry came in on 19 June 1896. Or was there a special ceremony in those days before the Life Peerages Act? I must find out.

When I sit in here, two benches behind Labour Party veterans, I try to look with fresh eyes at the adornment of this chamber, attempting to recollect how it was for me when I first came in and how it must have been for Henry. The paintings don't impress me and never did. We do have one Dyce in here, above the throne, but it's not so striking as his frescoes, representations of generosity, mercy, religion, that make the royal Robing Room so beautiful. Standing high up in gilded niches are black figures in chain mail with dust lying on their shoulders – can no cleaning device reach so high? – but they look more like characters from *The Lord of the Rings* than the archbishops, earls and barons they are, all of them present at Runnymede when King John issued Magna Carta in 1215. Below them and all round the Chamber, under the filigree railing of the gallery, are the armorial bearings of the sovereigns since Edward III and of the Lord Chancellors of England from 1377. Concealed lighting touches them and makes them glow as if they are lit from within. Sometimes I count the colours in the stained-glass windows. Once I thought only red, blue and yellow were there but since then I've discovered emerald green and dove grey and brown and gold.

I go out for tea at four and come back in again to hear the discussion on the position of Scottish peers in the House. I am speaking on an amendment whose effect will be to put off the date at which the Bill becomes law until the report of the Royal Commission has been considered by the House and I stand up when Baroness Blatch sits down. My speech lasts no more than three minutes. All I'm saying is that it seems wrong to abolish the voting rights of hereditary peers before we know what kind of chamber will replace them.

Before I go to the Home Room for dinner I phone Jude to tell her I don't know when I'll be back. The debate may go on through the night. I have to leave a message on our answering machine because she's not in. I sit for a while at the table where the phone is at the end of the Not Content lobby and think about Jude, my wife, who has become distant from me these past weeks. I know why it is but don't know what to do about it. So many things now I feel I can't say to her, so many subjects have to be avoided, or I feel they do, and this embarrasses both of us because she knows very well how I try and fail.

If Lord Weatherill's amendment comes to anything, will I be allowed to stay? Will I want to? Perhaps. No one knows yet – or, if they do, I've heard nothing – how the hereditaries who are to stay will be chosen. Voted for by their own peers would be the best way. But where and how? I suppose there's no reason why a polling station shouldn't be set up in the House. If that happens there will be many hereditary peers who have never been in one before. Being a peer and doing one's duty means a lot of work. I think now that if I wasn't who and what I am and if I had the choice no one ever does have of becoming a life peer or a knight, I'd choose the knighthood. And if I were a woman I'd choose a DBE. No work outside their jobs for knights and dames. The minimum of vilification in the media. And very little wrestling with nagging consciences, I suppose.

Henry was knighted by Queen Victoria in the spring of 1883 in what I imagine were the Birthday Honours. If they had them then. That's something else I must check. He was forty-seven years old, Physician-in-Ordinary to the Queen, Professor of Pathological Anatomy at University College Hospital and due to publish another book. I've tried to read *Haemorrhagic Disposition in Families* but its complex tables of inheritance and lists of family relationships are almost too much for me. Still, I haven't given up, only paused. I'm going to make myself read, say, five pages a day till I finish it. One item I have managed to digest and that's Henry's conclusion that claims of males being carriers of haemophilia are invalid. Where there seemed to be cases, for instance, where a haemophiliac man fathers a haemophiliac son, this is not a direct transmission from the father but comes through the mother who was herself a carrier. It's something that used to happen occasionally in communities where access and egress are difficult and inbreeding is common. This seems to be the first and perhaps the only new discovery Henry made in his chosen field. Still, it's rather a negative conclusion to reach and unlikely to lead to fame or further honours.

By the time he was Sir Henry he was on the point of parting from Olivia Batho, but not yet from Jimmy Ashworth. After the three pentagrams in May there are three more in June but before that, he had had a heroic encounter.

That is, Henry's behaviour was heroic. The whole affair reminds me of a passage from one of Trollope's novels. Someone (not Trollope) says somewhere that nothing ever happens to a man except that which is like him and this doesn't seem to me much like Henry. But what do I know? With all my researches, I know so little of his true nature or his inner life.

A short while before these events he had returned from his walking holiday in the Lake District, where he seems to have caught a cold. His diary entry for 23 May, a Wednesday, is brief. Not so *The Times* for that day. Henry wrote: 'Suffering from a cold in the head. Was able to give some assistance to a Mr Henderson who had been set upon by a ruffian in Gower Street.' Modest Henry. *The Times*' report is much fuller.

Mr Samuel Henderson, attorney-at-law, of Keppel Street, had a providential escape from injury or even death last night when he was set upon by a desperate villain in the neighbourhood of Gower Street, not far from the British Museum. We understand that Mr Henderson had just come from his business premises and was beginning the short walk to his home. Possibly in the belief that he was proceeding from the bank nearby and that he was in possession of a large sum of money, the miscreant attacked him, taking him unawares from behind and striking him with a cudgel.

Fortunately for him, help was at hand in the shape of none other than the distinguished Physician-in-Ordinary to Her Majesty the Queen, Sir Henry Nanther, KCB, FRCP. Sir Henry, who was coming away from University College Hospital where he is Professor of Pathological Anatomy, witnessed the entire scene. A powerful and vigorous man in the prime of life, Sir Henry immediately set upon the ruffian with his stick and made short work of routing him. Next he turned his attention to the unfortunate victim of the attack and ascertained that Mr Henderson had sustained no worse effects than bruising and a severe abrasion to the right shoulder. An errand boy who happened to be passing was dispatched for help and Mr Henderson was later removed to University College Hospital where he is happily recovering.

On his way home after perhaps delivering a lecture to a class of medical students, Henry can hardly have foreseen what a life-changing encounter this would prove to be. I'm tempted to dwell on the operations of fate and chance. Remember the Tay Bridge and the train he nearly boarded? Suppose, in Gower Street, he'd been detained for five minutes by a student who dared put a private question to the great man. Or his voice had grown hoarse through this 'cold in the head' and he terminated the lecture five minutes early. Poor Mr Henderson (my great-great-grandfather) would perhaps have been killed or at any rate left bleeding on the pavement. Help, if help there was to be, would have come from some other source. In any case, Henry would never have met the Henderson family and I and my forebears never been born.

There are some, of course, who would say it was 'meant' but I'm not one of them. Not destiny and therefore inevitable. Not fate but chance. Chance that the telegram sent to him arrived in time to keep him off the train. Chance which decreed that he and Samuel Henderson and the 'villain' met and encountered each other in that momentous way. A strange force, but that which determines all our events and adventures. Henry saved Samuel Henderson from serious injury or even death, and the result? As a reward the solicitor gave him his daughter's hand in marriage? That's not how it was, of course not, that's only the way it occurs in the romances read by Henry's housemaid.

Probably what happened was that when Samuel returned home Henry called to enquire after him. It would have been considered the most natural and courteous behaviour. It was what anyone would do in the circumstances. Nowadays we would phone; the Victorians were obliged to call at the house. The odd thing is that Henry doesn't record such a visit in his diary. Perhaps he's being modest. A man, if naturally humble and self-effacing, is so even in his private and personal jottings. Only Henry wasn't humble and self-effacing. He was proud of himself, what some would call arrogant. He'd have considered calling in Keppel Street (birthplace, incidentally, of Anthony Trollope sixty-eight years before) an act of condescension on his part, a stooping. Or I think he would, but maybe I'm wrong.

It was very likely at this time that he composed the first essay in the notebook, the one on altruism. I've bought a more powerful magnifying glass to make his writing easier to read. It is tiny, apparently deliberately made so, and this first contribution is, frankly, rather dull. Not interesting enough to make me settle down and try to decipher the rest of the notebook with the new glass. Jude, who hasn't read it either, calls the notebook Alternative Henry, though I can't see anything in this first bit to justify that title.

It seems to refer to his 'heroic act' of a week before, or that act to have given rise to these reflections. Nothing in it is new or, I should think, original. Very little hadn't been said before. Still, it does show what Henry thought about these things and perhaps the one interesting feature of it is the inevitable reference to blood.

Altruism [Henry writes], is there such a thing? Do we ever perform an action without thought of self? Is not everything we do done to aggrandize ourselves in the estimation of others or at least to leave them with an impression of our self-denying qualities? I believe it is. Sinful man is ruled by self in every aspect of his life. If women appear to be more altruistic this is only because they have been brought up from their earliest years to passivity, obedience, acquiescence and the placing of others first. God forbid that they should ever be removed from this sphere, but if they were and were encouraged into independence, self-determination and even dominance, their altruism would vanish and their nature come to resemble or even exceed man's.

If I hasten to the aid of some unfortunate passer-by whose pocket has been picked, perhaps by supplying him with the few coins necessary to assure his safe arrival at his home, or enquiring after his injuries, I am merely attempting to impress him in two ways. By offering him money I demonstrate my wealth and, by ascertaining the extent if any of the wounds he has sustained, reveal my skill as a medical man. Altruism does not enter into it, for I place myself in no danger, suffer no noticeable diminution of income and, since the entire exercise takes no more than five minutes, endure no appreciable loss of time.

Indeed, it might be that I even benefit from my act. Suppose the wounded man were by some chance a 'bleeder'? It is not likely but not impossible either. Let us at any rate postulate such a case. I should witness what I seldom have the good fortune to see elsewhere, the unstemmed and very probably unstemmable flow of blood from a wound *deliberately inflicted in malice a mere few moments before*. I should of course attempt to stem it, I am a physician, I should try the various methods at my disposal, but the interest to me would lie in being there on the spot, as one might say, to see the immediate reaction of subject and subject's mental processes to his misfortune. This would be an example of direct self-benefit combined with apparent self-denial. And as I hold the wound closed – I recollect a case recorded by Grandidier of a sister holding her finger against her brother's bleeding gum for

123

three days to prevent the excessive and perhaps total loss of blood which might have ensued – I would reflect with undoubted pleasure on how this *adventure* contributed to the sum of knowledge on the ever-fascinating study of haemophilia.

Samuel Henderson didn't have his pocket picked. He certainly wasn't wounded in the sense Henry writes of. The 'case' is hypothetical, something we can be sure never happened and never would. The odds against it are too great. But if the allusion to blood is typical, there is one strange thing here. Why should this example come into Henry's mind just at this point? Samuel wasn't a haemophiliac and he wasn't bleeding. A bludgeon had been used, not a knife or some other sharp instrument. Or was Henry so obsessed with his particular specialization that he applied possible instances of it to all sorts of situations? I suppose that's the answer.

Returning to what *did* happen, there's nothing to indicate the time at which the attack took place. Not late, I suppose. If Samuel was leaving the chambers of Flinders, Henderson and Cox, and Henry coming away from delivering a lecture, it was very likely no later than six in the evening. Not dark then, not on 23 May, but broad daylight. Were there no other people about? The newspaper doesn't say and Henry doesn't. Still, we know that for every Samaritan there are a dozen priests and Levites. Passers-by notoriously do ignore the victims of an attack or a robbery. Isn't it true that we constantly read in the papers of tube-train passengers sitting indifferently by while one of their number is the subject of brutal assault?

At the beginning of last year I was approached by a relative I didn't know I had with a request to supply information for a genealogical table. This craze for making family trees seems to have reached gigantic proportions. Everyone is doing it, though no one in my family seems to have done it before.

David Croft-Jones is my second cousin. His mother is Veronica Croft-Jones, née Kirkford, daughter of Elizabeth and James Kirkford, he tells me, and Elizabeth of course was my great-aunt and Henry's eldest daughter. He seems to have begun his family tree through acquiring a new computer with a new programme that particularly lends itself to columns and tabulations. Or so I think, reading between the lines, though that's not what he says. He says he wants to do it 'for the record' and so that his children won't reproach him. As yet he hasn't any children, he's only been married about five minutes, but he takes his responsibility to a future generation very seriously.

I'd probably passed him round and about Westminster a good many times without knowing who he was. He's a civil servant at the Home Office and I walk past it when I make my way to the House by way of St James's Park. I've met him now, he and his wife came over for a drink last week and he brought with him the first draft of his table. It's an ambitious project and puts my own efforts to shame. He's not really aiming at tracing Henderson connections but concentrating on Nanthers and going back a couple of centuries. I was able to give him the names of the three wives of my grandfather Alexander (Pamela Goldrad, Deirdre Park and Elizabeth Pollock), my first wife Sally, and my sister Sarah's husband, John Stonor.

From his tree I found his aunt Vanessa and some second cousins of mine, Craddocks, Bells and an Agnew, descended from Henry through his second daughter Mary Craddock. In due course I shall be in touch with all these people in my quest for family letters. David Croft-Jones says that great-grandmother Edith seems not to have written a single letter in her entire life or, if she did, none has survived. If any of Henry's four daughters kept a diary it's been lost. David has lent me a bunch of letters from Mary to her married sister, his grandmother Elizabeth, given to him by his mother when he started the tree, but they are much more to my purpose than his. They have survived largely, I think, because Elizabeth and her daughters were the kind of people who never threw anything away. These hoarders are the biographer's friends, but only if what they haven't thrown away is worth keeping.

The summer of 1883, when Henry made the acquaint-ance of the Hendersons, was long before Edith, the second daughter, discovered her passion for photography. But among her 'accomplishments' was a small skill at draw-ing. She was the daughter who drew and painted, Eleanor the musical one. Thanks to Elizabeth Kirkford's hoarding everything and her daughter Veronica following in her footsteps, the drawing Edith made of her sister has survived. Apparently, Veronica wants it back but I shall only keep it long enough to photocopy it. It isn't dated but Eleanor is a grown woman, not a child; she's somewhere between seventeen and the age she was when her life was brought to a violent end.

My great-grandmother Edith used a soft smudgy pencil on thick paper which must once have been white and now is ochre yellow. Her subject is a pretty girl. Of course Edith may have beautified her sister and drawn a flattering portrait, but I'll credit her with sticking to Eleanor's regular features and copious hair. Blonde hair, as it happens. For, although Eleanor Henderson had a face not too unlike Olivia Batho's, her hair was light-coloured and her eyes too. Yet if I compare her with her sister in her wedding photograph, Edith has the advantage in looks in almost every respect. Her forehead is higher, her nose tip-tilted and her chin recedes less than Eleanor's.

'She's pretty but nothing out of the way,' Jude says, looking over my shoulder. 'Not a patch on her sister. What did your Henry see in her?'

'Charm, perhaps. Or she had a beautiful speaking voice or she made him laugh.'

'It's women who like men that make them laugh,' says Jude, 'not the other way about.'

She's looking very well, better than she usually does when she's got her period. *If* she's got it, I can't ask, but she will have. It comes as regularly as the sun rises. Instead I ask her if it's all right to ask David Croft-Jones and his wife to have dinner with us in the House, it's time I did that, he sent me the second draft of the family tree this morning, and she smiles and says of course.

'How old was she?'

I ask her if she means in the picture or when she died.

'When she died.'

'Twenty-four.'

'Poor thing,' Jude says. 'What was she like?'

I don't know. I know what she looked like but nothing much else about her. Only one letter from her to Edith has survived and there are none from Edith to her or from their mother or father. There's a difficulty of identification, or perhaps I should say specification, when writing about middle- and upper-class women of the nineteenth century. Most of them had a very limited education, no professions, they led sheltered lives, were kept ignorant, lived under the protection first of a father, then of a husband. They can't be differentiated as women could later, by their tastes, their travels, their activities outside the home, even their politics. They weren't 'all the same' as it's tempting to categorize them, but it's much harder to make a picture of an individual woman, to bring her out of the shadows into a hard outline and a clear light.

The diary entries don't help. Henry writes, 'Dined with Mr and Mrs Henderson' and 'Escorted Mrs Henderson and the two Misses Henderson to the theatre.' On one occasion, in July, the entry reads, 'Consultation with Mrs Henderson.' So, apparently, his new-found friends were availing themselves of his medical skills as well. Eleanor is never mentioned by name at this time. From her mother's letters to Dorothea Vincent, her sister-in-law, we know she was 'musical', whatever that meant, probably that she played the piano. She lived at home with her parents like most unmarried girls. No doubt she sewed, helped with domestic tasks, for the Hendersons were comfortable but not well-off, went shopping with her mother or her sister, occasionally attended a concert and performed at a 'musical evening'. She may sometimes have gone to meetings for the promoting of women's rights but if she did there is no evidence of it I've so far found. There is no evidence either that any man courted her before Henry.

There was a son too, the eldest of the three. Lionel Henderson was twenty-seven and a clerk in his father's practice. He too lived at home. According to David Croft-Jones's mother, the family was happy, the parents easy-going and tolerant for the age they lived in, the grown-up children very attached to one another. With them, also, lived William Quendon, Samuel's father-in-law, aged eighty-three, who had made his home in Keppel Street since the death of his wife some years before. The house is still there, four floors high with a basement, the rooms rather small and poky, the kitchen regions and servants' bedrooms below ground. The present occupants or perhaps those before them had the two ground-floor reception rooms turned into one and even so the resulting room isn't large. It's all bedrooms above now but probably, in the Hendersons' day, the entire first floor was given over to the drawing room. Old William Quendon, my great-great-great-grandfather, must have had a weary climb of it to his bedroom unless they managed to accommodate him in the basement.

This, then, was the household, grandfather, father and mother, son and two daughters, who no doubt welcomed Henry with open arms when he first began calling in June 1883.

In July, Jimmy Ashworth was two months pregnant. If Henry hadn't known before he would know by then. Did he see this coming event as a joy, a gratification, a nuisance, a threat, or was he not much affected by it? The last, I believe. There's no reason to think Jimmy was anything but compliant, subservient, grateful. An assertive woman wouldn't have held Henry for nine years. She was a convenience to him. No doubt he found her very attractive and still did. No doubt she brought him solace, comfort, relaxation and a total contrast to the rest of his life, the Palace, the hospital, his work. But in love with her he never would have been. By then, presumably, he was in love with Eleanor Henderson. Now he had to pension Jimmy off and find a father for her child. While he had Olivia he could keep Jimmy on. Eleanor was different and his relationship with her serious.

The final pentagram in the diary appears on 15 August 1883. That may be the last time Henry ever saw Jimmy Ashworth, but probably it wasn't. It's most likely he went back to Chalcot Road on several occasions: to present Len Dawson, to make arrangements for the wedding, to pay the lump sum. The date of his engagement to Eleanor, according to *The Times* in which the announcement appeared, was Thursday 23 August. I imagine prudent Henry, correct Henry, enjoying his final sexual relations with Jimmy Ashworth on a Wednesday, calling in at Keppel Street to continue his courtship on the Friday, returning to propose on the following Monday and receiving a favourable answer, asking Samuel Henderson for formal permission to marry his daughter on the Tuesday, and the announcement appearing on the Thursday. Not that there is any record of this in the diary up until then. On Friday 24 August the entry reads: 'My forthcoming marriage to Miss Henderson noted in *The Times* yesterday.' Cool Henry. On one hand he is organizing the future life and nuptials of the mother of his child to a hospital porter, on the other participating in arrangements for his own, not to mention doctoring the Queen and instructing his students. Busy Henry.

The question remains, though, and I need to find an answer to it. Why on earth did he want to marry the daughter of a not very prosperous solicitor, with no 'real' money and no prospects, when he could have had Olivia Batho? Olivia, who apparently loved him. Olivia, who was beautiful and rich and more *his type*? Whose father was a baronet with a country mansion and seven hundred acres and could give his daughter thirty thousand pounds on her marriage. It's not enough to say he fell in love and there's no accounting for love. Suggestions that Eleanor might have been charming or clever or funny as well as pretty – fairly pretty but 'not a patch on' her sister – won't solve it, nor will saying that he fancied her and couldn't have her any other way than by marriage. He was a middle-aged man, an experienced man who for nine years had kept a mistress. Yet his head was turned by a pretty little thing *no man had wanted before*?

And why did he, otherwise so reticent, mark his occasions of sexual intercourse with Jimmy Ashworth by a five-pointed star?

9

Jude is pregnant. She told me this morning, at ten.

She's working at home today, the second Monday in May. This usually means she gets up a bit later in the morning but she didn't. She was in the shower at seven-thirty, brought me a cup of tea before eight and said she had to go to the chemist.

'You won't find one open before nine-thirty,' I said, and I asked her what she needed so urgently.

She didn't answer but pretended to be looking for something in the bathroom. I know my wife so well, I know what she's up to. If I ask her a question she doesn't want to answer, rather than lie she'll walk off quickly as if she's just remembered something she's got to do. But why should she want to lie? I was clearing away the breakfast things, hers and mine, when I heard her come back and go straight upstairs. It was about half an hour afterwards. David has sent me a bunch of letters from my great-aunt Elizabeth Kirkford that his mother found and I was in the study, arranging them in some sort of order, when Jude came in. Her face was brightly flushed. She looked enormously well. She said it.

'I'm pregnant.'

The trip to the chemist was to buy a pregnancy testing kit. She was ten days' overdue and she couldn't bear to wait another day. I jumped up and threw my arms round her and we kissed and kissed. I was going to say I've never seen her so happy but I have – last time and the time before.

Nothing was said of that, though, no caution, no dampening of joy. I forgot about work and so did she. We went back to bed, to make love and then to lie side by side, our arms loosely round each other, and I let her pour out her excitement while I listened and said it was wonderful and the best thing that's ever happened, and we laughed for joy, and then we got up and I took her out for a celebratory lunch.

It's not really like that for me, but I know the only hope for our marriage is that we have a child. And I know that if she doesn't have one her whole life will be blighted, she'll be embittered and unhappy, yearning for ever after for children and always feeling that if she's not a mother she's not a real woman. But in my heart I don't want a child. My selfishness is enormous, though harmless if I keep it to myself, and that's what I'm striving to do. I'm base. I don't want a baby that cries in the night and demands attention in the day. I know all about that (and she doesn't), I've been through it with Paul. Because I'm the one of us that's at home I'll be saddled with looking after it, or if we have a nanny and we'll have to have one, I'll be responsible. I don't want the napkins and the bottles and the sick and the sleepless nights and the awful mysterious illnesses small children get so that you're out of your mind with worry, tearing about in the night to Accident and Emergency. Because you love it, of course you do, you can't help it. It will put its fingers in the electricity sockets and pull pans of hot water off the stove and fall out of its high chair. It will have to be taken to school and fetched back *for thirteen years*. By the time it's sixteen, I'll be past sixty, wanting a rest and a bit of hush.

But while I was pretending to rejoice – and I was rejoicing, I was, for my dear wife's sake – I was also resolving that she shall never know, never be given the slightest tiny adumbration, that I am not as exultant as she is. I will be happy, I will be triumphant, I will play the foolish expectant father who boasts to his friends of his coming child. I will be as anxious as she that she carry it to full term, as watchful that she takes her folic acid, abstains from alcohol, takes exercise, rests, has the right diet. And I will instigate, even at the risk of being boring or when she's tired of the subject, conversations about names, decorating the nursery, christening robes, to pram or not to pram, and the inadvisability of ever allowing a small baby to sleep face downwards. I'll be even sillier than she is about all these things and when the time comes, like Jemima Puddleduck, I'll be an anxious parent. And maybe, as the months pass, the power of thought and determination will change me and make me look forward to our son or our daughter as much as she does.

I wish.

Today, 11 May, is the fourth day of the Committee Stage of the House of Lords Bill and we are due to debate the Weatherill Amendment. That's the one that seeks to keep 92 of the 750 hereditary peers in the House. The suggestion is that the Labour Party elect 2, the Conservative Party 42, the Liberal Democrats 3 and the Cross-benchers 28. It is also proposed to elect 15 hereditary peers ready to serve as deputy speakers – that is, to deputize for the Lord Chancellor on the Woolsack. With the Earl Marshal and the Lord Great Chamberlain the number comes to 92.

No doubt I shall be stuck in here all evening so it's as well I've got the Croft-Joneses coming in for dinner. Georgina Croft-Jones is in the seventh month of her pregnancy. I tell myself I've had a lucky escape and reflect on how I'd feel if Jude hadn't told me her news yesterday. Both women make a point of not drinking alcohol but Georgina has the House's peculiar homemade tomato juice mixed with horseradish and Jude has austere sparkling water. Jude looks well and years younger and altogether a great beauty, very like in fact Sargent's version of Olivia Batho Raven, her skin glowing with the same luminosity, only with more rosy pink about it, and her dark eyes shining. An elderly peer – one, incidentally, who forty-two years ago voted against admitting women to the House – lays his hand on her shoulder and tells her the sight of her does his old eyes good.

David isn't, in looks at any rate, a Nanther. He is small and neat and fair, with very blue eyes. Georgie, as we're to call her, is a bit taller than her husband, dark and very slim apart from the bump. Only on her it's not a bump, it's more like a sack of flour she's chosen to hang across her thin hips and cover up with a diaphanous clingy dark-green dress. Jude tells me afterwards that it's by a designer called Ghost. Her face is white and sharp-featured, her mouth wide and very nice when she smiles, as she does a lot. Jude looks like a famous painter's portrait and Georgie looks like a film actress, like Julia Roberts.

She holds one end of the now very lengthy family tree as David spreads it out and holds the other. Being insatiably inquisitive, as always, everyone else in the Peers' Guest Room turns to stare at us. I take Georgie's end from her and David and I study the Quendon-Henderson section of it. The women seem relieved we're occupied and turn to discussing pregnancy and babies. I've quickly shifted from dismay at this baby to straight horror but I'm happy for Jude just the same, filled with joy for her and very nearly moved to tears by the look on her face. I give a sort of gasp and gulp and expect David to look at me in wonder but he doesn't. No doubt he's been through it himself – but with somewhat different feelings, I hope.

He's not interested in Olivia Batho but when I tell him about Jimmy Ashworth and that her child Mary Dawson was almost certainly Henry's he perks up quite a lot. Do I think Laura Kimball would consent to a DNA test? I tell him he can ask her if he likes, I'm not going to. These genealogists, amateur or otherwise, become so obsessed with their branchings and linkings and twigs going this way and offshoots that way, that they lose all sensitivity as to how family members actually feel. I can see from the look on his face that he wonders if he ought to add to his table a kind of bend sinister jutting out from Henry and culminating in Janet's grandson Damon, but would rather not. It's messy, and what about all the other ancestors who might have had 'entanglements'? He wants to know if I think it would be in bad taste but I absolve myself from involvement in this question.

Everyone orders more drinks but before they come the division bell rings. So I make my way to the Content lobby because we're voting on the Weatherill Amendment to retain ninety-two hereditary peers, and I'm more content with it than with its alternative which would mean curtains for all of us. A lot of chat usually goes on as we're passing through to be counted but no one is very talkative today. I'm silent too, lost in thought, and suddenly I understand something. Our child was most probably conceived that night Jude was acquiescent and I, for once in our recent mode of living, positively desirous. And my desire had been stimulated by that erotic dream of the Henry-me character watching the *tableau vivant* of the *Three Graces*. Ah well, I say to myself, they all *looked* like Jude and, anyway, it can't be helped now. Back in the Peers' Guest Room Georgie is asking why everyone is allowed to smoke in here. Haven't they heard of passive smoking and its effect on the unborn child? I think of telling her that my mother smoked forty cigarettes a day all the time she was carrying me, but I don't. That would be comparable to the tales I often hear in this room of some peer's noble grandfather, a heavy smoker who died in his sleep at the age of ninety. Someone says over my shoulder that we won the vote by an enormous majority, one of the biggest the Government have had, though in fact it was a cross-bench amendment, supported by the Government.

Jude has, of course, told Georgie and David about her pregnancy. She'll tell everyone, I know that. Lorraine will get to know the minute she sets foot in our house tomorrow morning. And why not? Part of one's joy in success, in something achieved, is telling other people. I'm fearful because I remember, though I can never speak of it now, the last time. She carried the foetus for two months and a week and then, one midnight, it bled away from her. Blood – if anyone asked me what I see when I hear or read the word I'd have to say I think of the blood in our bed, all over both of us, and Jude's tears, her dry sobs and then her tempests of tears.

But no one is going to ask me. Henry might, but he is present at this table (and in David's table, the genealogical one) only as descendant and ancestor, offspring and progenitor. David cares nothing for him as a man or a doctor. Now he has decided against DNA testing attempts, he dismisses the long liaison between Henry and Jimmy Ashworth as 'the way those Victorians went on'. But Georgie, who is naturally I suppose interested in these things at the moment, says how happy Henry must have been to know his first child was on the way and looks indignant when I say it's unlikely.

'I'd have thought he'd be happy,' she says. 'I mean, *thrilled*. He's forty-seven, didn't you say? Forty-seven and this is his first child. He must have been happy.' This is approaching too closely my own case for comfort. I contrive a smile.

'He could have married her. She wasn't a low sort of person, was she? She wasn't a prostitute.'

'She probably had been,' I say.

'Well, she was no worse than him. He's a real example of someone with a double standard, isn't he?'

We go into dinner then. Useless to tell the Georgies of this world that it's impossible to judge the morals and manners of a hundred and twenty years ago by those which prevail today. Henry's attitude was time specific and that's all there is to it. David has unfolded his tree and folded it up again mapwise so as to expose only the relevant section. 'Henry, the one who became Lord Nanther,' he says, 'got married the following year. In the October.' Rather impatiently he goes on, 'I don't see there's anything mysterious about it. He announces his engagement in *The Times* in August 1883 and gets married in October 1884.'

'It would have been a very long engagement for the time,' I say. 'Long engagements were supposed to be bad for the girl. People thought the man was keeping her hanging on and that was bad for her reputation. But all that's beside the point because it was Eleanor he got engaged to and her sister Edith he married.'

There's a mistake in the tree here and David seems suitably chastened. Jude and Georgie want to know why the marriage didn't take place, though this must be politeness on Jude's part because she knows already. Our wine and our first course arrive and a waitress with a basketful of the awful bread you get here. Stanley Farrow, passing, pauses at our table and whispers to me what I already know, that we won the vote. David, tucking in to smoked salmon, says, 'I don't see how I can get an engagement into my tree. I'd better just forget it, hadn't I?'

'You'd better if you're not going to include Jimmy Ashworth. He wouldn't have had sexual relations with Eleanor, you can be sure of that.'

This is something else Georgie finds hard to believe. All engaged people do. Everyone she knows moved in to live with the person they were engaged to. I shrug my shoulders and mutter something about times changing. Georgie must have had some sort of answer to her question from Jude because she says, 'Jude said she died. Eleanor, I mean.'

'Yes, she died.'

Georgie says people often died young in those days. They got tuberculosis or something you'd have an operation for today or in childbirth. The faintest shadow passes across Jude's lovely face and I'd like to stick my steak knife into that silly woman's neck. 'They got pneumonia,' Georgie says, 'and took three weeks to die and *knew* they were going to die, they knew there was no help for them. You can't imagine, can you?' I see she's an inveterate reader of historical novels of the sensational kind. 'And then they sort of wasted away, they had something called the green sickness.'

'Eleanor died a violent death,' I tell her. 'The way she died wasn't just typical of her time. It's the kind of thing that happens today. She was murdered.'

'Oh, do tell!'

But I don't tell. I shake my head and smile. Perhaps because I know Georgie Croft-Jones would get excited and say Henry must have done it or otherwise speculate in wild and inaccurate ways. I say instead that I'm still researching that bit, which isn't true, I've researched as far as I think necessary. But I'm not so circumspect as Jude, I don't mind white lies in a good cause. And keeping me from losing my temper is a very good cause.

We have coffee. At last the Croft-Joneses want to know what's happening in the Chamber. It's the House of Lords Bill, I tell them, what we in here call the Reform Bill. Georgie thinks this means everyone with a title is going to lose it, eldest sons are no longer to inherit and the aristocracy will lose their property. No one's going to be called 'Lord' and 'Lady' any more, the whole aristocracy will be swept away in a kind of bloodless French Revolution. As I set her to rights I think to myself that this will very likely be what the whole country thinks before we're finished with the Bill.

She doesn't seem at all tired and wants to know where we're going next as if I had a nightclub in view. But I take them round a bit, show them the House's treasures, Charles I's death warrant that we keep in a glass case in the Royal Gallery, the Dyce frescoes, tell a few anecdotes and ask them if they'd like to go into the Chamber. Georgie is keen to go in but loses her enthusiasm when I tell her she and David will have to sit on the right below the bar and Jude on the left in the peers' spouses' seats. Rules of the House, I'm afraid. She seems to have taken a shine to Jude and says that rules are made to be broken. I tell her that if we break this rule a doorkeeper will come and either move them or move Jude, and we go downstairs to say our goodbyes in the Peers' Entrance, David promising to send me the tree when it reaches its next stage.

The House is very quiet now and there's a tense feeling in the air, everyone having either gone home or disappeared into the Chamber. I tell Jude I'll go in myself for a bit, see what happens, and would she like to go home? She says she'll stay with me, she's not tired, she's so happy she doesn't want to waste her time sleeping. Walking slowly up that august red-carpeted staircase, I take her hand and say very quietly, 'I love you. I'm so happy for you.'

'I hope you're happy for yourself too,' she says shrewdly, too shrewdly, but I tell her I am, I am.

10

This story has been as famous in the family as Henry's heroic rescue of Samuel Henderson. My father told it to me when I was thought old enough not to be given nightmares and I'm afraid he told it with Gothic relish, in which mode – probably – his father had told it to him. You could call it a very Victorian murder.

Trains were the preferred form of travel in the nineteenth century, indeed the only fast form of travel. Twice they brought disaster into Henry's life – at least, it would seem like disaster to anyone else. There is no way of knowing what he felt about these two particular incidents. Rather cryptically he mentions Eleanor's death in his diary but gives no details and still less indicates his emotions.

Still, I'm assuming that the tragedy affected him at least as deeply as Hamilton's death in the Tay Bridge disaster. He was in love with Eleanor Henderson. Love is the only possible reason for his wanting to marry her. They were engaged and the wedding was to take place in February. Did Henry reflect, did he *remember*, that this was the month in which Jimmy Ashworth Dawson was to give birth to his child? No one knows. The engagement ring Henry gave to Eleanor is in the possession of my sister Sarah, a clumsy piece of jewellery, the diamonds half buried in the thick heavy gold. It was taken from Eleanor's finger before her funeral and somehow found its way back to Henry, there to become, in its turn, Edith's engagement ring.

This is something assumed in my branch of the family.

My grandfather Alexander knew it and passed it on to his son. Confirmation comes from Mary Craddock's letter to her sister Elizabeth Kirkford. Her mother Edith had told her the ring she wore had been Eleanor's. This piece of information is wrapped up in Victorian sentimental flummery, which may have been Mary's, not Edith's, about the sacredness of Henry's first love and Edith's own desire to have the ring so that she and Henry would never forget it was her dead sister who brought them together. That's one way of looking at it. Another is that Henry, having got the ring back by some means or another, saw no reason to spend money on a new one. Thrifty Henry.

The closest relation the Hendersons had, outside the immediate family, was Samuel Henderson's only sister Dorothea. David Croft-Jones's genealogical table shows me that Louisa Henderson, the girls' mother, had one sister and a brother, who died at the age of seven. These people, of course, were Quendons, the children of William Quendon and his wife Luise, née Dornford. Dorothea Vincent belonged on a rather higher social plane than the Hendersons. She was a comfortably off widow who lived with her two daughters in the village of Manaton in Devon, where her late husband had been the squire. She was Eleanor's godmother and closer to her than she was to the other Henderson children. Eleanor was in the habit of going to stay with her for a couple of weeks every year in the late summer, in her early years accompanied by her mother, later on by her sister Edith. This was only the second time she had gone alone.

Most of my information about this visit and its consequences comes from newspapers. The relationships between the various people I've gleaned – and 'gleaned' is the word if that means what I take it to mean – picking out tiny usable grains from a mass of chaff – from David's mother's and grandmother's letters. Unfortunately, there's not much in them about what people felt and thought, no more than a shocked referring back to the 'terrible tragedy' and a reflection on Veronica's part that if Eleanor hadn't died they wouldn't exist.

Eleanor's habit was to visit her aunt in August, but there was an obvious reason for her not going in the August of 1883. Perhaps she planned to go but postponed her visit when it seemed likely Henry would propose. Instead she went in early October, travelling by the Great Western train that went, and still goes, from Paddington to Penzance, and she travelled first class. Ladies Only compartments existed in 1883 but not on that line. At Newton Abbot she changed on to the local line to Moretonhampstead and got off at Bovey Tracey, which in those days was simply called Bovey. She was met at the station by her aunt with the pony and trap. Her visits must have been a pleasant change for Eleanor, coming as she did from a London that was often fogbound in winter and hot and dusty in summer. Manaton in those days, and to a great extent still, is in beautiful country on the edge of Dartmoor, a place of high tors, deep leafy lanes and trout streams. Aunt Dorothea's was a more luxurious home than her own in Keppel Street. She employed a cook and two maids and two men to do the garden. The family wanted for nothing. The pony carriage was nice to go about in and there were beautiful places within easy reach of Moor House to walk to. Eleanor got on well with her cousins and the purpose of her visit was, in part, to ask them to be her bridesmaids.

Her wedding was fixed for 14 February, St Valentine's Day, though less was made of that as a lovers' festival in the nineteenth century than today. As things turned out, the wedding never took place, so the fact that Jimmy Dawson gave birth to her daughter Mary on the 13th isn't as significant as it might have been. Jude, who is perfectly happy now to discuss anyone and everyone's babies, who prefers baby-discussion to all other types of conversation, says that the prospect must have hung over Henry. He must have felt guilt as well as an excited anticipation. How could he simply turn his back on his own child?

'I don't think men felt the same then,' I tell her. 'The divide between good women and bad women has so entirely changed it's difficult to imagine it, but it was very marked in the eighteen eighties. And the divide between the children one's wife had and the by-blows or wrong side of the blanket children was very wide. Henry would have given Jimmy money, probably in the form of an ongoing income to her husband. There may have been a condition that he himself was never to see or hear of the child. At all costs its existence must never get to his wife's ears.'

Jude says she can't imagine being married to one man and carrying another man's child. 'They'd never have been able to talk about it the way we do. She must have felt frightened and ashamed all the time.'

'It happens just as much now as it did then, women having children by men they're not married to or living with. Probably more. And as for Henry, I don't suppose he made the connection between the expected birth and the wedding day. He wouldn't have thought about the two events on the – well, the same plane.'

'Hateful Henry,' says Jude. 'Must you write his life? He's so dreadful.'

I tell her I must and that Henry wasn't any worse than other professional men of his time. As for guilt and shame, I feel plenty of that myself over my feigned enthusiasm for *our* coming child, but at the same time I'm revelling in being able to talk to my wife again, to say anything I like about anything, not to keep breaking off in mid-sentence and blushing the way no man of my age ever should.

If Eleanor wrote to Henry from Manaton her letters haven't survived. I wonder how many times I'm going to write that sentence, changing only the names and the place? Biographers get to feel that letter writing should be compulsory on everyone's part and letter preserving even more important. Still, she wrote one letter home and that single one to her sister Edith. It exists only because, probably, its date is just before the murder, and for this reason Edith kept it.

We don't know how Eleanor passed the time in Manaton. Jude says, and I agree with her, that it's hard to know how any middle-class Victorian woman passed the time. If you have servants and no job, what do you do all day? Read, sew, write letters, read, walk, talk, sew, I suppose. Eleanor mentions none of this in her letter to her sister. Its main purpose seems to be to tell the family she'll get a cab home from Paddington station. It is as follows:

Moor House,
Manaton,
Devon

St Luke's Day

Dearest Edith,
    The weather is beautiful. Aunt says the fine weather in mid October is called St Luke's Little Summer. That is why I have put St Luke's Day instead of October the eighteenth

at the top of this letter. You have been here so you know how lovely the countryside is. I should really like to live in this neighbourhood once I am married but Henry cannot be away from London where his work is. Perhaps one day we could have a house here, though I think he would call that no more than a romantic dream.

Isobel and Laetitia have consented to be my bridesmaids, indeed they were very happy to accept the invitation. You, of course, will be the third, my dearest sister. You have already said you will, so I do not *think* I am being presumptuous in taking it for granted! Henry talks of Italy for our honeymoon and I dare not suggest we come down here. Of course, it would not be nearly so nice in February.

I have had one of 'my falls'. It happened out walking with I and L. I stumbled in the middle of a field, caught my foot in a rabbit hole, and fell headlong. Mud all over my blue serge frock but the worst was (of course!) the bruising. I am black and blue. The bruises on my left side and leg are a sight to behold, but luckily no one but me does behold them!

I shall return on Saturday by the 11.14 train from Bovey. The journey takes hours and hours, as you know, but it is due to reach Paddington at five minutes past five. There is no need at all for Father to meet the train. I shall be quite safe on my own and will take a cab. My dear love to Father and Mother, Grandpapa, Lionel and your dear self.

Your affectionate sister,
Eleanor

She mentions Henry as a Victorian wife-to-be should. His work was paramount, he made the decisions. When she says she 'dare not' suggest they come to Devon for their honeymoon she doesn't sound seriously fearful. She says it much as a present-day wife would say she daren't ask what's-his-name to go out to dinner again this week. From the sound of it, she and Henry had a simple and cheerful relationship. Perhaps the passion was all on his side. There is nothing in her letter to betray her love or even her pride in landing such a prize. Perhaps she'd said all that to her sister beforehand. Still, I find it hard to believe that the Henderson family as a whole weren't ecstatic that one of their number was making this amazing match. A knight! A royal doctor! A rich man – at least, in their estimation. The daughter who was already twenty-four, on the shelf, dowry-less, a burden for ever on her parents, was about to become Lady Nanther and in the following year would be living in a house fine beyond their dreams.

For Henry was house-hunting once more. His friend Barnabus Couch had a post as Visiting Professor of Anatomy at the Owens College in Manchester once attended by Henry himself. To him he wrote as follows on 18 October 1883:

My dear Couch,

I have to thank you for your kind letter of congratulation on my engagement to Miss Henderson. You will like her. She is gentle, charming and quiet, very far from the 'New Woman' we hear so much about these days. I doubt if she knows what the franchise is, still less would she wish to play a part in choosing a member to send to Parliament. I am confident she will do her duty by me as my wife and will never exhibit the restlessness and, worse, neurasthenia, you and I see so much of in those female patients whom modern notions of 'freedom' and emancipation have so adversely affected. At present she is staying with her aunt in Devon where plans are afoot for the coming nuptials, but will return on Saturday.

I have been looking out for a suitable residence for us and would like to have settled on a property by the end of January. Then, if we spend six weeks away on our wedding journey – I have Rome and Naples in mind – all transactions could be complete by the time we return. However, I shall take a house somewhere until midsummer by which time my wife will have purchased furniture, carpets and whatever else may be necessary for our future home. Our permanent residence will, I think, be somewhere in that district I consider the most salubrious of anywhere in North London – St John's Wood. I had thought of the Eyre Estate or the almost rustic Loudoun Road but tomorrow I am to be taken on a conducted tour of a very fine place in Carlton Hill, at present the property of Mr Hapgood, the brother of a colleague of mine.

You will remind me, my dear Couch, of St John's Wood's reputation as the hiding place for a gentleman's *belle amie*. On being told that the philosopher Herbert Spencer had taken up residence there, a bishop is said to have asked, 'And who is the lady?' But I believe its disreputability, if such it has been, is passing. After all, the great T. H. Huxley, with whom I am proud to have some acquaintance, has been living there at various addresses for the past thirty years. My wife and I will no doubt attend St Mark's Church, Hamilton Terrace, that place of worship made distinguished by the incumbency of Canon Duckworth, who also resides in the neighbourhood and whom I had the honour of knowing while he was tutor to His Royal Highness, the Prince Leopold. So I believe we may take up residence without danger to our morals!

I trust you are well and that Mrs Couch's health is keeping

up. Bear February the fourteenth in mind! You will receive
Mr and Mrs Henderson's invitation in due course.

Yours most sincerely,
Henry Nanther

Jude's comment on that is, 'I don't know how he had the
nerve,' referring, of course, to Jimmy Ashworth whom
Henry had only recently pensioned off. The answer is that
he was not necessarily a hypocrite; he was not one person
but many people who lived alongside one another inside
his lanky frame and noble head.

'Very fine' the house may have been, but Carlton Hill
was scarcely Park Lane. In 1883 St John's Wood wasn't
considered part of London as it is now, but a suburb, and
much of it, especially on the western side of Maida Vale, a
building site. In the event, Henry didn't buy Mr Hapgood's
house. The woman who was to choose its furniture and
carpets met her death the day after her fiancé went to
look at it.

On the morning of Saturday 20 October, her aunt drove
her to Bovey station to catch the local train for Newton
Abbot. They must have set off quite early for Eleanor to
make the connection at that little Devon junction on to the
Great Western express. Once again she travelled first class.
The train came into Paddington on time and Samuel
Henderson was there to meet it, in spite of Eleanor's injunction to her sister that this wouldn't be necessary. She wasn't
on the train and Samuel went home. There would be one
more train arriving but not until 10.20 in the evening. After
some sort of consultation with his wife and other children,
he telegraphed to his sister to find out if Eleanor would be
on that train instead. Telegrams, which were still used but

lost their novelty with the coming of phones, were an efficient form of communication in the late nineteenth century, yet it was not until the Sunday morning that Dorothea's answer reached Keppel Street. Long before that Samuel Henderson had been back to Paddington in the hope his daughter would be on the 10.20 train.

By Sunday morning the police had been called in. Before they had done much, a farm worker in east Devon had spotted a woman's body lying on the railway embankment somewhere between Alphington and Exeter. It was identified by Samuel Henderson on the following day, the Monday, as that of his daughter. Here is a rather sensational account of the inquest from a national daily paper, though not so sensational as my father's:

The inquest took place in Exeter yesterday on Miss Eleanor Mary Henderson, aged twenty-four years, of Keppel Street, London, whose dead body was discovered on the railway embankment at Alphington on Sunday last. The coroner's jury brought in a verdict of murder by person or persons unknown.

William Newcombe, a cowman of Alphington, said he saw a dark-blue object like a bolt of cloth on the grass of the embankment and supposing it was a portmanteau or other piece of luggage fallen from a train, negotiated the fence which divides the embankment from the meadow and went to investigate. To his horror he perceived it to be the body of a young woman clothed in a dark-blue costume and cape of similar colour. Wisely refraining from touching the tragic cadaver, Mr Newcombe went for help to the nearest police station which, unfortunately, was some miles away.

Heavily veiled and speaking in a low, often scarcely audible voice, Mrs Dorothea Jane Vincent, the dead woman's aunt, told the court her niece had been staying with her for the past fortnight.

She personally drove Miss Henderson to the station at Bovey to catch the 11.14 train. She cautioned her to enter a first-class compartment of the Great Western express, departing from Newton Abbot at 11.50, and Miss Henderson undertook to do so. She saw her niece board the local train and then she drove back to her residence in Manaton.

Dr Charles Warren said he had examined the body. It was that of a well-nourished and formerly healthy young woman in her early twenties. He had no doubt that death was by strangulation. It was his belief that Miss Henderson was dead before she was thrown from the train. No marks on the body, apart from the disfigurement of her face and neck, had been made prior to death. There was bruising, but the physician's opinion was that this occurred several days earlier. When asked by the coroner, Mr Swithun Miles, to give a time of death, Dr Warren said that officials of the Great Western Railway would be more accurate arbiters of that than he. No doubt, Miss Henderson's assassin, having committed the dreadful deed, wasted no time in ridding himself of her body. Estimating the time of death should merely be a matter of ascertaining at what time the express passed through Alphington. For his part, he would suppose death to have occurred during the late morning of Saturday, the twentieth of October, say between noon and twelve-thirty.

(No doubt the doctor had done some detective work of his own, for it turned out that the train had passed through Alphington at twelve twenty-five.)

Only one witness came forward to say he had seen Miss Henderson on the train. Mr Christopher Morris, a solicitor's clerk of Heavitree Road, Exeter, travelling from Plymouth to Exeter St David's, said he saw a young woman in dark-blue garments board the Great Western express at Newton Abbot. She was carrying a small black portmanteau and he believed a porter was beside her, holding a larger suitcase, but of this he could not be sure. He noticed her because, although some two dozen persons were among those waiting on the platform, she was the only woman travelling unaccompanied. In answer to the coroner's question, he said he did not observe what carriage she entered, whether it was an ordinary third-class compartment or a first-class compartment. He never saw her again.

Mr Frederick Formby, a guard on the Great Western express, said that a small portmanteau and a large leather suitcase were among the four pieces of unclaimed property found on the train at Paddington station after the passengers had departed.

The coroner said that this was the most dreadful and shocking case that had come to his attention for many years. There could be no question of accident or *felo de se* for it was as impossible for Miss Henderson to have inflicted such injuries upon herself as it was that she was somehow strangled by chance while falling from the train. At some point in the short journey from Newton Abbot to within a few miles of Exeter an individual entered the compartment, where no doubt she was alone, bent on carrying out his nefarious work. The jury must draw their own conclusions as to what happened at this encounter.

The jury was out for no more than five minutes before returning a verdict of murder.

It's not possible to know for sure what were the reactions of the Hendersons and Henry to Eleanor's death. Imagination will have to do what knowledge can't.

That Samuel was a devoted father is shown by his insistence on meeting the train his daughter was due to return on, in spite of Eleanor's telling him not to do so. The sisters were close. We know virtually nothing about Samuel's wife Louisa except that she was pious and fond of referring to

'Providence', but there's no reason to think she was a less than loving mother. They must all have been, to use the current popular word, devastated. But it's a word that sometimes means exactly what the dictionary defines it as: 'laid waste'. These parents, this brother and sister, would have been laid waste, ruined, broken. But even in extreme grief, people retain their prideful feelings, their snobbery, their vanity. For the Hendersons Eleanor wasn't just a beloved daughter and sister, she was the promised bride of a distinguished physician and professor, a royal doctor, a knight and (to them) a wealthy man. With her death all that hope went too. Samuel would never now hear his daughter called 'Your Ladyship'. There would be no visits to the grand house in St John's Wood and no visits to Bloomsbury by Eleanor in her own carriage. Her chances of finding a husband for her sister Edith and promotion for her brother were lost. Edith herself would probably have cared least about that aspect of things. For her it would have been a matter of simple grief at the loss of a beloved sister.

What, then, of Henry? How did he react to the death of the girl he was engaged to? His diary ought to give us something to go on but it doesn't, or not much. By Sunday 21 October everyone was seriously worried at Eleanor's disappearance, Dorothea Vincent's telegram having arrived with the news that Eleanor had boarded the 11.14 train. Later that day a body was found. But it wasn't till Monday the twenty-second that the body had been positively identified by Samuel. Henry's diary entry for 21 October reads: 'I was at home in Wimpole Street at seven in the evening when Mr Lionel Henderson brought me the alarming news [of the discovery of a body]. I, of course, accompanied him back to Keppel Street.' One wonders why Henry didn't accompany the man who was to have been his father-in-law to Exeter. Perhaps he had pressing business at Buckingham Palace or at University College Hospital, but what audience or lecture could more profoundly affect his life than the murder of his fiancée?

However, from this day forward, as they say in the marriage service, Henry's character seems to have undergone another change. Hamilton's death in the Tay Bridge disaster had made him colder and harder than he was before. Now the diary entries changed to being chill and laconic. He became relentless, single-minded, ambitious, a man apparently without much family feeling, having a large acquaintance that included Huxley, Darwin and the painter Lawrence Alma Tadema as well as Canon Duckworth and Sir Joseph Bazalgette, but if not friendless, numbering only Barnabus Couch, Lewis Fetter and perhaps the Henderson family among his friends. He had courted and danced attendance on Sir John Batho and his family but dropped them cold for no apparent reason. The woman who had been his mistress for nine years he rid himself of once she became pregnant with his child. A general practitioner in Stamford, Wilfrid Thorpe, one of his students at University College Hospital in the eighties, wrote in a letter to his future wife of Henry as 'alarmingly cold, repellently austere, and without a vestige of that wit and humour which can so enliven instruction and make learning less a labour than a delight'. Unpleasant Henry, then. Chilly Henry. On the other hand, Lady Bazalgette wrote to her daughter that she and Sir Joseph had dined with Henry and found him, 'Such a charming man with so much conversation and a model of courtesy to us ladies.' Many-sided Henry.

Still, it could have confidently been expected of him that once Eleanor was dead and he'd correctly attended the funeral he'd turn his back on the Hendersons and never see any of them again. The reverse was true. Two or three times a week from 21 October onwards Henry's diary entries read, 'Called in the evening upon Mrs Henderson' and 'To Keppel Street where I sat for two hours with Mr and Mrs Henderson.' Plainly, he went there to comfort them, to show perhaps that in losing their daughter they hadn't lost what their daughter had brought them, his friendship. It's out of character, it *isn't* Henry. Good conversationalist he may have been, but he wasn't the sort of man who cared about other people's feelings, especially when those other people were a shabby solicitor making ends meet in an overcrowded house near the British Museum. But it *is* Henry, it happened. The diary entries alone mightn't constitute sound evidence but future developments in his emotional life do, and so does a letter Louisa Henderson wrote to her sister-in-law Dorothea Vincent in December 1883. Only the second page of it has survived. Mrs Henderson has evidently been saying that Christmas will be a sad season for the family this year.

. . . only to dread. There can be no festivities in this house of mourning. If we have any comfort – for I cannot regard the arrest and appearance in the police court of Bightford as comfort – it is in the continued kindness and attention of Dr Nanther. Henry, as I have learned to call him and as he insists I continue to do, is a constant visitor to our house and never appears without some little gift. We are so spoilt by him that we have almost come to take flowers and sweetmeats for granted but yesterday he appeared with books, new novels I am glad to say, not his own learned volumes, though it is ungrateful in me to say so. If anyone could have persuaded me that we must not question the works of Providence but accept what He sends with a humble heart, it is Henry, who has talked so beautifully and eloquently to us of God's mysterious ways and the working out of His purpose to a final glorious end. Samuel has sometimes said to me that he would not have summoned the strength to go about his daily work without constantly reminding himself of the words of comfort and *true religion* from Henry the evening before. It is true that we cannot see the end in the means, Henry says, but must only have faith and in the inner . . .

Henry had been brought up as a Wesleyan Methodist. In his letters to Couch and in his homilies to the Hendersons he presented himself as a religious man. He makes references to God in the notebook and occasionally in the diaries. Strange then, that in a letter to T. H. Huxley, written within a few months of Eleanor's death, he expresses his own position as 'agnostic', the term Huxley himself coined a few years earlier. Two men again, I suppose, or several.

My great-great-grandmother Henderson mentions someone called Bightford as having been arrested and awaiting trial. This was Albert George Bightford, an unemployed railway porter, whom the police had discovered a few days after the inquest living rough on Dartmoor. He'd gone home to his parents where he'd confessed to strangling Eleanor Henderson and throwing her body out of the train. His father was resolved against protecting him and told the police. By that time Bightford was missing but was found when he attacked and threatened a shepherd who refused him food.

At his trial in Exeter, the test was applied to Bightford that if he knew what he was doing when he killed Eleanor, did he know it was wrong? The prosecution successfully contended that the answer was yes to both. Bightford himself was not permitted to give evidence. His counsel said that his dismissal from his post with the Great Western Railway, for insolence to a superior, preyed heavily on his mind. He'd boarded the train at Plymouth and gone into several carriages, speaking to passengers and trying to enlist their sympathy, contending that a great injustice had been done him. Several witnesses told how they'd been alarmed by his wild looks and aggressive manner. Counsel said Bightford entered Miss Henderson's compartment, sat down opposite her and began on his tale of woe. Miss Henderson was seriously alarmed and threatened to pull the communication cord. To silence her Bightford, by this time no doubt in a panic, strangled her with her own scarf. Somewhere between Alphington and Exeter, when the train slowed a little, he opened the door and threw her body out on to the embankment.

The jury found Bightford guilty. There was really no other choice about it. He was hanged for the murder of Eleanor Henderson in January 1884.

Meanwhile, Henry was in attendance at Windsor and at Osborne. In April the Queen went to Darmstadt for the marriage of Princess Victoria of Hesse to Prince Louis of Battenberg. At that wedding Queen Victoria's youngest daughter, Princess Beatrice, was to meet the bridegroom's brother, Prince Henry, and fall in love with him. If my great-grandfather foresaw that the Queen's favourite child and companion was to do the unthinkable and marry, he must have looked forward with great interest to Princess Beatrice's future offspring. The Queen was a haemophilia carrier, her daughter Alice had been a carrier, one of her sons and two of her grandsons had been 'bleeders'. Was Princess Beatrice also a carrier and, if she had sons, would they too inherit the haemorrhagic disease?

Henry wrote a paper entitled 'Inherited Epistaxis'. He was regularly contributing to medical journals, he gave a lecture to the Royal Society that was attended by Herbert Spencer and Charles Bradlaugh, and another to the Royal Society of Physicians. He was attentive to the Hendersons. Once the period of mourning was past, he organized a picnic on Hampstead Heath to which they, along with Dorothea Vincent who was in London for the 'Season' with her daughter Isobel (she who married the American and may have given Edith a Kodak camera), were transported in carriages. He notes in his diary that he gave a dinner party in July at which the guests were, 'Mr and Mrs Henderson, Miss Henderson and Mr Lionel Henderson, Dr and Mrs Fetter and Miss Fetter'. Far from abandoning his house-hunting on Eleanor's death, he had been busily continuing with it. At the end of July he notes in the diary: 'Took possession of a house in Hamilton Terrace, St John's Wood today. Mrs Henderson has undertaken to engage a cook and two maids for me, who, with my manservant and coachman, will constitute my little household.'

Hardly 'little' today. Considering the 'establishment' she kept up, I'd be surprised if my great-great-grandmother knew much about choosing suitable servants, but Henry seems besotted with the Hendersons. They can do no wrong. He records dining alone with Lionel Henderson in a hotel, escorting Mrs Henderson and Edith to a dance given by Dorothea Vincent, and, more significantly, transferring all his legal business to Samuel's firm. One of them he obviously valued above the others. In August he proposed to Edith and was accepted; this almost exactly one year after proposing to Eleanor, probably in the same room.

Did he place that ring on her finger, the one taken from her dead sister's hand? He must have done. Did she ask if she was second-best, if it was only that she reminded him of the woman who was gone? I don't know. No one knows. There seems to have been general rejoicing in the family. Louisa Henderson wrote to her sister-in-law, now returned home to Manaton, that 'Providence' – my great-great-grandmother was devoted to Providence – sent Henry to them in their trial and has now 'set the seal on our satisfaction' by wishing to 'ally himself more closely with our family'. Eleanor doesn't go unmentioned. She would have 'rejoiced to see her beloved Henry comforted and destined for a happy future with our dear Edith. Don't think me foolish, dear, if I say she knows.'

Why did Henry propose? There are a number of possible reasons. He liked the Hendersons. No doubt he'd sat many evenings alone or almost alone with Edith, talking about the dead girl. The two young women were quite a lot alike to look at, both fair and well-built, but Edith was prettier and had the large, if not the dark eyes, of Olivia Batho and Jimmy Ashworth. She may, too, have been 'gentle, quiet and charming'. Henry had a house, he needed a wife, and here was a compliant, trouble-free woman, who would cause him no more problems than her sister would have done. It was time he married, more than time. In two years he'd be fifty.

'I don't believe a word of it,' says Jude. Her dislike of Henry seems to grow every time we discuss him. 'He was up to something. He'd probably found out in some underhand way that she was likely to inherit her aunt Dorothea's money. And there'd be more of it now her sister was dead.'

I am alone in Alma Villa, looking at a bunch of letters sent to me by David Croft-Jones. The address on his covering letter, thanking me for dinner at the House, isn't far from here, a garden flat in Maida Vale. For some reason I thought he lived in Westminster. Jude wasn't surprised, she'd found out while I was off to the division lobby, and is over in Lauderdale Road now, having coffee with Georgie. She's gone on foot. Someone or some newspaper has told her walking is the best form of exercise and it's all part of her new health regimen.

We're very happy. We haven't been as honeymoon-happy as this for at least four years. I ought to be thankful and not bother with analysing it. And I *am* thankful, but . . . All the unhappiness we've had, all the rifts between us and all the silences, have been due to Jude's passion for a child. There, I've put it into words. It's true but not entirely true. I'll rephrase it. All our unhappiness is due to *my not being able to cope with Jude's passion for a child*. I suppose I feel that if two people love each other and live together and marry they ought to go on loving each other through adversity. Adversity ought to strengthen their feelings, it's the old marriage service stuff about better and worse and richer and poorer. It doesn't work for us. Am I really saying we can only be happy when things are going well? Or we can only be happy *when things are going well for her*? The truth, and I'm ashamed to confess it even to myself, is that I think I ought to be enough for Jude, just as she's enough for me.

★

Today is the fifth day of the Committee Stage of the House of Lords Bill and we'll probably be late, later than we were on Tuesday, but I'll not go in until Jude's come back from Georgie's and we've had lunch together. Meanwhile I read the not apparently very interesting letters David has sent me. They were sent to Veronica from her first cousins, the Craddock women, Patricia and Diana, the daughters of Henry's second daughter Mary. I'm now in possession of a great many letters Veronica received from her mother Elizabeth Kirkford, her aunt Mary Craddock and these first cousins. That makes me wonder why there don't appear to be any from Veronica's sister Vanessa. Did the two women live so near each other letters weren't necessary or was Vanessa like her grandmother and never wrote letters? That Veronica didn't keep them isn't the answer. It looks as if she hoarded everything that came to her through the post. Of course the existence or non-existence of these letters is irrelevant to Henry's life, I'm sure. It's just that when you're researching for a biography all kinds of odd little questions keep coming up and, if you're like me, you want to solve them even if they're only distractions.

David has also enclosed the latest version of the family tree and two photographs. These have the relevant details written on the backs of them in his neat civil servant's hand. One is of Patricia Agnew and her daughter Caroline and the other of her sister Diana Bell with her husband and their two little girls, Lucy and Jennifer, born in the sixties. It may be a bad photograph but Patricia looks heavy-faced and with an outsize chin while the child is plain, more like a boy than a girl. The Bell family are all handsome, their good looks not of the Nanther type, and the little girls are very fair. These people, my cousins, are rather too far removed not only from me but from Henry to be of much interest –

not a question that must be solved. Not one of his grand-children was born in his lifetime, the result of marrying so late. All there is to be said of the people in the photographs is that they are healthy looking and apparently prosperous. There's nothing astonishing in the letters, but in one from Patricia Agnew a small query arises. I must ask David about it.

Dear Veronica,

I didn't write to you when your baby was born. Frankly, I was just so afraid that all might not be well and I might put my foot in it. Now Diana tells me David Roger is quite all right and I am so happy for you. I know that things aren't what they were and all sorts of things can be done to help these people lead normal lives but it would still be a grave handicap.

Tony and I couldn't be happier for you now that things have turned out all right. I'm sorry if I've said too much but perhaps that's not important in a private letter. You'll burn it, I'm sure.

I do hope to have the chance to see young David one day. How sad it is we live so far apart. Give my best to Roger and my fondest

love to yourself,

Pat

I check on the tree and find that Veronica was forty-three when she gave birth to David in 1960. Patricia Agnew had presumably been afraid of Down's Syndrome, knowing that older women are many times more likely than younger ones to give birth to affected children. Did they know that in 1960? Did they have amniocentesis by then to discover it in the foetus? Patricia Agnew sounds like a pessimist to me or

163

maybe just a very nervous woman if she was so confident her cousin would have a Down's Syndrome child without any evidence for it. But wait a minute, there *was* evidence for it, or evidence perhaps in Patricia's eyes. There was Billy, Henry's young brother, the little boy who spat blood on to his pillow. If he didn't have Down's he had something Patricia must have believed – her mother must have told her – David could have inherited. Anyway, it's probably quite unimportant.

Will Jude have an amniocentesis? She's thirty-seven now, so I suppose they'll advise it. The trouble is that in women inclined to miscarry it's not a very safe procedure. That woman's letter has reminded me of Jude's miscarriages, the first one at eight weeks, the second at three months. I'd so much rather not think about this and wipe it from my memory but the pictures come unbidden: the rush to hospital the second time, the first and somehow worse occasion, when Jude came back into our bedroom wrapped in bloody towels, holding in her hands, carrying it in her open hands, the little foetus, bird's egg-sized in its net of white membrane. No. Stop. Take that image away.

At dinner in the House I find myself sitting at the long table next to Lord Hamilton of Luloch. We've never really met before, never spoken at any rate. He'll lose his seat here just as I will, though his family have had their title for centuries longer, and now, holding out his hand across the soup and dreadful House of Lords bread, he says in a gloomy depressed voice, 'Hamilton. How do you do? I know who you are.'

We talk for a bit about the reform bill. If everyone abides by Weatherill, and we get ninety-two hereditaries left in the interim house, he says he'll stand for election and he's thinking of writing a personal manifesto. All this positive forward thinking is delivered in the same low dismal tone, which is maybe habitual with him even when he's happy. I tell him I'm not going to stand and he nods as if this is perfectly understandable. He's about twenty years older than I am, short and stocky, with one of those walrus faces, big drooping moustache and bunchy jowls, a lot of white hair over his ears and down the back of his cranium but none on the top of his head. To my surprise he says he knows all about my writing a biography of my great-grandfather and am I going to put anything in it about Richard Hamilton?

Certainly, I say, he was an important influence in Henry's life.

'Queer as a coot,' he says. 'But of course you know that.'

I tell him I didn't know it. How does he know? I'm sure Henry had no homosexual tendencies.

'We all have 'em,' says Hamilton in his gloomy voice. He asks me to call him Lachlan. Apparently all eldest sons of Hamilton of Luloch are called Lachlan. 'We all have 'em if we're honest. Most folk aren't honest, I grant you that. My grandfather's cousin Richard, *your* chap, he was engaged but he never married the girl, couldn't face it, you see. That's par for the course. Maybe it was as well he went down with that train. It was no joke being a queer in the 1870s. How *old* is this bread?' This last to the waitress who says she's sure it was fresh in the morning, my Lord. 'It's been submitted to an ageing process then,' he says, and manages a laugh as dry as the bread.

I ask him if he has any evidence for Richard Hamilton's alleged homosexuality and he says no, but it was common knowledge. He hasn't got a diary either or any letters, and from the biographer's point of view he's a dead loss, but I like him. I like his dry rather hopeless manner and his occasional bursts of laughter. We finish our dinner, and Lachlan tells me about his grandfather being in here when the Liberals threatened that if the lords rejected a bill to reform their power they'd swamp the House with five hundred new peers. Herbert Asquith called the Lords 'this ancient and picturesque structure' and said it had been condemned to demolition by its own inmates.

'However, we're still here,' he says in his lugubrious way, and we both go back into the Chamber, he to the Tory back benches, I to the cross-benches and my place behind the Labour Privy Counsellors. I go outside once to phone Jude but come back again and finally leave for home when the House rises at a quarter past midnight.

Edith Nanther, my great-grandmother, was a woman of mystery. She kept no diary, wrote no letters, and succeeded, though hardly deliberately, in keeping herself out of other people's letters, diaries, memoirs. What records she kept were through photography and these of the most mundane kind. From them and from her silence we can infer that she was completely wrapped up in her husband and family, but there may be other explanations. For instance, I've no idea if she wanted to marry Henry or was coerced into this 'good' marriage by her parents. He wasn't, as far as I can tell, a lovable man, but he was good looking and, for all I know, may have been sexy. We always think of Victorians as having undeveloped sexuality or none at all, but I'm sure we're wrong there. Perhaps Edith married Henry because she longed to go to bed with him or for money and position and to be called Lady Nanther. Or because she thought life at home would be unbearable if she didn't. As for the family, women in the 1880s had children because they came, not because they wanted them.

The first of these arrived in August 1885 and was born, like all babies at the time, at home. No doubt Edith was delivered of the child in the principal bedroom, its handsome window just above the pediment of the covered way whose etched-glass roof protected visitors arriving in a carriage from the weather. One of the first of these would have been Edith's mother Louisa Henderson who, unless she came in a cab, may have used the newly built Metropolitan Railway from Baker Street, and walked from Lords station or Marlborough Road. It's possible, of course, that she was staying at Ainsworth House for the birth.

The child was a girl. If he was characteristic of his time, Henry would have preferred his first child to be a son. In his diary he records the event: 'E. delivered of a daughter.' That's all. No further comment. Nothing about Edith's health, his delight, if he felt any, or his disappointment if he didn't. The baby was baptized in October with the names Elizabeth Louisa but Henry has nothing to say about that either. In the letter he wrote to Barnabus Couch in December, a routine Christmas good wishes letter, it seems, he had more to say about the royal family than his own, and there everything he wrote was in the most discreet of terms. Princess Beatrice had been married in the past summer to Prince Henry of Battenberg. Henry writes of the Queen's pleasure at the match to a man many thought unsatisfactory because he was aristocratic but not truly royal, the child of a morganatic marriage. The Queen believed in the infusion of new blood into her family, a subject that Henry with his fondness for anything to do with blood, dwells on. As to his own affairs, he describes Elizabeth as his wife's child, following the fashion of the time, as if there was something not quite manly, something of the milksop or the effeminate, in acknowledging the presence of a baby in the house. 'My wife and her daughter are well.'

The Princess and her husband lived at Court. It seems to have been a condition Queen Victoria imposed in consenting to the marriage. She couldn't do without 'Baby' or 'Benjamina' as she called the Princess, and Henry, as Victoria's Physician-in-Ordinary, was in attendance on Beatrice as well. Although he never says so, he must have been on the alert when a son was born to the Battenbergs in November 1886, for he knew of the gene – though not to call it that – which Victoria and her second daughter Alice carried, which her daughters the Crown Princess Frederick of Prussia and the Princess Helena did not, but which Beatrice, the youngest, well might. A phenomenon of haemophilia, according to Henry and other authorities, is that only rarely do boy babies who have it suffer abnormal bleeding from the umbilicus at birth. So he may have had to wait some time before he knew whether the little boy was affected or not. But 'Drino' as the baby Alexander was called – he later became the Marquess of Carisbrooke with a seat in the Lords – was not a haemophiliac, and since the Princess's next child, born a year later, was a girl, he was still as far off knowing.

His own second child came along in the same month and within two weeks of Drino. 'Another daughter' is how he records the event in his diary. Mary Edith was born in November 1887 and merits a brief mention in Henry's Christmas letter to Couch.

Jude comes in while I'm mulling over all this to say she's going to the doctor to have her pregnancy confirmed and then on to work. She reads the line in the diary and asks if I want a boy or a girl.

Neither, though I'm desperately hoping that will change as the birth approaches. 'I've got a boy.' I can say things like that now. 'I'd like a girl.'

'Didn't Victorian people ever want children just for the sake of children? Why did this heir business always have to come into it?'

I tell her that I expect there were some who preferred girls to boys. It's just that Henry wasn't one of them. And what Edith thought we don't know.

'But he wasn't a lord then. He didn't have any land or a big country house or anything.'

'He had Godby Hall, for what that was worth. Men used to want a son. There are a good many people now who'd rather have a son first and a daughter second.'

Jude starts speculating about that so that I wish I hadn't said it. Maybe, now she's managed to get pregnant, she has time to have *two* children. I don't answer, I've nothing to say, and at the moment I feel I couldn't speak on that subject if I tried. Instead I tell her to give me a ring when she's seen the doctor – or would she like me to come with her?

No, darling, she says, kissing the top of my head and promising to phone. After she's gone I get out a book I've got on Queen Victoria and haemophilia, published ten years ago, and browse through it. Henry would probably have loved to write such a book himself but it was impossible. Even if any company had been prepared to publish it, it was more than his job was worth. I don't suppose he even stuck his neck out so far as to tell Princess Beatrice of the risks she ran in having children, though he'd have been quite justified in telling her and Prince Henry to stop now they had their son and daughter, for the next Battenberg children were both boys and both haemophiliacs.

Jude phones at midday and tells me the pregnancy's been confirmed. The baby's quite likely to be born on Christmas Day. At any rate that's the due date. The doctor has told her of the importance of pre-natal screening. She can have chorionic villus sampling, whatever that is, or an amniocentesis and something called an alpha-fetoprotein test. A Bart's test will also be done but I've already forgotten what that's for. The risk to the pregnancy of the chorionic thing is greater than amniocentesis, so she's opting for the latter. Oh, and there'll be an ultrasound too. I can't think of anything to say so I tell her I'll take her somewhere nice for dinner. I'll call for her as I'm not going into the House today.

Victorian women had nothing of that. They concealed their pregnancies from almost everyone, even to the extent of not going out of doors in the final months. I start thinking about Princess Beatrice, wondering if she ever averted to her brother Leopold's sickness and death when she was pregnant for the third time? Or thought of her nephew Frittie, Prince Frederick of Hesse? The pattern of transmission of haemophilia was known. Although there were a good many fallacies and old wives' tales about, that a haemophiliac's son could inherit his father's condition, that haemophilia and scurvy were identical, for instance, there was also sound medical knowledge, much of it still accepted today. And the widely held view that women can be haemophiliacs, denied for decades, is now known to be true. Perhaps Henry's books were too abstruse for Beatrice or else her mother stopped her reading anything of that nature. And the babies just came, there being no reliable contraception till well into the twentieth century.

Henry's babies went on coming too. And they went on being girls. The two my father referred to as his 'maiden aunts' arrived in 1888 and 1891, Helena Dorothea first, then Clara. Helena may have been named after the Princess Helena, Victoria's third daughter, whom Henry seems to have liked, and also after her great-aunt Dorothea Vincent. Clara was given the second name of May. Henry's choice probably, for the future Queen Mary was known as Princess May. After that fourth birth comes a gap of four years. Because Henry and Edith, after the births of four children, no longer slept together, the surest form of contraception there is? Or Edith did conceive but miscarried? Or children just failed to come, always one of the possibilities in this mystifying area.

Queen Victoria, long mourning the Prince Consort, lived mostly at Osborne in the Isle of Wight at this period of her reign. Henry was often there, though not as chief physician. James Reid had succeeded Sir William Jenner to that post in 1889. The Queen particularly liked Henry. In letters to the Princess Frederick, by now the Empress Frederick, she refers to him as 'my dear Sir Henry' and even as 'my favourite among my doctors'. Is it too much to infer that, although she would never admit to haemophilia being in the royal family, still less that it came in through her, she valued Henry's expertise in this particular field? That, notwithstanding Prince Leopold's death, she trusted him to be able to deal with it if it occurred again? Henry, as we know, could be charming to women when he chose, and in the case of his sovereign and golden goose he certainly would have chosen.

I've turned my attention back to Alternative Henry, the notebook with its essays in tiny handwriting. This one, from which I quote, is the third and of course undated. It touches on frustrated ambition and on the last thing one would expect from its author, sex.

The other day I heard a man describe another as being 'on the wrong side of fifty' so I may say of myself that I am on the right side of sixty. Men say I have achieved much and it is true that, like the unhappy Macbeth, I receive 'golden opinions from all sorts of people', but I ask myself what I have truly achieved. Success, elevation to the top of my profession, which it cannot be denied is a noble one, a substantial body of work, the valued favour of Her Majesty, a satisfactory domestic situation and a family of four children. Notwithstanding all this, I have scarcely made any new discovery, have merely recorded, albeit meticulously and in scholarly fashion, discoveries made by others. To use a metaphor that, I suppose, derives from the peasant at the plough, I have broken no new ground. There have been anomalies and phenomena of disease I have guessed at but been unable to verify scientifically. Providence has denied me the opportunity I hoped for. It has been the fault of no one but I feel it as a chronically bitter blow.

When I was young I was already irresistibly drawn to blood. For me it possessed mysterious connotations with the act of generation. I believed with the ignorance of youth and lacking any experience *de sexu* that the generative fluid which passed from male to female in the act was none other than blood itself, that it was the crimson ichor which flowed from the male member *in uterum* and that if conception failed to occur, it was this male blood which was shed in menstruation. A more logical procedure, is it not, than that which in truth occurs?

This belief I held until my medical studies commenced. I look back on it now with the weary amusement of age. Many years have passed since then. Others have made the discoveries: evolution, the source of embryonic eggs, types of parthenogenesis, Lister's revolutionary advances in surgery. It sometimes seems to me that only I have lagged behind, yet few could do more than I have done to make some momentous advance possible. Age has brought to me no diminution of ambition, but I am aware of a weakening of my vitality.

The words 'elevation' and 'noble' lead me to think that Henry had his sights on a peerage. Perhaps the Queen had dropped hints, unlikely though this seems. His extraordinary notion about blood as against semen made me feel queasy the first time I read it and Jude, who was horrified by the idea of blood gushing from the penis at the moment of ejaculation, says it could put her off sex and she wishes I hadn't told her. Henry seems to have picked up the habit from his mother-in-law of referring to Providence, but what does he mean about his being denied the opportunity he hoped for? And what is this bitter blow? The last line puzzles me too. If someone had written that today we'd think only that he was tired and age was telling on him. When Victorians wrote about 'weakening of vitality' they often meant something rather different. It sounds as if Henry is afraid of becoming impotent.

Next day Paul is at Alma Villa when I get home from the House. He's staying the weekend with his friend in Ladbroke Grove and has phoned to ask one of us to post him a bunch of CDs he left here at Christmas. Jude, who's powerless to be discreet about her pregnancy, said she'd something to tell him and if he wanted to hear it he'd better come up to St John's Wood. Like most of his contemporaries, Paul conducts his life on the phone, talks into his mobile as he walks along the street and all the time he's driving – which, thank God, happens seldom as he hasn't a car and I won't lend him mine – and wanted to know why she couldn't tell him there and then. She said no, and curiosity drew him.

He's in our living room, sitting opposite Jude, and instead of the sparkling water he lives on, he's drinking whisky. When I come in he gets up, which is far from habitual with him, and says he thinks we're mad. Jude has told him and he says he's horrified. Well, what he actually says is that he thinks it's 'horrendous'.

'I'm nearly nineteen,' he says, 'or hadn't you noticed?'

That's unfair because I've never forgotten his birthday and never would and he knows it. I fetch myself a whisky, though I never drink the stuff.

'Jude wants children,' I say, almost wincing at my own use of the plural. 'Why not? She's young enough. When she married me I don't suppose she thought your existence disqualified me from having any more.'

'*I* want them,' says Jude in a strained voice. She's addressing me. 'What you've said sounds as if you don't.'

Paul ignores her. He's staring at me. 'And what about when your marriage breaks up?' He takes no notice of Jude's smothered gasp. 'What's the kid going to suffer? Have you thought of that?'

There are all sorts of things I could say, such as that I didn't leave Sally, she left me, that any sufferings he had weren't my fault, but I'm too angry to be coherent. I shout at him to get out of the house if he's going to talk like that. I don't want him, I didn't invite him here, and God knows what Jude was thinking about even to tell her news to a little shit like him.

I'd forgotten, I always do forget, how he thrives on abuse. A smile of satisfaction spreads across his face. 'I'll help myself to some more of this,' he says, 'if you don't mind,' and he carries his whisky glass over to the cabinet, comes back with what you'd call a meagre amount if it was orange juice. 'I just happen to feel that there ought to be a law against people who've been bad parents having any more kids.'

Jude counters this – bless her – with a calm and well-considered defence of me, telling him he can't possibly call me a bad father when his mother took him away and did her best to deny me access. My anger has suddenly disappeared because I've realized something. Paul's been rude and insulting and wildly slanderous, but what he hasn't done is imply that things may go wrong and this baby never be born. I love him for that and ask him to stay to supper. He won't, of course, but once he's made a few of his essential phone calls and to my surprise heartily kissed Jude, he slopes off to a pub that does Thai food to meet one of the people he's been talking to on his mobile.

Jude and I sit on the sofa, holding hands. She's looking more like Olivia Batho than ever. Pregnancy has taken years off her, her skin glows with a pearly sheen and her eyes are clear and bright. She asks me if I've noticed she's had no morning sickness and points out – this is her first reference to previous failures – that 'last time' she vomited every morning. This is a sign, she thinks, that everything is going to be all right.

'You do want this baby, don't you, Martin?'

I curse myself for my tactlessness half an hour ago and tell her that of course I do, I'm as excited about it as she is. And, though this is an exaggeration, I do have a feeling that considering the one I've got, another child might be different and might give me a chance to be a better father this time.

12

Last evening David Croft-Jones appeared on our doorstep, minus Georgie but bringing the latest version of the tree. Like most people, Jude and I don't much like visitors turning up unannounced but we made the best of it. The tree is now several feet wide and growing by the week. I ask David about the letter from Patricia Agnew to his mother when he was three months old and he had another look at it. But he was as mystified as I am and a bit miffed too.

'I obviously don't have Down's,' he said rather stiffly.

'No, but was that what Patricia thought you had?'

'I really don't have the faintest idea.'

I said that perhaps I could ask her. No, you can't, he said, she's dead. She's been dead twenty years, and there's a peevish note in his voice that implies I'd know that if I'd studied his tree properly. I suggested that her daughter, an only child, might know, but David poured scorn on that and said I'd have to employ a private detective because no one knows where Caroline is or what's become of her. He didn't explain what he meant by 'no one', though later on when he'd insisted on taking me relative by relative through the tree, he indicated he was sporadically in touch with Diana's daughter Lucy.

He stayed so long that it was bedtime before he went. I fell asleep at once and some time during the night had a vivid dream. I was in a train – what else? – with Jude. We were on our way to some hospital in Scotland where she was going to undergo a test but I don't know what kind of test because we seemed to be in the nineteenth century. At any rate, though I was in the sort of clothes I generally wear, Jude was in a crinoline and wearing a bonnet. She's called Olivia but she looks more like Jimmy Ashworth than herself. In fact, she's turning into Jimmy. It was evening. It was getting dark. A great gale rose, a storm of wind and rain. I suddenly realized what train we were in and where we were going. We were heading for the Tay Bridge and this was the night it's going to collapse and take us with it.

I shall have to tell Olivia, I don't want her to know, but I have to stop the train. A ticket collector comes in and I tell him my fears but I can't tell him how I know. I don't know how I know. Of course he doesn't believe me, he thinks I'm mad. The bridge is new, he says, the bridge would stand a hurricane. I say, doesn't he know who I am, I'm Lord Nanther. That makes it worse.

'There's no Lord Nanther,' he says. 'He's lost his seat.'

After he's gone I decide to pull the alarm handle, only it's not a handle it's a chain, a communication cord. Jude-Jimmy-Olivia has gone, disappeared, so there's no one to stop me giving the alarm. I'm pulling on the cord when I wake up and find myself tugging on the bedlamp lead.

Two sons eventually arrived for Henry and Edith, so his fears of impotence were groundless. All Henry's children looked like him and both boys, if Edith's family photograph is anything to go by, were clones of their father. Edith's features disappeared somewhere in the complexity of genetic inheritance. Only her large, beautiful and myopic eyes were replicated in some of her descendants. Both my father's aunts, the maiden aunts, had fine eyes and both had worn glasses from their early youth. I've no way of knowing what Mary Dawson looked like, but she too must have passed on whatever genes she had of Henry's facial appearance to her children.

His first son Alexander was born in 1895, when his mother was thirty-four and his father fifty-nine. The diary entry for 27 February, the day after the birth, reads only: 'I have a son.' Henry noted his arrival not much more fulsomely in the notebook. The baby, christened Alexander Henry, was three months old when Henry wrote in the notebook:

My son, like most infants, is obstreperous, noisy, greedy and apparently ill-tempered, always either in tears or asleep. Nurse has been instructed to keep him out of earshot. Were all things equal and were I able to manage our lives prudently and wisely, were I without these painful needs and desperate ambitions, I might settle for the *status quo*. But I thank Providence too that I was wrong when I felt my vitality diminished. It was no more than that I was tired and had been overworking. HM makes great demands on me. I am sent for to Osborne, to Balmoral, and these are not summonses to which one returns a refusal.

Providence has reared its head again. But what is the *status quo*? Obviously some family situation. From time to time Henry's typical reticence finds its way into Alternative Henry as well as the diary. It very likely only means that while he considers his family complete, Edith wants more children. Or is there something I know nothing about? A legacy promised from someone or other to a second son? That would just about cover 'painful needs and desperate ambitions'. The only wealthy member of the family was Dorothea Vincent and she had daughters of her own. There was never anything in Jude's suggestion that Edith might inherit her money. But was there a settlement somewhere that only devolved on a second male child? Obviously I must find out.

Something else interesting, which I hadn't noticed but Jude pointed out, is that, with the exception of the Queen and her daughters, no woman is ever mentioned in these essays, not just Edith. Not Olivia, not Eleanor and not Jimmy. One supposes that Henry considered 'bad' women beneath his notice and 'good' women of insufficient interest to merit a mention. Which category was Olivia Batho Raven now in? In 1896 she ran away from her husband to join a lover, leaving her three small children behind. Henry must have known, it would have soon become common knowledge. In the light of what I know of Henry, it's needless to say he doesn't mention it in either the diaries or the notebook.

Undoubtedly it's true that Queen Victoria made great demands upon him, though one wonders why in the early nineties she required his presence so often. Haemophilia was by now his speciality but at that period there were no haemophiliacs in the royal family in England, though several abroad, of course. Carriers there were Princess Beatrice herself and her daughter Ena; the Queen's granddaughters, the Princess Irene of Hesse and her sister Alix, mother of the ill-fated Tsarevich, and Princess Alice, Leopold's daughter. Henry had claimed to detect her heredity in Princess Beatrice's appearance but modern medicine would call this impossible, so any ideas that he might have been able to recognize 'carrier-ship' in Irene and Alix on their visits to their grandmother, or in the baby Ena, must be nonsense. Nor would he have passed on his belief to the Queen. It was a subject she'd have refused to discuss. In any case, beyond the largely ineffective plugging of wounds, application of ice and horrific cauterizations, there was nothing approaching alleviation, let alone cure.

The answer probably is that Victoria liked his company, liked having him there. Tall, handsome, very masculine men had always attracted her. She was fond of discussing ailments (not haemophilia) and may have spent many pleasant hours in her seaside retreat talking about rheumatism and her failing eyesight. By 1893 this had become acute. She could hardly read at all and asked her correspondents to write 'in as black ink as you can'. These health problems were not in Henry's specialization, but he was a doctor of medicine and would understand. If she trusted her chief physician Sir James Reid always to tell her the truth and not that which might be more palatable, perhaps she also enjoyed Henry's courtly optimism. He had another talent the Queen would have valued. Like Sir James, he spoke German. Many connections of the royal family, from small princedoms and Grand Duchies visiting Osborne or some other royal residence, had only limited English. Henry could have talked to them in their native tongue if they needed medical advice during their stay.

At any rate, she took the extraordinary step in 1896 of ennobling him.

It seems strange to us today, the violent opposition which existed in the nineteenth century against conferring peerages upon worthy commoners. In 1856 the Queen had tried to make a judge, Sir James Parke, into Lord Wensleydale, but the Committee for Privileges considered the proposed life peerage contrary to usage. (Life peerages had been given before, despite the belief of those who think this first happened in 1958.) The committee decided that Lord Wensleydale's letters patent did not entitle him to a seat in the House of Lords and that was that.

Things gradually began to change. With the changeover

in England from an agricultural to a manufacturing society, industrialists began to be regarded as of greater worth. Sir Arthur Guinness, the brewer, was ennobled under Disraeli and in 1892 the scientist Lord Kelvin was sent to the Upper House, followed three years later by the first of many newspaper proprietors, Lord Glenesk. The poet Tennyson was the first literary figure to receive a peerage. Still, Henry's elevation was unusual for its time. A year later Sir Joseph Lister became the second doctor to be ennobled.

In the Queen's Birthday Honours of 20 May 1896, Henry was invited to accept a barony. No doubt he agreed to this with alacrity and, in a visit to Garter King of Arms at the College of Arms, would have chosen his title and his armorial bearings. Of this, in the diary, he writes only: 'Her Majesty has graciously bestowed upon me, her humble servant, a barony.' He never had his coat of arms framed and hung. It still remains curled up in its long red-leather box. I wonder why. From the photographs I've seen he'd had all his other certificates and diplomas framed and hung up on the study walls. Surely none of these equalled in his estimation his coat of arms, beautifully executed, hand-painted and lettered in gorgeous colours. For the time in which he lived, it would have cost him a lot, yet he kept it in its box, hidden from all eyes.

Soon afterwards he'd have received his Writ of Summons. Written in feudal language and in use since the fourteenth century, it's still in use today, though it's been considerably shortened and simplified. Henry's read like this:

Victoria, by the Grace of God of the United Kingdom and Ireland Queen, Defender of the Faith: To our right trusty and well-beloved Henry Alexander Nanther, of Godby in Our county of Yorkshire, Chevalier, greeting. Whereas for certain arduous and urgent affairs concerning Us, the state and defence of our said United Kingdom and the Church, we did lately, with the advice and consent of Our Council ordain Our present Parliament to be holden at Our City of Westminster on the eleventh day of August in the sixtieth year of Our reign, which Parliament hath been from that time by several adjournments and prorogations, adjourned, prorogued and continued to and until the twenty-fourth day of March now next ensuing, at Our city aforesaid, to be then there holden; We strictly enjoining command you upon the faith and allegiance by which you are bound to Us, that considering the difficulty of the said affairs and dangers impending (waiving all excuses) you be personally present at our aforesaid Parliament with Us and with the Prelates, Nobles, Peers of Our said Kingdom to treat and give your counsel upon the affairs aforesaid. And this as you regard Us and Our honour and safety and defence of the said Kingdom and Church and despatch of the said affairs in nowise do you omit.

Henry would have brought his Writ of Summons with him to his Introduction and worn his own robe. The one he had made, trimmed in those days with real ermine, not rabbit which is used today, is the robe I still wear at State Openings of Parliament, though of course will wear no longer. He was introduced 'between', as it's still put, a junior and a senior supporter, two of his soon-to-be fellow Peers. How did he come to choose them? Did they offer their services? Did he know them previously? Were they perhaps his patients?

The procession, as it enters the Chamber after prayers have been said, consists of the Gentleman Usher of the Black Rod in black tail coat and knee breeches, Garter King of Arms dressed like the Knave of Hearts, then should come the Earl Marshal and the Lord Great Chamberlain, but mostly they don't come, the Junior Supporter, the new peer carrying his Writ of Summons, and the Senior Supporter, the last three all in their robes and carrying black cocked hats. At the Bar each member of the procession makes a court bow – that's a nod of the head – to the Cloth of Estate. Henry and company would have proceeded up the Temporal side of the House and gone towards the Wool-sack, bowing again and again – but I can't go on with this, it's really a bit tedious and can be ludicrous if anyone makes a mistake or loses his voice or stumbles. In Henry's day, and up to a couple of years ago, new peers had to kneel before the Lord Chancellor to present their Writs of Summons. But many of them were too old for this and too stiff in the joints. They could kneel but they couldn't always get up again.

Henry would have knelt. Slender Henry. Agile Henry. He'd have taken the Oath of Allegiance. Whether the watching peers in those days graded new ones according to their performance I don't know but I've no doubt it was in a ringing voice that Henry uttered, 'I, Henry Alexander, Baron Nanther, do swear by Almighty God that I will be faithful and bear true Allegiance to Her Majesty Queen Victoria, her Heirs and Successors, according to law, so help me God.'

After a lot more bowing and cap-doffing, as much as fifteen minutes for the whole thing, Henry had become Lord Nanther amid the congratulations of his peers. In the following year, he records in his diary for the end of June and early July how he took part in some of the celebrations of Queen Victoria's Diamond Jubilee. These entries, perhaps needless to say, are more fulsome than anything he wrote about his wife and children.

On 23 June he joined the procession out of the House of

Lords' Chamber to the Peers' Entrance in Old Palace Yard where the Lord Chancellor entered his state carriage and the peers followed in their private carriages. Henry mentions the gold lace and cocked hats, the Levee dress worn by Privy Counsellors, and I detect a wistful note as if he wished he too might have been privileged to wear it. They proceeded to Buckingham Palace, hardly a novelty to Henry, to present an Address to the Queen. Nothing is said by him as to the weather but according to Her Majesty in her journal, 'the heat was dreadful'.

The Houses of Parliament must be almost alone today in still giving the name Whitsun to the Sunday and Monday seven weeks after Easter. The Church calls it Pentecost and the country the Spring Bank Holiday but we still call it Whitsun. Parliament has a week off and after that, when we go back, tea is served on the terrace. Not before, no matter how warm it may be, but always after Whitsun. Visitors usually ask if they can 'have tea on the terrace', a request that puzzles me because this embankment above the Thames is set about with grimly functional tables and hard chairs, is complicated of access and when you get there by a cold winding staircase and through kitchen regions, has one of the least attractive views on the river. Facing you is St Thomas's Hospital, the old part and the new, reminding MPs and peers that this is where they'll take you if you have a heart attack climbing the stairs. I much prefer the Peers' Guest Dining Room, Puginesque red and gold, carpet on the floor and a lofty ceiling. But the food at teatime is delicious wherever you have it, smoked salmon sandwiches and strawberries with the largest portions of thick golden clotted cream, positively slabs of it, you'll get anywhere.

Coming out of the Chamber I encounter Lachlan Hamilton in the Peers' Lobby and he suggests tea on the terrace. We make our way down the staircase that probably has a name but I don't know what it is. Bright hot sunshine meets us and blazing light coming off the river. Lachlan is humming a tune. I don't recognize it but a Viscount sitting at the nearest table to the door does. He says, 'You need not be quite so sickeningly appropriate, Lachlan,' and manages a hollow sort of laugh. The woman with him, probably the Viscountess, is as puzzled as I am. She looks up from her strawberries and gives us the sort of long-nosed icy look you only get from a certain kind of peeress.

'The *Götterdämmerung*,' says Lachlan as we sit down.

Are we gods? I'm sure they didn't have glorious summer days like this in Valhalla but a kind of perpetual twilight. I order strawberries and sugar and cream and therefore, according to Lachlan, am like the young lady who sewed a fine seam.

'Must have been a bloody good doctor, your great-grandpapa,' he says, 'to get a peerage out of Victoria.'

'He was a courtier.'

'Must have been. Did he cure any of that lot of anything?'

I say that I believe the Queen thought he could cure her grandsons' haemophilia. Of course he couldn't, no one could. 'Perhaps today they can do it by transplanting a gene but this was over a hundred years ago.'

'Who were these grandsons? The Tsarevich would be one, right?'

'He was a great-grandson. His mother was the Tsarina, Princess Alice's daughter. Her sister Irene was a carrier, one of her sons bled to death aged four and another, Waldemar, was also a haemophiliac. There were two Battenberg grandsons. Princess Beatrice's sons. They both lived into their twenties. Leopold died in a car crash and Maurice in the retreat from Mons. Beatrice's daughter Ena married the King of Spain, Alfonso the XIIIth. Two of her sons had it.'

Lachlan looks thoughtful and even gloomier than usual. 'And now it's just died out? Of the royal family, I mean.'

I say that considering Queen Victoria had five daughters and all but one of them had a daughter or daughters, it was astonishing how few males of the family had haemophilia and how relatively quickly it had simply disappeared. 'One or more of the Russian grand duchesses would almost certainly have been a carrier but we'll never know because they died in the cellar in Ekaterinburg. Princess Helena's sons were free of it. Of *her* daughters, one had her marriage annulled because her husband was homosexual and the other never married. They may have been carriers. By the end of the nineteen forties all the haemophiliacs were dead and all the carriers either childless or daughterless or dead or past childbearing. Queen Victoria brought it in or a mutation in her genes or her mother's did and within forty-five years of her death it had gone.'

'Your great-grandpapa,' says Lachlan, 'did he do anything to make those Battenberg boys live long enough to be cannon fodder or drive cars?'

'I don't see what he could have done apart from telling the parents to be careful they didn't fall or cut themselves.'

'What happened if haemophiliacs had to have their appendixes out?'

'They died.'

He gives his dry laugh that has no hint of humour in it. It's a signal with him that the subject is to be changed. His walrus face settles into bags and pouches. 'You realize, do you, that if you and I want to come here next year we'll have to come as Lord or Lady Life Peer's guests?'

I hadn't thought about it but now it casts a faint chill over me. Surely not, I say, with more optimism than I feel. We'll still be able to come and eat and drink – won't we? Not on your nelly, says Lachlan. And if we want to see someone in here we'll have to wait inside the Peers' Entrance and ask the doorkeeper to let someone know we're here. 'We'll be told to clear our desks and hand in our computers and take our name cards off our coat pegs because this is the end, my boy. The Twilight of the Gods. I'm sure I don't know what your great-grandpapa would have said.'

'Or your remote laird of an ancestor.'

'They'll both of them be turning like spits in their graves,' says Lachlan.

What shall I do with my robe when I have to go? Robes aren't the same for every rank of peer. Barons have two rows of 'ermine', Viscounts two and a half, Earls three, Marquesses three and a half and Dukes four. There's a fuss if any Baron or Baroness is spotted wearing a borrowed robe with, say, three rows of moth-eaten white fur. These things are very important to some hereditary peers who stand about in huddles on State Opening day listening to the scion of a noble house holding forth on who wears what and why.

I doubt if I'll ever drape myself in Henry's again. By the time the Queen next comes to the Palace of Westminster, I'll be gone.

13

Henry was sixty when he was made a peer. An outsider, viewing his life, might have said that he had everything a man's heart could desire: worldly success, a position at the top of his profession, a sufficient income to live in comfort, good health, a wife and four daughters and an heir. His son would inherit more now than his name and wealth; he would be a peer from the moment his father died. But Henry wanted another.

That son came along in 1897. Henry noted the birth in his diary even more curtly than last time: 'Son born'. Instead of waiting three months as they had with Alexander, the parents had him baptized at six weeks. Certificates of baptism for both boys were in one of Henry's trunks. I found none for the girls, though all the children were certainly christened. The new baby was named George Thomas.

Looking at these certificates, prettily engraved in red and blue and green with a minimal decoration in gold leaf, like a baby's own coat of arms, makes me think about names for our child. I shall let Jude choose. I chose last time. What I mean is, I overruled Sally who wanted Paul called Torquil. Now I'm getting used to the idea of becoming a father again. Jude's joy is so beautiful to see and it's such a pleasure to know that she'll be as happy when she wakes up in the morning as she was the night before, that I'm halfway to forgetting about broken nights and nappy-changing and the chronic anxiety children bring you. I suppose the truth is

I'm so uxorious (or I am with this *uxor*) that I can put up with anything so long as she's pleased.

And she's well. The two previous times she wasn't. She was sick in the mornings and always tired. I see her continued health as the best omen of all that this time it's going to be all right. *She's* going to be all right and that's all I care about.

Georgie Croft-Jones has given birth to a huge boy weighing nine and a half pounds or, as she insists on putting it, four kilos and a bit.

'You'll all have to buy everything in kilos next year,' she says briskly, 'so you may as well get into the habit now.'

'He's for sale then, is he?' I ask her. 'Shall we buy him, Jude, to be a companion for ours?'

Jude likes jokes like that now. She loves holding Galahad Croft-Jones and listening to Georgie talking about her delivery, what a breeze it was, how Galahad was nearly born in their new BMW, how the maternity hospital staff said he was the loveliest child they'd seen for years, and so on. When they've gone we decide we shall privately call the Croft-Jones baby the Holy Grail.

Jude's having the ultrasound next week. This is a kind of photograph of what's inside the womb and apparently they can tell if the foetus is normal by the shape or position or something of a fold at the back of its neck. If that's all right, and for some reason I'm confident it will be, there'll be no need for an amniocentesis.

Henry had none of this to worry about in his wife's pregnancies. With babies, in the 1890s, you took what came. There were no tests, beyond, I suppose, swinging a pendulum over the woman's stomach or trying to detect if she was 'carrying forwards'. Nor would Henry have been present at the births of his children. Perhaps he paced outside

189

the bedroom door in the tradition of excluded fathers, but somehow I don't think so. He'd have been relieved the new baby was a boy. A second boy was what he wanted but it wasn't so that the child could inherit some relative's money. I've made enquiries about the Vincent family and found there was very little money there at all and that the Manaton property was entailed on the late Squire Vincent's nephew. A son was probably welcome to Henry because he already had four girls. In order to make the family better balanced this child should be male.

The elder one, Alexander (my chain-smoking philandering hedonistic grandfather) was a thriving lusty boy, big for his age, if the many photographs his mother took of him are a guide. She wrote no letters but she recorded the progress of her elder son, the apple of her eye, in pictures that dominate her 1896 to 1900 album. There is one on nearly every page, the legend underneath in her sloping Victorian hand: 'Alexander aged nine months' and 'Alexander one year old today!' and 'Alex' – he is known by his diminutive now – 'walking at thirteen months, the earliest of the children to walk'.

It was George who was the less healthy one. Had he been sickly from birth and does that account for the prompt baptism? His mother seldom took photographs of him. This may have been because he wasn't a favourite like Alexander or, more likely, because the few likenesses she took show him as thin and puny. He mostly appears in those sibling groups so dear to the Victorian heart, sitting on a sister's lap while another sister rests one arm across the wing of the chair, her head on one side, and all looking soulfully at mother with the camera. Except that George doesn't look soulful. He wears on his face that indescribable look of suffering and endurance chronically sick children can't hide, not today or ever. He isn't well. He has never been quite well and never will be. Tuberculosis has taken hold. Henry mentions it in the notebook. He calls it 'consumption'.

I very much fear my younger son is a victim of consumption. Fortunately, the air of North London, of much higher elevation than the city itself, is beneficial to this condition. However, I must consider the prospect of Switzerland and its mountains as a possibility for him . . .

Whether or not he did isn't known. Though things had changed a lot as far as travelling in Europe was concerned since Henry's mother rejected the Alps and took the consumptive Billy to the Lake District; nowhere in the diaries or the notebook is any stay in Switzerland set down, nor does Henry, with or without George, apparently repeat his visit to that country of the early eighties. Tuberculosis was incurable, though life could be prolonged by mountain air, rest and, they believed, lack of excitement.

George was born much the same time that Henry would have received his coat of arms from the College of Arms. Maybe I'm conjecturing too much, taking too big a leap in the dark, but isn't it possible Henry had no compulsion to frame and hang up this beautiful document because worry over his second son made him apathetic? Because he was beginning to see, late in the day, that his family might be more important than objects, however rare and valuable?

It's a curious thing how often, throughout my family, an only or younger son has died in childhood. There's no inheritance connection. It has to be coincidence. First there was Billy, dead of tuberculosis at six, and contemporaneous with him, Louisa Henderson's little brother, the cause of whose death isn't known, though it may have been scarlet fever. Henry's son George was destined to die at the age of eleven and his daughter Elizabeth's son, brother of Vanessa and Veronica, of diphtheria at nine. It suddenly occurs to me that this could account for Patricia Agnew's nervousness about Veronica's son, a superstitious dread that boys in the family were fated to die young. The objection there is that they obviously weren't. How about Henry himself and Lionel Henderson and Alexander and my father?

Lionel had been married for ten years in 1898 and had three sons, all of whom grew up healthy, married and had children. They are vigorously present in David's tree. His second son, born in 1890, lived into his nineties and died leaving behind him a quiverful of healthy descendants.

Samuel Henderson died a few days after his daughter took a photograph of him with his wife and Elizabeth, Mary and Helena in 1892. His death certificate gives stroke as the cause. He was just sixty, four years older than his son-in-law, Henry. The Providence she so often talked of preserved his widow for another seven years, but she died of ovarian cancer in the last month of the old century.

Queen Victoria had another year to live. She continued to keep Henry at her beck and call. Her health was failing, her eyesight worsening. On 12 January 1901 she wrote in her journal for the last time. It was not Henry but Sir James Reid who took the responsibility of telling Ponsonby's office that the Queen was ill. She died ten days later, all her surviving children at her bedside.

Princess Beatrice's husband Henry of Battenberg was also dead. He had succumbed to fever off West Africa in the year Henry got his peerage. After the Queen's death Henry ceased to be Physician-in-Ordinary to the widowed Princess and her children, only one of whom, the eldest, Drino,

Marquess of Carisbrooke, was free of haemophilia. The other two boys, Leopold aged twelve, and Maurice aged ten, both had the disease, the elder being the worse afflicted. In the daughter Ena it was of course concealed. No one could tell whether or not she was a carrier. When she was eighteen, in 1905, Alfonso XIII, King of Spain, came to Britain looking for a bride and his eye first lighted on Princess Patricia, daughter of Queen Victoria's son Arthur, Duke of Connaught. But, although the chances of her inheriting the throne were remote – dozens of claimants would have got there before her – Princess Patricia was considered too close to the crown to be suitable. Undeterred by the rebuff, Alfonso had another go. This time his choice was Ena.

Henry wrote in his diary in the autumn of 1905, *Audience with His Majesty, King Alfonso of Spain*. No more than that, no details, no hint at his purpose in meeting the King and no mention in Alternative Henry that he was no longer Ena's doctor. But in an essay he wrote,

I considered it my bounden duty to warn HM of the risks involved if he persisted with his suit to her Royal Highness the Princess Ena, and did so. I felt from the first he was a young gentleman who would not take advice or listen to counsel even from one speaking on a subject on which he was an acknowledged authority and old enough to be his grandfather. The facts were laid before him. I pointed out to him the cause of the death of HRH Prince Leopold, Princess Ena's uncle, and the sufferings he endured in his lifetime; I enlightened him as to the delicate health of her two brothers, telling him that they had inherited haemophilia through their mother, who was a conductor and, finally, that though it was not certain the Princess he wished to marry carried the disease, in my opinion the chances of her doing so were very great. Of any children they might have, half the boys were likely to be haemophiliacs and half the girls conductors.

He listened to me but gave no indication he had heard, still less that what I said had any effect on him. I was not thanked. He merely nodded his head to an equerry and indicated that I should leave.

Good God, that any man should knowingly and willingly bring this grief upon himself! Should bring into the world a poor child whose daily lot is pain and incapacity, whose very innocent play may be the cause of torment and disablement, whose tumbles swell and distort his limbs and whose cuts and bruises, the simple hazards of childhood, result in the copious and unstaunchable gushes of blood comparable to those from wounds on the battle-field. I, who have seen it, know. And to consider that this poor fool, this *Majesty*, will rush headlong into a doom, not for himself but for those who come after him, for no more than a whim, a sudden passion for a girl he scarcely knows, makes me despair of humanity and this world and long, yes, long, to depart.

Very strong words for Henry, weren't they? Passionate words for once, full of real feeling. Blood is no longer the ichor that once fascinated him to a degree of unhealthy obsession. Throughout a lifetime he had seen haemophilia and what it did, he continues to see it, in his work both in and out of royal households. He has had enough of it and is ready to die. But he has another four years to go, another four years before the heart attack takes him.

As for King Alfonso, he married Ena, in spite of Henry's warning. Their first son had haemophilia, their second was a deaf mute, the third, probably also a haemophiliac, died at birth, the fifth was a haemophiliac. Only the fourth, father of the present King of Spain, was healthy. Unfortunately for Ena, Spaniards placed great importance on 'blue blood' and purity of descent and Queen Ena was blamed for bringing what we should now call defective genes into the Spanish Royal House. A gruesome story, almost certainly apocryphal, went about at the time that a Spanish soldier was sacrificed every day to infuse healthy blood into the King's haemophiliac sons.

Henry, who would have known about the eldest prince's inheritance, if not about the subsequent children, may well have remarked that Alfonso had only himself to blame.

14

It's the House of Lords Bill again, first day of Report Stage, and we're debating – what? It's hard to say because what is really happening is that the Opposition is using every chance to delay the passage of the Bill. As the Leader of the House has just said, we seem today to be quoting previous remarks. Not that that's unusual in any debate in here. Many peers have no compunction about saying the same thing at Third Reading as they said at Second Reading, Committee and Report Stages.

Lord Campbell of Alloway wants the Act not to come into force until the people have approved it in a referendum. This makes me wonder if things will drift off into a discussion, which once happened before, of whether the plural of this increasingly popular word should be 'referendums' or 'referenda'. I remember a bunch of elderly noble lords who ought to have known better hissing 'Da, da, da!' when the first construct was used, though Fowler unequivocally recommends it.

We vote on Lord Campbell's motion and the Not Contents, who are most of us, win. The amendment is accordingly disagreed to. It's too late for tea, so Lachlan Hamilton and I go to the Peers' Guest Room for a drink. I tell him about my progress with Henry and mention that sudden unexpected gush of emotion over Alfonso XIII's refusal to listen to his advice. Lachlan says he's not surprised, but he means over the refusal not the emotion.

'Royalty never take advice,' he says in a voice more

gloomy even than usual. 'They're taught not to at their mother's knee. It's about the only thing their mothers do teach 'em.'

I agree, though I don't know if this is true or not, and ask him why he thinks Henry got so passionate, he being such a cold fish normally.

'He'd seen a lot of suffering,' he says. 'Bound to, being a doc. Didn't you tell me he'd a small brother who died young?' Lachlan has a wonderful memory. 'And his own boy was delicate, wasn't he?'

'Yes, but he had tuberculosis.'

'I daresay he thought it was just a damn' shame. Alfonso getting wed willy-nilly, I mean. He probably liked kids. Some men do.' He says this as if it's a truth scarcely known to society. 'I do myself. Don't like to see 'em suffer. No doubt your great-grandpapa thought that poor bloody Alfonso a sort of murderer in advance, if you see what I mean.' He glares at me. 'He was under twenty at the time, you know.'

'Who was?'

'Alfonso. He was a posthumous child, born in 1886 after his father was dead, born king, in fact. His mama was Regent till he was sixteen. Dogged he was, poor devil, by attempts to assassinate him. They say he was brave. All these family defects lost him his throne.'

'How do you know all this?' I ask him.

He looks dour. 'I just do. Still, he was lucky. It was only his throne, not his head.'

With that we both go back into the Chamber for the resumed House of Lords Bill and hear a newish Labour peer called Lord Randall propose that all hereditary peers should remain in the House until they die but not be succeeded by their heirs. I whisper to Lord Quirk that he'll be in trouble with his whips for this and get a grin of complicity. We debate this for an hour or so. Then, after I've eaten a foul dinner in the Home Room, I phone Jude and go home.

She's looking pale, a white and wan version of Olivia Batho, and I have the horrible idea I wish I didn't have, that this is how Olivia may have looked when she was deserted and alone and ill. 'I'm just tired,' she says. 'Would you mind if I gave up work sooner than I said?'

Of course I wouldn't mind, I'd be glad of it. I sit beside her on the sofa and put my arm round her and she says, do I realize she's been pregnant three times and she's never yet felt the baby *move*. I forget how far she is, she tells me three months and one week and I say that as far as I remember it's too early yet but it ought to be soon, within the next three or four weeks. She wants to know what it will feel like. She's asking *me*, a *man*? I tell her that so far as I know, at the beginning, it's just a flutter, the kicks and punches come later.

'I wouldn't mind how much she kicked and punched me,' she says.

So it's to be a girl, is it?

I'm dreaming again. Not about Olivia or Jimmy Ashworth or Henry this time. And I'm not in a train about to cross the Tay Bridge. I'm in a house that I think is Grassingham Hall in Norfolk, country home of the Bathos. Someone has told me it's Grassingham, though whoever that was has disappeared and I'm alone, walking along a gallery high up in the house and the wall to the right of me is hung with weaponry of a medieval kind, sabres and cutlasses and things I think are arquebuses and muzzleloaders. Over the gallery rail I can see down into misty depths but, through the cold haze, engines and instruments are visible, part of a great wheel, the top of what may be a guillotine, a section of some metal structure covered in spikes. It's like one of those Piranesi prison pictures, grim and menacing.

I am looking for something and my unconscious mind knows what, but in some strange way I'm aware that my unconscious hasn't told my consciousness what that something is. When I find it I will know, that at any rate is plain to me. The passage goes on after the gallery is passed and now there are doors on either side. I open one door and then another and look inside. It's getting dark, it's dusk, and there are no lights on. I look for electricity switches, gas brackets, oil lamps, candle sconces, but I don't see any. If you want light in this place you have to bring your own.

The rooms I look into are bedrooms, full of dark furniture with white curtains and counterpanes. Outside their windows the sky is a clear blue-grey like the inside of a mussel shell. I open a third door. At first I think someone has drenched this room with water or rain has come in through a hole in the ceiling, for everything is soaking wet, the bed, a nightgown on the bed, the pillows and covers, the rug on the floor and the floor itself. I can see the wetness gleaming a little though the light is no longer strong enough to show me colours. I take a few steps into the room and touch with one finger the sodden nightgown, dipping it into a pool that lies in a fold and bringing the finger close to my eyes. The wetness is black. When I smell it I smell iron and when I taste it I taste blood. The room, the bed, the nightgown, the rug, are soaked in blood as if something has had its throat cut in here or the someone who wore the nightgown has . . .

I wake up soundlessly but with a violent jerk. Jude isn't there but the bedlamp on her side is on. The bed isn't soaked in blood but there's a lot of it on the sheets and a big still damp stain where she's been lying. I sit up and for about a minute I do absolutely nothing. I don't even think. My mind is blank, a reddish-black screen. Then I get up and go into our bathroom. Jude's lying on the floor, naked and bleeding and weeping, her nightgown, which looks quite a lot like the one in my dream, thrown into the bath.

I say, absurdly, 'I'm so sorry, I'm so sorry, I'm so sorry,' and I go back into the bedroom and dial 999 for an ambulance.

She's in the hospital overnight and for one day and another night. They don't know why she lost the baby or why she always loses babies. They tell her there was probably some defect in the foetus to account for it, as if this is comforting. Her obstetrician says it certainly doesn't mean she can't conceive again and carry a child to term.

To me she says bitterly, 'Funny, isn't it, I'm actually using those words "my obstetrician" like other women do. As if I'd had a baby. I looked the word up in the dictionary and it comes from the Latin, *obstetrix*, a midwife. I looked it up at home when I thought I'd really have a baby this time. And I've never had a midwife, I don't think I've ever spoken to one. I was happy when I looked the word up. I was starting to be happy.'

I can never think of anything to say to her but I say all sorts of things just the same. That I love her, that she's all in all to me, that it hurts me to see her so unhappy. Then she starts apologizing to me *for not giving me a child*. I'd like to say I don't give a toss about a bloody baby and I'd ten times rather not have one, but that wouldn't help. I'm steeling myself to ask her if she wants to adopt, if she wants us to try for a child from Vietnam or Peru or whatever.

Once she's home friends come and see her, her mother

comes and her sister. Then the Croft-Joneses turn up. They've left the Holy Grail behind with David's mother. He's conspicuous by his absence, his parents' tact sticks out a mile, it's worse than if they'd brought him. I wish they'd just stayed away. Just as Georgie was the most pregnant woman I've ever seen, so she's now the most obvious wet-nurse, her breasts huge bolsters on that thin frame. After a while these bulbous udders begin leaking milk and damp patches form on the bodice of her skimpy green dress. Her embarrassment is a pretence, she's immensely proud of herself, and although she's very obviously made a pact with David before they came not to mention babies or anything to do with them in front of 'poor Judith', she can't resist murmuring with mock shame that she's got enough milk for two.

I want to kill her, I want to throw them both out. I'm so anxious to get rid of them that I forget all about telling David I'd like to meet his mother before she goes back, I'd like to have a talk with her about *her* mother, Henry's eldest daughter, see if she has any stories about Henry and Edith and their other children. But I forget this in my desire to say goodbye and don't hurry back. Of course I don't say this. I thank them for coming and say we must meet again soon and when I've closed the door behind them and it's too late I remember about wanting to talk to Veronica Croft-Jones.

Jude's miscarriage put an end to all Henry research for a time. Nor did I go into the House. I missed the further consideration of the House of Lords Bill on Report but read the debate in Hansard. A letter has come from Stanley Farrow, saying he missed seeing me in the House and he'd heard my wife was ill. I ought to reply but I don't because

I don't know what to say. Jude doesn't want anyone 'outside our immediate circle' to know about her miscarriage, only those who knew she was pregnant in the first place. Someone she didn't tell was Paul. He called round without warning and knew at once, she says, from her face and from her thinness. She has discovered unexpected depths of tenderness in my son who, now the possible half-brother or sister has vanished, claims to have been looking forward to 'taking it out in its buggy'.

I sit with Jude, I hold her hand. We sleep with our arms round each other as if we're afraid something will come in in the night and prise us apart. But we have no sex. It seems an indelicate idea. Besides, I don't know if I ought to use a condom or if she ought to go on the pill or what, and I'm afraid to ask. I take her out to her favourite restaurants and pay black market prices to get into plays we haven't seen. I've joined Blockbuster Video and we watch old and new films night after night. Our childless friends are assiduous in asking us to drinks or dinner. The fecund ones maintain a tactful silence. After a month of this she doesn't do what I'd like and what I've started waiting for, that is make a sexual advance on the sofa where we sit side by side watching *Casablanca*, but as we're putting out the lights and starting up the stairs, she says in the sort of voice she'd use to suggest we book ahead for our Christmas holiday, that it's time to try again for a baby.

I ought to be impotent, I ought to be a candidate for Viagra, and I don't know why I'm not because I thought I would be. I anticipated total failure, but I didn't fail. I suppose I simply find my wife the most attractive and desirable woman I've ever known and that's that. Good. Three loud cheers from all and sundry.

I can't sleep and I lie beside the sleeping Jude, thinking

about Henry and Victorian men in general. Impotence is mostly supposed to be psychologically rather than physically caused. So if it's true nineteenth-century women were without sexual feelings they would have presented a man with no challenge, nothing for him to rise to, if you'll excuse the pun, and therefore he'd never have been incapable. But I don't suppose it is true, it's just what nineteenth-century men preferred to believe. For most of this past century men have been expected to be 'good at it'. I wonder if Henry was, if he tried, if he ever thought about it. Did Jimmy Ashworth teach him? You can only teach if you have a receptive pupil and somehow I don't think Henry would have submitted to being taught. Edith, presumably, would have accepted what she was offered, and if she expected great things, was perhaps disappointed. Marriage, as someone said in Henry's day, is the price men pay for sex and sex is the price women pay for marriage. It sounds grim.

It's the middle of July and I've begun going into the House again. Since I'd told no one I expected to become a father in December, there's no one to commiserate with me. Stanley Farrow comes up to me at the long table at teatime and asks after Jude – he thinks she's had a bad go of summer flu – and I tell him she's better. I sit in the Chamber for a couple of hours, listening to the progress of the Greater London Authority Bill, listening at any rate with half an ear, while I contemplate various of my fellow hereditaries and wonder which of them will be elected to stay and which will go. And I ask myself, suppose a banned hereditary came back, came to the Peers' Entrance and walked in and hung his coat up on his old peg, what would the doorkeepers do? Would they, respectfully, stop him? Or try to stop him? But suppose he resisted, refused, walked on and turned to the left and went up the red-carpeted staircase, would they – unthinkable, surely – *manhandle* him? Or call the police? I wonder if the promoters of this bill have thought of that.

Henry seldom came into the House. These days new peers are encouraged to make their maiden speech as soon as conveniently possible, to find a bill entering its second reading or a Wednesday afternoon debate and put their names down on the speakers' list with an 'M' after it in brackets. The debate in question should be on a subject the new peer knows something about or can mug up and the maiden speech should be non-controversial, not lasting more than ten minutes. Henry made his in July, exactly one hundred and two years ago. His theme was, appropriately enough, public health: the improved health of British city-dwellers as a result of efficient drainage. By this time Sir Joseph Bazalgette was dead. He had died in 1891. But he had been the great engineer of London's sewers and embankments and Henry's neighbour in Hamilton Terrace and they'd very likely often talked on this subject. Reading the maiden speech today, you can find evidence in it of technical knowledge that may have been acquired through conversations with Sir Joseph.

He spoke again a year later on new discoveries in bio-chemical research, then in its early stages, on the coagulation of blood, and three years afterwards on Mendelian laws of heredity, which had apparently been ignored for thirty-five years but in 1900 were rediscovered. It was in this, extremely long, speech, that Henry made his notorious remark, for which he's since been ridiculed: 'What is the answer? That is the question.' After that, he seldom spoke in the House.

He seems never to have written another book either, though there is evidence that he started one and that he regarded it as a highly significant work. The diary entry for 2 March 1900 reads, 'Began my magnum opus this morning.' Some months later he is writing in Alternative Henry,

I am agnostic, not a believer, though I pay lip service to religion, but certain sayings of Jesus Christ I recognize as words of great wisdom. For instance, one that springs constantly to mind is one of the last phrases He is alleged to have uttered; Father, forgive them, for they know not what they do. I knew not what I was doing when I did what I did, though I believed I knew only too well.

I shall never be a pioneer now, a great discoverer. My ambition has come to nothing. I cannot write. I can carry out no experiments. The child's crying is a constant disturbance to me. It rings and echoes through this house, it penetrates the thick walls. No matter where I go I cannot escape from it. Sometimes I think I shall lose my mind. Oh, how I am punished!

Why? How? What has he done? I don't know, and the rest of the Alternative Henry papers, only two of them, give no clue. Those last lines sound like the witness of someone in the ghost stories of M. R. James, some wretched haunted creature who has seen the demon yet again and seen it come closer. Or is he only saying, as a thoroughly selfish man might, albeit with unusual near-hysteria, that his three-year-old son's crying is a nuisance and a hindrance to his work? Perhaps. Still, the terms he uses are extreme. By the standards of the time, he was an old man. It may be that he was on the verge of making some new discovery and the presence of two small boys in the house interrupted the process. Even with a staff of servants, it's no joke to be a father of a five-year-old and a three-year-old when you're sixty-four. This makes me think of myself and my own situation and what I now know to be Jude's aims, to have a child whenever and by whatever means she can. I know I'm getting things out of proportion but I can't help thinking that if she finally succeeds when she's forty-seven, I'll be fifty-five, and not far short of Henry's age when it's five.

A package has come from Janet Forsythe, containing a wad of smudged photocopies, a photograph and a covering letter. I've forgotten who she is and the address at the top of the letter means nothing. But the first sentence tells me how much she and her mother enjoyed tea in the House of Lords and she apologizes for not having thanked me before. And of course I remember she's Laura Kimball's daughter and Jimmy Ashworth was her great-grandmother. She's a sort of cousin of mine, a fact she's unaware of, or so I think. But when I read the letter I find this isn't so. She says she's always suspected Henry was her great-grandfather but she's never liked to mention this to her mother who has an 'exalted idea' of Jimmy. For her part, she'd be proud to be descended from 'the distinguished doctor'. The photocopies, she writes, are from *The Times* of various dates in 1883 and she goes into a long explanation of being interested in some other aspect of family history – she is another of these amateur genealogists, apparently – of investigating newspaper accounts and of coming on pieces I might 'find fascinating'. In due course she'll send me a draft copy of the family tree she's making because she's sure I'll be interested.

Before I go through these copies I look at the photograph. It's of Janet when young – or is it of her mother? For a moment I can't tell but I think it's Laura by the clothes which are unmistakably 1930s. But what grabs my attention is the brooch this woman, mother or daughter, is wearing on her dark dress. It's a five-pointed star in brilliants, almost certainly not diamonds, and Janet has written on the back: 'This is Jimmy's brooch Sir Henry gave her and which came to my mother when her mother died.' So now I know where the idea of marking his dates with Jimmy came from, a brooch he gave her. Or did the pentagrams come first and he chose the brooch to match them? Perhaps it was a joke between him and her. And it opens up the idea of tenderness and affection in Henry's attitude to Jimmy. Jokes, a pretty gift, drawing the five-pointed star in his diary at appropriate times, maybe even a secret sign between them, the present bestowed and Henry saying: 'I bought this for you because it reminded me of our special sign and now when you wear it you can think of me making the sign of love in my diary . . .' All imagination on my part, of course, all a romancing worthy of Laura herself.

I go through the copies, finding it necessary once more to use a magnifying glass. Many of the paragraphs are concerned with Henry, lectures he's given, announcements of new books he's published, the notice in the Court Circular of his knighthood. There's nothing new for me in any of this. The last cutting is about the appearance in the magistrates' court of a man called Joseph Edward Heyford Brewer, aged twenty-six, of Palmerston Buildings, Euston, on a charge of assaulting Mr Samuel Henderson in Gower Street. Brewer was found guilty and sent to prison, but not for long. No doubt he'd have got years if he'd committed robbery at the same time, the English always valuing property above human life and wellbeing.

This is quite useful to me, I'd have had to find it for myself sooner or later, and I write back to Janet Forsythe immediately, thanking her for the cuttings, agreeing with her about her grandmother's paternity but saying nothing about the pentagram brooch or how thrilled I'd be to see her family tree. I put her photocopies in one of the Henry box files. These are five now, variously labelled Work, Royal Family, Personal History, Children and Descendants, and Miscellaneous and Marriage. Janet's stuff goes into Personal History, though I hesitate as to whether the last wouldn't be a better home for it, the heroic rescue of poor Samuel being the trigger which set off Henry's marriage.

I take the letter to the post and Jude comes with me. A hundred-yard trip becomes a walk. She's looking well again, though she's very thin, her waist a narrow stem like Olivia's in the portrait, but Olivia's was like that because she wore a corset. Of course the streets are full of women with babies, black women and white women and Asian women, all pushing their infants in buggies or carrying them in baby-carriers on their chests. There's even one with an old-fashioned pram, the child's face round and pink amid lacy froth and flounces. I feel like telling Jude what a nuisance Henry found his kids, how they get in the way of great enterprises (as Bacon or someone says). I feel like it and that's as far as it goes.

We go into a health food shop and Jude buys folic acid and multi-vitamins and gingko biloba and echinacea and St John's Wort. She used to have a getting-fit-for-the-birth regime and now she has a getting-fit-for-the-conception one. Twice a week she does the Alexander Technique and she's visiting a herbalist. We come back across Abercorn Place into Hamilton Terrace, talking about how there are certain plant substances which are claimed to prevent mis-carriage, or Jude is talking and I'm listening. I tell her it can't do any harm but maybe to check with her doctor, and we turn aside and stop outside Ainsworth House, now renamed (absurdly) Horizon View, and look up at the millionaire's windows and at the millionaire's covered way in which the stained glass has been replaced with clearer and brighter colours.

The front garden is chock-a-block with the kind of flowers in tubs you plant when they're already in bloom. Their colours match those in the roof of the covered way, something that must be intentional. None of the windows is open, though it's a hot day, but no doubt the millionaire has air conditioning. The curtains inside are festoons of silk and velvet and lace. You can't see much inside. Last time I looked at this house I saw a dispirited young Asian woman at the window of the room that was Henry's study, but there's no one today.

I desperately want Jude to say something. I want her to make some comment on the house or Henry or the changes that have been made. I want her to ask a question about what this room was or that and who slept where, anything but babies and her prospects of having a baby. But she says nothing, only takes my arm and draws me close to her, and I bend and kiss her, there in the street outside my great-grandfather's house.

15

There's been more discussion in the House today of the Lords Bill, as amended on Report. Lord Mayhew, a former attorney general, rose to move whether questions of hereditary peers' rights should be referred to the Committee for Privileges.

I spoke, briefly, more or less echoing the words of Lord Goodhart that what the motion proposed was a waste of time. Everyone knows the Bill's intention and what its effect will be – to get rid of us as anachronisms and white elephants. Cries of 'Oh!' greeted this, especially the white elephants bit.

But Lord Mayhew presses it to a division and wins. We go on after that, this time about the Treaty of Union and a fundamental principle (apparently) in it guarantees Scotland specific representation in this House. The idea now is that the Committee for Privileges should look into this as well, a ploy which tries the patience of Baroness Jay, the Leader of the House. Another vote is inevitable and the pro-Committee for Privileges faction win yet again. But that's the end of the Bill until after the long summer recess. We'll resume sometime in October, and meanwhile we hereditaries are still here. Henry's line carries on.

It's 27 July and the House gets up on Thursday. The Labour Working Peers, always heavily whipped and roster-driven, are panting for their holidays – and so am I. Jude and I are going walking in the mountains of the Tyrol and then for a week on a Greek island. It was fixed up long before the miscarriage and she pretends she wants to go but I know she doesn't. I can tell.

We're off today. Our flight goes in the early afternoon and we're ready to leave. But just before the cab comes two letters arrive in the post, one from Veronica Croft-Jones and the other, enclosing her draft family tree, the one I didn't ask her to send, from Janet Forsythe. Veronica, whom of course I've never met, writes that she understands from her son that I'd like to talk to her about the family. She'll be back visiting David and Georgie and Galahad in September and would be very happy to fix up a meeting. Anyway, she says, we're such close relations really, we ought to get to know each other better, and she signs herself, 'Your affectionate cousin, Veronica.'

I leave this letter behind but for some reason I stuff the family tree into my pocket, the cab comes and we depart for Heathrow. We're in the aircraft, going over some alps, before I look at the tree again. I soon see I shall have to take great care of it as it's obviously the top copy. This genealogical table is done in a fancy way, more like a real tree than a table, with branches and twigs hanging down and coloured brown and green instead of standing up because the trunk part has to be at the top. The male characters are each encased in a leaf shape and the female in an apple. Jude looks over my shoulder and says in a cold voice that it's nauseating. At first I can't see any names that I recognize. Then I spot Jemima Ann Ashworth and Leonard Dawson. Their daughter Mary (or Henry's daughter) is there and so are all the other children that are truly Len Dawson's, and on a twirly little twig, Janet Forsythe, branching out of Laura Mary Kimball and Robert Arthur

Kimball, with her husband and her son Damon. Jimmy Ashworth appears to have had no siblings, but Len Dawson had no fewer than eleven brothers and sisters plus two half-brothers and two half-sisters born after the death of his father and when his mother, a glutton for hard labour apparently, had married again. I can't see much to interest me in the tree and I put it into my flight carry-on bag, neatly folded this time.

Jude worries about walking, just as she worries about everything else that involves bodily motion. She worries particularly about four-wheel drive vehicles bouncing up bumpy mountain tracks. I remind her that she can't be pregnant because she hasn't yet had a period since the miscarriage. Whether this is true or not, I mean the bit about not possibly being pregnant, I don't know. Neither does she and she sulks disdainfully. I find myself looking north across the mountains to Switzerland, to where I think the Graubünden must be. Did Henry come walking here? Jude is sitting on a rock, scowling.

I say to her, 'Why are you being so disagreeable?'

To my astonishment she bursts out laughing like the old Jude, like the one I first fell in love with. 'I love you,' she says. 'You're always using these crazy old-fashioned expressions. Disagreeable! I ask you. No one, but *no one*, says "disagreeable" but you.'

So we hug each other and go back to the hotel and make love like we used to before all this baby business. We make love every day and often at night as well and each time it's like it used to be, so I start thinking it always will be now, this holiday is the beginning of our new happiness. We write postcards to all our friends, we even write one to Paul who despises them, and we sign them off 'with lots of love'.

Love is what we're engulfed with, soppily, and we even have some over-spill.

Jude's period comes when we're on Skyros but she's fine about it, she's glad to see it. She says nothing about babies. 'Baby' is now a banned word. It mustn't pass our lips. It's as if we're children and our mother has told us we're not to say that naughty four-letter word. We swim and lie in the sun, slathered in factor fifteen, and drink things that taste disgusting at home, ouzo and retsina, and Jude says not a word about alcohol poisoning her hormones or whatever.

On our last day a newcomer to the hotel comes up to us while we're sitting by the pool and introduces himself as Julian Brewer. 'Soon to be Lord Brewer,' he says with an expansive smile. Apparently, he's just been made a peer and he'll take his seat in October. I get up and shake hands and tell him I'll be departing just as he comes in. We order drinks from the waiter who comes round to the tables and I answer his questions about the Lords as best I can, but my mind is only half on what he's saying, only a quarter, because one of those revelations has just come to me, one of those flashes of enlightenment. I want him to go away, I want the sun to sink and the wind to get up so that we can all go indoors and I can get up to my room and find Janet Forsythe's family tree in my carry-on bag.

Eventually he goes, but not until I've made wild promises to have a drink with him after his introduction, meet his wife and children and show him the ropes – that is, where the lavatories are and how to put down a starred question. Anything to get rid of him. Jude is looking at me strangely because I don't usually do this sort of thing. I explain when we're in the lift. Brewer, I say to her, Brewer. His name is

213

Brewer and that triggered off something. I've got to check it out. If I'm right it's going to put a whole new complexion on Henry's life.

There it is, in Janet Forsythe's tree: Joseph Edward Heyford Brewer, second son of Joseph William Brewer and his wife Mary Ann Dawson, née Heyford. These two had four children and they all had Heyford among their names. But the important, the astounding, point is that Mary Ann Dawson had been married to Clarence George Dawson and by him become the mother, among twelve children, of Leonard Dawson, husband of Jimmy Ashworth. Therefore, the man who assaulted my great-great-grandfather Samuel Henderson in Gower Street, and was interrupted in his nefarious work by my great-grandfather Henry Nanther, was Len Dawson's half-brother.

I haven't got the cutting from *The Times* about the appearance of Brewer in the magistrates' court but I remember the name perfectly. It's the Heyford bit that's stuck in my mind, I don't know why. His age has too, twenty-six. According to Janet's tree Joseph Edward Heyford Brewer was born in 1857, which makes it about right. I shall have to check his age and where he was born but they have to be the same man. They have to be. Anything else would be too enormous a coincidence.

Does Janet realize? She must do. That is, she must have noticed that the man who attacked Samuel Henderson was Len Dawson's half-brother. But has she put two and two together and seen that Len Dawson's half-brother was convicted and sent to prison for an assault on *my great-great-grandfather and Henry's future father-in-law*? Somehow I doubt it. I talk to Jude about it and tell her there was nothing in the police court proceedings about Henry, he wasn't mentioned, and she agrees with me. Janet very likely hasn't made the connection.

'But why did she draw your attention to it by sending you that cutting?'

I've thought about that and I tell her I'd make a guess it's because, when we met, her mother seemed to censor everything about Jimmy Ashworth, make her come out pure and innocent, while she, Janet, is more of a woman of the world than that. 'She wants to show me her family had their black sheep. Most people would think anything like that in their family history quite amusing. Jimmy being a kept woman and this Joseph a Victorian thug. Only Laura Kimball wouldn't. Janet wants to show she's broader-minded than her mother. Besides, Joseph was barely related to her.'

'He wasn't related to her at all if what you say is true and Henry was her grandmother's father.'

I ask her to tell me what she thinks was behind it all and she's silent for a moment. Then she says things look black for Henry. 'I mean, is there any other way of looking at it but that Henry put Joseph up to it? Paid him? Joseph was a sort of contract mugger and Henry paid him to waylay poor old Samuel in the street, knock him around a bit but not too much, and then gallant Henry the white knight comes along and rescues Joseph's victim.'

'I suppose so,' I say.

'Well,' she says, playing the devil's advocate, 'you could look at it the other way about and say Henry was innocent. He only met Joseph Edward Heyford Brewer *because* he knocked Samuel down. Maybe he was one of those Victorian philanthropists who were prison visitors and he sought Brewer out in jail, got to know him and his family and met Len Dawson.'

'Only there's no evidence at all that Henry was a prison visitor,' I tell her, 'and quite a lot of evidence to the contrary. One of the letters to Couch is devoted to a long diatribe on the treatment of prisoners. In Henry's view it was too lenient. He actually says he thinks prison visitors are misguided. Criminals on whatever level, in his view, should be ostracized by society even more than they were.'

'I'm glad. I want Henry to turn out a villain. Didn't I always say he was up to something? And now we know what it was.'

She goes off to have a shower and I sit on the bed and think about that one. Where and how did Henry meet Joseph Brewer? Or did he meet Len Dawson first? I doubt if I'm ever going to find out. I suddenly remember that Joseph Brewer's address was somewhere in Euston but that doesn't help. Maybe he was one of those 'exhibits' doctors had up before their students and asked them to observe certain anomalies or deformities about their anatomy. But I've no reason to believe Joseph had any deformities or was in any way peculiar. He was very likely a completely normal young man.

How much did Henry give him to 'do the job'? A hundred pounds would have been a fortune to a man like that. Later on he rewarded his half-brother with marriage to Jimmy Ashworth, accommodation and no doubt a considerable down-payment. Why pick on Len? Why not Joseph himself? Possibly because Joseph was married already. I take another look at the family tree and see that of the Dawson and Brewer children nine were male and seven female. In 1883 the oldest male was forty-one and the youngest nineteen. The five oldest were all married by 1883, another was widowed and left with five children. Len was single and I notice something I didn't see before. His youngest full brother had died aged fourteen and a brother a year younger than he died aged one year. Of the Brewers, two were girls. Joseph had been married three years. The nineteen-year-old Albert was still single. Henry wouldn't have foisted a widower with five children on Jimmy, even he would have stopped short at that, and the nineteen-year-old was too young for her. Hence, Len was the only possible choice.

He didn't meet Len because he was a hospital porter. He was probably a porter at Euston Station and Henry met him when Joseph introduced them. Why hadn't Len married before? Perhaps there was something about him that didn't appeal to women, he had a birthmark or a wart on his face or something. I must find out if Laura Kimball has a photograph.

Henry can only have had one motive in fixing this assault and his own heroic intervention: to meet the Henderson family. There were other ways he could have done this but perhaps none so effective. He could have arranged an interview with Samuel to consult him on some legal aspect of his medical research. But how to make such a consultation lead to friendship and invitations to the Henderson home? It would have taken a long time, nothing might have come of it. In fact, it's hard to see how Henry could have thought of a sounder and surer plan of action than the one he arranged. Nothing could be more likely than that he earn the gratitude of the whole family. Nothing more natural than that he call at the Henderson house to ask after the health of the victim.

What it doesn't tell me is why Henry so much wanted to know the Hendersons that he, a hitherto law-abiding man, an eminent figure, a professor, a royal doctor, would stoop to criminal conspiracy to gain access to their home. What was so attractive about them? They were very ordinary people. A solicitor was far less respected then than he'd be today and Samuel wasn't even doing very well. They were middle-class, not rich, living in an overcrowded poky house in an unfashionable part of London. None of them would have been accepted in the kind of society the Bathos belonged to. The girls were pretty but so were a thousand young girls in London, many of them far more eligible.

Another curious factor in this business comes to mind. Henry must have known of the Hendersons before he set up the encounter in Gower Street and he could only have known of them by making enquiries about them. Did he use a detective agency? Someone on the lines of Sherlock Holmes? I've a picture in my mind of a rather sinister figure, very Victorian, a character out of Wilkie Collins, following Samuel, watching his house, maybe striking up an acquaintance with old Mr Quendon when he went out for his 'constitutional', eyeing the girls from a shop doorway. But why? What for?

I decide to sleep on it, knowing from experience how different things can be in the morning. Tomorrow it may all fall to the ground, it may turn out to have been in my head, a think-piece, as the journalists say. But I sleep and get up early because we've a plane to catch, and things are just the same. Henry is still a conspirator and a villain and I still don't know why he wanted to know the Hendersons.

Devious Henry. Criminal Henry.

16

At home there are no personal letters awaiting us, no more titillating revelations, only bills, a pile of appeals for my time and money sent on from the House of Lords and two books from a literary editor for me to review. I'm glad to see them, this history of the parliamentary system in Great Britain and a biography of Bonar Law. The two reviews will earn me a thousand pounds or a bit less. On the way back, in the plane, I've been thinking, not of Henry, but of money.

Jude hasn't given up her job. Sadly, she didn't have to. I was in publishing myself once, until I left on the strength of the flash-in-the-pan success of my first biography. My latest one won't even go into paperback and research takes so long I don't anticipate beginning the writing of the Henry book until the end of next year at the earliest. What occurred to me in the aircraft was something that simply hadn't struck me before, though no doubt it's struck many wiser than I. When I'm chucked out of the Lords I'll lose my expenses. A peer who goes into the Chamber four times a week and five times if the House sits on a Friday, can claim expenses of ten thousand a year or more, and it's tax-free. I may have to get a job – if I can. I can't depend on my wife to keep me. Besides, what about this baby? The baby that's never come yet but may come.

Lamb wrote an essay called 'Dream Children' about the family he never had. It's sentimental but it has its finer moments. Ghostly children gather round to listen to his tales of the people who might have been their ancestors if they'd ever been born. They want 'stories about their pretty dead mother' but at last they fade mournfully away saying, 'We are nothing; less than nothing, and dreams. We are only what might have been, and must wait upon the tedious shores of Lethe millions of ages before we have existence, and a name.'

I don't know if Jude knows this essay. Of course, I'd rather she didn't. There are no two ways about it for me; I must want her to have a child, I must stop it any longer waiting on the tedious shores of Lethe, I must teach myself to want it as much as she does, because that's the only way we can survive together. I must stop being relieved when another day passes and she hasn't used the dreaded four-letter word. More than that, I must begin using it myself, show enthusiasm for what dismays me, pretend a longing I don't feel. Even that must change. The dismay must go and my whole attitude towards our life be altered. I must get myself into Henry-the-father mode, think of how he longed for a second son, though he had four daughters and a son already. It would be better too if I stopped telling myself it was easy for him, he had a wife at home and nannies for his children, and remembered his involvement with George the youngest, the sick boy, the child whose crying so distressed him.

But do I want that distress? Do I want someone to enter my life and bring me pain? Suddenly I remember Paul having croup at a year old and rushing him to hospital and the touch-and-go tracheotomy the surgeon carried out. That agony will be mine again, or something very like it, if Jude gets what she wants and I must teach myself to want. Because I shall love the child. I shall adore it and there's the pity of it all. But if she doesn't get what she wants, it will be worse.

★

It's September now, a Sunday morning, and David and Georgie have called. They've brought the Holy Grail with them, having apparently decided tact can only be maintained so long. He's the biggest ten-week-old I've ever seen, not that I've much experience in these matters, he's the sort of baby Renaissance painters used as models for their *putti*, presumably because this was the ideal and few fifteenth-century Florentine infants actually packed this amount of fat on to their bones. I admire him so extravagantly that Jude, whom my transports are designed to impress, gives me a suspicious look. While she and Georgie talk babies, feeding routines and the ever-absorbing subject of Georgie's superabundance of milk, David tells me his mother is coming on the twentieth to stay for a week. Will we come to dinner while she's with them? I can't really turn this down, though I'd like to, but I stipulate that I also need to have the private interview with Veronica she suggested in her letter. I want to tape our conversation as I've a feeling it may be very useful. I consult Jude, interrupting a mini-lecture from Georgie on efficient methods of expressing milk, breast pumps, et cetera, and we fix on Saturday 25 September for the dinner. The Croft-Joneses are now established as our friends.

'Our cousins who are also our friends,' as David alarmingly puts it.

I'm tempted to put to him my problem about Henry's motivation in introducing himself to the Hendersons. After all, he's just as much his great-grandson as I am. But something stops me and I almost laugh out loud when I realize what it is. I've the same sort of inhibition as Laura Kimball has about Jimmy Ashworth. I don't want it to get around that my celebrated and distinguished great-grandfather was party to a criminal conspiracy, that he paid a villain to attack an innocent and harmless man. It may have been a hundred and sixteen years ago, it was still my ancestor and a disgraceful thing to do. After the Croft-Joneses have gone Jude wants to know what I was 'grinning about'. I tell her and she too laughs.

'It's called empathy,' she says.

But what does it bode for my Henry biography? If I don't want to tell my second or third cousin or whatever he is, I'm certainly not going to want to tell the world. Or those inhabitants of it that constitute my readership. It's something I've never thought of before. I suppose I simply assumed Henry's life would be blameless. In a way, of course, I'm presented with a choice: a dull (and untruthful) biography that few will want to read or an exciting truthful one that will sell. There isn't really a choice, it has to be the latter – or not happen at all.

I've made a table for myself, rather like the details of evidence compiled by investigating officers in old-fashioned detective stories. On one side I've listed everything I knew about the Hendersons as they were in 1883 and on the other the known facts about Henry's involvement with the Dawson–Brewer family. I've been looking at it every day since we got back from Greece and still I can't see why Henry wanted to know the Hendersons and what they had that he couldn't find elsewhere. I've concentrated on the son Lionel and even wondered if Henry *was* homosexual, if that was what his friendship with Richard Hamilton was really about, and having seen Lionel he'd fallen in love. But considering the broods of children both he and Lionel later had and the lack of any evidence for homosexuality in either of them, not to mention Jimmy Ashworth, I've abandoned that. I've even asked myself if there could have been something in the house in Keppel Street Henry wanted, if there was something hidden there known to him but not them. This again is the stuff of old-fashioned (very old-fashioned) detective stories. Was the old man William Quendon in possession of some information Henry needed? That really comes into the same category as the last supposition.

I'm looking at the two detective story columns again today. We're going out for lunch, to find somewhere we can eat outside, and I'm sitting at my desk staring at the table while Jude gets ready. And suddenly I see. It's so simple and so obvious when you know that I'm ashamed of myself for not cottoning on before. He'd seen Eleanor somewhere, fallen in love and decided he wanted to marry her.

'At his age?' says Jude as we're walking up to Blenheim Terrace.

'I fell in love with you at first sight,' I say, and it's true. I saw her across the room at a publisher's party.

'You weren't forty-seven,' she says.

'No, I was ten years younger. But old enough to know better, only it wouldn't have been better any more than it would have been for Henry.'

This muddled thinking and confused phrasing she rightly receives in silence. But when I take her hand she gives mine a squeeze. 'I can't see you getting a hit man to bang my father over the head in order to meet me.'

I say we don't have to do things like that these days. I went up to Jude at that party, I didn't even find anyone to introduce us, I just asked if I could fetch her another drink and we talked and when it got to eight I asked her if she'd have dinner with me. 'You couldn't do that in 1883,' I tell her. 'Girls didn't go to parties on their own, they had chaperones, and, anyway, she and Henry wouldn't have gone to the same parties. He couldn't have gone up to her in the street. He couldn't have knocked on the front door and asked to talk to her. I can see he'd have thought this the only way.'

She nods, but abstractedly. I know I haven't gone far enough to convince her. But I've almost convinced myself. Henry was tired of Jimmy Ashworth and bored with Olivia. Why not? One day, making his way to the hospital in Gower Street, he sees a pretty girl with a mass of beautiful blonde hair, a girl with a fine figure and the air of a lady. He can't get her out of his mind and he employs a private detective – he may even have employed Brewer – to find out who she is and where she comes from.

'If what you say is true,' says Jude as we go up the steps of the restaurant, 'how did it happen that once Eleanor was dead he transferred his affections to Edith?'

'For the reasons we've been into before. They had their love of the dead in common, they talked, they were often alone together. Besides, by this time Henry was set on marriage. He was forty-seven going on forty-eight, he'd no time to waste and I don't suppose he met many young women.'

'No, and he couldn't keep on knocking old men down in the street in order to meet them.'

We're shown to our table, outside, as we'd requested, and the waitress has brought us each a glass of unexpectedly well-chilled white wine. It pleases me to see Jude drinking it, not adhering to this dreary healthy eating regime she started on before we went away. 'Why not go back to Olivia?' she says. 'If he wanted a wife, that is. According to her sister, she'd have had him. Why did he have to have a Henderson?'

I say that this is a strange way of putting it.

'Is it? It seems reasonable to me. I've been reading these memoirs – in manuscript I mean, at work – they're about a bunch of aristocrats who were all friends of Edward the Seventh. His eldest son, he was called Albert Victor – there was a tale went the rounds that he was actually Jack the Ripper, but that's another story. Anyway, he was engaged to Princess Mary of Teck, always called May, but he died and Princess May transferred her affections to his brother. They married and turned into King George the Fifth and Queen Mary.'

'Yes, but that was dynastic,' I say. 'She was probably told it was her destiny not to marry the individual man but to marry the future king. It was her duty.'

'It certainly wasn't Henry's duty,' says Jude. For one so slim, she has an inordinate passion for pizza and has enthusiastically begun on a margarita. I'm more austerely getting to work on a Caesar salad. 'It was his choice,' she says. 'He had to have a Henderson just like Princess May had to have a future king. I bet it was her choice too. Imagine if you're the daughter of the Duke of a little German duchy, even if your great-grandfather was a king, and your fiancé who's going to be King of England dies of pneumonia – think of the disappointment even if you didn't love him. You'd jump at the chance of marrying the next one in line.'

I tell her she's losing her parallel, it's getting less and less like Henry's case every minute. George the Fifth was a great catch for anyone. Edith wasn't. All she seems to have had going for her was that she was slightly prettier than her sister. Jude says she doesn't know, she can't fathom Henry but she's willing to bet he was up to no good. We sit about in the sunshine, drinking rather a lot of wine, and feeling as if we're in some Mediterranean place. Jude says she knows it's not considered the thing to say but if this is global warming, she's all for it. At home, in a somewhat fuddled state, I take another look at Henry's diary for the year 1883, specifically at those entries for the late summer when he became engaged to Eleanor, and for the autumn, made after her death.

There's no mystery about any of them. All they show is a callous and relentless nature as well as a determination to reveal nothing in a diary someone else might find and read. On Thursday 14 June he breaks with the Bathos. 'Feeling unwell, I cancelled my evening engagement.' Two days later comes, 'Called to enquire after Mr Henderson's health,' and on the 20th, 'Dined with Mr and Mrs Henderson.' Then come more visits to Keppel Street but the only entry that arouses the slightest curiosity is for 27 July, 'Consultation with Mrs Henderson.' What was she consulting him about? All the family seem to have been healthy. I suppose it must have been about Samuel Henderson, who perhaps suffered headaches and dizziness as a result of Joseph Brewer's attack on him, and Louisa Henderson, like a good wife, was worried about him. I seem to have answered all my own questions and I ought to be satisfied, but somehow I'm not.

Later on, Jude asks the question I was afraid Georgie Croft-Jones would ask that evening we had dinner together in the House. 'Now you've found Henry was capable of criminal conspiracy and fixed up the assault on poor old Samuel, has it occurred to you he might also have engineered Eleanor's murder?'

'You mean, paid Bightford to do it and later on let Bightford be hanged?'

'Well, yes. Bightford would have been hanged anyway, he did the deed, but I suppose Henry would have been hanged along with him.'

I say that if our theory that Henry fell in love with Eleanor after seeing her in the street is correct, he'd have wanted to marry her, he wouldn't want her dead. Besides, there's no discernible connection between Bightford and Henry.

'There was no discernible connection between Brewer and Henry until you discovered it.'

Bightford would have told the police, I tell her. He'd nothing to lose. While in police custody at Exeter he'd have come out with the whole story, if story there was. I can't believe it, it doesn't ring true. Henry wasn't *married* to Eleanor, he wasn't irrevocably bound to her. If he wanted to be rid of her he could have jilted her. After all, he'd more or less done it before with Olivia.

'It was just an idea,' she says.

While she watches her favourite Sunday night television serial I give her theory a bit more thought. Suppose the mysterious 'consultation' wasn't about Samuel and his headaches at all. Suppose Louisa Henderson had confided in Henry that her daughter Eleanor had some disease or disability. She'd been injured as a child, for instance, and would never have children. But that won't work because Henry wasn't engaged to Eleanor on 27 July when the consultation took place, he didn't propose until quite late on in August. If Louisa Henderson had told him Eleanor was incapable of having children or was malformed in some way – for instance, lacking a vagina, which happens sometimes though very rarely – Henry would surely just have abandoned her, as was his habit. He'd dumped two women so why not a third? In any case, why would Louisa say such a thing to an eminent medical expert she'd only known for about six weeks? She'd have had no reason then to believe Henry was contemplating marriage.

Or would she? Mightn't it be the case that, even so early on, Henry had asked both parents for consent to pay his addresses (or however those Victorians put it) to their daughter? It was only afterwards that Mrs Henderson asked to speak to him in private and to lay the unpalatable truth before him. Even if that were the case he could still get out of it. *That would have been the point of telling him*. So I don't know and it may be that I'll never know.

Veronica Croft-Jones is the kind of woman of whom people say that she's wonderful for her age. She's tall and upright and her trimly cut hair is tinted a uniform pale blonde, fitting round her head like a golden velvet cloche hat. Her skin is like crumpled tissue paper and she wears very dark red lipstick which has 'bled' into the lines round her mouth. She's evidently proud of her legs, which are very good still, and she sits at angles to show them off, crossing her legs and letting her foot, in an absurdly high-heeled shoe, swing provocatively. Her voice is very upper class, plummy yet fluting.

None of those directives for mothers-in-law, specifically those about not interfering or criticizing, have reached her. She tells Georgie she hopes she's feeding David the food he likes and not neglecting him now she's got Galahad. Then she wants to know why the vegetables in this household are boiled and not steamed. What has become of the Chinese steamer she gave Georgie last Christmas? Galahad's name, and no wonder, has evidently never gone down well and when she pronounces it you can detect the quotation marks hanging in the air. He's too fat, something Veronica can't understand because breast-fed babies don't get overweight. Georgie must be supplementing his feeds with something.

To my surprise, Georgie takes all this very well, answering enquiries either with a 'I suppose you're right' or 'I shall have to do something about that'. David is an only child, born late and fourteen years after his parents' marriage, and plainly, as Veronica points out to me, as if I couldn't see it for myself, they 'adore' each other. From time to time they exchange conspiratorial smiles. And if David doesn't exactly side with his mother he doesn't stick up for Georgie either. Jude and I watch it all avidly, knowing what fun we'll have dissecting it later.

Veronica dampens my spirits somewhat by telling me that when we have our tête-à-tête she hopes I'm not expecting any family secrets because there aren't any. However, I can think of one and shall confront her with Patricia Agnew's letter when the time comes. We eat. Georgie's a good cook and the food is delicious. The meal is marred only by Veronica asking if her daughter-in-law has forgotten she's allergic to asparagus and never touches butter anyway. She drinks a great deal. Not just for a woman of her age, but for anyone. Lots of gin and tonic before the meal, wine all the way through, liqueur brandy afterwards and whisky and water just for passing the evening.

When she's settled with her drink I expect her to light a cigarette and wonder what Georgie's reaction will be, but she doesn't. She announces to anyone who may be interested that she gave up smoking three years ago, not for the sake of her lungs or her heart, but because she's read that cigarette smoke wrinkles the skin. Then she says to me, 'I never knew my grandfather, you know. He died *ages* before I was born.'

Eight years, I tell her. I know that.

'By all accounts he was a frightful bore. I can't think why you want to write his life.'

'I don't think he was boring,' I say. 'He was peculiar, an extraordinary man.'

'Oh, well, *chacun à son goût*,' she says, and then Georgie brings in the Holy Grail. I'm more favourably disposed to

Georgie than I've ever been, it must be sympathy with the underdog that has got to me, and I tell her how beautiful the baby is and how proud she must be of him.

'I hope you're not going to do that in public,' says Veronica, presumably referring to an imminent suckling session. But Georgie says meekly that she's done it already, it's the reason for her absenting herself, feeding Galahad is what she's been doing for the past half-hour.

Veronica says with a rudeness that takes my breath away, 'People don't always notice your absence, you know. You can't be the centre of attention all the time.'

We arrange to meet later on in her stay for the interview. Going home – we're walking because it's such a fine night – Jude says she doesn't envy anyone who's going to be alone with Veronica Croft-Jones, but I tell her one good thing is that after that neither of us will ever have to see her again.

17

I've been re-reading the letters Mary Craddock wrote to her sister Elizabeth Kirkford. Mary lived in the Fulham Vicarage while Elizabeth was far away in Yorkshire.

The first one is dated 1923, a few months after Mary married her vicar. She writes about life in Fulham, still a place with a good many rustic open spaces, about her work in the parish and how she helps at the school. Visits to their mother are mentioned and to 'the girls', as she always calls her sisters, Helena and Clara. Towards them she has the typical disparaging attitude of the early twentieth-century married woman to spinsters. Plainly, in her eyes, they are 'surplus women', of no use in the world, and she wonders what they find to do all day.

By the time she writes again she is pregnant or, as she puts it, 'expecting'. She feels very well, unlike Elizabeth herself who apparently suffered from morning sickness for months on end. And she makes much of this in her sharp way. Women make too much fuss about what is 'an absolutely natural event'. But she wishes she wasn't so far away from Mother and the girls. Presumably, the other side of London feels a long way away to her.

In April 1924 the baby is born. It is Patricia Agnew who, thirty-six years later, is to write the mystifying letter to Veronica. All the family have been to see the baby. Mary's mother Edith stayed in the house for the confinement and was 'a tower of strength'. In any case, she writes robustly, her labour was neither prolonged nor at all unbearable.

Clara is still with her 'to help out'. Mary thinks she and Helena will never marry. 'They have got some nonsense into their heads about, among other things, not handing themselves body and soul over to a man.' In any case, she goes on rather callously, it may be just as well to have come to a decision as all the suitable young men have been killed in the Great War. Clara reads their father's books. It must be 'showing off' as Mary is quite sure she can't understand them. Now, if you please, she's saying she'd like to be a doctor herself, a notion to which no one gives serious consideration.

Her next letter is mostly about their mother Edith, Lady Nanther, who, by 1925, was in her sixties. Mother, she writes, is wonderful, always so cheerful and practical. She, Mary, still thinks it was disgraceful of Alexander to sell Ainsworth House 'absolutely over Mother's head, with no compunction'. It's no joke to be obliged to move at her age but she took it so well. Of course in Mother's eyes Alexander can do no wrong. What does Elizabeth think of his marrying 'this American woman'? Mary believes they have been living together, which is very wrong and shocking, but at least she has money, plenty of it, and money is what Alexander is in dire need of. Mother says she's pleased he's found someone at last, 'though what she means by "at last" I don't know. He's not yet thirty.'

The sisters' father, dead for sixteen years, is only mentioned once more in this correspondence, and the reference comes as part of Mother-praise. 'Of course it's well known that only she could manage Father. He never listened to anyone else. I sometimes wonder what kind of a tyrant he would have become if he had been a less devoted husband and she not been there to teach him wisdom and tolerance.' She adds, 'Mother has taken up her brush again, is in fact having drawing lessons, and has produced a lovely study of little Patricia.'

From all this a picture emerges of Edith and adds a little to the build-up of Henry's character. According to his daughter, who would surely know, he was devoted to his wife, the woman he had come to prefer over her dead sister. There's nothing very surprising in that. I feel I'm getting to know my great-grandmother; a sensible woman, brisk and practical, with a personality strong enough to keep Henry under control. Not in awe of him, not under his thumb. A good and affectionate mother, without strong passions, unemotional, yet with a decided feeling for artistic expression. She was a photographer from the start of cameras becoming available. She took hundreds of photographs, particularly of her children and her nephews and nieces, the children of her brother Lionel. One of the remarkable things about them is that they're not sentimental. With a few exceptions, her subjects don't look 'soppy', but natural and *real*. And somehow she's managed to catch the cheerful niceness of Elizabeth, her mother's daughter, the grandeur and sharp malice of Mary, her father's child, and in Helena and Clara a kind of mutiny that was never to take positive form. The pictures of Alexander show simply a confident contented boy, his mother's favourite, a preference I'm sure she strove earnestly to conceal from the others. Who included, of course, George, the baby, the semi-invalid. All that shows in her photographs of him is stoicism and pain.

The portrait she made so long before of her sister I thought the only one of her drawings to survive. But I'm wondering now if the two pretty watercolours which hang in our dining room and which hung there when I inherited the house are her work. It never occurred to me before, I've hardly glanced at them. I go into the dining room and

233

look at a study of what may be the Yorkshire dales near Godby and another that's plainly Hampstead Heath. They don't seem to be signed, or so I think at first, and then I look more closely and see a tiny E.N. in the lower right-hand corner of each. What did Edith think of her husband falling in love with her sister at first sight and when that sister died turning to her? And taking her to the same honeymoon destination as he'd planned for her sister? Perhaps she didn't mind. She wanted a husband, she wanted children, and a wealthy successful eminent husband was on offer. I'm sure she came to love him. And he came to love her deeply, as we do when we depend on someone for comfort and peace of mind and security and a safe haven. She had given him too the two sons he wanted. We can be sure she never learned the story of the hit man and the set-up that led to Henry's first calling at Keppel Street.

When I ask Veronica Croft-Jones if she minds my recording our conversation she gives me a strange suspicious look as if I'd suggested bugging her phone. 'It seems so business-like,' she says. 'So official. You'll have to let me see what you intend to put down in this book of yours. I mean, the actual words.'

I promise to do this. She is wearing a white suit today made out of a sort of nubbly material and with a very short skirt. Her legs are crossed at the knee and she has an irritating habit of swinging the dangling foot. I start the recording device, test it and ask her about her parents. Who was James Bartlett Kirkford and where did Elizabeth Nanther meet him? She knows their history and doesn't mind talking about it. Have I ever heard of her great-aunt Dorothea Vincent? Trains come to mind and poor Eleanor's death and I tell her, yes, she was the one who lived in Manaton,

Samuel Henderson's sister. Well, she says, Kirkford was a friend of her daughter Laetitia's husband, though much younger than he. They met at Laetitia's house in Wimbledon. 'Daddy', as Veronica still calls him, was in the Customs and Excise but 'he had private means'.

I ask her about her brother Kenneth. Her foot starts swinging again. She can't remember Kenneth at all, she says, she was very young when he died.

'It was diphtheria,' she says. 'A lot of children died of it in those days. Poor Daddy couldn't fight in the war, you know, the Great War, but he longed to be at the front. He had a bad leg but people didn't know that and someone sent him a white feather. It was all quite ghastly.'

Veronica married in 1946 at the age of twenty-nine but her son David wasn't born till fourteen years later. I point out – daringly – that this is a coincidence as it is precisely the length of time that elapsed between Henry's parents' marriage and his birth. The foot swings slowly, the way an angry cat's tail does. 'One has nothing to do with the other,' she says. 'My husband and I were all in all to one another. We were perfectly indifferent as to whether children came along or not.'

I tell her I'd like to show her a letter and produce the one Patricia Agnew wrote to her soon after David was born. The foot stops swinging and is positively stamped on the floor, her knees drawn up close together. 'Where did you get this?'

'From David. It was among a lot of family letters.'

'I suppose you mean you got it from Georgina. That would be typical. One simply has no privacy left in the modern world. I gave those letters to my son purely for his family tree.'

I ask her if she'd mind answering one question about it.

She looks mutinous and her white papery face has gone quite red. 'Go ahead,' she says. 'If I don't like it I shan't answer.'

She reads the letter as if she's never seen it before. 'What did your cousin think might be wrong with David? Down's Syndrome?'

'Is that being mongoloid? They have such ridiculous names for everything nowadays. Yes, that's what she did suspect. Or I suppose so. She was a very silly hysterical woman, I must say, though she was my own cousin.' Veronica has completely forgotten this conversation is being recorded. 'I mean, how absurd can you get? David, who's simply the most intelligent man in London.'

I manoeuvre her back to her grandparents and she reminds me that Henry was dead long before she was born. Her grandmother Edith she was fond of, chiefly it seems because she allowed her to play the piano in the drawing room at Alma Villa while her grandmother Kirkford expected children to be seen and not heard. She remembers Edith painting, 'Not with an easel and a palette and all that, you know. With a paintbox.' She, Veronica, refused to sit for her grandmother and made a scene about it. Edith only laughed and said to leave the child alone but Veronica's mother was cross. Edith sometimes spoke about Henry, she remembers she always called him 'your dear grandpapa'. Her mother Elizabeth didn't recall him as a tyrant and she can't imagine what Mary means by suggesting he would have been but for Edith's intervention. Elizabeth said her father spent more time with his daughters than was usual with a Victorian paterfamilias and often told them stories. One was about a drop of blood travelling around the human body and the obstacles it encountered on its journey from the heart and back again.

This is the kind of story that makes me feel squeamish. Still, I ask for more details. But of course Veronica can't remember. Her mother tried to tell her this story but admitted failing to give it the vitality Henry had, she couldn't give the blood drop life and personality as he had, and she lacked the anatomical knowledge. All this interests me quite a lot because it sheds new light on Henry. I'd never have suspected him of wanting to be with his children.

When we're finished and I'm on my way home, something occurs to me. Veronica never once mentioned her elder sister Vanessa. Didn't they get on? I take another look at David's tree and see that though Vanessa's recorded as having married in 1945, a year before Veronica, her husband isn't named and no children are listed. I have three second cousins as well as David on the Nanther side, all more or less my contemporaries, Patricia's daughter Caroline as well as Lucy and Jennifer, the two daughters of Patricia's sister Diana. If Vanessa had children there would be more. How far down the line into the subject's descendants does a biography have to extend? All the way, I suppose, so I shall have to find out what these people do for a living and whom they've married, if they have. That latter detail will no doubt be in the next stage of David's tree.

By a coincidence that's explicable as just a coincidence I hear about one of those second cousins on my third day back in the House. We return on 11 October, a Monday, and on the Wednesday I encounter Lachlan Hamilton sitting by himself in the Peers' Guest Room with a pile of books and papers on the other chair at his table which happens to be the only available one in the place. He greets me with a lugubrious nod, picks up the pile of stuff and deposits it on the floor. The room is crowded as it always is these days, people propping up the bar, 'the last days of the Raj,' as Lachlan puts it.

'I don't know why they come in,' he says. 'It's pure masochism.'

'They hope for a last-minute miracle,' I say. 'Come to that, why do you come in?'

'I'm a masochist.'

'I don't think I am. I'm interested.'

Lachlan is silent. He smiles very slightly, an unusual event with him. I ask him why he's not drinking and when he shrugs I order whisky for him and a beer for me. The drinks are a long time coming and when she brings them Evelina looks harassed, but polite as always. Lachlan raises his glass a couple of inches and nods, the nearest he ever gets to a toast, and says he met a cousin of mine the other day. It was in Vermont. Somehow I've never imagined him going out of the United Kingdom and it seems even odder when he says he and his wife went to see the autumn colours.

'Who was this cousin?' I ask him.

'Chap called Corrie. Dr Corrie. A PhD and a medico.'

'I've never heard of him.'

'He's heard of you. Or rather, he knows he has a cousin who's a lord. It's because I'm one he happened to mention it to me. This pal of mine introduced us. It was at a party on what they call a campus, I daresay you know what that is, and my pal said, "This is Dr Corrie. John, this is Lord Hamilton," and this chap Corrie said, "I've a cousin who's a lord, maybe you've met him. He's called Nanther."'

I ask if he's American, this cousin, and Lachlan says he must be, he was born there, his mother was a GI bride. John Corrie looks to be on the right side of fifty. He doesn't know what kind of a cousin he is, second or third perhaps. It means nothing to me, as far as I know there's no one on the Nanther side he could be, so I suppose he's some connection of my mother's.

'He's a scientist,' says Lachlan. 'Something to do with gene therapy, whatever that is.'

We talk a bit more about the twilight of the gods and speculate about what all these bar-proppers will do when they've lost their seats in the House and have to go home and live on their estates. If they have estates. It worries me a bit that for some it will mean real financial hardship, me among them. Thoughts of dwindling resources cause me to walk to Charing Cross and take the tube home rather than a taxi. Jude's in the Alma Villa kitchen, drinking wine and cooking risotto from a recipe in the *Evening Standard*. Few women realize (and would be furious if they did realize) how sexy men find them wearing an apron and standing at the stove cooking. Knowing one ought not to feel like this, that it's anti-feminist and actually against one's principles, a nasty identification of 'real' women with domestic tasks, makes no difference. I put my arms round Jude from behind and kiss her neck and she nearly overturns the risotto pan. Of course all this has made John Corrie slip my mind and I don't remember him again until hours later, after some highly satisfactory lovemaking and while Jude is sleeping the sleep of the just. I creep downstairs and find David's family tree among the stuff on the dining-table desk.

I know John Corrie isn't there. I've come down here to see who he could possibly be, where he could fit in. I've half decided he must be a Rowland from my mother's side, there are dozens of them, most unknown to me. I unroll the tree and see he could be a son of Vanessa's. If Vanessa married a man called Corrie and had a son. The last chapter of my biography ought to deal with the lives of Henry's descendants and if this scientist, this John Corrie, is following in his great-grandfather's footsteps, he'd make an interesting footnote. After all, gene therapy is just a few logical steps on from what Henry himself was doing when he examined heredity and factors he believed were carried in the blood.

Do I need to meet John Corrie? Probably not. Certainly not if it means travelling to the United States expressly for that purpose. I can't afford it.

Henry lived for nine years into the new century and they seem to have been years of semi-retirement. All his life he'd been a strong healthy man. At least, no illness more serious than a cold is ever mentioned in the diaries, his letters or letters he received. The single cold that he seems to have had on the day he 'rescued' Samuel Henderson may only have been an excuse for leaving early, as may his 'feeling unwell' when he was supposed to dine with the Bathos.

Edith took a photograph of him with Alexander and Elizabeth in the garden at Ainsworth House and though it's not dated it's possible to guess the approximate date by assessing the ages of his son and daughter. Elizabeth is tall and handsome, dark with her father's strong features, a grown woman of eighteen or nineteen, while Alexander is about eight, a big healthy-looking boy in a sailor suit. Since she was born in 1885 and he ten years later, this makes the date of the photograph 1903. Henry has aged. He isn't yet seventy but he seems to have shrunk from his former superior height, his hair is thinning and his face pinched. He still holds his chair of pathological anatomy at University College Hospital but very likely seldom lectures. It is seven years since he published his third book, but there is evidence that he intended to publish again.

Two letters from Barnabus Couch refer to this book. In

one, dated May 1901, he asks how Henry is progressing. 'Knowing your prolificity as I do,' he writes, 'I have no doubt that if you are not yet nearing completion, an unlikely event in the light of the magnitude of your task, you have, if you will forgive the slang, "broken the back of it".' Couch must have received a denial, and perhaps in sharp terms, for in the following year he's writing, 'You may reprimand me again, old fellow, but I cannot resist enquiring as to the progress of the Great Work. Admirers among your readers – and this means *all* your readers – avidly await its publication and the revelations contained in its scholarly pages.' Couch certainly knew how to lay it on with a trowel but whether Henry liked flattery or merely bore it we'll never know.

His admirers waited in vain; the *magnum opus* was never published. Did Henry begin to write it but gave it up or was it never started? Was this because his health began to fail or from some other cause? There are no manuscripts in the trunks, complete or unfinished, and only one more letter from Couch. He suffered a stroke the following year and remained incapacitated until his death. It was the time in Henry's life that comes to all men who live long enough, when his friends and acquaintances are sick or dying, first Ernest Vickersley, an occasional dinner guest in Wimpole Street and Hamilton Terrace. Lewis Fetter and Sir Joseph Bazalgette had both died in 1891 and Huxley in 1895. His mother-in-law and his wife's aunt Dorothea Vincent lived on. They were both of them his contemporaries but Louisa Henderson was younger than he. His brother-in-law Lionel with his growing family flourished, but Caroline Hamilton Seaton, who had perhaps been his first love, was dead of uterine cancer at the age of sixty-two. A letter from her husband informs Henry of her illness and her death, referring to their 'long friendship', so apparently the two families sometimes saw each other or at least corresponded. But no other letters from Cameron Seaton survive.

From 1903 onwards Henry's diary entries grow briefer and more taciturn. Weeks go by without a single entry. Those events which are recorded are social engagements and various royal births, marriages and deaths. Henry never noted his children's birthdays in the diary, nor, come to that, his wife's. What he did write were more of those essays in the notebook. I've decided I'd better get around to reading them, in spite of having to use a magnifying glass, and that's what I'm doing now.

It's been a disappointment. They're rather dull, typical Victorian (though actually Edwardian by now) disquisitions on the vanity of human wishes, the paths of glory leading but to the grave, the decline of religious faith. The abstract virtues appear often and in capital letters, Courage, Honesty, Determination, Humility. I am reminded of the Dyce frescoes in the Robing Room, which also depict these sort of things, and wonder if Henry was inspired by them. There's nothing extraordinary about any of it. Or so I think until I'm about to close the notebook, feeling rather miffed. Tedious Henry. Then something strikes me as odd. You don't, surely, buy yourself a notebook to write essays and reflections in, write until you get to the foot of the last page and then just stop. But that is what Henry seems to have done. The last line in the book comes at the very foot of the last page. It's 'A humble heart tends to worldly success more surely than arrogance ever does.' And that's it, there it stops.

Now this may be the last line of the Humility essay and it may be that Henry was such a neat orderly-minded man that when he got to the end of his notebook he made an end to this essay and never wrote another. The 'humble heart' sentence may be a final rounding off, an exit line. On the other hand, it may not. It's hard to say. But doesn't it seem far more likely that Henry continued into a *second* notebook? That he either wrote more on humility or else began another essay? Why would he have finished when he seems to be in full spate of writing just because he came to the end of a notebook? And in that case, where is the next one?

When I decided to write Henry's life I emptied all the trunks he left behind him and Edith brought here with her. They weren't the only contents of the attics, there were boxes and crates and other trunks of things obviously not his, women's clothes, ornaments, discarded pictures, quantities of photographs. I went through these too but not very assiduously, there seemed no point. I've always meant to do so again, sort stuff out and give what's worth saving to a charity shop.

Now is the time. Not in the interests of tidiness and not hoarding but to try to find that second (and maybe a third?) notebook.

18

The attics have disappointed me. Searching this time, I took everything out of the remaining packing cases and boxes, the stacks of Edith's dresses, reeking of camphor, fur tippets, skirts, things I think may be called spencers, hats, their crowns stuffed with brown tissue paper. Do mothballs last a century, only shrinking a little? These have. Now I can't get the smell out of my nostrils.

I was distracted from my task by the photographs, as one always is, even if they are of people one doesn't know and has never heard of. Edith had labelled some or written names on their reverses: Quendons, a Dornford cousin, schoolfriends of her daughters, Kirkfords and Craddocks. The children's school books were there, or some of them, and books of drawings made not by Edith herself but by people of no obvious talent. Was I going to keep all this?

Of course I didn't find the missing notebook. If there was one. If Henry finished that essay. If he didn't just stop when he came to the foot of the last page and, tired, old and disillusioned, decided that enough was enough. That's what Jude believes. She's sure that a second notebook, if there had been one, would have been with the first, maybe the two of them tied together with string. The clothes interest her more. Not because she's dress-conscious in the way Georgie Croft-Jones is but because she says, when she's had a look, that Edith's are well-preserved and moth-free, probably quite valuable. Some museum might like them.

Or we could sell them, I suggest, my mind as usual these days intent on getting money from somewhere.

Another letter has come from Janet Forsythe with a photograph enclosed. It's of Len Dawson and Jimmy Ashworth Dawson, taken in middle age. She is seated, he standing behind her and slightly to the right. Her dress is black silk, stiff and shiny and uncomfortable-looking, but she is still handsome, her mass of hair still dark. Len hasn't a mole on his face or a birthmark. He's a squat rotund man with a head rather large for his body. Not hideous but no great catch either. A substitute, a compensation of a kind. Above all, a father for a child. She must sometimes have looked back to her Henry days and thought, or in words to that effect, that compared to her husband her old lover was Hyperion to a Satyr.

Question time starts a bit late today as two new peers have been introduced, one of them that Julian Brewer I met in Greece. I'm sitting in my usual place in the Chamber, half-listening to Lord McNally on the LibDem benches ask about football hooliganism while I read a letter I received yesterday. It's from Barry Dreadnought, the millionaire, and I've already answered it. In fact I've made an appointment with him for 5.30 this afternoon, by which time I calculate we'll have done with the House of Lords Bill for today.

He says he answered the letter I wrote him more than a year ago, but his reply in its envelope fell down behind a filing cabinet in his office. For which offence, he adds rather pompously, his assistant has been 'admonished'. What must I think of him in failing to reply to my perfectly reasonable request to visit his home, formerly the property of my great-grandfather? What I think of him is, vulgarly, that we've got a right one here. He's happy to get my phone call and will be delighted to show me round the house this afternoon. Fortunately, he'll be at home himself, 'pressure of business being slightly relaxed at this moment in time'. I put the letter back in my pocket and hear Lord Bassam, the Under-Secretary at the Home Office, say he's beginning to feel like a referee. Then he says his ten-year-old son reminds him every week of the stupidity of hooliganism, a statement which is met with muffled murmurs of approval from all sides.

Now we're on to the House of Lords Bill and the two motions which are before the House. The Duke of Montrose gets up and says in spite of the so-called simplicity of the bill of which 'the Government were so proud', it's not really simple at all. He looks every inch a duke, which is more than you can say for most of them, a tall handsome man with a fine figure (according to Jude) and whenever I see him I think of his ancestor who was loyal to Charles I, called him 'Great, good, and just' and died horribly for his pains. The present Duke, speaking mellifluously, is suggesting that this is a hybrid bill and therefore should be referred to examiners. The bewigged clerks at the table get out their Erskine May (the great authority on parliamentary procedure) and leaf through it. The Duke moves his motion and Lord Clifford of Chudleigh gets to his feet. Lord Clifford's ancestor was the first of Charles II's first ministers – Clifford, Arlington, Buckingham, Ashley, and Lauderdale – whose surnames' initial letters spelt the word CABAL. Lord Macaulay wrote of them that they 'soon made that appellation so infamous that it has never since their time been used except as a term of reproach'. Lord Clifford, very different from his forebear, says it's a pleasure to follow the noble Duke, the Duke of Montrose. We're excessively polite in here, something that causes mirth in the Commons. Among those who admit to knowing we exist, that is.

Lord Clifford defines a hybrid bill, which is a relief to most of us who still don't know what it means. He says that hybridity is concerned with making, in a public Bill, a distinction between the manner in which the Bill affects the private interests of one or more members of a class and the manner in which it affects the private interests of other persons in the same class. In other words, it applies different treatment to some peers from that which it applies to others. The woman next to me, a Baroness who's teetering on the edge of taking the Government whip, whispers that anyone can see with half an eye these motions are just further time-wasting moves designed to hold up the progress of House of Lords reform.

Sleep threatens and I go outside to wake myself up. If I can't make myself stay awake at forty-four, what am I going to be like at sixty-four? Will you still feed me, will you still need me, as the Beatles said, but of course they won't need me, I'll have been banished twenty years earlier. Like in three weeks' time. I return in time to hear the always witty Earl Ferrers being wittier than ever. Like Bennett's *The Card* he is here in the 'great cause of cheering us all up' and I hope that, at least over the interim, he'll still be here as one of the remnant while I'm gone. He's now involved in a much funnier explanation of hybridity than Lord Clifford's, with a long account of what might happen if he were invited to stay with the Attorney General in Wales and they both went to Paddington and bought first-class tickets for Cardiff. If the Attorney General went on to Cardiff while *he* was turfed off at Swindon it would be quite wrong, but that is exactly the same as what is happening to hereditary peers. All peers have a Writ of Summons, their equivalent of a

247

first-class ticket, and therefore none of them should be thrown off halfway through their journey. After Lord Onslow, another wit always worth listening to, has said he's supposed to be doing his duty to the nation and he's not a corner shop in Scunthorpe (a place he often mentions with unholy glee), and Lord Pearson has pointed out that the very word 'peer' means 'equal', we vote and the motion is rejected by an enormous majority.

It's nearly five, so I slip away and take the tube up to St John's Wood, noting of course that the Jubilee Line still isn't open to Westminster and I still have to change. By the time it's open I'll never need to go on it. The day is damp and grey, but still light. The clocks will go back in ten days' time. But the leaves are still on the plane trees of Hamilton Terrace, still a tired-looking dark green, flapping with a leathery slapping sound in the wind. In the front garden of Ainsworth House or Horizon View two big clear plastic bags cover the palm trees against the frost which has been threatened but never comes. The outer gate in the wall has already been unlocked for me. I go up the steps under the red-and-blue glass canopy and at the unsuitable door, more like the barred and studded entrance to a medieval fortress after the drawbridge has been crossed, I pause and ring the bell.

Luckily, Edith took a good many photographs of the exterior of her house as well as the interior. The door was painted panelled wood then with an etched glass pane in the centre of the upper half. And I'm sure her doorbell worked from an iron pull and rang rather than what this one does, twittering like a nest full of fledglings. Barry Dreadnought answers it himself and almost immediately. He's a fat man but muscular and tough-looking, his face the kind that would be all right on a woman; as things are, the little nose, fleshy mouth and short upper lip give him a sinister air. His hair, though receding from a massive forehead, is rather long, dark brown and curly. He's wearing jeans, belted in below his belly, and a bright-red polo shirt with a designer logo on the breast pocket. I realize that I, in my House of Lords uniform of dark grey suit, white shirt and discreet tie, must appear outrageously formal in his eyes. Maybe I'll be expected to dress like him after the Bill of Banishment has gone through. Maybe I'll want to.

He apologizes all over again for the mislaying of his letter, only this time it's not the filing cabinet it's fallen behind but the back of a drawer in his assistant's desk. This assistant doesn't seem to be in the house and nor does a wife, child or indeed anyone else at all. I am alone with Barry Dreadnought and if I wasn't six inches taller than he and probably about five years younger, I wouldn't much like it. His name isn't exactly a misnomer. I daresay he isn't afraid of anything much, but he instils fear into a companion. I couldn't claim to dread nought in his company. If I were a woman I'd think him not the kind of person I'd like to meet in an alley on a dark night.

And the house, now I'm inside it, isn't at all what I expected. It isn't what Jude would call a friendly house, though it's warm enough, far too warm for my taste. It was fairly new when bought by Henry, probably hadn't been built more than twenty years, and the eighteen sixties weren't good years for architecture. The rooms are large but still too small for the height of the ceilings. Dreadnought, or the interior designers he employed, have aimed at Victoriana seen through twenty-first century eyes rather than how it actually might have been, or that's how it looks to me. And, worse, it's almost a parody of eighteen sixties décor so that you feel those designers were laughing up their sleeves at him. Everything is too ornate, too bright and crude, even the ceiling mouldings picked out in pink and green and gilding. The drawing-room carpet is Stuart tartan, as if they'd had Balmoral in mind. There are wax fruit and stuffed tropical birds under glass domes, lengths of densely embroidered fabric hanging over cupboard doors, pelmets (I don't know what else to call them) suspended from mantelpieces, busts of Roman emperors and busts of soulful maidens, masses of Venetian glass and more occasional tables than most people have teacups.

'Pretty well in period,' says Dreadnought. 'Don't you agree?'

I nod non-committally. If I told him what I really think he'd throw me out. Then he calls me 'my Lord', which would silence me if the décor hadn't already done so.

'This way, my Lord,' he says, showing me to the kitchen, which I don't much want to see, it being as different from how Edith's cook's kitchen would have been as laminated plastic is from cast iron. Only it isn't laminated plastic. All the surfaces are highly polished pink granite. Burnished copper pans hang from the ceiling along with a couple of what look like hams. These *are* plastic, as Dreadnought explains after asking me to guess whether they're real or not. I haven't guessed. I've said I couldn't give an opinion from this distance, but he rejoins with a smirk that that's tantamount to saying they're real.

'No one ever guesses right,' he says triumphantly. 'The only way you could tell would be if you tried cutting them with a knife.' He smiles craftily. 'And I'd like to catch anyone doing that.'

Again I'm thankful for Edith's photographic talents. Every room in this house has been photographed. I'm half wishing I'd brought her pictures with me, though showing them to Dreadnought would have been almost cruel, they're so unlike what he's achieved.

'I'll lead the way, shall I, my Lord?' he says, and we go upstairs.

There is someone in the house, after all. It's the dark-skinned woman I saw at the window of Henry's study. She's cleaning one of the bedrooms, or at any rate she's dusting it, as there's no vacuum cleaner in sight. When she sees Dreadnought she stands still with her head bowed. He knows what she expects from him and she gets it.

'Run along now, scoot,' he says. 'Chop, chop.'

She does actually run. Dreadnought watches her departure with some satisfaction. We go into what Dreadnought calls the master bedroom. It's at the front. In fact, it covers all the front and is obviously the old principal bedroom and another knocked into one. Here all Henry's children were born. Whether Edith had difficult or easy labours isn't recorded, nor is the number she failed to carry to term or were born dead, if any. One thing is for sure, they weren't delivered in this vast fourposter, festooned in striped satin and pale pink lace. Dreadnought has an erotic picture of nymphs and satyrs on the inside of its tester but at least there are no mirrors on the ceiling. He is obviously awaiting admiration but all I can manage is to mutter, 'Very nice.'

Who slept where I've no way of knowing. There seem to have been ten bedrooms if you include the servants' rooms on the second floor, but one of the ten became Henry's study and under the Dreadnought administration (or before) four turned into bathrooms. One of these bathrooms has peacocks on its window blinds and a bunch of green plastic bananas suspended over the handbasin. The study, which is really what I've wanted to see, overlooks the garden full of elaborate topiary-work animals at the back and the street at the front, for it covers the entire right-hand end of the first floor. It's still a study – Barry Dreadnought's. He has filled it with computers, printers, screens, photocopiers and other technological marvels so that it's impossible to imagine it as it appears in Edith's photograph. Where now is all that mahogany and brown velvet, ormolu and chinoiserie, leather and gilt inlay, pen holders and inkwells, the turkey carpet, the bearskin rug, the books and the crystal skull? Gone with the wind. Disappeared into other people's homes, antique shops in Church Street and junk shops in Kensal Green, ground up in the mills of refuse disposal trucks.

Barry Dreadnought is describing to me – or I think he is – the vast quantities of software and CDs he possesses for doing almost everything possible 'on line'. I haven't heard of any of it but I nod and say it sounds very interesting, a comment my mother taught me to make when shown a work of art one can't in honesty admire. Do I want to go on up to the top floor? I shake my head and say, I hope politely, that I've seen all I came to see.

'You're welcome any time, my Lord,' he says. 'Just give me a bell. Now you'll want to go round on your own to take your photos.'

He's astounded when I say I haven't brought a camera and he gives me the kind of look you'd give Rip Van Winkle if you met him in the street. 'You know your own business best. But I'm going to insist you bring your partner over to dinner in the very near future. You have got a partner?'

'I've got a wife,' I say, rapidly imagining Jude's reaction to the idea of wasting an evening here.

Dreadnought repeats his offer and says his partner will contact my partner and fix a date. 'That's a promise, then.'

The place has knocked the stuffing out of me and feeling I've been lamentably feeble, I assert myself by insisting he stop calling me my Lord. 'My name's Martin.'

He's so delighted that he calls me by my christian name no fewer than five times in the ceremony of saying goodbye. I walk home up Abbey Road and when I let myself into Alma Villa find Jude has company. David and Georgie are there with the Holy Grail and all but he are drinking champagne. Apparently, to quote Georgie, whose comments on her mother-in-law David doesn't dispute, they're celebrating the departure of Veronica. She's finally gone home to Cheltenham. Jude looks enigmatic. She's been rather mysterious lately, as if she's harbouring some secret, though not an unpleasant one, and I've no idea what it can be as she's certainly not pregnant again. She made a great point of informing me when her period arrived. Anyway, she's back on the pill to give herself a six months' rest. So I'm pleased to see her drinking champagne and enjoying herself, the abstinence and diet regime abandoned for the time being.

Up till now she's avoided taking much notice of the Holy Grail and I know that's because it's sometimes painful for her even to look at him. But now, because he's whingeing and squeaking in his Moses basket and Georgie has lifted him out, Jude takes him on her knee and cuddles him and talks to him. He stops crying and smiles up into her face. He's really a very handsome baby, I must admit, with lots of dark shiny hair and dark-blue eyes. They make a beautiful picture, the two of them, a Madonna and child set-piece, for Jude is wearing a flowing blue silk garment, her hair, the same shade as his as if she were his mother and not Georgie, pulled up and knotted on the back of her head. I'm enraptured, I can't take my eyes off her, and I'm almost persuaded that a baby would be all right, would be bearable, if I could see such a sight as this at my fireside.

However, I pull myself together and regale them with an account of my visit *chez* Dreadnought. Jude says there's no way she's going to dinner at Ainsworth House, aka Horizon View, so she hopes I didn't make any promises. I tell David about John Corrie, the gene therapy cousin Lachlan met, and to my surprise he looks very cagey. Georgie doesn't, though. She's in an ebullient mood and she lets out a crow of laughter.

'I know who he is,' she says. 'He's the son of my esteemed ma-in-law's sister who stole her fiancé.'

The most intelligent man in London says, 'Oh, *Georgie*,' rather feebly.

'Oh, Georgie, nothing. You told me the story yourself. You never said I wasn't to talk about it.'

'There's such a thing as discretion,' says David.

Still, discretion isn't to be allowed to prevail and the story comes out, both of them contributing. Now I know why Veronica didn't speak of Vanessa and why, according to her dictates, the name is never to be mentioned. It's a family quarrel that's been going on for fifty-four years.

Veronica got engaged to an American serviceman called Steven Wentworth Corrie in 1944 when she was twenty-seven. Her sister Vanessa, five years older than she, and also in the WAAF, the Women's Auxiliary Air Force, was stationed far from where the Kirkfords lived in York. She came home on leave at the same time as Veronica, met Steven Corrie and the two of them fell in love. Instead of confessing to Veronica, Vanessa and Steven were married secretly in London and it wasn't until Corrie had returned to the United States at the end of the Second World War that the truth came out.

'My mother was very badly treated indeed,' says David.

Even Georgie concedes this but adds that it served her right. 'The amazing thing is not that he'd have been happy to have got shot of Veronica, anyone could understand that, but that he preferred a woman five years older. She was even older than him.'

'Has age to do with love?' asks Jude, but only I know she's quoting Nancy Mitford.

No one answers her. Georgie's usual attitude when anyone makes a remark or asks a question she doesn't understand is to ignore it. Still, I'm losing my dislike for her. I suppose it's because she's showing herself to be so human and so vulnerable. She must have suffered a lot of humiliation while Veronica spent that month with them. 'Anyway, it's time you forgave poor Vanessa,' she says to her husband. 'It's not your quarrel.'

'She's probably dead by now,' David says. 'She'd be all of eighty-seven.'

Georgie says airily that that's nothing these days and naming a restaurant in Blenheim Terrace, suggests we all go there for dinner. We can take Galahad because the restaurateur is 'child-friendly'. She belongs to the school of thought – as Sally and I did with Paul – that when a baby's small you can take him out with you in the evenings because he must perforce remain in his carrying cot, while once he starts walking you've had it for the next fifteen years.

I don't much want to go but I can see Jude does. On the way we all discuss family quarrels to David's discomfort; Veronica's marriage 'on the rebound' to his father and speculate as to how many children Vanessa would have had. I decide to write to the University of Vermont at Burlington for help in discovering the whereabouts of John Corrie.

*

We've had a water disaster: a pipe suddenly leaking into one of the upstairs ceilings and bringing part of it down. When I phone the plumber we always use I recall that in a debate on House of Lords reform Baroness Kennedy said she wouldn't employ a hereditary plumber and she suspected that a great many people up and down the country shared that view. The analogy is clear. Why give a man a job to do because his ancestor had that job, was in other words a hereditary peer? When it was my turn to speak I said that was exactly what I would do and did. My father – maybe not my grandfather, who knows what Alexander did? – employed my plumber's father and that's why I employ him. The same might well apply to the hereditary peerage. Muffled 'hear-hears' greet this and someone says that's why eldest sons sit on the steps of the throne: to learn the ropes before Dad drops off his perch.

The plumber comes. He's much more of a scientist than his father was and he says, incredibly, that the cause of the leak was 'spontaneous mutation' in the pipe. While he's working I sit at my dining-table desk and look once more at Edith's photographs of the rooms of Ainsworth House – the authentic Victorian interiors. The plumber calls me with his usual, 'Are you there?' and I have to go upstairs and answer a lot of questions I can't really answer about replacement of lead pipes with copper ones and where do the electricity cables run.

It's a quiet sort of day, as the weather forecasters say when it's not wet or windy, and I poodle through most of the morning, studying photographs, adding Steven Corrie's name to the tree and John Corrie's with a question mark after it, and in the late afternoon I go into the House. Apparently, it's St Crispin's Day, and Lachlan amazes me by declaiming Henry V's speech on the eve of Agincourt.

Not in the Chamber, I don't mean that, but in the Bishops' Bar, where everyone stops talking to listen to him until his voice grows hoarse with the smoke that pervades the place.

'I always do that,' he says when the applause dies away and we've brought our drinks to a table in the corner. 'I sort of feel I owe it to them. Harry the King, I mean, Bedford and Exeter, Salisbury and Gloucester. They'd all have been in here. They *were*. In my flowing cups they're freshly remembered.'

He has tears in his eyes. I remember he hopes to be elected among the peers chosen by *their* peers to remain in the interim House, so I ask if he's got his manifesto with him. He cheers up and produces a sheet of paper rather like a CV. A code of conduct was issued for the hereditary elections and this code states that 'each candidate may submit to the Clerk of the Parliaments up to seventy-five words in support of his candidacy'. Lachlan's tells me he's called Lachlan John Andrew Hamilton, he's sixty-one and he's the eighteenth Lord Hamilton of Luloch. He's only had one wife – a mark of distinction in these degenerate times – Kathleen Rose Hamilton née MacKay, and they've six children and fifteen grandchildren. I'd no idea Lachlan was so philoprogenitive. He sits gloomily sipping whisky while I read. The manifesto goes on to state he has two engineering degrees, four honorary degrees, is the patron or chairman or president of eleven organizations, has been something or other at the United Nations and his interests are Robert Burns, Celtic languages and golf. Seventy-four words. If I were a Tory I'd vote for him and I tell him so.

He takes the manifesto back without a word on the subject but says he hasn't forgotten my interest in 'that Dr Corrie chap'. He's asked his wife who's got a far better memory than he has. Kathleen Hamilton remembers John

Corrie perfectly and that he's the JGP Fellow at the University of Pennsylvania, an MD and a PhD. I make up my mind to write to him as soon as I get home.

But I'm not going home yet. Like Adam and Eve, doubtless, after the fall but before the expulsion, I'm going to make a little tour of my soon-to-be-lost domain. Because, once I'd made up my mind not to stand for election – on the grounds that whatever I may *feel* I know that no one should play a part in the government of his country because his father and his grandfather played that part – because of this I also decided I shan't haunt the place once I've no legitimate right here. Not for me a seat in the gallery or on the steps of the throne, wistfully waiting for some life peer or one of the precarious ninety-two to offer me a drink. If I come back it must be as someone's lunch or dinner guest and even those invitations I shall seldom accept.

The Committee Corridor isn't exactly a place steeped in history, so I don't bother with going upstairs. Instead, I hang my pass round my neck – necessary when entering 'the other place' – and stroll along the marble and between the statuary to the Central Lobby. The Commons are sitting and I think of going in, up into the Peers' Gallery, where we're always welcomed. But it's just gone seven and if they're going to divide the Commons usually do so at seven, and as I hesitate I hear the division bell and see the green bell-shape come up on the screens. So it's back to the Peers' Lobby where everything is slow and quiet now. Dinner guests are coming in and parties are gathering on the red-leather seats in the corners. There's no one in the Moses Room and its doors are unlocked. I walk in and stand looking at Herbert's huge paintings. Moses bringing the tablets of the law down the mountain and the 'Judgement of Daniel'. I've always liked these two, especially the animals in them, the gazelle and the lynx on a lead, wearing an embroidered coat like a little dog. Herbert was one of those painters who have a recurring woman in their pictures, a model or wife, I suppose, and his looks a lot like Jude, a slender creature with a beautiful classical face and shiny dark hair. She's always got a child or children with her as I expect young women did on Mount Sinai or in ancient Babylon.

I walk past the Earl Marshal's room that's now a retreat for women peers and the staircase where the public go up into the gallery, and make my way along the Not Content lobby and out on to the blue carpet of the Prince's Chamber. The blue carpet is sacred, or rather the room it covers is, because it's the ante-chamber of the Chamber itself. No one may smoke here and the public, passing through, may not linger or speak above a whisper, though peers themselves talk as much and as loudly as they please. On each side there's a fireplace where once, no doubt, coal fires burned. They're gas now. A high fender with a leather-padded top guards each fireplace and on a chair nearby on the temporal side (why not the Government side? I don't know) sits the Labour whip when a two- or three-line whip is on and peers must be prevented, if possible, from going home. High above, all round the walls are portraits of James IV of Scotland and his Tudor Queen, their son James V and Mary Queen of Scots.

Pugin and Barry arranged things so that, if all the doors were open, the Lord Chancellor on the Woolsack could look through and see straight ahead of him the Speaker of the House of Commons on the Speaker's Chair. I don't suppose anyone's ever put this to the test. Certainly it's true that when you come out of the Robing Room and walk down along the Royal Gallery you come face to face with a huge, grossly flattering statue of Queen Victoria, flanked by figures representing Justice and Mercy, which dominates the Prince's Chamber. The woman who employed Henry as her doctor didn't look much like this white marble nymph.

I enter the library where it's quiet, smoky, gorgeous with gilt and leather and dark glowing colours. Peers are asleep in armchairs, newsprint sheets over their faces, or sitting at tables poring over papers. Outside the windows it's a wet grey dusk, the river black and glittering, St Thomas's drowning in mist. The Millennium Wheel that we're supposed to call the London Eye is still lying on its side above the water level, awaiting its elevation to some monstrous height. If I sat down here between the river and the books I think I might follow Lachlan's example and the tears in my eyes begin to flow. I didn't know till now, this moment, how much I mind.

The tour wasn't, after all, a good idea. I wander down the corridor towards the Salisbury Room with no clear purpose in mind. No one's using either of the phones on the oval table, so I sit down, pick up the receiver and ask for international directory enquiries. It's more to distract me, lift me out of this sentimental journey, than for any pressing reason that I ask for the number of the University of Pennsylvania. The time on the eastern seaboard of the United States will be two-fifteen, a very suitable hour to call. I'll have to pay for the call, we only get free calls from here to places in the United Kingdom. I ask the voice that answers for a fax number. She wants to know which department but of course I don't know. Genetics? Biochemistry?

'John Corrie,' I say. 'Dr Corrie.'

'Professor Corrie,' she corrects me and I write down his fax number, firmly rejecting an e-mail address I've no idea how to use.

In the Salisbury Room, sentimentality forgotten, I sit in one of the hideously uncomfortable leather armchairs, glossy as mirrors and slippery as oil, and write on House of Lords headed paper:

Dear Professor Corrie,

I believe you are my second cousin, the son of my father's cousin, Vanessa Kirkford Corrie. What I know of you comes via my friend Lord Hamilton, whom you met recently in Vermont.

I am currently undertaking research for a biography of my great-grandfather and yours, Henry Alexander, 1st Lord Nanther. I understand you are working on a research project concerned with gene therapy and would be most interested to know more about this. It seems that you are the only descendant of Henry Nanther to follow to any extent in his footsteps. You must forgive me if you don't see your own work in this light. He was, for his time, an expert in diseases of the blood, as you possibly know, and a royal doctor with a particular brief to attend the haemophiliacs of the royal family.

I would be grateful if you could confirm that you are indeed my second cousin and also furnish me with some details about yourself, your personal and professional history.

Best wishes,
Martin Nanther

I write Jude's publishing company's fax number at the foot of the page. I'm a bit ashamed to say I don't know where the fax machines are in here. One of the doorkeepers soon tells me and the fax goes straight through without a hitch or even a single recall. Considering I want this information only for the last chapter of a biography I haven't even begun to write, and considering it makes little difference to the final work whether it's there or not, I've been very expeditious about this. Is it because I expect to discover something unlooked-for, surprising? I've no reason to. Maybe I'm excited to have found a new cousin. Odd if I am. The last one to turn up, David Croft-Jones, hasn't exactly illuminated my life. Then what is it?

I go downstairs and pick up my coat, reflecting that my name will be above this peg for only about ten more working days. Yet what else is there in this House to identify me and keep the memory of Nanthers green? A few speeches in Hansard no one will read. It's quite dark outside now and the pavements are wet and shining. The doorkeeper at the desk says, 'Goodnight, my Lord.' I'm going to have a cab home, I can't face the tube. The policeman at the pavement edge presses the switch that sets the orange lantern flashing at the gate, the signal to taxi drivers that there's a fare waiting. Richard Coeur de Lion sits astride his stone horse, eyeing the Victoria Tower or maybe the Holy City of Jerusalem. I always tell guests who are coming in for the first time to make for the entrance by the equestrian statue of Richard I. I shan't do that any more, that's over.

But in the cab that's taking me along the Mall and past Buckingham Palace I put all this maudlin harking back behind me once more, and ask myself what it is I think I'm going to get from John Corrie. Something, I decide, something I don't expect. There's no reason behind this, it's a gut feeling, my intuition, which Jude once told me during a quarrel that I don't possess. I want it to be world-shaking, I want it to be my breakthrough.

19

The Earl of Burford is the son and heir to the 14th Duke of St Albans, a direct descendant of Charles II by Nell Gwynn. He's a young man with fair hair and a beard. The story goes that when Nell had her baby she took him onto a bridge over a river, held him over the parapet and threatened to drop him unless the King promised to make him a duke.

During questions Burford's been sitting on the steps of the throne, as is his right, and just as business is about to begin he leaps up, jumps on to the Woolsack and shouts, 'This Bill, drafted in Brussels, is treason! What we are witnessing is the abolition of Britain. Before us lies the wasteland. No Queen! No culture! No sovereignty! No freedom! Stand up for your Queen and country and vote this Bill down!'

Lord Onslow, always to the rescue and often suppressing incorrect behaviour, does his best to pull the bearded fanatic off, but he's past sixty and Lord Burford is thirty-four. I can't help remembering how Onslow said at the start of the Bill that he'd behave like a football hooligan to ensure that 'whatever comes after me is much much better'. He's put that behind him now. It takes two doorkeepers to grab Burford but by then he's done what he came to do and quite gracefully allows himself to be escorted out by Black Rod. Of course the whole House, which is packed for the last day of the Bill, is convulsed and gasping. None of that will find its way into Hansard, which will no doubt record it as an 'interruption'. I hear later that a reception committee of the media was awaiting Lord Burford, who is destined for a couple of days of the fame he's never had before.

This is our last formal opportunity to debate the measure. All that will remain will be for the Bill to return with Commons amendments but no one thinks there'll be a serious attempt to defeat the Bill again. Lady Jay is certainly treating the House as if this is farewell time, saying to hereditaries that the hour has come to say 'thank you and goodbye'.

Barry Dreadnought has wasted no time. The woman he lives with phoned Jude this evening and gave her so many dates to choose from that she couldn't get out of it and picked next Saturday.

'Get it over,' she says on the phone to me at the House.

'I thought you were so set against it,' I say.

I've never included Jude in that category of people who pass their lives teetering between 'highs' and 'lows' but she seems to be on a high at present, laughing at nothing, uttering joyful gasps and singing in the shower. Now, when she says she's changed her mind, she wants to go, it will be 'good for a laugh' she giggles and adds that she doesn't really care, she's feeling so good this simply doesn't affect her. 'Shall I call Roma back and tell her we can't?'

'Roma?'

'That's her name. I know, it's like the capital of Italy or a perfume or something – so what?'

I'm not sure I can cope with all this ebullience. I tell her that now she's accepted we'll go and I ring off, feeling like a mean-minded curmudgeon. Of course I've forgotten to ask her if she got a fax at work from John Corrie, but it's a bit early to expect one yet. I go back into the Chamber where throughout the afternoon we've had a number of amendments on the composition of the interim House. It's past five-thirty now.

This is deliberate time-wasting, to hold up the Bill as long as can be. A Labour life peer, Lord Peston, angers the opposition by comparing what's going on to a debating society 'beloved by sixth formers'. He believes the House should become an elected assembly and says he won't stand for election and, rather than 'clinging to the furniture', is quite willing to go when the need arises. Most hereditaries aren't in the least willing to go, including among them Lord Ferrers, who looks every inch the general and commanding officer he never was. If Wellington looked like that it's no wonder we won the Battle of Waterloo. His amendment proposes that life peers should be elected by their fellow life peers, a democratic process that would make everyone legitimate, and he calls for a division.

'I just want to see all the noble Lords on the Benches opposite,' he says, 'traipse through the Division Lobby in order not to be elected.'

So we traipse – a wonderful old word my grandfather Alexander used to use – through the Not Content lobby, lifers and hereditaries alike, and disagree to the amendment, having wasted another three hours. Instead of going back into the Chamber I leave the House, resolving to come back later and vote on the passing of the Bill. On the tube home – I deny myself the luxury of a cab this time – I take my thoughts as well as myself away from the Upper House and transfer them to John Corrie. If the reply I get from him is at all interesting why shouldn't I go to Philadelphia and talk to him face-to-face? After all, I'm going to have to set out Henry's theories on diseases of the blood as best I can. It won't be possible to write his life without an exposition of his discoveries in the field of haemophilia, for instance. Do

I, at this stage, even know precisely how haemophilia is inherited? To put it in layman's terms, how the gene pattern works? John Corrie will know. Even if these diseases aren't his speciality, as they probably aren't, he's an MD and he's got a PhD in something to do with genes. He could surely explain this stuff to me much better than a book. Probably I can get a bargain flight, a package to New York which will include two nights, say, in a hotel. And from there I can do as I once did as a student and take the train, the Metroliner, down to the City of Brotherly Love.

I make it home in record time. Jude says that if I'm going back to the House at nine-thirty she'll come with me, take her seat below the bar and watch me expel myself. She's still very much on her high and it's taken away her appetite as it always does when it rules her. Her face is flushed and her eyes bright. While I eat she tells me she's phoned Roma and told her we'd love to come on Saturday night. There won't be anyone else to dinner, just the four of us. I don't know whether to be glad about this on the grounds that friends of Dreadnought are bound to be appalling, or sorry because there won't be any leavening of conversation (sure to be about money, the Internet and shopping) at the dinner table. Jude wants to stay on the subject, she's as keen to go to Ainsworth House now as she was dismayed when I passed on the invitation, she thinks it will be 'an eye-opener' but I slip in my question when she draws breath and ask if a fax has come for me from America. It hasn't. It's early days, isn't it, she says, and I shouldn't expect anything till the end of the week.

I ask if she'd mind my going alone to New York and, knowing my generous-hearted wife as I do, I'm anticipating an unqualified, 'Of course you must go, darling.' What I get is rather more grudging, not to say mystifying.

'You mean to see this Corrie? *If* he ever answers, I suppose. When the time comes you may not want to go.'

'Why do you say that?'

'I just think you may not,' she says and she goes off to call us a cab, having flatly refused to get into the tube 'at this hour'.

Jude is the best-looking peer's wife in the House. I *would* say that, I daresay, but others have told me so, an ancient Tory hereditary volunteering the opinion that if there was a peeresses' beauty contest she'd win. I've never dared tell Jude that. She'd be infuriated at the violation of her feminist principles. I part from her in the Peers' Lobby and when I'm in my usual place I see she's stationed herself no more than a couple of yards away from me. A lot of old men turn their heads and crane their ancient necks to look at her in her blue dress and pearls.

The House is packed. So were the bars and dining rooms, but everyone's in here now. The new Lord Brewer sits rather self-consciously on the Opposition benches, hoping someone will tell him what to do. There are a number of amendments, all finally withdrawn, and then it's time for compliments and regretful speeches. Lord Longford, who's nearly ninety-four and has been in the House for fifty-four years, says there's something about the culture of this place that people respond to, intellectual, moral and religious. He will vote in favour of the Bill because he shares my feeling that there must be reform, he won't try to interfere with its passage. Lord Longford has a noble head still and the voice of an aristocrat but even he isn't the oldest peer here. The reform measures recommended in the coming Wakeham report will probably advocate a maximum age for remaining in here and it's more likely to be seventy-five than ninety-five. As more changes to the Bill are proposed only to collapse, I sense in the atmosphere a nearing of the end, the tide of power's withdrawing roar. These are not the last days of the Bill but its last hours. After six hundred years those who up until 1958 *were* the Upper House are about to be expelled by those who came forty years ago. Within an hour or so the Bill will pass to the Commons and return here only to consider a group of Commons amendments, all probably unacceptable to the diehards. For all intents and purposes, in all reality, the deed is done.

Courtesies are being exchanged now as well as gratitude and admiration expressed to Lord Weatherill whose amend-ment it was to retain the 92. Lord Ferrers gets up.

'At the end of all that,' he says, 'we must have a House which works and, for goodness' sake, a House which is happy and content. Happy the Houses which smile at each other. Far too often there has been a tendency for vitriol to creep in.'

Of course, a good deal of the vitriol has come from him. He advises against voting against the Bill 'in any great measure' but for all that, when it comes to the final division, he doesn't vote at all. Lady Jay has got up and begged to move that this Bill do now pass. I leave for the Content lobby, a departure for me, as my usual course is to vote Not Content, and in turning to the left and walking in the direction of the throne I fail to pass Jude below the bar, as I have always done in the past. Omens mean nothing to me, so why do I so much dislike this turning of my back on her, this walking away from her to take my place and vote for my own banishment?

The vote was won by 221 to 81. It's all over. On the Opposition front bench Lady Miller of Hendon is in tears and Lord Kingsland holds his head back in a rictus of agony. Labour life peers aren't cheering, just waving their order papers in triumph. I'm surprised there haven't been more disturbances and more hooliganism during the passage of the Bill. Nothing much happened really and it passed faster than I expected. We've been dispossessed not with a bang but with a whimper, with tears and despair.

I say nothing about this feeling on the way home. I'd be ashamed, anyway, to voice these irrational fears. This is a bad sleep night for me and in the small hours I sit up and read. Nothing wakes Jude but even so I put the bedlamp on as dimly as I can and still see the print. But after a little while I put the book on the floor and look at her. Closed eyes can be as beautiful as eyes when they're open, the lids as fragile as moths' wings, the lashes lying in a dark delicate fringe on white pearly skin. Her lips are folded but not quite closed. I lay one finger an inch from them and feel the warm breath on my skin. In the dark once again, I can no longer see her, only the outline of her head and the darker mass of her hair. A surge of love for my wife doesn't excite me at all but makes me want to hold her very tightly in my arms, only I know it can never be tightly enough. I turn over, trying to sleep, and eventually do.

The dream I have shows her to me as she was when she sat with Galahad in her arms. The child with her this time isn't he but much older, maybe two or three years old, and he's our child. No one speaks. The atmosphere isn't pleasant, we've been quarrelling, we've said things that can't be forgiven, yet I don't know what those things were. The little boy looks at me with large reproachful eyes. Then Jude gets up and, taking him by the hand, goes to the front door and down the steps and out into the street. It's summer and warm, the trees are in leaf and flowers are out. I stand there, holding the front door open and watching them walk

269

down the street until they turn the corner and disappear. I know I have to follow but I've no shoes on and I can't find the key or any money, and when I run down the steps barefoot I can't get out of the front gate, it's locked. The door slams behind me and I wake up.

It's seven in the morning and Jude isn't there. The dream still lingers with me and I'm absurdly frightened. I call her name and she comes at once out of the bathroom in a white towelling dressing gown. 'I can tell you now,' she says.

There's only one thing it can be. A voice inside me is saying, O God, O God, O God . . .

'I'm two months pregnant.'

I say stupid things, knowing as I say them they can't be true. You had a period in September, you're on the pill.

'No, I'm not. I deceived you. It was bad enough me waiting to see, I couldn't have you waiting too.'

I *feel* deceived, I feel I've been made a fool of and I don't like it. Sally and I deceived each other all the time or tried to. No, I haven't been spending money, I didn't go to such-and-such with so-and-so, I wasn't there, I wasn't here, I didn't hear the phone, I phoned but you didn't answer, I never lie to you, you know that. For Jude and me things are different. Or so I thought. I thought we were open and honest with one another always.

'Have you done a test?' I say dully.

'Three weeks ago.'

More deception, or am I making a ridiculous fuss? She hasn't been unfaithful or lost a thousand pounds gambling or had liposuction. One thing, I'm only making the fuss inside and with myself. 'You've seen the doctor?' For some reason I can't remember her obstetrician's name.

'When I'd done the test. I asked him if I ought to stay in bed for the whole pregnancy, I said I would if it would help but he says not.' She looks at me almost fearfully. 'You're cross, aren't you?'

I ought to say I'm not and I love her. I love the prospect of our son or daughter. But I can't. Memories of the dream keep intruding and how mysterious she's been lately and how excitable and 'high'. 'You should have told me a month ago.' I say it like a sulky child.

'Can't you understand I didn't want to disappoint you again?'

Could there be a less appropriate word? At the moment I mind more about the deception than the pregnancy but I know that will change and I'll be back watching her and worrying and counting the days and the weeks. What was the longest time measured in days she carried a child? Ninety days, a hundred? And when and if the hundred's past this time shall I be happy or dismayed?

It's Saturday night and we're at Ainsworth House, having pre-dinner drinks. The pre-dinner period has been going on since half-past seven when we arrived and it's now nearly nine-thirty. Roma has only left for the kitchen within the past ten minutes 'to do something about food'. The Dreadnoughts are the kind of people for whom the eating part of inviting guests for dinner is the least important. Every kind of alcoholic drink I've ever heard of is on offer from the bar in the drawing room, disguised on my previous visit as sideboard or cabinet in reproduction early Victorian mahogany. We are shown all over the house again, drinks in hand. I'm aware of something unusual to me in a private house. Background music is playing and it follows us as we move from room to room. It's the kind of music that gets played in hotel lounges, always the same tunes, 'La Vie en Rose', 'Never on Sunday', 'Un Homme et une Femme'.

The conversation is on the subjects I feared it would be but I'd no conception of how much shopping people can do and how much they casually spend. Barry's record is £30,000 in one evening at Harrods but Roma has come very close with a credit card bill for only £2,000 less after an afternoon's wandering down Bond Street. Like Imelda Marcos, her passion is for shoes and she buys them at Jimmy Choo and Manolo Blahnik.

As we were walking here I warned Jude not to tell Barry and Roma about the baby. 'Would I?' she says.

There are all sorts of things I could say, such as, 'You did last time' or 'You told Georgie last time,' but I don't because last time isn't to be mentioned. She's even said that we're to behave as if last time didn't happen and nor did the time before that or the time before that. We have to forget 'old unhappy far-off things' and act as if this is the first time she's conceived.

I've apologized profoundly for ungracious behaviour, for making a fuss about not being told. I've been forgiven. And she hasn't said a word to these two. No doubt she's sensed that she's dealing with a very different pair from David and Georgie. Barry and Roma have no children either separately or together. Children are what other people have, though they don't understand why. Roma is a painfully thin blonde with a strained stretched face and long bony legs, famous name shoes on her long bony feet. Her jewellery is breath-taking, huge diamonds encrusting rings, earrings, a necklace and a bracelet. They flash under the matching chandelier and make small spots of light dance up and down the walls.

Jude is drinking sparkling water. She's worried about that champagne we had the other day with the Croft-Joneses and the wine she drank at the restaurant afterwards. Will the baby be harmed? Why was she so criminally foolhardy

272

as to drink when even then she *knew* she was pregnant? I remind her (I've told her before) about all the whisky my mother drank when she was pregnant with me and all the cigarettes she smoked, and about Sally's fondness for beer and the occasional joint, but she's not reassured. She just thinks my mother and my first wife were criminally fool-hardy too, but their excuse is that they knew no better. Anyway, she's indulging copiously in fizzy water now which may account for her glum expression, though Dread-nought's conversation about buying a car on the Internet is as likely to be responsible.

At last, at a quarter to ten Roma comes back and says, '*Madame est servie*,' in a phony French accent. The food is quite good because it's obviously all been bought from Harrods food hall – part of the £30,000 expenditure? – and heated up in the microwave. Somehow I feel that this is more successful than Roma's cooking would be. I drink too much, not because I've a tendency to alcoholism or Barry's wine is specially nice, but because I'm bored. Drinking doesn't alleviate boredom but it gives you something else to think about, such as how not to fall off your chair and how to keep your speech from slurring. On the way home, which doesn't happen, which we're quite unable to make happen, before half-past midnight, Jude tells me, but very gently and kindly, that I'm drunk.

'Good,' I say, 'then perhaps they won't invite us again.'

'Do you think it's bad for me to stay up so late now?'

I tell her I don't see how it can be bad if it doesn't happen often. I apologize again for being drunk, for being cross on Wednesday, for lacking the enthusiasm I ought to feel about the baby. She says she knows it's just 'my way', a statement I don't understand but am too fuddled to analyse. On our doorstep she opens her bag to get the key and pulls out a piece of paper she meant to give me last night but forgot all about. It's the fax from John Corrie.

I'm too far gone to read it and I fall into bed, already half-asleep or, at any rate, half-conscious. At four I'm awake again with banging head, pounding heart and dry mouth. After I've drunk several pints of water from the kitchen tap I take an alka seltzer and four aspirins, so it's not till late Sunday morning that I'm fit to look at the fax.

He begins, *Hi, Cousin!* Which puts me off from the start. This is because, says Jude, I'm a stuffy old peer and a snob. I don't deny it but think to myself that if Corrie had had a PhD in the arts he'd have begun, '*Hi, Coz*' and that would have been worse.

Hi, Cousin!

I definitely am your cousin, first, second or third, I'm not sure which but I expect you will. My mother was Vanessa Kirkford but I didn't know much about ancestors, family etc. till your fax came. All I knew was that my cousin was a lord in the UK.

Mom never talked about her family except to mention there was an aristocratic branch. I knew great-grandpa Henry was an MD and something to do with the royals, but not that he worked on diseases of the blood. As to following in his footsteps, it is pure coincidence that I am involved in a similar line of study. I am the JGP Fellow here at Penn and the focus of my research is targeting Factor VIII gene therapy to the epidermis. Sort of meaningless, I guess, to the layman but pretty exciting pioneering work to us here.

I am fifty-one years old and have been married to my wife Melanie (a psychologist) for over twenty years. We have no children but she has two, Craig and Lisbet, by her

274

first marriage. Our home is in Media, Pa. Do you ever come to the US of A? It would be good to meet with you.

Cordially,

John

I find all this deeply unsatisfying. John Corrie – older than Lachlan thought – must mean that he too is researching blood disease but not because Henry did. It seems too big a coincidence to be credible. I pour myself another glass of water – that's the fifth I've drunk since I got up – and Jude comes in. She gives me a reassuring kiss on the cheek and a pat on the shoulder. Being a complete louse, I feel a hot and bitter surge of resentment. I want to go to the States, I want to talk to this new cousin, stay in his house in Media, wherever that may be, get the answers I need. But I can't because Jude's going to have a baby. I can't leave her even for two nights. And actually, she's *not* going to have a baby, she's going to have a miscarriage. *She always does*.

Even thinking this is outrageous. I ought to want to stay with my pregnant wife. Any other man would. I'm an unnatural monster. I hug Jude and kiss her and tell her a whole string of lies about how happy I am for her and how it's going to be fine this time. She seems to believe me, I suppose she wants to. She's going to make coffee and then take me out for a hangover-curative walk. I go into the study and look up this Factor VIII in the medical dictionary. It takes me a long time because I don't know where to start looking, but eventually I find it and discover that it's a clotting factor, one of many allied substances numbered I to XII, missing from the blood of haemophiliacs.

So John Corrie's not only researching blood disease but the *same* blood disease as his great-grandfather Henry. And he expects me to believe it's coincidence?

20

The first hereditary peers' elections take place today and tomorrow. These are for those ready to serve as Deputy Speakers and other office holders, and everyone in the House who has taken the Oath, life peers and hereditaries alike, may vote. There's a polling station set up which is mystifying to some ancient hereditaries. Some of them have never cast a vote in their lives. Their fathers died and they inherited their titles before they were twenty-one, the then age of majority, therefore being banned from returning a member to the House of Commons. So now a polling station is as alien to them as this House would be to their tenants and they've no idea what to do with a ballot paper. When I consider that these timid tyros won't just have to put a cross in a slot but choose fifteen from the candidates and number them in order of preference, I wonder not how many ballot papers will be spoilt but how many will get through at all.

Ballot papers, we're told, will be invalidated if any number is used more than once, any number is missed out or the paper is illegible or ambiguous. The idea of ambiguity intrigues me and, going into the polling room with Lachlan, I speculate as to whether some will put down three ones or others number all thirty-three candidates.

Results will be available on Friday in the Printed Paper Office and the library but I shan't bother to come in for them. Monday will be good enough for me. Or even next

Wednesday when hereditaries start to vote for hereditaries, those seventy-five who are also to stay. I suddenly remember Henry's robe.

'D'you think I could sell my robe?' I ask Lachlan.

'Dunno,' he says. 'I've got one. It's two hundred years old, falling to bits. Nobody'd buy it.'

There's only some point in having an ancient robe if it's been in your family all its life. A lot of kudos comes from wearing a tatty old garment. When the Queen comes to open Parliament I've seen young peers walk proudly into the Chamber in a moth-eaten antique, the white fur looking as if it's been chewed by a pack of hounds.

'They'll all be the same in future,' Lachlan says in his mournful tone. He's referring to the number of ermine rows according to rank. 'All those old robes'll be rubbished because no one's the right to wear 'em. Just a bunch of Life Barons in double rows of rabbit it'll be.'

'You'll be elected,' I tell him, though I'm not at all sure about this. 'You'll be coming to the State Opening for years yet.'

He shakes his head. It's weeks since I saw him smile. 'Dressing up'll be the next thing to go. A tenner that by two thousand and two no one'll wear robes any more.'

I take him on, though I think he's right. Peers who haven't got their own robes borrow them if they can or hire from Ede & Ravenscroft in Chancery Lane. Hiring costs over £100 and I'd never have been able to afford it if I hadn't got Henry's. If I sell mine I might get enough to pay for my flight to the United States. Then I remember I can't go because I can't leave Jude. That's what she meant when she said the other day that I wouldn't *want* to go. She was wrong there because I do want to. But I won't. I'll stay here and spend the robe money on buying her something nice and school myself into wanting this baby, this foetus that's still securely in the womb.

And virtue is rewarded. I feel quite proud of myself for being good and never once protesting aloud. My recompense is that another fax has come from John Corrie. Contrite over the time she kept the last one before remembering to give it to me, Jude phones from work about this one. It's just arrived and it says he's coming over here to a conference on gene therapy. Some other research fellow has dropped out and he's taking his place. The conference is in London, so maybe we can meet?

My usual course would have been to invite a guest in here for lunch or dinner. I'm not sure if I can do that now. I certainly won't be able to after Prorogation, the end of the present session, which is happening next Thursday. By the State Opening on 17 November I'll have been banished. Suddenly, ridiculously, I feel embarrassed about having to tell John Corrie that. He won't understand. I barely understand myself. I try to explain to taxi drivers, some of whom believe that *all* peers are to be got rid of and replaced with a wholly elected assembly. It's extraordinary what a large proportion of the general public seems never to have heard of life peers and believes everyone in the Upper House is male, old, rich, a landowner, of ancient lineage and set to pass on his title and estates to his eldest son. John Corrie, of course, may have heard of lords but never of a House of Lords. If I get to give him dinner it will probably be somewhere in the neighbourhood of this conference.

The Clerk of the Parliaments announces the election results this afternoon, the successful seventy-five who are to stay along with the fifteen Deputy Speakers elected last week. Earl Ferrers is in, polling 190 votes, the most of anyone, and so are the Earl of Onslow, Earl Russell and Lady Darcy de Knayth. Lachlan Hamilton's manifesto must have had its charms or else voters were persuaded by his hard work and constant attendance, for he's returned with a respectable 110. I congratulate him and he says he wishes I'd stood because I'd have got more votes than he.

I've done a deal with Julian Brewer over the sale of my robe. He's beaten me down to £50, pointing out like someone dropping in to the Oxfam shop that there's a moth hole in one shoulder and one of the rows of ermine looks as if some rodent's been nibbling it. Brewer pays me in cash and I walk home via Bond Street where I buy Jude another kind of robe, a dark-blue satin dressing gown, that defeats my purpose entirely as it costs me five times what Brewer gave me for mine.

When I get home Lorraine's still there, vacuuming the living room. She's tidied up the study, in spite of being asked not to touch any of the papers on the dining table. I untidy them again and when the droning of the vacuum cleaner stops I dial the phone number John Corrie has given me. It's two-thirty here, so nine-thirty in the morning in Philadelphia. After three rings I get his answering machine. I leave a message to call me, which he does at ten in the evening. I've given Jude the dressing gown and had three hours of the pleasure of seeing her in it, curled up on the sofa.

It's 'Hi, Cousin' again, which I'm churlish to mind. He has the Ivy League voice, the US equivalent of our public school and Oxbridge. In my mind's eye I can see him, tallish, thin, with a boy's face still, very short hair, no eyebrows, glasses, a buttoned-down collar, an Armani jacket and blue jeans. He's probably not like that at all. The conference starts on Monday 15 November and he's arriving the day before, the Sunday. When I ask him where it is he says, 'It's in London, Chelmsford.'

I tell him I'll come to Chelmsford, to the Conference Centre that's not in the town but outside in a place called Writtle, and as I do I reflect that while I'm in the train the State Opening of Parliament will be going on and for the first time in fifteen years (for I usually went when my father was alive) I won't be there.

Jude's had a bleed. Very slight and now apparently over. But they took her into hospital and kept her overnight. Not for one moment – and I congratulate myself on this – was I glad, not once did I hope that this pregnancy would go the way of the last and the one before that and the one before that. If nothing else could have put me firmly on her side, her fear did, her panic and grief, as she held me and hung on screaming, like a child in a war zone. Then, waiting for the ambulance I'd called, she grew utterly calm, willing herself, she told me afterwards, to keep the baby, telling herself that if she wanted this hard enough it would work and all would be well.

Since then a scan's been done with satisfactory results and she's been given something that's supposed to help prevent miscarriages, and told to rest and carry on taking the tablets. Only she won't, because she's afraid of the thalidomide effect. When she was in her teens her parents had a neighbour who'd taken thalidomide and whose daughter was born without hands. While she tells me this, something she's never told me before, she's shaking and shivering and her teeth are chattering. In the middle of all this Paul comes.

'You're always asking me,' he says, 'so I've taken you up on your offer and come for the weekend.'

I'm sure the offer didn't stipulate a day's or even an hour's notice. This means I can't complain. Jude is lying on the sofa, looking beautiful in the blue satin dressing gown, and he sits next to her and, rather oddly, holds her hand. He doesn't ask what's wrong but seems to assume it's the flu. I get lunch for us all and hunt through the permafrost depths of the freezer for something for dinner, as Jude can't go out and for once, it appears, Paul is staying in. He wants to talk about the end of the hereditary peers and how did I feel about being in there on my last day. I give him a copy of Hansard but have to tell him I wasn't there but here, at home, looking after Jude.

Having moved, it seems, into the hereditaries' camp, he asks me how I could bear to stay away on those grounds. 'Just because your wife had flu?'

I expect Jude thinks she's standing up for me, I know she does, but I wish she'd kept quiet. 'I didn't have flu, I had a threatened miscarriage.'

He says nothing but flushes a deep dark red.

'Paul,' says Jude, 'we want to have a child. I don't think my life will be worth living if I can't, it's as desperate as that. Can't you try to understand?'

He's been holding her hand again but he lets it go and something in his face tells me he'll never want to hold it again, never want to kiss her again. He turns to me. 'I really came here because there's something you've got that I want. Great-great-grandad's robe. Now you've been demoted I thought I could have it. You won't need it again.'

Jude catches my eye, though her face doesn't change. 'What do you want it for?'

'I just want it.' Like a child who asks for something to eat he's never asked for before and won't say why.

'I've sold it,' I say. 'I sold it to a life peer. It was rather shabby.'

He's furious. His face goes even redder. 'And what you've done is rather shabby. It wasn't even yours to sell, it belongs to the family. One day it would have belonged to my son and his son.'

This is the first mention I've ever heard of *his* dream children. It's useless to defend myself or the sale, particularly as I'm now feeling I shouldn't have done it, I should have told him first. Jude, who never intervenes in our scraps, now does so and tells him she thought he was a Marxist who despised what she calls 'the trappings of the aristocracy'.

Strife usually raises his mood to a point of cheerfulness but not this time. He looks the way he did when he was five and told he couldn't have another slice of chocolate cake. He announces that he's going over to see his pals in Ladbroke Grove and may be back tonight or may not. I wonder aloud to Jude if the time will ever come when my son and I will be able to be together like civilized beings, talk to each other, maybe smile at each other's jokes, and not walk out in a rage halfway through a discussion.

'When he's thirty,' she says. 'You'll have another son by then. Or a daughter. Let's hope you'll have better luck next time. After all, your marriage isn't going to come to grief like your first one did.'

Of course I take her hand and kiss her, I kneel down by the side of the sofa and hug her, but I haven't liked her talking about our marriage ending, even though she said it was impossible. I suppose I'm superstitious, though I always deny that I am. And all sorts of fears and resentments come creeping in as I kneel there. Does she *blame* me for Sally's leaving me and leaving Paul? Does she really think having another child at my age, against my will, a child I can't afford and don't want, will heal the breach between Paul and me? Or am I supposed to write Paul off as a failure? The child she has will be the one I really always wanted. Is she that obtuse?

21

I'm sitting in the train going to Chelmsford. It's not, of course, a first-class carriage but one of the new ones (not very new now to judge by the state of the upholstery) in which the seats face the backs of the seats in front, as in an aircraft. If one were fat it would be very uncomfortable. As it is, the seat back ahead seems unpleasantly close to one's face and liable to smash one's nose if the train had to stop suddenly. The view from the window is dreary in the extreme, Essex conurbations, grey fields and trunk roads.

If I were in the Heathrow Express I could watch the State Opening on television. As it is, I'm obliged to see it in imagination and memory. I run it before my eyes. The Queen wearing her crown and regalia will enter the crowded Royal Gallery at 11.27 precisely. If she's late it's said they stop Big Ben and start it again so that she *does* walk through at the right time, but she's never late. She always wears white satin and pearls and a white fur robe. The Duke of Edinburgh is with her and other royals, the Leader of the House in her robes and the Captain of the Gentlemen-at-Arms in uniform and a procession of other dignitaries. The Queen may never enter the House of Commons, so after she's taken her seat on the throne she says, 'My Lords, pray be seated,' whereupon the Lord Great Chamberlain raises his white wand as a signal to Black Rod who then goes to knock on the door of the Commons Chamber, a door that's been slammed in his face, and summons members to 'attend her Majesty immediately in the House of Peers'. The Commons pour out, led by the Prime Minister and the Cabinet, and some of them talk and laugh and make a lot of noise as they pound across the Peers' Lobby and into the Chamber below the bar. The whole assembly of peers in red and white Parliament robes and peeresses in long gowns and tiaras are seated there, gazing at the Queen as she begins to deliver her speech.

Except in memory or on television I shall never see it again. Henry went every year for eight years, from 1897 to 1904, but wearing his new robe that was made for him only for four years in that time. Years passed when Queen Victoria never opened Parliament and when she was absent and a commission of lords presided, no robes were worn. But after the Queen's death Edward VII opened every Parliament until *his* death nine years later. The new King loved colourful ceremony and there was gorgeous pageantry at his first State Opening, peers being told to arrive fully robed and in their finest carriages. For his part, he made a dramatic entrance through the East Door, resplendent in red velvet state robes and cape of white ermine, carrying a white plumed helmet. He made his speech from the throne, a custom his mother had given up forty years before.

Did Edith also attend State Openings? If she did, was there a tiara handed down among her jewellery? I must check. It's all in the possession of my sister Sarah and some other Nanther female descendant. Veronica? Certainly not Vanessa, the renegade runaway. The most likely thing is that Edith sold it during the twenty-three years of her widowhood. This reminds me of the robe, cause of such dissension between me and Paul that he never returned from Ladbroke Grove and is now, presumably, back in Bristol academia. If Jude has a daughter will she, one day, want the tiara? The train is pulling into Chelmsford. It's spitting with rain and rather cold. I find a taxi with a driver willing to take me to the Manor House Conference Centre.

It's a huge Victorian Gothic place, angry red brick, its grounds thickly planted with big conifers. Wellingtonias and Scotch pines stand black and ragged against a sky of unvaried pale grey. Inside the house it's warm in the way no private person except Barry Dreadnought and his kind can afford to maintain the heating. A blanket of warmth meets and enfolds me as I enter and am shown to a deep sofa in the lounge where I sit and wait for John Corrie. I've brought him two presents: one of the copies of Henry's *Diseases of the Blood*, and a folder for keeping two photographs in. It's bound in red leather and stamped in gold with the House of Lords portcullis crest and I bought it in the shop near the Home Room on my last day. Jude took the attitude that I couldn't give someone an empty photograph case and when I ridiculed that, pointing out that he wouldn't want pictures of her and me, she suggested one of Edith's photographs of Henry. Edith took hundreds, most of which were in one of the trunks, so I carefully cut one to size and slipped it inside the partition.

John Corrie's not the least like I imagined him. He's tall but dark, he's got a short dark beard and he looks a lot younger than he is. He doesn't wear glasses but maybe has lenses, for his eyes are a strange unnatural green, a colour never seen in the unenhanced iris. When he smiles he shows the usual magnificent American teeth. I hand over the presents, which he calls gifts, and he reacts with transatlantic grace, enthusing over the photograph case and wanting to know who 'the old guy' is. Henry's book brings just as much gratitude, but when he opens it and looks inside, reads a phrase or two and glances at a chart, I detect the twenty-first century scientist's superiority tempered with indulgence this nineteenth-century bumbling about in the dark is bound to arouse.

He takes me into the conference centre bar, a Stakis Hotel kind of place now filling up with biochemists or whatever they are. A television screen, hanging up in one corner, is showing the State Opening, focusing on the Leader of the House carrying the Cap of Maintenance, a kind of hat that symbolizes the hold one of the early Edwards had on Normandy and Aquitaine and now our retention of the Channel Islands. The ceremony is coming to an end, the Queen has spoken, the Chamber is emptying and the camera moves. A film star who's also a peeress swans down a crimson corridor in long gown and pearl tiara. They are all going off to have lunch in the Cholmondeley Room.

No one but me in this bar is looking at the screen, they're all drinking and talking genetics. I'd have bet anyone willing to take me on that John would drink sparkling water or Coke but I'm wrong and while I have red wine he has a gin and tonic. He knows very little about the family history we share and seems never to have shown any interest until this moment. Would I draw him a plan? I tell him I can do better than that as I've furnished myself with a photocopy of David Croft-Jones's genealogical table. He's delighted and pores over it while helping himself to nuts and crisps.

'I suppose you know the story,' I say, 'of how your mother stole her sister's fiancé and ran away to marry him in secret?'

He doesn't and for a moment he looks disconcerted as if not knowing whether to take this with a smile or intense seriousness. Then he raises his eyebrows, silently asking for more. I tell him what I know. He's never heard any of it before. 'Mom's been dead nearly twenty years,' he says.

'She and Dad died within a few months of each other in 1980. They were so devoted, one of them couldn't go on living without the other.'

'He was engaged to your aunt Veronica first.' Remembering her, I grin to myself. 'I think he made a wise choice.'

This makes him laugh. 'And here's this great-grandfather you're writing about. I'm really happy to have his book. Did he write any more?'

'Quite a few. He was one of the leading authorities of the day. Hadn't you heard of him?'

'I remember Mom saying her grandpa was a doctor and attended the royal family, that's about all.'

'Nothing about blood diseases?'

He shakes his head. He's found himself and me on the tree. 'May I add my wife and my brother and his wife and their kids?' In a very small neat hand he writes after his own name, 'm. 1977 Melanie Strozzi,' in the blank space beside his name, 'Rupert Steven, b.1946, m. 1977 Lauren May Bowyer' and under their names, 'Clay, b.1978 and Wilson, b.1984'.

He himself is a childless man. I don't seem to come across many. 'What exactly is this research you do?'

His grin is the scientist's smile, the not quite patronizing smile of one learned in an abstruseness he knows his audience haven't a clue about. 'How much do you know about haemophilia?'

I think I know a lot, but daren't say so to him. 'The basics, I suppose.'

'The focus of my research is targeting Factor Eight gene therapy in haemophilia A. I'll explain. You know what the epidermis is, the outermost compartment of the skin? Right. The epidermis is a good target because it's highly accessible and able to secrete gene products into the bloodstream. I've carried out experiments with mice – I'm trying to clarify this for you – and results suggest that the epidermis can synthesize functional Factor Eight which can then enter the systemic circulation.'

'Yes,' I say.

'There are problems. The transgenic mouse model has limitations. But my results demonstrate that a localized area of skin alone can serve as a source of Factor Eight and support the feasibility of cutaneous gene therapy. Now I'm looking ahead to the best ways of delivering Factor Eight to the epidermis. Shall we go and grab ourselves some lunch?'

The screen's still showing the State Opening. The one o'clock news has started and it's the principal item. I go into the dining room with a picture of red robes and flashing diamonds still printed on my retinas. A buffet lunch is laid out. I help myself to chicken and various other cold meats and salad. John has curry and rice and chicken and spinach, all on the same plate. For a moment it looks as if he's going to lead me to take my place at a table where twenty delegates to this conference are already sitting, but he's only stopped to exchange pleasantries with a woman in a red trouser suit and an older man who looks important. It's a bit like the long table in the House where I'll never sit again.

John and I are lucky. Most people seem to want to sit with their fellows and gossip or maybe swap theories, so we have no difficulty in finding places in the embrasure of a bay window with a view of the grounds. I'm not very hungry and wonder how I'll get through what's on my plate but John attacks his food with enthusiasm. Ever since he told me he knew no more about Henry than that he was a doctor in attendance on the royal family, a question's been hovering in the back of my mind. I postponed asking it while he was describing the nature of his research and now, just as I'm planning how to phrase it, he begins telling me how haemophilia is inherited, something I already know.

'Look, I'll write this down for you,' he says. 'Or better still, we'll pick up a brochure from the US National Hemophilia Foundation on the way out. That'll give an explanation for the layman.' Suddenly he shows an unexpected sensitivity. 'I'm really sorry, I guess all this talk of blood and sperm and whatever could put you off your food.'

'It's not that.' I make myself take a mouthful of chicken and mayonnaise-covered roquette. 'It's – well, if it wasn't being Henry Nanther's great-grandson, what was it drew you to researching haemophilia? I mean, he was the great haemophilia expert of his day. You're researching his subject yet you didn't know it was his subject?'

I'm noticing something else about him. He has about as completely an open and honest face as I've ever seen on anyone. He's transparent. Now he stops eating and laughs. The answer I get stuns me. Possibilities leap out and dance up and down like floaters when you turn away from a bright light.

'I'm a haemophiliac,' he says.

'It's very different than it once was. I haven't a severe form. The risk is internal bleeding that can lead to arthropathy – that's joint damage – and that's prevented by infusions of Factor Eight or Factor Nine. When I was a kid I had to be hospitalized for infusions, but in 1965 there was a medical breakthrough. Dr Judith Graham Pool discovered cryoprecipitate.'

I'm staring at him, not I hope open-mouthed.

'That's the factor-rich component of the blood. It meant

less fluid had to be transfused into the patient and by the early seventies you could get it in freeze-dried form which made it possible to infuse at home. I never had any joint damage. You could say these discoveries came just in time for me. There are a lot more clotting factor products and there's prophylactic treatment.'

'And your gene therapy.'

'And my gene therapy, as you say. I use a product for mild to moderate haemophilia A called desmopressin acetate, DDAVP. There's genetic testing too. But in my case if I'd had kids there'd not have been much point. *Any* daughter of a haemophiliac is a carrier, so mine would inevitably have been one. I chose not to reproduce but luckily I married a woman who already had two kids by her first marriage.'

'But how did it come to you?' I wish I knew the language better. I'm sure I'm using all the wrong terms and I start with a mistake I ought to know better than to make. 'Who did you inherit it from? Was your father a haemophiliac?'

'Wouldn't have affected me if he was. You'll have to study the brochure. All the daughters of a haemophiliac are carriers because they have his X chromosome but his sons won't have the condition. They have his Y chromosome.'

'Then your mother was the conductor?' I've inadvertently used the word Henry and his contemporaries did and I correct myself. 'Carrier, I mean?'

'She must have been. Of course it was the result of mutation.'

I've read a book about haemophilia in the royal family in which the author dismissed the possibility of a mutated gene in Queen Victoria's genetic make-up. 'But surely that's very rare?'

He smiles that same smile. 'Haemophilia itself is pretty rare. That said, mutation is common. About thirty per cent of haemophiliacs have the disease because of a mutation in the mother's gene.'

'And that was true of your mother?'

'Sure it was. She was asked about that when I was a baby. But she didn't know of any family history of haemophilia. It was a mutation. Let me give you an example, in a study done of five hundred and forty-three persons with haemophilia A – that's my kind – two hundred and ninety-six unique mutations were discovered.'

I'm looking at his additions to David's tree. 'And your brother?'

'Rupe's not a haemophiliac. He was lucky. Mom had two X chromosomes as a female, remember. He must have gotten the one that's not carrying the mutated gene.'

By this time I'm reeling from genetics. I've eaten nothing, which John puts down to my squeamishness. I don't know what I put it down to. We go and help ourselves to pudding – 'dessert' I ought to call it. I think I can manage crème caramel. He has that and cheesecake and chocolate mousse and a banana as well. This time I manage to eat what's on my plate. The subject has been changed to family history and I tell him about Henry's life, his medical training, his friendships, the Tay Bridge disaster, his attendance on Prince Leopold and his women. He seems to have no idea of historical specifics and finds the Jimmy Ashworth episode shocking by his present-day standards. The foisting of Jimmy on to Len Dawson is unforgivable. He wants to know why Laura Kimball doesn't have DNA testing to establish that she and I are related and can't understand when I tell him it's better for her not to suspect, to retain her belief in Jimmy's chastity.

'Isn't the truth always best?' he says.

Is it? I abandon truth for the time being, it's too big

a concept for the way I feel today. 'Henry was fascinated by blood,' I say. 'It was what his life was about. Blood. Isn't it a big coincidence that you, his great-grandson, have haemophilia and also devote your life to working on blood?'

'Genes, not blood,' he corrects me. We go back into the lounge where coffee comes. 'Maybe it's a coincidence that he was an expert on haemophilia – if expertise was possible at that period – and I'm a haemophiliac. Coincidences do happen. On the other hand, look at all the family he has who aren't haemophiliacs or carriers.' It's obvious from his expression that he thinks people like me, non-scientists, authors, biographers, meaning the imaginative, the woolly-minded, are always on the watch for the sensational. If it's not there they'll manufacture it. If it's insignificant they'll enlarge it.

He's smiling at me, handing across the table a dish of chocolate mints. Suddenly I think of Jude, maybe because she hates after-dinner mints, she says they taste like tooth-paste. And I have one of those premonitions others have but I seldom do, I know they mean nothing except maybe that the omened thing won't happen. This one tells me Jude needs me, she's tried to get hold of me but she can't. It's getting on for three.

'Are you OK?' John says. 'You've turned pale. It's all this talk.'

'No. No, I'm fine. But it's time I went.'

He says he'll have them call me a taxi and he'll pick up that brochure for me on his way. As I finish my coffee, I try to think about what he's said but I can only think of Jude. She's at work. I haven't got a mobile with me, I always forget to carry it, or perhaps purposely don't carry it because you're supposed to keep them switched off while you're inside the Palace of Westminster. I won't be there again. Hooray, I'm free to carry a mobile!

I could phone from the call boxes, inside one of which John Corrie is summoning a taxi for me. He comes back, says the cab will be ten minutes. I try to phone Jude, I get through to the company but the next step is her voicemail and all I get from that is that she's not at her desk at present. Unable to restrain my frustration, I tell John how much I hate modern technology, am a Luddite (I'm not really), despise e-mail, don't possess a fax, have never succeeded in penetrating the Internet further than viewing a page of a newspaper I've never previously heard of, and avoided like the plague the House of Lords Parliamentary Video and Data Network. John, of course, loves it all, sometimes receives twenty e-mails in a day, has already sent two to his wife this morning by means of a tiny computer he carries that's a phone and fax as well.

The cab driver comes in, looking for me. I can't dislike John Corrie, no one could, but we've nothing in common. I doubt if we'll ever see each other again. But he congratulates me on finding him and I congratulate him on finding me and if we don't exactly swear eternal friendship – we're stuck with the cousinship – we faithfully promise each to come and stay with the other when I go to Philadelphia and he comes to London. Any help he can give me on blood disease he'll be only too happy to provide and he's thrilled to have 'great-grandpa's opus'.

The train's ten minutes late. But when it comes there aren't so many people in it as there were this morning and the seats are the old-fashioned kind, pairs facing each other with a table between. I lay the brochure on the table and open it. It's a brightly coloured glossy booklet, the size of a newspaper's weekend supplement, with illustrations of happy people, all young, handsome and smiling, who've presumably come to terms with their haemophilia through the marvels of modern medicine. I find the bit I already knew about X and Y chromosomes and read on into the complications of the different types of the disease. But concentration isn't coming easily because all the time the coincidence of Henry, the great Victorian expert (whatever John says) on the condition and his great-grandson being a haemophiliac keeps bugging me. The coincidence of Henry's granddaughter having a mutated gene that resulted in her son being haemophiliac bothers me too. Such an occurrence of events, given that in John's own words the disease is rare, is something I can't accept. And if he can accept it this is only because he's not one of us imaginative, sensation-seeking authors but a scientist who's not really interested in the peculiarities of human beings' interior lives.

Once the train pulls in to Liverpool Street, having made up the ten minutes it's lost and loudly trumpeting this victory on the public address system, my worries about Jude come back. By now it's half-past four. I go into a phone booth, try her number and get her voicemail again. Then I try Alma Villa. First the answering machine, then Lorraine breaking in and telling me Jude's been taken ill and gone to hospital. She doesn't know what's wrong but I do. Oh, I do.

Nowhere like ninety days this time. Her obstetrician's told her it was too soon to try again. She should have given it six months. They keep her in hospital overnight but she's not really ill, there's been no pain – no physical pain, that is – only blood and a tiny foetus too small to see its sex, not much more than a bag of jelly. That's her description, not the obstetrician's. It makes me feel nauseous. I've drunk a lot of whisky and coffee since I got off that train but I haven't eaten anything. There's been too much talk of blood these past two days and I wonder how doctors can bear it, how they get on while they're becoming used to it. I even dreamed about blood last night, sleeping alone in our bed. I was in a transfusion centre, lying on a trestle and the man lying on the next one was Henry. It didn't surprise me seeing him there, I knew him, we were friends, and he was also what he truly was, my ancestor. A nurse came by and said how young he looked to be my great-grandfather and he said, the way some women do, that he'd not been much more than a child when he married.

They started taking the blood from my arm and his. Mine was ordinary but his was a much darker richer red. The nurse held the glass bottle it was flowing into up to the light and a doctor looked at it and said you could see that it carried a gene of aristocracy. A son of this man would be noble and sit in a gathering of lords, as would his grandson and his great-grandson and all his descendants for ever. But when Henry's bottle was full his blood wouldn't stop coming out. It overflowed, it splashed on to the floor, it began draining his body dry. He sat up, he got up and shouted at them to stop it, to staunch the flow, didn't they know he had haemophilia? Did they want him to bleed to death? I woke up then, half-expecting to find myself in a bloody bed, as I'd been before, but I was alone in clean white sheets.

I fetched Jude home. There's no point in her staying in bed. She's not ill. It's just, as she says in a voice of simulated practicality, brisk and philosophical, that she's a perfectly healthy woman who's four times conceived a child and four times lost it in a flood of blood. It's ridiculous to make a fuss, the same thing's happened to other women and they've had healthy babies in the end. She's only thirty-seven, there's heaps of time. I find this determined cheerfulness harder to take than her grief. It's a stance which is bravely assumed in advance of her first counselling session. This is to take place at the end of the week. I want to know what a counsellor can possibly say to her that I can't or that she doesn't know already. Or is she just doing the politically correct thing?

'I'd like to know what an outsider thinks,' she says, 'someone who doesn't know me or you.'

I suppose it can't do any harm. But I keep thinking of how she deceived me over the conception of this recent, lost child. That feeling went into abeyance while she was pregnant and was happy and confident but now it's returned and I think of how she could do it again. I'd like to ask her to promise me not to try for a baby for the six months the obstetrician advises, but we've never asked each other for promises and this is no time to begin. Something else has happened which worries me more than anything else.

There have been articles in the papers about whether a husband or partner should be present at the birth of his child or not. For a good many years now it's been received wisdom that he should be. I was with Sally when Paul was born. It was taken for granted by both of us that I would be, I don't remember any discussion about it, she'd go into the maternity hospital when her labour started and I'd either go with her or she'd contact me at work – I was in publishing then – and I'd come straightaway. Now the gynaecologist who's written these newspaper pieces says it's a bad idea for various reasons. One is that men get distressed by the woman's pain, another that men make inappropriate conversation and the third, the one that's enraging the feminist lobby, that seeing the process of birth diminishes the woman's sexual attractiveness. Her man will never feel quite the same about her again.

I can't say I was affected like that. But by the time Paul was born Sally and I were already becoming alienated, we both realized we'd made a bad mistake. Her sexual appeal for me had practically gone by then. But it's not far off the experience of the birth-attending man which is troubling me now. I feel a shift in Jude's attraction for me, only 'attraction' is the wrong word. I'd rather say my total, utterly compelling, absolutely exclusive, almost obsessive, passion for her. That's what it was and putting it in the past tense like that gives me physical pain. I've never seen her give birth, worse luck, but I've seen too much these past months, years, too much blood and mess, heard too much talk of hazardous wombs and dilated cervixes and menstrual anomalies, and the accumulation of it has done something to the curious mechanism of attraction. Appalling of me, isn't it? Callous and insensitive, the worst kind of male attitude. I know all that and it makes no difference. There is no one to whom I could say this, no intimate friend. I couldn't say a word of it to Jude, my dear love whose only offence is that she wants to be a mother, in line, it seems to her, with every other woman in the world.

I couldn't say to anyone what this has revealed to me, that I know now why men want virgins, the untouched, the pure. In order to make them impure, sullied, bloody? Perhaps. I know why Orthodox Jews submit their women to purification rituals after childbirth. But I don't want to learn these unpalatable things. I want my passion for my wife back, not this tender, pitying, brotherly love.

22

While I don't believe in the coincidence, I can't find anything to put in its place. Perhaps it doesn't matter. I'm thinking of my last chapter – so very far off being written – and saying something like:

Only one of Henry Nanther's descendants followed in his footsteps and became a doctor of medicine. John Wentworth Corrie, son of his granddaughter Vanessa Kirkford and her American husband Stephen Wentworth Corrie, is at the time of writing the JGP Fellow and a research geneticist at the University of Pennsylvania. By coincidence he is himself a haemophiliac, the result of a mutation in his mother's gene, and gene therapy to haemophilia A is his particular study.

I don't like it much. Also it reminds me that I don't know if it's true about John Corrie being the only descendant to have a career in medicine. I must check. For instance, what does John's brother Rupert do? I should have asked but I was too stunned by the coincidence to think of it. Then there are Caroline, Lucy and Jennifer, granddaughters of Henry's second daughter Mary and as much my second cousins as John and David, but I know very little about them. All I know is that they're on David's tree. They may all have husbands or partners, they may have children, and one of them may be a doctor of medicine, a nurse, a radiographer, the chairman of a health authority or a paramedic. Jude's willing enough to ask the Croft-Joneses to supper (which means dinner eaten in the kitchen) and doesn't mind their bringing the Holy Grail. This time she was more discreet and didn't say a word about her pregnancy to Georgie, so there'll be no hard-to-take commiseration.

I've had another idea that doesn't seem to have occurred to John. Or if it did he didn't mention it. Why was the mutation assumed to have taken place in Vanessa's gene? Why not in that of her mother Elizabeth Kirkford, née Nanther? John would say I know very little about haemophilia but I'm learning and it seems to me from studying the brochure that a male's condition may owe as much to an alteration in the grandmother's genetic make-up as in the mother's. If this were so *both Vanessa and Veronica may have been carriers.* Of course, the coincidence then would be even greater, for it would mean that one of Henry's daughters had a gene mutation which made her a carrier of the very disease, the rare disease, which was the subject of his life's work.

Galahad has become an engaging baby. He's a constant smiler. It's as if he's discovered what a charming habit smiling is and how it calls forth approval, indeed from his parents ecstasy, so that he can't do it often enough. He laughs too, a bubbling quite musical sound inspired by anything bright or shiny brought within his orbit. At nearly six months he's sitting up and, according to Georgie, about to begin crawling. He seems not to have inherited his father's rather sullen temperament nor his mother's volatility but is a sunny soul, happy and placid. Veronica, gone this past month but far from forgotten, has told Georgie that placidity and 'good' behaviour in a baby bode ill for its intelligence. Bright people are diabolically naughty in infancy, as David was.

'Can you imagine anything more cruel?' says Georgie.

We can't. We shake our heads, though we're not surprised. Even David, who at last seems, according to Jude, to have taken to heart the biblical injunction to leave his mother and cleave unto his wife, says Veronica can be very cruel. He's quite sure he didn't behave badly when young, that's another invention of hers.

'I'm longing for you to get pregnant,' Georgie says to Jude as if Jude wasn't. 'Mind you, when you do I'll be so excited I'll go and have another one just to keep you company.'

David pulls a long face. 'Don't I get consulted?'

'Of course you do, darling. More than consulted.' She laughs and so does Galahad. 'You'll be a participant like you were last time. Don't you remember?'

Galahad laughs so loudly that Georgie, like those people who say their pets understand every word they say, is convinced her son has a precocious knowledge of reproduction. We move on to a slight, if not total, change of subject. David has brought the latest genealogical table with him but it seems to me largely unchanged from last time. I add the Corries and ask him about the three women of whom I know no more than the names but he knows only that Lucy is married – he was invited to her wedding – and believes Jennifer isn't. Of Caroline he knows nothing but says he'll look her up at the Family Records Centre and I decide I may as well let him do that for me.

'My mother doesn't know. I asked her. It sounds as if she fell out with Patricia and maybe Diana too.'

An even more contentious woman than I thought. I tell him I ought to talk to Veronica again. Immediate alarm. 'I really don't think we could have her, Martin. Not at the moment, certainly. Not for a while.' He lowers his voice, though Jude and Georgie are in the kitchen and only just visible on the other side of the serving hatch. His sibilant whispering makes Galahad laugh. 'You may have noticed that she and Georgie don't get on. My mother has an unfortunate turn of phrase sometimes. And Georgie can be rather emotional.'

'I was thinking of going to Cheltenham to see her.'

His face clears. 'Oh, well, why not? Good idea. She's very hospitable, you know. Go to tea and she'll be baking for days before you get there.' He wants to know what I'm going to ask her. It's plain he's not interested in anything but avoiding Veronica's presence in his house. He may even be planning visits to Cheltenham on his own or putting her up in a hotel next time she wants to come to London. 'I'll give you her phone number. And her address. You may prefer to write first. She'd like that, I think, a preliminary letter. And by the way, though I'm sure you wouldn't, don't mention Vanessa, will you?'

I let him remain in his state of certainty that I won't, though of course I must, that's one of the reasons I'm going, and I tell him I already have her address. I've had a letter from her. When I get there she may refuse to discuss her sister but that's a chance I have to take. She may not even know Vanessa is dead. She may not care. I'm having all sorts of wild ideas about these sisters and their cousins and my great-aunt Elizabeth Kirkford, but I suppress them. I don't want to waste thinking time on speculations that may all come to nothing once Veronica has talked to me. If she talks.

As far as my research goes I'm coming to the end of Henry's life. There are gaps, of course, big ones that somehow or other have to be filled, but the course or stream of his life has only half a dozen years to run. He spoke again in the House of Lords, once in a debate on the motor car, which he called a 'flash in the pan', and once on the folly of proposing to give the vote to women. There was nothing new in this speech, made in 1904. Henry dilated for nearly fifteen minutes on the delicacy of women's health compared to men's, their regular 'incapacity', which kept them in his view in a permanent state of mild invalidism, their peculiar talents for home-making and domestic arts and their intuition as against man's rational attitudes. None of this had much to do with allowing women the franchise, it was directed more at keeping them out of universities and the professions, but no one questioned its validity. Earl Ferrers' view of women as potential legislators, given fifty-three years later, was only a slight advance on Henry's. Several subsequent speakers congratulated the noble lord, the Lord Nanther, on his wise words which, one of them said, derived from his expert knowledge as a 'medical man of awesome repute'. Misogynistic Henry. Though no doubt pleased with this reception by his peers, he spoke no more. Although I've trawled through Hansard for the remaining years of his life I can find no evidence that he ever entered the House again.

He was giving up, giving in to age. In February 1906 he became seventy and he records his birthday in his diary. 'The years of man's life are threescore years and ten. Today I reach my allotted span.' For an avowed agnostic, he quotes the Bible surprisingly often, but no doubt this was a hangover from his Wesleyan youth. He was no longer in attendance on the royal family, for his service seems to have been terminated when Edward VII came to the throne in 1901. Someone else had been appointed to care for the Battenberg princes, Maurice and Leopold. In the spring of

1906 Barnabus Couch died. Henry records in the diary: 'By rail to Edinburgh. Attended poor Couch's funeral.' Did he reflect while he stood in the churchyard, and watched his old friend's coffin lowered into the grave, that now there was no one to ask him how his *magnum opus* proceeded? He could abandon it without shame and without excuse. As for the women who might have enquired how 'papa' was getting on, their opinions didn't count. They were incapacitated invalids, relying on intuition.

That he'd started this book is known. In the early days, the end of the nineteenth century and the beginning of the twentieth, he notes: 'Worked on *A History* and good progress was made' and 'Six chapters of *A History* completed.' But by 1903 there are no more entries like these. We don't even know what its full title would have been. *A History of Blood Disease*? *A History of Haemophilia*? He still saw the occasional patient and still gave the occasional lecture. His name is listed as among the contributors to the haemophilia section of that vast work *A Treasury of Human Inheritance*, always known in medical circles as 'Bulloch and Fildes' after its main instigators, though it wasn't published until three years after his death. But his work was done and it seems that he considered his life was over.

In the year he became seventy and Couch died, Henry's eldest daughter Elizabeth, aged twenty-one, married James Bartlett Kirkford at St Mark's Church, Hamilton Terrace. Henry gave her away. He notes tersely on a Saturday in June: 'Gave E. in marriage.' Her husband took her to live in Yorkshire. Mary, Helena and Clara remained at home, Clara being still at school in St John's Wood. Alexander, the heir, was also at school, a prep school in Arkley, prior to going to Harrow, but George, the sick boy, was never considered well enough to go to school. A tutor called Mr

Beckwith came every day to instruct him in Latin and mathematics while a Mademoiselle Parent taught him French. Henry, who had been at home as little as possible in his daughters' early years, now scarcely went out. It seems that when George wasn't at his lessons, he spent his time with his father.

The letters exchanged between Elizabeth Kirkford and her sister Mary Nanther have been a rich source of information on family life. They wrote to each other once a month for many years, though there are gaps in the correspondence, notably during the summer of 1910 and again in 1917 and 1919. But in August 1910 Mary refers to 'Your letter of June' and in December 1917 to Elizabeth's mention of 'Vanessa's whooping cough' some months before, and those letters are missing. There are no letters in the collection between May and August 1910 and none between September and November 1917. Nineteen nineteen is another blank year with only one letter from each woman surviving. Of course they may just be lost. There is no reason to think that they were purposely destroyed. Those that remain for the years prior to Henry's death give a detailed picture of family life at Ainsworth House and of Elizabeth's marriage. James Kirkford walks with a limp. Apparently, he had one leg a fraction shorter than the other. This keeps him from serving in the Great War of 1914. 'I never expected to be thankful for poor James's disability but now I am,' Elizabeth writes. 'He of course frets about it, especially as some Beast has sent him a white feather.' Four years before she has given birth to a son.

I suffered for two days and was awfully afraid but at last he was born and my agony was not so great as to disincline to give him a brother or sister. James wants him to have his name and I agreed but Kenneth must come first. It is fashionable but nothing he will ever be ashamed of.

By then Henry had been dead a year. Throughout 1907 and the early part of 1908 Mary writes of their father's ill-health. She calls it a 'malaise'.

I don't think even Papa himself knows what is wrong with him. It is a malaise that cannot be defined. He sometimes suffers a mild pain in his chest and down his left arm, which points to heart trouble, or so he says.

At Christmas 1907 she tells her sister,

We shall miss you here but all understand of course that you must spend the festive season with James's people. We are to have no guests and to go nowhere. Poor Papa seems to have nothing to employ him – unless you count George. He spends all his waking hours with him, mostly reading aloud to him which George likes, though he has been able to read perfectly well himself since the age of four. He has been in terrible pain and sometimes in the night lets out bloodcurdling screams which wake the whole household. Papa has ice delivered here and applies fresh packs of it for hours on end. It seems nothing is too much trouble . . .

In February she is writing,

They play extraordinary games. The latest is to count how many times certain words appear in the plays of Shakespeare. For instance, 'green' and 'milk' in Macbeth! George enjoys it and claims to have found a secret code in one of them. He is such an intellectual child, which none of us was and Alexander certainly is not.

George died in July 1908. To his father it was the worst blow of his whole life. Mary writes,

It is a dreadful thing for all of us but worst for poor Papa. Mother is always so phlegmatic, though perhaps philosophical would be a kinder word. Nothing seems to upset her for long. I can't help wondering what Papa's reaction would have been if any of us had died. Rather different, I think. Could anyone deny that George was the only one of his children he cared a jot for? You were very seriously ill with scarlet fever in the early nineties. I was only five but I remember very well that Papa hardly came near you, claiming he was afraid of infection, though he had had the disease himself. I was with Mama when she came to tell him you were out of danger and he hardly looked up from his book.

Not very kind if Elizabeth had no prior knowledge of Henry's callousness. He died in 1909, six months after George. 'Of a broken heart,' Elizabeth suggests to her sister. Mary isn't having any of that.

Father [she never calls him Papa again] may have died of a broken heart but it was heart disease, not grief, that broke it. Whatever Mother says I believe he had a heart attack soon after George died. At any rate, she found him lying on the sofa in the study, clasping his hands to his left side and his face a most peculiar purple colour.

The next one, in the following January, killed him. *The Times* carried a long and sycophantic obituary and Princess Beatrice sent a wreath. Henry left most of what he possessed to his son Alexander, by then Lord Nanther. The exceptions were small legacies, providing incomes to his unmarried daughters and a life interest in Ainsworth House to his widow as well as a considerable sum in life insurance. Edith put up a gravestone to him, leaving room for her own name to be added later. It reads conventionally: 'Henry Alexander, Baron Nanther KCB, beloved husband of Edith, born 19 February 1836, died 20 January 1909. Blessed are the merciful for they shall obtain mercy.' I think I understand my great-grandmother well enough by now to know that no irony was intended. Her husband had been a doctor so this particular Beatitude was appropriate.

Two or three terraces of cottages remain opposite the main gates of the cemetery. They and a couple of big houses are all that survive to give an idea of what Kensal Green was like when Henry was buried there. But even then the warren of streets in the hinterland was there and the rows of shops, many now run-down, their windows boarded up. You can walk the length of the Harrow Road, from Paddington to Harlesden, and, with the exception of a butcher with a queue to his door, not pass a shop you'd dream of going into, still less buy anything from. There's a hairdresser's with the plaster dropping off its walls, innumerable betting shops, fast-food places, hardware stores where the hardware is all plastic. The area has become depressed, almost sinister in its atmosphere; litter and chewing gum on the pavements, every building ugly or mean, every surface in the neighbourhood of the tube station savagely coated with graffiti in primary colours. People who live here would prefer to live almost anywhere else and their discontent, not to be wondered at, shows in their grim faces. The cemetery is a green haven in summer but now bare branches shiver behind the kind of high wall you'd expect to see round the grounds of a prison.

A fine drizzle is falling, only a little wetter than a mist. I know roughly where Henry's grave is but still I need the cemetery plan I'm given to find it. This place is huge, some of the tombs as big as the cottages outside the gates and not a very different shape. Obelisks and angels surround me, weeping widows in pock-marked limestone, broken columns, and everywhere the ivy and the ilex, eternally evergreen, dark, ugly, apparently immortal, unlike the occupants of the ground beneath my feet. I think of it as harbouring bones and rotting wood, rich with larval life, and wonder what they thought they achieved by it, those Victorians. Was their aim to overcome death? If so, they conspicuously failed, for this place is his abode, where the living man feels that he intrudes, yet must make haste if he wants to come out alive.

His is not a very impressive gravestone. It stands between an obelisk very like Cleopatra's Needle commemorating an Egyptologist and the weeping muse of an obscure poet. Ivy and brambles blanket the spaces between. Henry shares his with his widow Edith and his son George. George's epitaph shows more feeling than the inscription the widow devised for his father. No doubt it was composed by Henry himself, for there is no mention that he had another parent. 'George Thomas, beloved son of Lord Nanther, aged eleven. Do ye hear the children weeping, O my brothers?' The quotation is from Browning, I think, and as far as I remember from a poem about the suffering of factory children. I'll look it up. Edith's epitaph was probably put there by Alexander during one of the short periods he lived in London. 'Louisa Edith, Lady Nanther, widow of the above, 1861–1932, a dearly loved mother.' No doubt the married daughters are buried with their husbands. But what of Helena? What of Clara? They lie elsewhere, neglected, unwanted women, of not much account to their family or their collateral descendants.

But what really surprises me is the vase of flowers. The grave looks as if it's been untended for a long time but not two-thirds of a century, nothing like that. On the mossy slab at its foot is a small stone vase, half-full of greenish-brown water, in which stands a bunch of dead rosebuds. They're withered but still pink and their leaves aren't shrivelled. Who can have put them there? Not my great-aunt Clara, the longest-lived of her generation. Though nearly a hundred, she died in 1990, and these flowers have been there not more than a few weeks. Another small mystery and one I'd like to solve.

On a curious and untypical impulse I go back to the gate where a man is selling flowers from a stall and buy a bunch of chrysanthemums. While I arrange them in the rainwater in the stone pot I decide I'm putting them there not for Henry or George but for Edith. I used to see her as a fortunate woman, making a better marriage than she might have expected, living in a fine house and wanting for nothing. Her husband was devoted to her and her children affectionate and, by her daughters' accounts, she was of a placid equable temperament. She was an accomplished photographer and painted at least to her own satisfaction. But now I'm beginning to think of her as a wronged woman, duped and taken advantage of, though I don't as yet know why.

23

True to David's prediction Veronica has invited me to tea. I'd have liked to have Jude with me on this trip. We could have had a weekend in the Cotswolds and I could have left her behind briefly in the hotel at Stow while I went to Cheltenham. But Jude won't. She makes several excuses where one would do, so I know she doesn't really want to come. It's too expensive, she says, we can't afford holiday weekends. Besides, on the Friday she's due to have tests done to see if she's got some recessive gene that causes these miscarriages. It's after she's hinted that I may have to have a similar test that she says she'd rather stay at home, she's been up there too often anyway to the Cheltenham Literary Festival.

And she needs the car, so I go by train. It's twenty minutes' walk from the station to Veronica's and as I stroll along (because I'm early) I think about genes and wonder what this test is, telling myself in the base way we talk to our inner selves, that there can't be much wrong with *me*, I've fathered a healthy child. Perhaps I should phone John Corrie and ask him to explain. But I'll have the test first, to please Jude.

Instead of one of the pretty Georgian terraces that abound here, Veronica lives in a nineteen-seventyish 'town house' with picture windows and an integral garage. She's been watching or listening for my arrival, for she answers the door faster than she could have done if she hadn't been just inside it. Great care has gone into her appearance. Her hair is newly tinted, her nails freshly painted and she's dressed in what I'd guess is the latest fashion for women some forty years younger than she, a sort of padded skirt and jumper with frayed edges. I'll describe her clothes to Jude who'll tell me if I'm right. David was quite correct about the sumptuous tea. Veronica has provided smoked salmon sandwiches, scones with jam and cream, flapjacks, carrot cake and shortbread. Now I shan't have to eat dinner, always supposing I could get it, on the train.

While we eat, she talks family history, which must be her own bland, diluted, expurgated version of events, for no collection of human beings in any age could be quite so virtuous, conformist and dull as she makes out the Nanthers and the Kirkfords to be. Henry, as she's told me before, she never knew. Her grandmother Edith she remembers as being particularly tolerant of what children did but not as playing with her or even having much time for her. She had other things to occupy her, which Veronica can well understand, her photography, her painting, and she's sure Edith was 'as happy as the day is long'. As to her appearance, Veronica believes that 'in those days women always looked their age'. Her grandmother never went out without a hat. Her once copious blonde hair was white and thin, worn in a 'bun' on the back of her head. She was a churchgoer and Veronica remembers the vicar of St Mark's coming to tea at Alma Villa.

I interrupt here and ask her about the engagement ring, expecting her to say she doesn't remember and that children never notice things like that. But she does remember and no, her grandmother never wore any rings but her plain gold wedding band. Of course this may mean no more than that she found the wearing of rings a nuisance. Many women do. On the other hand, it may be that she resented Henry's handing on to her the ring he bought for her sister and discarded it as soon as he was dead.

Veronica's own mother and her aunt Mary were both very good looking, the reason no doubt for their getting husbands in an era when young men were in short supply. She seems to have forgotten – deliberately? – that her mother married eight years before the Great War started. Veronica's childhood was idyllic, her father James Kirkford a saint, who never complained though suffering badly from arthritis in his foreshortened leg. She speaks always as if she'd been an only child. I wait until she's finished and we've finished tea and I'm about to mention John Corrie when she suggests I might like to 'see over' the house and garden. This is the last thing I want to do but I submit with a good grace.

The place is oppressively neat but there seem to be more cupboards and chests than is usual and these, I suppose, are the repositories of all those letters and photographs and maybe David's early scholarly efforts. We go up two flights of stairs, pausing to look at a bedroom and a bathroom and another bedroom, this one rather creepily already decorated for Galahad's future occupancy with sailing boats on the walls and fish on the curtains. Has she mapped out a marine career for him? She tells me airily she's sure he'll be coming to stay quite often with his 'gran' and, of course, on his own. Perhaps it's natural or a kind of life assurance that she speaks as if she were sixty instead of over eighty. The garden is depressingly neat, everything clipped or shaved, shrubs, though quite mature, retaining their labels and name tags. Do I think she has room for a swing or maybe one of those, what-are-they-called, climbing frames? I begin to see her as pathetic, which I never did before.

We go back indoors and I'm fast getting the impression

she's anticipating my departure. In the next ten minutes, at any rate. What is there left to do? He's eaten his tea, seen over the house, heard his family history. Her smile is growing strained. Would I like to see the letters David wrote her while at boarding school? His first 'compositions'? Photographs of herself and David and her husband? Perhaps later, I say. That makes her impatient, she's probably got her favourite television serial coming on in half an hour. I sit tight, keep my eyes on her but not searchingly, and ask if she knows who John Corrie is.

She's one of those people who blush when surprised and it's not becoming. 'I suppose he's my nephew. Why?'

'I do need to talk about this, Veronica. I'm sorry if it's painful.' The blush is fading. She looks displeased but I plunge ahead. 'You do know your sister is dead?'

'I heard,' she says, though not how she heard. From Steven Corrie, the faithless fiancé? I'm going to avoid mentioning him.

'Her son John is a scientist. He does research into gene therapy.' Now it's coming. 'For haemophilia.'

The blush is back. She sits very upright, pressing her knees together. I perceive her distress in her breathing, which I can hear regularly rise and fall. I say, 'He is himself a haemophiliac.'

'No!' The negative comes quick and sharp like a gunshot.

'I'm afraid yes.'

Strange things are happening. I'm trying to read the way she's thinking, the options her mind is dealing with. If she really doesn't understand, if it's new to her, she'll ask me what haemophilia is. Something wrong with the blood, she'll say, but she's never known anyone . . . She's silent, turning possibilities over. Then she says, 'Where does it come from?'

I don't want to tell her John's theory. If I do the discussion could shut down. So instead of talking of a mutation, I say he doesn't know, but it must somehow be through his mother. Her face shows me she knows much more than she's told me so far. There's a family secret here, hidden for God knows what reason, but known, I suspect, to some, though not all, of its female members. She may throw me out or at least ask me to leave if I put this question but I take the risk.

'What did your brother Kenneth die of, Veronica?'

No answer. She's not looking at me any more but down into her lap. Astonishingly, she says, 'Would you like a drink? Sherry or gin or something? I'm going to have one. After all, as my husband used to say, the sun is over the yard arm.'

It has just gone half-past five. The sun passes early over the yard arm in Cheltenham. I accept sherry, hoping it's not the sort served by Violet Farrow, and get a big schooner full of the cream variety, no doubt so that she can have a big one too. 'Will this be in your book?'

'I don't know. Probably. Does it matter?'

'What d'you mean, does it matter?'

'I mean, is it important now that so many family members are dead?'

'I suppose,' she says grudgingly, 'it might be a relief to talk about it. Perhaps you didn't realize, I've had no one, but no one at *all*, I could tell. David wouldn't have been interested.' Out comes another nautical metaphor. 'It's pull up the ladder, Jack, I'm all right with him. I suppose it's understandable. He would have known Galahad couldn't be affected. Oh dear, I do feel such a *fool* every time I have to use that absurd name.' She's been stalling but she knows it's no use. Now she's speaking in a small young voice like

315

that happy child she once was. 'What do you want to know?'

I try to match her tone in diffidence. 'I asked – well, about your brother.'

'I was only two when he died. I don't remember him. I only know I did have a brother.' For some reason she looks guilty. 'It was diphtheria he died of but he'd always been ill. Once he fell over and bled from grazed knees for two days. That got better but the joints inside didn't. Arthropathy is what they call what he had.'

'If you can't remember him how do you know?'

'My mother told me. Not till I was going to get married.' She lifts her head and looks at me. In ten minutes she's aged and become a very old woman. 'I was engaged to this John's father. Did you know that?' I nod. 'I suppose Georgina saw fit to pass that on. He jilted me for my sister. When I first got engaged my mother told me there was haemophilia in the family. Men got it, women conducted it, that's what she said. If I got married I might have a son with haemophilia like Kenneth and she was going to tell Steven. It was her duty, she said, to tell Steven. If I'd known the suffering she'd endured with Kenneth I wouldn't even want to get married.

'It was a great shock. Imagine it, a young girl, happy and carefree. I was in the WAAF and *loved* every minute of it. I was in love with Steven.' She's in the swing of it now. She wants to talk, let it all come out. 'Imagine being told a thing like that. It made me hate my mother. I made her promise not to tell Steven and she said she wouldn't so long as I promised to tell him myself. Well, I never did. I never got the chance. My sister stole him. I don't know how she did but I suspect witchcraft. Oh, yes, you needn't look like that, she had some strange beliefs, the stars ruling our lives, horoscopes and all that. It was funny, though, wasn't it? It's just struck me, the irony if that's the word. Maybe if he'd married me his children would have been all right. David is, couldn't be healthier. But Steven married my sister and God punished him. They were both punished. Vanessa never knew, our mother never told her, she didn't get the chance. How old is this John?'

'Over fifty, I think.'

She says brutally, 'Why is he still alive?'

'They can do a lot for haemophilia these days.' I press on. 'Was that what your cousin Patricia meant when she wrote congratulating you on David's being all right? It wasn't about Down's Syndrome at all, it was about haemophilia?'

She nods, says sharply, 'I'm not one of these conductors.'

The fact that she's had one son without the faulty gene proves nothing. I don't say this aloud. 'But you thought you might be. Was that why you waited so long to have a child?' I realize this is a rather over-the-top question. 'I'm sorry, I don't mean to be impertinent.'

'Bit late for that, isn't it?' She sniffs. 'My mother had frightened me. She died a year after I got married. I didn't grieve. I just thought, now she can't tell anyone.'

'Tell anyone what? That there was haemophilia in the family?'

She shrugs. A yes or a no? 'I wanted a child. Why shouldn't I? It was my right. When I got married to David's father, to Roger that is, I told my mother I'd told him. I'd done it and she wasn't to mention the subject. We'd agreed not to have children, though the fact was we'd agreed to no such thing. I never had told him, I dared not. Then my mother died and I felt I'd been let off the hook. But I wanted a child.' She leans towards me. 'My grandmother had had four girls before she had a son and my mother had two girls to one boy, my aunt Mary had two girls. And if it's the man determines the sex of a child it would be all right because Roger had four sisters. I reasoned I'd have a girl.'

I interrupt. 'A girl might have been a carrier.'

'That would have been her problem, wouldn't it? Not mine.' Her callousness is chilling. I try to imagine being in Georgie's shoes and nearly shudder. 'It took a long time. Conceiving a child, I mean. I'd almost given up and then I found I was pregnant.' She looks at me with a mixture of defiance and triumph. 'I didn't worry. I felt it in my bones I wasn't a conductor. David was born, a perfect, beautiful and absolutely normal little boy. Patricia wrote me that ridiculous letter. I don't even know how she knew I'd had a son, let alone that he was a perfect child. I suppose her sister Diana told her. I was quite friendly with Diana then – until she let me down, that is. She was just one in a long line of treacherous women.'

I don't know what Diana did and I don't want to. 'Where did this haemophilia come from?'

'Don't ask me. I'm not a doctor.'

I say slyly, 'I think you know quite a lot about it, though.'

'I used to read a lot about Queen Victoria and the Tsarevich and all those royals who had it. Where did their haemophilia come from? Not one of Queen Victoria's ancestors had it, it started with her. It must have started with my mother.'

Because I think – wrongly – that news of hopeful break-throughs will please her, I tell her as much as I understand of John Corrie's research, how carriers can now be detected and embryos examined to establish whether they carry the 'bleeder' gene. This would mean that in a couple of genera-tions haemophilia could be eliminated.

'I shan't benefit, shall I?'

'Your cousins' children and grandchildren might.'

She shows more interest. 'Diana's dead now but she had two children, you know. Both girls. I see you knew that.' She's disappointed, thwarted of scoring off me. 'I can't remember their names, something typical of the time they were born. They'll be in their thirties now.'

'They may be carriers.'

'They're not descendants of my mother's so they can't be.'

I don't comment on this. It's based on an assumption, not evidence. I thank her for the tea, leave half the sherry – I'm pretty sure she'll finish it when I've gone – and fetch my coat. She tells me as she sees me off that she has no objection to my putting all of this in my book, now I've wormed it out of her, I'm welcome. After all, as she strangely puts it, she's nothing to be ashamed of, she's not a carrier.

It's past seven. The rain has cleared and it's turning cold. I've half an hour to wait for a train. I sit for a while and then I walk up and down the platform and think about haemophilia. On the back of a bill I find in my pocket I draw from memory part of David's family tree, starting with Henry and Edith. I write in the names of their first four children, the girls Elizabeth, Mary, Helena and Clara. If the gene mutation started with Elizabeth only her descendants can be affected, as her son Kenneth was and as is her grandson John Corrie. But if Mary's children, grandchildren and possibly great-grandchildren, or one of those people, is or are affected, the mutation can't have occurred in Elizabeth because her sister's descendants also have the faulty gene. So it must have occurred further back.

The train comes. I put the improvised tree back into my pocket and concentrate on gene therapy and what it would have meant to people such as Prince Leopold and Veronica's brother Kenneth and the Tsarevich, who suffered so much pain and fear before, in the case of the first two, their disease killed them. My mind wanders to Jude and the tests she's been having. I'm not usually the kind of person who fantasizes worst-case scenarios but it does occur to me that there may be some genetic disorder to account for all these miscarriages. Is that what they've been testing for?

What a strange thing it is to be like Veronica, proud of yourself for not carrying genes of disability and ashamed of yourself for carrying them. Look at me, she's saying, I who am pure and healthy and perfect, I who have perfect children. Yet nothing could be further from her own volition or beyond her control. Both known carrier and apparent non-carrier are in a state of utter innocence and, moreover, of ignorance too. For I've read somewhere that all of us have in our DNA about twelve defective genes we are capable of passing on to our descendants, but the chances are we know nothing of them. They lie dormant, as they have lain in the bodies of mankind and animals for millennia. They will never show themselves unless we reproduce with someone whose DNA matches ours in some tiny particular, the reason that lies behind incest taboos and strictures in all faiths against marrying close relations.

In my mind I've been condemning Veronica for assuming she isn't a haemophilia carrier on the strength of having had one son with normal blood. But there's no difference between this attitude of hers and mine when I tell myself Jude's miscarriages are nothing to do with me, my genes are all right, Paul proves it. I'm behaving like Veronica, congratulating myself on my purity without any foundation for doing so. I too have one son, an only child, just as Vanessa had one son – until she had a second one. Veronica and I act as if we created ourselves in the image of God instead of being the result of thousands of years of mixing and selecting and rejecting and surviving.

24

Christmas is past. Paul decided to come and spend it with us and things went rather well, due perhaps to his bringing his nice new girlfriend with him. I realized I'd never talked to him about what I do, apart from what I *did* in the House of Lords, and realized too that if I had, this might have saved our relationship. So I told him about the Nanthers and the haemophilia; he was interested and, for once, not scathing. It helped a lot that Sam, the girlfriend, is a medical student and fascinated by gene therapy and its potential. They both know a man who's a haemophiliac and is now HIV positive through being given a transfusion of infected blood.

To my surprise Jude talked about her own tests, and was completely open and frank about them. She gets the results next week. Everything shuts down over Christmas and the New Year, especially this one, the start of a new millennium, so she's had to wait a long while. Mine are due to be done about the same time. At least I know she's taken to heart the sternly delivered advice not to attempt to conceive again yet. Her attraction for me, once so overwhelming, is back. There were an awful few days – or nights – when a kind of panic seized me that with her, in bed, in the dark perhaps, I'd have to fantasize, run in front of my unseeing eyes some self-involving video, as at the end of our relationship I did with Sally. But there was no dark, the lights were on as they mostly are for us, and her beauty and her essential Jude-ness worked their magic, and I think it was the same as it always was. I think so.

★

David Croft-Jones is furious with me for mentioning John Corrie to his mother. I 'undertook', he says, not to do this. I remind him that when he asked for an undertaking I didn't answer him and then I add that whatever his mother may have said to him since, she was perfectly happy to talk about it once she'd got over her initial awkwardness. Georgie is saying something in the background – no doubt about Veronica's general unreasonableness – and David is mollified. He wants to hear my version and can he come round? I can't very well say no. Of course it turns out that Veronica has let something out about haemophilia in the family, but been cryptic and secretive and now he wants to hear the truth of it. He's seriously worried. It was the first he's heard of it, it's 'devastated' him, and Georgie wants to know if any more children they might have could be haemophiliacs.

'Absolutely not,' I tell him. 'It's not even known if your mother has the gene and if she has she didn't pass it on to you. It's died out in your branch.'

'So you say,' he says rather rudely. 'I shall check it out. I shall ask my GP. All this has been a shock.' He talks about our family's inheritance as if it were a small animal, a hamster maybe, that has escaped and is lurking somewhere. 'Where is it now, this haemophilia? Is it hidden in someone's blood? What's happened to it?'

It's on the tip of my tongue to tell him to ask his GP. After all, he doesn't believe me. But I don't. I answer quite mildly that it may not have begun with a mutation in his grandmother's genes but earlier and his great-aunt and mine, Mary Craddock, may have also carried it. Therefore, so may either of her daughters, Patricia and Diana, and hence her granddaughters, Caroline, Lucy and Jennifer. Always precise and didactic in these matters, he says in rather a peevish tone that 'those girls' are his second cousins just as they are mine. He and his mother were invited to Lucy's wedding in 1997. Diana wrote to them, urging them to come on the grounds that though they'd never met the bride they were family and families should 'stick together'.

'Then you'll have her address.'

'No, I won't. I must have lost it.' Then he adds, surprisingly, 'I could have her traced for you. If that's what you want.'

Could he really? Perhaps he's more important in the Home Office than I thought or perhaps any of them can do this sort of thing. Of course I readily accept.

'It would be useful to me too,' he says. 'She may have a child by now that I could put in my tree.'

'Did you go to the wedding?'

'What wedding?'

'Lucy's.'

'Good God, no. All they asked us for was to get a present. I never believed all that family rubbish.' He's his mother's son.

'And Diana's dead now?'

'She died last year. My mother told me.'

I ask him how his mother knew, seeing she isn't in touch with either Lucy or Jennifer or their cousin Caroline. He says she saw the announcement in the death columns of the *Daily Telegraph*, of which she's apparently an avid reader.

Whether he went to his GP I didn't ask and he volunteered no information but he traced Lucy Skipton much more quickly than I'd expected. I phoned her and she's agreed to meet me. Time was but is no longer when I could have taken her to lunch in the House of Lords. She's a solicitor with a firm near the Law Courts, so I suggest a restaurant in a street just off Aldwych. I wonder if she knows she's in the same profession as her great-great-grandfather and, incidentally, as my father. How astounded, how disbelieving, Samuel Henderson would have been if he'd known one of his *female* descendants was following in his footsteps. More shades of Earl Ferrers' speech with its diatribe against possible judges 'drawn from the serried ranks of the ladies' and women eating their way like acid into the professions.

Our date is a fortnight away. I haven't told her much, only that I'm writing Henry's biography, but she didn't need any more. She knows quite a bit about Henry from being an inveterate reader of biographies of eminent Victorians, in many of which he's mentioned. Lucy is thirty-six, about a year younger than Jude. I'm looking forward to our meeting in a way I didn't look forward to seeing John Corrie or renewing my acquaintance with Veronica. In fact, I'm impatient about it because she's told me something on the phone I didn't expect.

'I'm a carrier.'

'You're a carrier of haemophilia?'

'That's right. There's no secret about it. My mother told me and my sister we might be and I was tested before I got married.'

They haven't told Jude the results of her test, though it appears they have them. They've asked her to wait until the results of mine are known. She sees this as sinister and frightening, though to me it seems just like mysterious medical behaviour, the kind of way people who seem to have no empathy and no understanding of natural anxiety inevitably go on. It may even be that they want to confront us both with broad smiles to tell us there's absolutely nothing wrong with either of us. Everyone likes being the bearer of good news.

'It could take weeks,' she says.

'Look at it this way. If there was something that was wrong with you they wouldn't need to test me. They're testing me in case the fault lies with me.' If I hadn't had those thoughts on pride in one's personal DNA I might have added that it doesn't because I've already got a healthy son. That's something I've learned not to say.

We decide to share a bottle of champagne without having anything special to celebrate. Its aftermath, a dry mouth and faint ache behind the eyes wakes me up in the small hours. Having been indoctrinated as a child with the theory that anything that doesn't come from the main tap is toxic, I make my way down to the kitchen for real water and sit there at the table drinking my second glass and thinking about what Lucy told me.

It means that Diana Bell was a carrier and therefore her mother Mary Craddock must have been a carrier, since we know her sister Elizabeth Kirkford also was and Mary's husband Matthew Craddock can't have been a haemophiliac. So where did it come from? First of all, is it absolutely out of the question that Henry was a haemophiliac? It's an explanation that covers almost everything. It would account for his devoting his life to a study of the disease in search of a cure. All his daughters would have been carriers and it's likely that they were. Helena and Clara never had children but we know Clara had resolved never to marry and the reason may have been because she suspected she had the gene – or 'the blood', as she'd have put it.

The flaw in this theory lies with Henry himself. In the mid nineteenth century, a hundred years before the discovery of Factor VIII supplements, a haemophilia sufferer could hardly have lived the life Henry lived, walking the twenty miles from Versam to a village high in the Alps, intervening to save a man who was being assaulted, pursuing rigorous studies, taking hiking holidays. By the time he was thirty he'd have been crippled by arthropathy through bleeding into the joints. The third piece of evidence against his being a haemophiliac is Jimmy Ashworth. *All* his daughters, in or out of wedlock, would have carried the gene. If Mary Dawson had done so, surely one of her male descendants would have been a haemophiliac. But Laura Kimball was adamant that they all 'grew up healthy'.

So Henry can be dismissed as the source. In which case it must have been his wife, Edith Henderson. The more I look at her as a candidate the more reasonable it sounds. If she carried the gene all her daughters might have carried it or only two or three out of the four. There would have been a fifty-fifty chance of any son of hers having the disease. Alexander did not. Did George? So we've come close to proving Edith was the carrier.

I go into the study and trawl through the diaries and Alternative Henry and Mary's letters. Once you know George *may* have been a haemophiliac, there's plenty of evidence that he was. In the family group, photographed by Edith, he has the patient stoical look of the 'bleeder'. Henry writes of his screaming in pain, Mary of his being confined to bed as the result of a fall and of her father applying ice packs, presumably to his joints, a known though ineffective remedy. The conspiracy of silence on the subject becomes evident when you know what to look for. All the references are oblique or veiled. Was the reason that Henry didn't want the world to know that he, the great haemophilia doctor, had a son with the disease, and a disease which he, despite his knowledge, couldn't remedy? It sounds only too like him. This would be why it was put about that George suffered from tuberculosis.

If Edith was the carrier, where did she inherit the gene from? If her father Samuel Henderson was a haemophiliac his daughter would inevitably carry it. But if this was so he'd scarcely have been able to practise as a solicitor well into his fifties. And when he was attacked in the street the blow to his head would have resulted in bleeding that might have been fatal. And Henry, in his essay on courage and altruism, would hardly have presented the haemophilia hypothesis as to what would have happened if poor Mr Henderson had been a 'bleeder'. It's far more likely the carrier was his wife, Louisa Henderson née Quendon. Her son Lionel was very evidently not a haemophiliac but that doesn't mean his mother wasn't a carrier, for her chances of passing on the gene to a son were fifty-fifty. Her daughter Edith was a carrier and so, possibly, was her daughter Eleanor. I go to the larger of the correspondence files and find the letter Eleanor wrote to her sister from Manaton.

She has had a fall while out walking. 'The bruises on my left side and leg,' she writes, 'are a sight to behold, but luckily no one but me does behold them!' On another occasion Henry notes in the diary that Mrs Henderson had a private consultation with him about this daughter. Is it too far-fetched to guess that she was confiding to him her worries about Eleanor's heavy periods? Maybe. I need more evidence. But it is known now, and perhaps was even then, that some haemophilia carriers bruise very readily and bleed heavily in menstruation. It may be that both Edith and Eleanor carried the gene.

So was it a mutation in the cells of Louisa Henderson? My head is spinning by this time. I can't think any more

and it's four-thirty in the morning. I fetch another glass of
water and go back to bed, kissing the sleeping Jude on her
upturned cheek and falling asleep at once.

25

The news from the hospital has blown our lives to pieces. Nothing else is significant. It's as if everything has fled: our day-to-day existence in this house, Jude's job, Henry, my lost much-regretted seat in the Lords, my son, our friends, even – temporarily, I hope – our love.

When something like this happens to you, you become only a body, hardly a thinking being, and that body diseased and flawed. It harbours an unseen but outrageous deformity. They told us, using that tired old formula: do you want the bad news first or the good? The way you answer defines you as a pessimist or an optimist on the lines of whether you say the bottle is half-full or half-empty. We both chose the bad news.

So they told us. We each carry a gene of something neither of us has ever heard of. It's called Spinal Muscular Atrophy, or in these days of acronyms SMA. Any child we might have together has a one-in-four chance of being affected by it. And SMA isn't like having an operable heart defect or asthma or, come to that, haemophilia. It kills. If a baby was actually born alive it would be severely disabled and die before it was a year old. At best. Most foetuses abort and that accounts for Jude's miscarriages.

Poor Jude says, 'But that's only twenty-five per cent. There's still a seventy-five per cent chance of a baby not having whatever it is.'

The consultant looks at her. His face wears that expression newscasters put on when the next item they have to talk about is some famous person's death. 'You haven't been in the seventy-five per cent so far, have you? Would you risk it? Would you risk trying to nurse a child twenty-four hours a day only for it to die at six months?'

'Why do I have these miscarriages?'

He doesn't want to say it but he has to. 'It's your body's way of getting rid of disabled foetuses, Mrs Nanther.'

I am unreasonably, ridiculously angry. Why should I care if he doesn't get it right and call her Lady Nanther? Or, come to that, Miss Cleveland? Why do I object so much to 'getting rid of'? Getting rid of hereditary peers, getting rid of foetuses, getting rid of people. Isn't there some other, better, way of saying it?

'But I have a healthy son,' I tell him.

'Yes, we have it in your notes. You were lucky. You were married to a woman who didn't carry the gene.'

If I'd been the grandson of one of Henry's daughters instead of one of his sons I might have been a haemophiliac. But I've missed out on that and got this much worse thing. To anything but my own gratification, I had been right when I speculated as to what was wrong. Where did it come from? I don't ask. Somehow I know he'll give me that mutation business. 'What's the good news?'

'I expect you've heard of Preimplantation Genetic Diagnosis. You'd call it "designer babies".'

You're at a party and you see a beautiful woman across a room. You may think even at that point – I did, I really did – that you'd like to spend the rest of your life with her. Because once you've looked on that face you know no other will do, not ever, not even as it grows old and other young faces are there, no other will be imprinted on you as this one is. This is your standard against which all others are compared and found wanting. You see it in likenesses as I used so often to see Jude's in Herbert's paintings in the Moses Room, and when you do it lifts your heart.

What you don't see is that this woman may be the last woman you should choose for a life partner and you may be the last man she should choose – if you or she or both of you want a child. For her sake, you ought to turn and run out of the room, disappear, plead a pressing engagement elsewhere. You aren't so much a poisoned chalice as a reagent, a substance harmless in itself but toxic when added to another relatively harmless substance.

I ask myself if it was like this for Henry. Did he see Eleanor that first time he called in Keppel Street to ask after her father, and seeing her, succumb? But there the parallel ends, for it was Edith, the second choice, the substitute, whose body held the hidden flaw. It's as if I, unable for some reason to have Jude, made do with her sister. But this was something I could never have done. No other would have been the woman for me. And as I dwell miserably on this, I ask myself, perhaps absurdly, if these very deformities in our cells, Jude's and mine, drew us inexorably to each other by some mysterious alchemy. Or was it nature's way of achieving the end of two tainted lines, ensuring they breed no more?

So to the good news, except that to me it's the worst news in the world. Not that I can say so to anyone. And I'm thrown more violently than ever before up against the block that wrecks marriages: the inability of one to confide true feelings to the other. More than that, the impossibility of continuing to love and live with my wife if I tell her that the dearest wish of her heart fills me with – well, yes, with terror. With horror but with both more and less than that, a simple revulsion from the idea of becoming maybe next year or the year after the father of triplets. It sounds ridiculous put like that, doesn't it? The stuff of comic postcards. There's the poor sap standing hangdog outside the delivery room and a pretty nurse in a mini-skirt and black stockings is putting three squalling babies into his arms.

The consultant's face reminds me of that description in *Hamlet*: a man 'may smile and smile and be a villain'. He's not of course a villain to Jude but her saviour. 'The treatment begins with IVF,' he says, 'to generate and fertilize a number of eggs. Then we take one cell from each egg and check that it's free from disorder. Three healthy embryos would then be implanted in your uterus.'

'*Three?*' I say.

'Usually one or two won't take hold,' he says, with that villain's smile. 'If all goes well the result is a healthy child – or twins if you're lucky.'

'I'll be thirty-eight in May,' says Jude.

'I'm not saying it wouldn't be better if you were twenty-eight but you seem to have no trouble in conceiving and that's very much in your favour.'

Luckily for me, I'm so sorry for Jude, I feel such an all-pervading pity and love for her, that my horror of what she's contemplating is – temporarily, I suppose – drowned in it. And then I watch that other smiling villain, Hope, come to her rescue. She's hoped before and it's all been in vain, but that doesn't deter the smiler with the knife, he's indestructible, he knows he's one of the cardinal virtues and he basks in his undeserved reputation. Never mind that he makes the heart sick. Never mind that every time he throws open a door his opposite number, Despair, slams it in your face. He's back again, riding high and Jude in the saddle with him, his knife pointed at her back. But she doesn't know that or she refuses to believe him. He's

333

promised her her heart's desire and this time *nothing can go wrong*.

The nasty mean-mindedness of my position is that I want things to go wrong. I want the door to slam for the final time or the knife to go in. There's not a soul I can tell. I wince when I tell myself. During the pregnancies and the miscarriages I managed more or less well to fake enthusiasm or wretchedness and sometimes I really was enthusiastic, I really was miserable. But this news – the 'good' news more than the 'bad' – I see as the ruin of our lives, hers as well as mine. It will be bad enough for her – what do I call it? Mental equilibrium? Peace of mind? Sanity? – if these implanted embryos refuse to 'take', it will be worse than the miscarriages. She will be wrecked.

Only a totally mercenary bastard would think about the cost and I must be one because I do. With this process there's not a money-back guarantee. You pay for it and if it doesn't work you try again and pay again. 'One cycle of treatment', as they put it, costs £2,500. What chance would we have to get funding out of our local health authority? None, at a guess. On the other hand it might be cheaper to throw away £10,000 on four cycles of treatment than to have two or three babies to bring up. Shall I have to sell this house? I lie awake in the long watches of the night wondering about things it would be better for me never to think of. Such as, how do you determine which of two people with opposing aims is the selfish one? It's the stuff of married people's quarrels and it's not going to be the stuff of mine. But am I selfish in wanting my beloved wife to myself in relative comfort, with enough to live on in my family house in a quiet London square? Or is she selfish in wanting a child at all costs, at the cost of comfort, peace, a pleasant home, and, perhaps, her marriage?

334

Most people would be on her side. And I pretend I am because I don't know what else to do. I don't *do* anything, I've lost all my powers of concentration and I'm quite relieved when Lucy Skipton phones and asks if I'd mind putting off our lunch for another couple of weeks. She's very apologetic but she has a client whose home down in Wiltshire she has to visit on that day. If she hadn't phoned I fear I might have forgotten all about her and our date.

I must be regaining my equilibrium because I don't forget I'm dining with Lachlan Hamilton. The papers say the House of Lords feels empty these days, now the hereditary peers, or all but ninety-two of them, have gone. I can't say I notice it but that may be because the day I go in they're debating a controversial clause in a bill and the Opposition have summoned all their troops. The Local Government Bill doesn't sound likely to make a dramatic impact but one aspect of it does just that. It's an amendment opposing the repeal of Section 28, a provision stating that a local authority shall not 'intentionally promote homosexuality' to young people. The Government wants it repealed, the opposition want to keep it. The fur is flying and such words as 'necrophilia', 'bestiality' and 'sodomy' are being bandied about.

I'm not there to hear it, of course. Not at first. This is the first time I've been back since they chucked me out in November. I vowed then never to return, whatever the circumstances, but I've come back. I need a reason to get out of the house, Alma Villa I mean, to get away from the claustrophobic atmosphere of talk of eggs and implants and multiple births. I'm ashamed of thinking this way, of course I am, but I'm weary of being ashamed, weary of the self-reproach with which I lash myself when at home. Coming here is a change. And there's another reason for it. I have to get back to Henry but I can no longer talk to Jude about him and the mysteries in his life. She doesn't care, she doesn't want to know. She pretends, she puts on a show of listening but it's as if she says to herself, I'll give him five minutes of this – I see her looking at her watch – and then we'll return to the important thing, to *reality*. Her life now is the hugely wonderful crowning achievement she sees herself approaching, the giving of birth. What does it matter if everything is subsumed in this, career, home, me, sex, love, friends, conversation, fun? The purpose of woman's existence is to give birth, carry on the race. *And now she can do it*. Thanks to the wonders of medical science she can have not just one healthy baby but two or even three. No wonder she thinks of nothing else.

So when Lachlan asked me to dinner I thought, I'll try Henry out on him. He, at least, doesn't want babies. He's had six. First, though, I have the embarrassment I knew I'd have of sidling in at the Peers' Entrance, uttering a greeting in response to the doorkeeper's cheerful, 'Good evening, my Lord,' and sitting humbly down on the bench at the back where visitors wait. I'm too weary of self-reproach to remind myself that *I* voted for it, *I* approved it. Anyway, I don't have to put up with it for long, as Lachlan appears on the stroke of six-thirty.

With his walrus face and landowner's manner, he looks the last person to vote for the repeal of Section 28 but he's going to. His appearance is deceptive. I recall our conversation about Richard Hamilton and Lachlan's assertion that all men are a bit 'queer'. Now he says homosexuality is inborn. You're 'that way' or you're not and no amount of promotion or encouragement will change you. I'm not in the mood for hearing any more about genetics just at the moment and I'm pretty sure I won't be in the

Chamber where crusty ancient hereditaries (some of the élite and elected ninety-two) are blithely confusing homosexuals and paedophiles. I'm allowed to sit on the steps of the throne where I haven't sat since I was a boy of twelve. Someone next to me I've never seen before – he may be a young hereditary or a peer's eldest son – whispers that he's gay himself and that Earl Russell has just made the best speech he's ever heard in the House in favour of repeal. Just my luck, I say aggrievedly, not to have been here to have heard it.

But I don't like sitting here. It embarrasses me. Like one of those gay schoolboys Government speakers say suffer from bullying under Section 28, I feel everyone is singling me out and staring. It's a relief when Lachlan gets up and goes out at the end by the throne and I can follow him.

It's just like old times. The Opposition have mustered their troops, peers who never come in except when heavily whipped, and here they are hastening through the Prince's Chamber with their wives that they've brought in to dinner. You'd have to be an expert to know the House had been reformed at all.

Lachlan buys me a glass of red wine and himself a whisky. I can't reciprocate, of course. I can't pay for dinner or share the cost. I'm no longer eligible to pay for anything in here and I ought to be pleased. Another forty or fifty quid will be saved towards anti-SMA procedures. I seriously think for a moment of telling Lachlan all about it but as quickly dismiss the idea. Instead I revert to Henry.

'So what do you think? I mean, about the coincidence?'

He always speaks slowly and with steady precision, in the Chamber and out of it. 'How common an affliction is haemophilia?'

I don't know the answer. 'The only figures I've got are

for the United States.' They're the ones John Corrie gave me. 'About fifteen thousand people out of whatever their population is – two hundred and fifty million? – are haemophiliacs.'

'A rare disease then.'

'The incidence has been much higher in communities largely cut off from the rest of the world, such as alpine valleys in Switzerland. And it seems to be more common among Teutonic people and Jewish people. There used to be a theory, which could be false, that haemophiliacs and carriers were more fertile than others.'

I tell him about Henry's youngest child George, his mysterious illness, the references to his ill-health in his sisters' letters, Alternative Henry's cryptic allusions to it, the family's conspiracy of silence. Why? Why?

'He was a medico at University College Hospital? Could the lady he married have been his patient?'

'Women don't really have haemophilia,' I say. 'They have bleeding disorders but I can't imagine a Victorian woman going to a doctor with something like that, a problem she'd just cope with at home. Besides, Henry didn't meet the Hendersons by that route. He got to know them because he came to Samuel Henderson's aid when he was attacked in the street.'

Suddenly I remember who Samuel's attacker was. Jimmy Ashworth Dawson's brother-in-law, someone Henry very likely paid to do the deed or else we're up against another coincidence. But it's time to go in for dinner where the talk buzzes with Section 28 and people keep coming up to our table to greet me, to ask how I'm getting on, some to say what a shame I can't vote, they need me. The debate has been going on for more than four hours and they're still slogging it out.

Lachlan's been looking at some of the notes I've made. 'He engages himself to Henderson's elder daughter, the girl who bruises easily? You mention that here. Significant, is it?'

'I don't know. Some haemophilia carriers – they're called symptomatic carriers – have mild bleeding problems, excessive bruising, nosebleeds, that sort of thing. The family seems to be aware of Eleanor's propensity to bruising. If Henry knew of it he might have suspected she was a carrier. But on the other hand, she could have had a far commoner disorder like Von Willebrand's disease or epistaxis. That he happened by chance to fall in love with a girl who was a haemophilia carrier would have struck him, as it does us, as too huge a coincidence to be viable.'

'He didn't marry her, did he?'

'He would have done. She was murdered.'

There's to be no more talk of this because a Tory pal of Lachlan's comes to the table and sits down in the third chair, after only the most perfunctory request to ask if he may. The rest of the meal passes against a background of Lachlan and the pal arguing, not particularly amicably, as to whether homosexuals are born or made. 'Did you hear the one,' says the pal, 'about the queer who went to a psychiatrist and said his mother made him a homosexual? The psychiatrist said, if I get her the wool will she make me one too?'

Nobody laughs. I think of Richard Hamilton and Henry and wonder. Can there be a gene of homosexuality, carried on one of a woman's X chromosomes? If there is they haven't found it yet. It's nine o'clock and I see on the monitor that the minister Lord Whitty is on his feet.

Lachlan says, 'Would you mind if we went back?'

I suppose I can get used to the steps of the throne. The discomfort ought to distract me from the humiliation and perhaps it will. As soon as I've sat down Lady Young, whose amendment this is, gets up, speaks for a few moments and says she's going to divide the House. I hear what the Deputy Speaker says with new ears. I've never noticed what a resonant piece of prose it is.

'The Contents will go to the right by the throne and the Not Contents to the left by the bar.'

There are hundreds of Opposition peers filing towards the Content lobby. The LibDems are going with the Government but fifteen Labour peers aren't. It's strange and rather unpleasant to watch it and not be one with it. Foreign nationals think us very odd not to have electronic voting, but to stroll, often laughing and talking, down a passage and give our names to a clerk, who if he knows you will have crossed it off before you pass. The name of Nanther will have been struck off the list three months ago. Lachlan comes to talk to me, then sits on the step beside me. The Government – I nearly said 'we' – have lost by forty-five votes.

'We tried,' says Lachlan at his gloomiest.

I leave alone, not needing him to show me the way. The policeman at the gate asks if I need a taxi, my Lord, but I shake my head. I'm going to walk, not all the way, but a good part of it, and maybe get onto the tube at Baker Street. The evening is dark and damp but the sky is clear. Having only just finished building the new Westminster tube station, they're digging up Parliament Square. No one seems to know why. There aren't many people about on foot and the Pinochet protesters who station themselves here in the daytime, the ones who want the old General extradited and the ones who want to send him home, have all gone for the night. I think about Henry, the reason for my walking.

It's a curious conclusion I'm coming to. Surely it's beyond

doubt that my great-grandfather arranged that assault on Samuel Henderson, paying his Victorian hit man to attack Samuel so that he could rush to the rescue and thus create a pretext for meeting the Henderson family. It wasn't Samuel himself or his wife or his son Henry wanted to meet but one of his daughters. He had seen Eleanor in the street and fallen in love with her, just as I saw Jude across a room at a party. Conspiring to assault a man seems a complicated, not to say criminal, way of getting to know a woman. Perhaps he simply couldn't think of any other or he was closer to the Dawson–Brewer family than appears and one of them had suggested it to him.

So where does the haemophilia come in?

Henry cannot have known Samuel Henderson's wife was a carrier. Or let's say I can't think of any way he could have known it. Of course it's possible Louisa Henderson *was* his patient, as Lachlan suggested her daughter might have been, and came to his consulting rooms in Wimpole Street because she was a symptomatic carrier and suffered, as such women sometimes do, from problems with her joints or bleeding gums. But if she had done so he'd have had no need to stage that street attack on Samuel, he would have known the family already. So Henry didn't know. He didn't know but he found out and the discovery appalled him.

How did he find out? Lionel Henderson, Eleanor's brother, wasn't a haemophiliac. Eleanor bruised easily, a sign of a symptomatic carrier, but there are many reasons for a tendency to bruise and Henry wouldn't have been alarmed by it. No, surely the answer is that 'consultation', as he calls it in the diary, which Louisa Henderson had with Henry after he'd begun calling in Keppel Street, when she confided in him that her daughter suffered from heavy menstrual bleeding. This worried her since she thought it might mean Eleanor would have problems in childbearing.

It must also be taken into account that Louisa *may not have known she was herself a carrier*. Her father William Quendon was not a haemophiliac. But Louisa had had a brother who died in infancy or when young. He was younger than she but how much younger? I must check, find out. If he had haemophilia and died as a result of it and if he and she were babies when he died, she may never have known the cause of his death. Altogether, it seems likely, taking into consideration the lack of knowledge among ordinary people at that time – I think of Queen Victoria adamant that the disorder wasn't 'in the family' – that Louisa didn't know.

But Henry, the expert, would have known. As soon as she told him her daughter had heavy periods and bruised easily, perhaps had nosebleeds too, and very likely added that she herself suffered from similar abnormalities, Henry would have suspected both were carriers. A few judicious questions from him, perhaps on the subject of family history, would have gathered more information. He asked about any brothers or uncles Louisa had and learned of her brother who died in infancy. What did he die of? His blood failed to clot like other people's, says his future mother-in-law. He had some illness, she can't remember the name. Henry can remember it, it's written on his heart in blood-red letters, and he sees the risk he's running.

But he wasn't engaged to Eleanor at the time. I should rather say that he wasn't *officially* engaged to her. All that is known of the date of his engagement is from the notice in *The Times* and his diary entry. He may very well have asked Eleanor to marry him as early as July *before the consultation*. First asked her parents' permission, explaining that he agreed with the possible objection that they had known each other only a short time but his mind was made up, and he believed his affection was returned. Then he asked her. The consultation took place the following week, Louisa Henderson believing the time had come to warn her prospective son-in-law of the difficulties her daughter might have in giving birth.

Henry is appalled. But it is too late now. The announcement goes into *The Times* and he notes his engagement gloomily in his diary. Six weeks later Eleanor goes to stay with her aunt in Devon. It's known that she wrote home to her sister Edith. Did she also write to Henry, her fiancé? And if she did was he also told about the bruising, the result of her fall, confirming – as if he needed confirmation – what her mother had told him? Two weeks later she attempts to return home but never does because she is murdered on the way and her body thrown from the train.

Henry is due to marry her in February 1884, just four months away. His discovery has profoundly affected his feelings for her. He sees her as tainted, diseased. He knows a great deal about haemophilia, perhaps more than any other living doctor. He knows what marriage to this woman would mean: any son they might have could be afflicted, any daughter a carrier. Marrying her would be a disaster he can't contemplate.

I'm at Baker Street but I can't get onto a train. Jubilee Line trains aren't stopping here because something's gone wrong with the escalators. I get a 189 bus instead. It'll take me closer to home than the tube would have. I don't at all like what I'm thinking about my great-grandfather, it's not something which distance and more than a hundred years can wipe away.

If Henry could arrange a street mugging in order to meet a girl, might he also arrange a murder to avoid marrying her? The crimes aren't really on a par. Samuel Henderson wasn't really harmed while Eleanor was brutally strangled. And why go to such terrible lengths? He could have just left her. Jilted her. But things were different then. An action for breach of promise was a very real possibility for a jilted girl and her family. An angry father could insert a notice in a newspaper, naming Sir Henry Nanther as a trifler with women's affections, someone to avoid, a man from whom to protect one's daughters. Olivia Batho's father is said to have contemplated such a step. Did Henry know of it? And here one must remember Samuel Henderson was a solicitor and would be familiar with such things. Henry, the royal doctor, was a man of considerable repute, and his livelihood depended on that reputation being sustained. Queen Victoria had been so rigid in her morality when she was young that she and the Prince Consort refused to receive a woman whose marriage was the result of an elopement. She would never have countenanced the behaviour of one of her physicians publicly announcing his engagement to a respectable and virtuous young woman with her parents' full consent, and then deserting her.

So, appalling as it sounds, can Jude be right and was Henry a murderer?

26

I wish I'd thrashed this out while I was still with Lachlan so that I could have another opinion. He'd have given the theory his measured consideration. And maybe he'd have said it was ridiculous, bizarre, because in Ibsen's words, 'People don't do such things.'

Of course there's no question of Henry's having murdered Eleanor himself – that is, killed her with his own hands. But doing the deed oneself is not a prerequisite for murder. Did he pay Albert George Bightford to kill her?

I haven't done sufficient research into Bightford. It seemed enough for the purposes of Henry's biography to read the newspaper accounts of Eleanor's death, the inquest, and the trial and execution. Still, it obviously won't be enough. One of the *Famous British Trials* volumes contains a more detailed assessment of Bightford, his life and death, included presumably, not because he was particularly interesting or the murder he committed bizarre, but due to the identity of his victim and her connection with the soon-to-be Lord Nanther. My next step must be to get this book from the London Library.

Before I've done that there isn't much point in speculating about whether, for instance, Henry had any connection with Devon or the Great Western Railway or if the Brewer–Dawson family had. There's no point in speculation at all. For all that, I'd love to talk to Jude about it. Once she'd have been only too happy to find any further evidence of wrongdoing against Henry and happily played the devil's advocate, but now I know very well she won't be interested, will even ask wearily if we have to talk about him *again*.

I get off the bus and walk round the corner into Alma Square. Jude is in bed and fast asleep. By the light from the landing I see a new jar has joined the other remedies and supplements on her bedside table. It's labelled Kava-kava and I've no idea what it's for.

I wouldn't have been surprised to wake up this morning and find the whole theory preposterous, ask myself how even for a moment I could have thought of my eminently respectable great-grandfather as a murderer. But I don't. I feel exactly as I did last night on the 189 bus. A man who'll plan an assault on a stranger and stage a rescue, who'll marry off his mistress and abandon his daughter, court a woman, enjoy her father's hospitality and drop her for another, isn't that man capable of worse crimes?

Usually, in the past when I've called at the London Library, I've taken my books, crossed the square and, by way of St James's Park and Queen Anne's Gate, walked down to the House of Lords. I can't do that now without some 'sponsor' to let me in, but I do walk as far as the park and stop in the middle of the bridge. It's a fine sunny day, the sky blue and a bright sheen on the lake. You can stand here and if you look northwards see, beyond the water and the trees, Buckingham Palace. Look south and beyond the water and the trees, the swans and pelicans, you see Horse Guards and Whitehall and the Foreign Office. Now the London Eye, the Millennium Wheel, rears up like a bow-shaped crane behind the white walls and green and silver rooftops. I try not to see it, to see the view through Henry's eyes, for I'm sure he often passed this way. The air was smokier then, the buildings dirtier, the streets car-less but soiled by horses, the sky above the same blue and the grass the same green. Did he ever think of what he'd done to get what he wanted, or rather, avoid getting what he didn't want?

I start on the *Famous British Trials* as soon as I get home, reading to the accompaniment of Lorraine's vacuum cleaner, droning away upstairs. The section on Bightford is by a man called Stewart S. Luke and it's called 'Murder on the Cornish Express'. Luke wrote it in 1909, the year of Henry's death, and I wonder if this is coincidence. I feel a little *frisson* of excitement. A good reason to await someone's death before writing on a subject connected with him is that the dead can't be libelled.

According to Stewart Luke, Bightford was born in 1862, the eldest son of Jane Bightford, born Edwards, and her husband Abel Bightford, coachman to Harold Merlin Clive of Livesey Place, near Tavistock. The name Albert, which had no precedent in the family, was probably bestowed on him in memory of the Prince Consort who had died the previous year. The Bightfords had many children but only three of them survived to adulthood, Albert and two girls, Jane and Maria. The entire family worked for Mr and Mrs Clive. Mrs Bightford helped out with the cleaning, her daughter Jane was under-housemaid and her daughter Maria worked in the kitchens, while Albert was employed as one of the assistants to the head gardener, Thomas Flitton.

The Bightfords had married very young [writes Luke] and were only just over forty when their son was hanged for the murder of Miss Henderson. Three years before Albert, then aged nineteen, had taken the unparalleled step in that family and at that time of declaring himself discontented in his employment and desirous of leaving it. It was his father in whom he confided, saying he hated gardening. The collecting and spreading of manure was distasteful to him and the bending hurt his back, which he had injured when he was fifteen lifting heavy sacks for his mother. He also averred that Thomas Flitton 'had it in for him'.

It would be no exaggeration to say that Abel Bightford was more frightened than angry at this disclosure. It was not, after all, young Albert's livelihood in jeopardy here but the whole family's, for if he were obliged to continue working under Mr Flitton he declared that he would run away to Plymouth and seek his fortune elsewhere or even abroad. Abel went first to Thomas Flitton, a fellow-worker for many years and a friend. Flitton was obliged to tell the father that his son had proved unsatisfactory. He was surly and uncivil and complained constantly about pain in his back, behaviour Flitton found incomprehensible in one so young. He advised Abel to seek an interview with Mr Clive himself.

It is easy to imagine the terror this notion inspired in Abel Bightford. Probably, he had never spoken to his employer except when first addressed by him, had taken orders but not commented upon them and if his master levelled harsh criticism at him, accepted it as a servant's lot. However, he plucked up his courage, and next day, while driving Mr Clive to a Landowners' Association meeting in Yelverton, asked if he might have a few words with him at Mr Clive's convenience.

How Luke knows all this he doesn't say. Perhaps it all came out at the Assizes. I shall see when I get to the trial. Harold Clive sounds in some respects a reasonable man, not the ogreish squire of certain kinds of Victorian fiction, for when Abel spoke to him about Albert he was sympathetic. Apparently, he told Abel that he had a high opinion of the Bightford family and would be most unwilling to lose their service. The two men were agreed upon that and Abel must have breathed more than a sigh of relief. Clive asked if he thought Albert would be happier away from home and when Abel said he would, promised to see what he could do for him. First, it appears, he consulted a neighbour, a Miss Withycombe of Tavistock, believing she might be in need of a general handyman, and this woman gave Albert a week's trial. He wasn't satisfactory, though Luke doesn't say why. With great forbearance, Clive tried again.

He was a director of the Great Western Railway. 'Or something of that sort,' as Luke curiously puts it. 'He enjoyed considerable influence over whom that body employed.' Whatever his position may have been, Clive secured a job for Albert as a porter at North Road, Plymouth station. One wonders at the wisdom, not to mention the kindness, in anyone's finding a porter's job for a man with a bad back. Stewart Luke doesn't question it. It's plain he's never on Albert's side. In his view Albert was lucky to get any sort of employment. He couldn't have complained if he'd been thrown out to starve. Anyway, he took the job, no doubt having little choice, and though he walked the ten miles or so to Plymouth his first day he couldn't walk there and back daily, so lodged with his aunt, Mrs Bightford's sister Maria Mollick, who had a cottage five minutes from North Road station.

Albert Bightford was by now twenty years old. He appears to have led a solitary and dour existence, portering by day but speaking little to his fellow station employees, returning to his aunt's house, eating his evening meal and retiring early to bed. There was a working men's club in North Road at the time but Bightford did not visit its premises nor attend its meetings. Several of his fellows at the station invited him to partake of refreshment with them in the local hostelry but he always refused. It was remarked upon that he was never once heard to call any of them by their names. Even the station master, an august personage in these circles, who was addressed as 'Sir' was not so called by Bightford. He complained from time to time of pain in his back and of the peremptory way passengers spoke to him. Otherwise, he hardly spoke.

It sounds to our more empathetic twenty-first century ears as if Albert was suffering from chronic depression. Perhaps he'd been depressed for years but things were worse now he was separated from his family, his old home and the friends he perhaps had at Livesey Place. He knew no one but this aunt in Plymouth, he had no girl and no friends. Anyone in his situation today would call up sympathy and perhaps help from many quarters, he would be less isolated, he could have sought training for a trade and once over eighteen, lived on benefit until he got a job. Or that's how it looks. Maybe it's not that easy, but it's certainly easier than it was in Victorian England.

Of course, from this distance in time and with so little evidence it's hard to tell. Luke gives no help. Depression to him is a hollow place between hills. Albert may have suffered from something deeper and sadder than depression. It's possible he was schizophrenic. The contemporary attitude would have been to tell him to pull himself together, be a man, that work and bettering oneself are what matter. A working man can't have 'nerves' like the gentry, like a young lady. Over the distance of a hundred and twenty years one's heart goes out to Albert Bightford, lonely and confused and in pain.

He was rude to his fellows and silent with the passengers. One day in early October 1883, when the express drew into North Road from London, a man called Sir James Thripp, of Caraman House, Plymbridge, alighted from a first-class carriage and told Albert to bring his bags out to his brougham that had come to meet the train. Albert said nothing but obeyed.

Later he said that his back had been painful. Whatever the cause, he dropped one of Sir James's leather grips on the platform, for which Sir James, justifiably but perhaps harshly, reproved him with the words, 'Look sharp, you damned fool! There are breakables in that bag and you shall pay to the last farthing if any are broken.' Whereupon Bightford set down the luggage he was carrying and replied in a loud carrying tone, 'Call yourself a gentleman? If there is any fool here it is yourself!'

Very evidently he'd reached breaking point and he broke. So also did a glass case of rare butterflies Sir James was bringing home, for what purpose no one seems to know. The whole matter was reported at once to the station master, who was probably delighted to have a reason for getting rid of Albert. Nothing more seems to have been said about paying for the broken butterfly case.

Albert went home to Mrs Mollick. What happened between them isn't known. He seems to have stayed with her for rather more than a week, during which time he left the house only to loiter, mostly in silence, about the station platforms. Finally, he was told to leave and not come back. While Eleanor Henderson was enjoying herself at her aunt's, talking of her forthcoming wedding, appreciating the luxury of the house and walking (and bruising herself) with her cousins, Albert was either closeted with his, constantly berated perhaps for his conduct and no doubt repeatedly asked what he was going to do next, or hanging about North Road station. Mrs Mollick seems to have been a sharp-tongued woman who 'stood no nonsense'. However it was, after nine days, she turned him out, telling him to go home to his parents. Albert protested that he couldn't walk so far, he was ill and in constant pain. She insisted and he left her house at about ten on the morning of 20 October.

What was wrong with Albert's back? It sounds like a slipped disc. Or possibly he'd damaged his spine even more seriously. Young boys in the Nazi concentration camps, forced to move heavy machinery or carry loads, often did damage to their backs which, if they survived, lasted into old age. No doubt a similar thing happened to Victorian youths who were set to manual work without thought that they might be too young and too vulnerable for it. Did Bightford have baggage of his own to carry? We're not told, but he could hardly have taken up more or less permanent residence with Mrs Mollick and brought no belongings with him. Perhaps this particular morning was breaking point rather than when he was rude to Sir James Thripp. He is out in the street, in pain, carrying his own luggage, unable to get home and, in any case, afraid to confront his father. When the London express drew into Plymouth he gets on it. Meaning to go where, do what? No one knows. It's likely he didn't know himself.

Apparently, he bought a ticket to London, Paddington, so he intended to get as far as that. This last rail journey he ever made was also the first time in his life he'd ever been in a train. He sat in a third-class carriage – but not for long. It's not known what made him get up and walk through the train, complaining to anyone who'd listen that he'd been unfairly dismissed from his portering job. It was atypical behaviour for this morose and usually silent young man. Mental disturbance changes people's characters and this has to be the answer. I suppose.

The train passed through Newton Abbot, Teignmouth and Dawlish, followed the few miles of beautiful route along the South Devon coast and approached within a dozen miles of Exeter. Albert Bightford entered the carriage where Eleanor sat alone.

Here Stewart Luke digresses to give some family background. To him, writing in Edwardian times, long before women ceased to be defined by the men connected to them, the most important thing about Eleanor is her link with the eminent Dr Nanther. He continually refers to him as Lord Nanther, though Henry wasn't ennobled until thirteen years later. He gets his degrees and orders wrong (describing him as KCVO, an order of chivalry not instituted until 1896), his position in Queen Victoria's household and his age, describing him as being forty-five at the time of the murder. But he obviously reveres him. Brilliant Henry. Courtly Henry. Although he calls Eleanor 'the unfortunate young lady' and expresses suitable Edwardian shocked horror at the mode and manner of her death, it's Henry's loss he dwells on, the blighting of Henry's happiness and Henry's amazing devotion to the Henderson family after the loss of his 'betrothed'.

No attempt is made to account for Bightford's strangling Eleanor. Motive, of course, is of little significance in British justice. Perhaps, even then, people knew how hard it is to explain human actions, why any of us do the seemingly inexplicable things we do. Psychology and psychiatry can account for some of them but not all. The great mystery remains. Albert Bightford had no girlfriend, had apparently never had one. Was he attracted to Eleanor and did he make an advance which she repelled? He pulled the scarf from her neck – did he do so during an attempt at an embrace? Or did she insult him as Sir James had? Not when he dropped something of hers but when he tried to confide his miseries to her? 'He saw red,' Luke writes, using the old bullfighting metaphor not very helpfully. Why he makes no attempt to explain. Albert strangled Eleanor, opened the door or just the window, and threw her body from the train.

The rest of Stewart Luke's piece is mainly concerned with the trial itself. First he tells how Albert left the train at Exeter and went home to his parents at Tavistock. How he got there neither he nor anyone else seems to know. Walking the distance would have taken a couple of days but people did walk long distances in those days – remember Henry in Switzerland – and some did so when not in the best of health. Once at Livesey Place Albert must have asked his father to hide him and perhaps told his father he'd be wanted by the police but not why. Or he told him why, because he was driven to desperation, struggled to give some explanation for the most heinous of crimes. Whatever it was, Abel refused, turned Albert out and left him to be discovered sheltering in a shepherd's hut on Dartmoor. It's a cruel, miserable story as much for Albert Bightford as for my great-great-aunt Eleanor.

But is there another possible motive? Was Albert employed by someone else to do the deed? He might have done it for money. Fifty pounds would have been a fortune to him, twenty a great deal of money. He could have gone to America on it, gone almost anywhere, begun a new life. But if he was a hitman, paid to kill Eleanor, wouldn't he have told his father, told the police? What did he have to lose? And he'd surely have been paid first, or paid half first. Why not use this money to hide himself, to lose himself, which was not a difficult thing to do in 1883? No money was found on him. That means nothing, he may have hidden it somewhere, or even buried it on the Moor. None of this accounts for his failure to say anything about a conspiracy when he was captured.

I'm thinking, of course, of Henry. Henry had motive enough for killing Eleanor. His whole future happiness was at stake. If he married her he chanced having handicapped sons and carrier daughters. If he jilted her he stood to lose his position with the Queen and his reputation. But why pick Albert Bightford to do it for him? Did he even know Bightford? Perhaps, but how is another matter. Possibly he was acquainted with Harold Clive or Beatrice Withycombe or Sir James Thripp, all 'gentlefolk' quite likely to have been among his acquaintance. On the other hand, it may have been that Maria Mollick was related to one of his servants or was once employed by him or connected to the Dawson–Brewer family. Public records are obviously to be consulted here – then *Debrett*? Or maybe something called *Kelly's Handbook to the Titled, Landed and Official Classes*? It seems impossible now that the real truth can ever be discovered, but if something in Henry's life could show me that in 1883, between January and October, he made a train journey to or from Plymouth it would be a help. There's nothing in the diaries and nothing in Alternative Henry.

How am I going to find out?

27

My wife is telling me, in a quietly conversational tone, that sex is no longer necessary for us. Has that occurred to me? The important thing is for her eggs to be taken and my sperm produced. Of course, she says, it wouldn't matter if there were sex, all she's saying is that it's not a 'prerequisite'.

'Thanks very much,' I say, because all this is making me angry now. It's happening after they've secured her eggs and I, in humiliating circumstances, as you'd expect, have supplied the fertilizing elixir. If it doesn't work I'll have to do it all over again.

'It's worse for me, darling,' she says.

It probably is, but she wants this baby and I don't. My face is stiff with smiling and pretending. Still, I don't see any way out of all this simulation. The alternative is the end of our marriage. These past few weeks I've come to see that losing Jude – even the changed Jude she's becoming – would be the worst thing that could happen to me, the thing I can't contemplate without panic, without a sense of standing on the edge of an abyss. But to keep her, can I bear anything? The loss of this house, maybe three squalling babies, the imperative to give up writing and get some sort of job? Can I bear no sex with her?

'You didn't mean that, did you?' I ask. 'That sex wasn't necessary?'

'Oh, darling,' she says, but she doesn't touch me, she doesn't take my hand and kiss it. 'I was only saying such are the miracles of science that to have babies we don't need each other in that way.'

Babies. 'In that way.' It sounds like the sort of euphemism my great-grandmother Edith might have used. Jude and I go back home, the process set in motion, the die cast. I ought to sit down with her. I ought to open a bottle of champagne. Make the most of it before it's banned lest the twinnies are born with Foetal Alcohol Syndrome. I ought to drink a toast to our future as parents and plan the nursery in the top-floor flat we'll no doubt have to buy in Maida Vale. But I can't face any more and I go into my study instead to contemplate the stacks of Henry-history.

For a little while I just shift papers about, open folders and look at them unseeing. But the mystery of Henry still has the power to distract me and presently I'm once more caught up in his life. I've said there's nothing in the diaries or the notebook about a visit to Devon but I'll have to check them again. There are hundreds of letters, neatly filed according to the year they were sent and the name of the sender. One consolation is that I don't have to examine any written before 1862, the date of Albert Bightford's birth, or after 1883, the time of the murder. I've photocopied every letter I've got, but even so many of them have to be read with the aid of a magnifying glass.

The best (or the worst) discovery to make would be that Henry knew Harold Clive. Suppose, for instance, he and Richard Hamilton had been on a walking tour on Dartmoor some few years prior to Hamilton's death in 1879? There are dozens of letters from Hamilton in the collection and thirty from him to his sister Caroline. Hamilton's handwriting is clear and upright, thank God, and doesn't need magnification. But although there are plenty of references to walking trips with Henry in them, all these seem to have

357

been in Scotland and Yorkshire with a single excursion to the Peak District. In one of the last letters Hamilton ever wrote to his sister, the date October 1879, he refers to a holiday he's taken in south Cornwall some years before but that was a very long way from Dartmoor then, and though it's likely he passed through Plymouth to get there, Bightford was an under-gardener at Livesey Place at the time and had never yet been in a train nor, presumably, on a station platform.

I go through Henry's letters to his mother and Elizabeth Kirkford's to her mother but to no avail, and then my conscience smites me as it has a way of doing. I put the letters away, find Jude and open that champagne. She's so happy and pleased about everything she hasn't noticed my lukewarm response nor my ill-concealed dismay and she actually asks, for the first time for weeks, 'How's Henry getting on?'

I tell her and she says she's not surprised. 'I told you he was up to something.'

'Yes, but you said that about his reasons for marrying Edith.'

'So? Maybe he murdered Eleanor so that he could marry Edith. That's being up to something with a vengeance.'

I say I can't believe in a man of forty-seven falling in love at first sight with a woman he happens to see in the street and then, a few months later, falling out of love with her and into love with her sister.

'What makes you think love comes into it?'

'Not because I'm such a romantic,' I say. 'I can't think of any other reason for his wanting to marry either of them. Can you?'

'Maybe not. But you have to think of a reason for his murdering Eleanor.'

'Would discovering his prospective bride was a haemophilia carrier be a reason?'

She asks if there's any evidence for it and I say that there is. My explanation comes out a bit diffidently because I can tell she's thinking of what she carries herself but she's also thinking things are very different today, so she smiles and says I'm on the right track. We drink the champagne and go out to eat and it's like old times. I can't help noticing that as we go downhill there's always the occasional good evening when we're like we used to be, but even these are a fraction paler, a little bit less fervent, the mutual love growing infinitesimally weaker. The lovemaking that follows is good because I force myself to forget how it used to be.

I spend the morning reading the rest of the letters and get nowhere. Mary Craddock writes to her sister Elizabeth Kirkford in 1936 about a holiday she and her husband intend to take in Torquay, but that and Eleanor's letter from Manaton are the only references to Devon in any of the correspondence. After lunch I go off to consult the Public Records. It takes me hours but I don't find much. Or not much in the way of answers to my questions.

I do discover that Abel Bightford, Albert's father, died in early 1885, not much more than a year after his son's execution. He was only forty-three. Both the sisters married but not men whose family names occur anywhere in the letters or diaries. Jane Bightford and her sister Maria Mollick had fourteen siblings, but again none of them was connected to names appearing in any Henry documents. Harold Clive had been born at Livesey Place but his wife Anne came from London. Before her marriage she had been called Dixon and her birth had taken place in Wimpole Street.

This establishes some sort of link with Henry but a tenuous one considering that she was born in 1829, some forty-three years before he set up in practice there. Still, I'll follow it up.

The Clives had no children. Nor, of course, did the single lady, Beatrice Withycombe, who appears to have been their friend. She was born in Tavistock and died there. If she was a distant cousin of Henrys there's nothing to show it. The only point of interest is that her grandmother's maiden name was Brewer, which brings me a feverish excitement at first, but as far as I can trace it back, from a completely different family from the Brewers of Euston (or, come to that, the Lord Brewer who bought my robe). Sir James Thripp was born in Highgate, seems to have lived in Richmond from the evidence of the births of his children there, and was married to a woman who had been a Justinia Gould.

If Henry paid Albert Bightford to kill Eleanor it looks as if he must have become acquainted with him on the platform at North Road, Plymouth when Bightford carried his bags from the train. But if he paid a visit to Plymouth, wouldn't he have noted it somewhere in his diary for 1883? It was just the sort of thing he did note. No emotion, not a scrap of feeling, insight, observation, but only economical comment on journeys he made or was about to make. And he was very fond of trains. But would he have recorded this trip if during the course of it he set Bightford up as his hitman? No, but he would surely have noted down that he was about to make the trip, not knowing then that he would encounter Bightford on the station platform.

The difficulty here is that it's preposterous. I try to imagine it and I can't. Here is this respectable and distinguished gentleman, a Knight and royal physician, forty-seven years old, probably wearing a tailcoat and high silk hat, suddenly taking it into his head that the youth who's humping his luggage would make a suitable murderer of his young fiancée. So he gets the youth's name and address and that same evening leaves his hotel or the private house where he's staying, pops round to Mrs Mollick's, and conspires with the youth to bump off Eleanor, paying him fifteen quid in advance. It won't do. It won't do for a moment. However it may have happened, if it happened, it wasn't like that.

Jude has alerted me to another difficulty. If Henry murdered Eleanor to remove the possibility of his becoming the father of haemophiliac children, why on earth did he stick around and marry her sister? For there was absolutely no reason why, simply because Eleanor was a carrier, her sister wouldn't be. Two of Queen Victoria's daughters were carriers as were two of the daughters of her daughter Alice of Hesse. Henry knew this better than anyone. And we now know that Edith was a carrier. The argument might be that he didn't kill Eleanor because he suspected she was a carrier, but because he'd fallen in love with her sister. I find this as preposterous as the theory that he met Bightford on a station platform.

The whole thing is a mystery because as it stands it involves people behaving out of their natures, the way people don't behave. They don't do such things. I present myself with an account of what I think would have happened, given the cast of characters. Henry saw Eleanor in the street, fell in love with her, found out who she was and rigged up the mugging of her father to get to know her. This I can just about accept. He engages himself to Eleanor, then finds out from her mother that she bruises and bleeds easily and that Louisa Henderson had a brother who died young from haemophilia. Immediately he realizes that his fiancée may be a carrier. But he doesn't plot to kill her. His whole way of life, upbringing and training, respectability and reputation, recoil from such an act. Anyway, it wouldn't cross his mind. He must extricate himself from the engagement.

This is tricky, especially since he's already stood up Olivia, and he postpones the interviews he must have with Eleanor and her father. Meanwhile, Eleanor is murdered in a train by a crazy boy, suffering from clinical depression or schizophrenia. That lets Henry out. Free, he can do the decent thing and commiserate with the bereaved parents. And the bereaved sister.

Out of the frying pan and into the fire, he marries that sister? No. Never. It's absurd. But he did.

Henry's practice was in Wimpole Street and Anne Clive was born there, seven houses apart. So the houses were not very far from each other. She was twenty-one when she married Harold Clive and that was in 1850, by which time it appears her family no longer lived there, since her father Richard Dixon died the following year in a house in Bloomsbury. I can't neglect this sort of thing, though I'm coming increasingly to believe Henry had nothing to do with the murder. Jude, on the other hand, is adamant that he did. But she hates him, in so far as you can hate a man who died half a century before you were born. I don't mind what she believes, I'm just so pleased she can talk about something other than ova and sperm quality and multiple births.

'You do realize, don't you,' she says, 'that you don't absolutely know what this talk Louisa Henderson had with Henry was about? All you know is from his diary that she had a consultation with him. It may not have been about her daughter. She may have thought she'd got cancer herself, she may have had a haemorrhage or she may even have just had a bad nosebleed. God knows, I've had enough bleeds and I'm not a carrier of haemophilia. Why shouldn't she just have asked him about something like I've had?'

It's true. I'd made what I thought was an intelligent guess. I'd no evidence.

'How old was she? Forty-five? Forty-six? She could have thought she was pregnant. Or having the menopause. You've thought this up because you can't think of any other way Henry might have suspected Eleanor was a carrier.'

'There was the bruising too.'

'Yes, but she mentions it in a letter to her sister Edith, not to Henry. She could have told him but you don't know that she did. You're adapting the facts to fit your theory.'

'Then how did Henry know?'

'He didn't know. That's the only explanation, the only one that fits the facts.'

'Then we come up against coincidence again. The enormous coincidence that Henry, the top haemophilia specialist, married by chance a woman who was a carrier.'

'Coincidences do happen, Martin.'

'And you still think Henry murdered Eleanor?'

'I do. But not because she might have been a carrier. Because he wanted her out of the way in order to marry her sister. It's an irony, if you like to think of it that way, a man murdering one girl because she was possibly a carrier and marrying, as a result of this act, another who certainly was.'

Then Jude says something highly significant, a change from her usual determined efforts to make Henry a murderer at any price. She's looking at David Croft-Jones's family tree.

'Where did the haemophilia come from?'

I say firmly, 'A mutation in Louisa Henderson's mother's cells.'

'Why should it have been a mutation at all?'

'No reason. It's just that John Corrie told me about a third of all cases of haemophilia result from mutation. Take Queen Victoria, for instance. There's no evidence of haemophilia in her ancestry, though all kinds of speculation are rife, one being that some young haemophiliac was her father rather than the ageing Duke of Kent.' Jude's not interested in Queen Victoria. She takes her republicanism to great lengths.

'If a third of all cases result from mutation, double that number don't. Have you tried tracing the haemophilia back?'

'It would be very difficult,' I say. 'We'd have to go back before records began. Louisa was born in eighteen thirty-seven.'

'Just the same, I think you should try. Do you know the names of her parents?'

'William Quendon and Luise Dornford.'

'You pronounced her mother's name "Leweesa".'

'In the German way, yes.'

Jude, who's a German speaker, obviously doesn't think much of my accent. She asks if I mean this Luise was German, do I know, and I have to tell her I don't, I just assume she was. It seems of no importance. 'I think I know the answer, anyway,' I say. 'I think it was this way. Henry was in love with Eleanor and he didn't know anything about her bruising or heavy bleeding or any of that. The consultation her mother had with him was about something entirely different, her own menopause or a cold in the head, anything. He and Eleanor became engaged with the approval of her family, she went to visit her aunt in Devon and on the way back was murdered in the train. Henry grieved along with the Henderson family and, seeing them so often, sharing their grief, realized that he had a duty towards them. He owed it to them, trusting him and admiring him as they did, to marry their surviving daughter. Duty was very important to these Victorians. And why not marry Edith? Remember he knew nothing of the haemophilia. No one did, none of the Hendersons did. It was just in there, lying dormant.'

Jude says, but gently, 'That has to be rubbish, my darling. He murdered her. He paid Bightford to murder her.'

28

I've reached an impasse with Henry. It's a month since I've done any real research. The last step I took to uncover the mystery of how haemophilia got into my family was to ring up Veronica and ask her if she knew the names of any of Edith Nanther's female forebears.

She sounded less than pleased to hear who it was. 'I've already told you everything I know and a lot more than I wanted to.'

'You haven't told me what your great-great-grandmother and great-great-great-grandmother were called.'

'All these greats,' she said in a very impatient way. 'It's ridiculous, it's so far back. Who cares any more? What can it possibly matter?'

'It matters to me, Veronica. It may be important.'

'Yes, I'm sure. In your judgement. Well, all right. But this is absolutely all I know. Lady Nanther' – this ancestress we have in common suddenly ceased to be a relative and became a peeress – 'Lady Nanther's mother's mother was called Dornford and *her* mother Mayback.'

Or that's what I heard. I asked her to spell it. She didn't want to but when I tell her David will want these names, they will be indispensable for his tree she becomes more willing.

'All right then. M-a-i-b-a-c-h.' Before I could get a word in she says, 'But she wasn't German, I can assure you of that. It's a very rare old English name like her christian name. That was Barbla.'

'Barbara?' I said, thinking she'd developed a lisp.

'No, Barbla. B–a–r–b–l–a.'

Veronica is seriously xenophobic. She kept and keeps on insisting Maibach wasn't a German name. I don't argue, there's no point. 'I have no foreign ancestry,' she said. The very idea, that I could even have thought of it shocked her. I was not to let David get the wrong impression. She'd phone him and tell him the whole family is pure English as far back as anyone can go.

But David, I later realize, has other things on his mind. Georgie is pregnant again. The Holy Grail is only seven months old and Georgie is still breastfeeding him, but still she is pregnant again. She pretends dismay, but in fact she's bursting with pride at her fecundity, a pure matter of physiology over which she has no control and has done nothing to promote. Much the same attitude in fact as Veronica's pride in her genetic purity and mine, before I knew the truth, in my own.

'I can't imagine how it happened!'

She's said it a dozen times with wide-eyed smiling incredulity. If she belonged rather lower down the social scale and was inclined to vulgarity she'd say David only has to hang his trousers over the end of the bed for her to be in the family way. Jude makes no comment on any of this. She hasn't even mentioned it to me when we're alone. I believe she feels none of it has anything to do with her, she's a special case. Not for her this simple trouble-free fertility. When the time is ripe she will have a designer baby. It's almost as if it's another kind of thing altogether, because it will start off very differently from David and Georgie's easy fruitful coupling and the result too will be different.

PGD is what she is going to have, Preimplantation Genetic Diagnosis. Only four clinics in the country do it at present and hers happens to be one of them. The last time she went there she came back and told me a heart-warming tale of a woman she met who'd had triplets as a result of the technique. David and Georgie are going to sell their flat and buy a house because the flat isn't big enough for two kids but, paradoxically, it would be for three or four (or so Jude thinks, I believe) so we could do a swap and they buy our house. Jude doesn't care. She doesn't think or speak of anything much but babies. Full of hope and anticipation, she is simply waiting, biding her time until they say, now is the moment, tomorrow or next week or in two weeks' time is the day we take your eggs and *his* sperm.

All this has brought me a kind of affinity with Henry, though. Poor Henry. Sometimes, surely, astounded Henry. That he of all people should marry a haemophilia carrier. The woman who was his wife and the mother of his children carried this tainted faulty thing, had now given birth to a haemophiliac son – and to how many carrier daughters? He who had warned King Alfonso not to marry the Princess Ena had himself done the very thing he cautioned the King against. Did he *tell* his daughters? Did he alert them to the consequences they might expect from marriage? In the case of the eldest did he warn young James Kirkford as he'd warned Alfonso? We don't know. But someone warned them or they somehow found out.

Isn't the fact that they knew of the family inheritance the true reason behind Helena and Clara's decision not to marry? I haven't done any research but I keep looking at my copy of David's amended tree, pondering and wondering. In the Quendon–Henderson line it doesn't go back any further than Barbla Maibach and the man she married, Thomas Dornford. David, temporarily indifferent to genealogy, couldn't find their forebears or he hasn't yet tried. Barbla

368

married Thomas and they had a daughter called Luise. They had three sons too. Next to one of them David has put the initials 'd.y.' for 'died young' and beside the others only question marks. He hasn't christian names for any of them. Luise married William Quendon and had two daughters and a son, Louisa, William and Maria. Louisa was my great-grandmother Edith's mother and Henry's mother-in-law. What happened to Maria isn't clear. William died aged seven. Of haemophilia is what I guessed when I was trying to prove Henry a murderer but it's only a guess. Louisa married Samuel Henderson and became the mother of Lionel, Eleanor and Edith.

Did William Quendon meet his German (or German-christian-*named*) bride Luise in this country or in Europe? When did he go to Germany or Austria, and why? People didn't pop across to Europe a dozen times a year in 1830 the way they do now, unless they were rich or grand or both, in which case they might have done the Grand Tour. Perhaps he was and perhaps he did. When I do get back into my research I shall have to look into this. I roll up the tree. It's no more use to me now.

I miss the House of Lords. Not in the recesses. Over Christmas and the New Year as well as in the slack times I barely noticed my banishment but now, at the end of February, when the House is getting busy again and the politics pages of newspapers are full of altercations among peers, *bons mots* from Earl Russell and quips from Lord McKay of Ardbrecknish, I feel great spasms of nostalgia and a real sense of the gates of paradise shut in my face. Not that it seemed much like paradise when I was in there, staying late at night to do a self-imposed duty, supporting a party I didn't belong to and whose whip I hadn't taken. I've given up taking Hansard, but I can't resist reading the papers.

I miss walking in through the Peers' Entrance, hanging my coat on the Nanther peg, mounting the great staircase, dropping into the Printed Paper Office to pick up the order paper and the amendments to a bill. But most of all I miss entering the Chamber, making a court bow to the mysterious invisible Cloth of Estate and taking my place on the cross-benches. Well, maybe not most of all. I greatly miss my expenses, which, because I haven't been in there since the beginning of November, would have amounted to not far short of five thousand pounds.

PGD is going to cost us £2,500 a go. And very likely there will be at least two goes.

Both Lachlan and Stanley Farrow have invited me into the House for dinner. I've said a regretful no. I've done it once and I don't feel like doing it again, facing the embarrassment of hanging about and waiting for them to find me in some area of the Palace open to the public. I can't face walking into the dining room and having to pause and chat with a dozen old acquaintances, not to mention sitting tight, and pretending to read the menu when the division bell rings and they go off to vote. So do I wish I was back there? Not entirely. Sometimes not at all. But perhaps what I do wish is that I'd never been in there in the first place, for I'm no adherent to the theory that it's better to have loved and lost than never to have loved at all.

The House was a club to me as well as a legislative assembly. I do still have the right to book a table in the guest dining room *once a month*, but I suppose I'm too proud to avail myself of it and invite David in for a drink or a meal when he phones and says he wants to talk to me. Jude won't have the Croft-Joneses to dinner here at the moment and I don't blame her. She says it's not that she minds seeing the

Holy Grail or hearing about the coming child, but that she's embarrassed by the way Georgie goes on, the pride she takes in conceiving 'without trying' and in that weedy owlish David's potency. So we must meet outside, in a pub or something, and he selects the Prince Alfred in Formosa Street.

He's there before me, drinking red wine, not being a beer man, and he launches straight into a request that Jude and I consider selling our house to them. Jude, apparently, in spite of her embarrassment at Georgie's boasting, has told her about the PGD. This doesn't exactly delight me as I don't much want the Croft-Joneses thinking we're on our uppers. I tell David I'm not thinking of selling. If Jude has a couple of children – I say it airily, great actor that I am – I'll need a big house. This takes him aback. His wife or mine must have given him the idea I'd jump at the chance. I take advantage of his silence to apologize for springing haemophilia on him and I explain how it's impossible for him and Georgie to have affected children. Of course it's not impossible, Georgie might herself be a carrier or a spontaneous mutation might take place in her cells, but I say nothing of this, only that he can't pass the family gene on.

'I've talked to my GP,' he says. 'He said what you said, only with expertise.'

Thanks. I ask him if this has put his mind at rest and he says it has, especially with the new baby on the way. Has he spoken to his mother again? Apparently, she phoned him, indignantly wanting to know where I'd got the idea from that her ancestors were German. She won't have it Barbla was anything but English, though she doesn't know, she's trusting to her instincts. She hates Germans even more than she hates Russians and Japanese, and come to that, the

French, she has done all her life. He says that she's told him William Quendon met his wife Luise in this country. Her father, Thomas Dornford, was a jeweller in Hatton Garden. Her mother Barbla had died in childbirth, giving birth to her second daughter, but David hasn't put her death date into his tree because he doesn't know it, and Veronica didn't know it. Nor did she know precisely where Thomas Dornford met Barbla Maibach.

Yesterday was the day. I managed it with some difficulty and, going into no details, it didn't take long. I suppose I'd worked myself up into such a state of horror at the prospect that the reality couldn't have possibly been so bad. The ancient hospital sample was the first pornography I've looked at since I was eighteen and I think it was the same magazine. Jude's eggs were taken and now we wait to know what can be grown out of the mix. I've decided I don't want to hear how many of the embryos whose cells they test have the abnormality – remember my sperm may carry it too – and Jude doesn't want to know either. All we want, all she wants, is to know they've found some healthy ones ready for implantation.

What would Henry think if he could know? Would he be fascinated, approving, delighted at this culminating breakthrough in a series of steps to put an end to inherited disorders? Or resentful that it didn't happen a hundred years before? Would his pleasure be overwhelmed by his knowledge of the suffering men and women used to endure from their inability to limit their families or prevent abnormality? Would he think of children like his son George who, with these techniques, would in a few years from now never again be born?

Strangely enough, I feel a lot better now the deed's

done or the die cast or whatever. Presumably, since there's nothing in Jude's reproductive process that makes her miscarry, only the fact that she carries damaged foetuses, once she's pregnant with a sound one she'll carry it to term. Or am I being naïve and ignorant? Does the implantation itself conduce to the foetus aborting? I don't know and I don't want to know. If I tell myself often enough that I want this child, I'm going to want it in the very nature of things. I reason it's a bit like the Alexander Technique. Repeat commands to the body often enough – 'let the neck be free', 'the head to go forwards and upwards' – and it will automatically respond. The same with the mind, surely. I want this baby, I want this baby, I even want *three* babies . . .

But I'm feeling better and able to get back to Henry research properly. To this end I've got out my Bulloch and Fildes and I'm checking that it's possible for haemophilia to lie dormant for several generations in cases when only female children are born. And it seems that it is, though in most cases the gene doesn't really lie dormant at all. Male children are born, they have haemophilia and they die young from it. In my own family we find William Quendon (probably) succumbing to it at the age of seven and later on Kenneth Kirkford doing the same, at the age of nine. While I'm going through the various tables, David phones. I ask after Georgie. She, as always, is fine, and the Holy Grail is fine and what do I think of Yseult as a name if the expected one is a girl? Not much, I say. No one will be able to pronounce it. I didn't know how to pronounce it myself until I heard him do it and then spell it out.

After that I go back to Bulloch and Fildes. Jude is in bed already. She's sleeping away the time, she says, until they implant in her the healthy embryos. I scan the tables, all the statistics from Tenna and the neighbouring villages the haemophilia investigators compiled. And it's then it happens. The name jumps out at me from all the other names: Maibach. And not just Maibach but Barbla Maibach. It can't be my one, my great-great-great-great-grandmother, the date's too early even for her, being back in the early eighteenth century, but it's a collateral ancestress of hers, her father's sister or aunt maybe. I must have seen it a dozen times before, I've been through these lists so often, but of course I'd no reason to notice it. There are a lot of other Barblas. It seems to be a local name, or a local diminutive of Barbara.

At least one of my questions is answered. Edith Nanther's great-grandmother wasn't German, she was Swiss. And she came from an area of Switzerland well-known for its concentration of haemophiliacs and haemophilia carriers. How on earth did she get to England and marry Thomas Dornford? People didn't leave the Safiental. That was the point, that was why in-breeding perpetuated haemophilia, carriers marrying 'bleeders' and producing whole families of afflicted offspring. Bulloch and Fildes says:

The Village of Tenna as described by Hoessli lies on the south-eastern slopes of Piz Riein in the Canton [sic] Graubünden and consisted of several widely separated groups of houses scattered over the meadow slopes. Communication between these houses and the outside world must be established over broken and in many places dangerous tracts. At the time Hoessli wrote, there were no driving roads, the journey having to be made on foot, and a traveller would require four to six hours to reach Versam . . .

It tells me to consult the accompanying map, so I do, but it's small, basic and not much help. I find our heavy world atlas and turn to the Switzerland page. Hoessli, a doctor practising in Thusis, was writing about the area in 1877, probably getting on for a hundred years after Thomas Dornford's visit or Barbla Maibach's escape, and then conditions would presumably have been worse. Why does the passage ring a bell with me? Why does the name Versam ring a bell? I don't know, but perhaps it's only because some friend went skiing there and sent us a postcard. The canton is Grisons and the nearest big town is Chur, and it doesn't look very big on the map.

I must go there. That's my immediate reaction. Look at the records, the archives. I must go there when the snows have gone. Say in late April or May. Then of course I know I can't, it's not possible, for Jude will either be in the early stages of pregnancy with these current implants or preparing for the next lot.

My difficulty about going to Philadelphia was solved by John Corrie coming here to me. I can't expect the entire population of a Swiss village to pop over, bringing their archives with them. I can't go and they can't come, but I *must* go.

29

I don't recognize Lucy when she comes into the restaurant. Of course I've never seen her before, though I've seen a photograph of her as a child, and somehow I expect the Nanther face and colouring to have taken over as she grew up. It hasn't. She's a plumpish little woman, blonde and very pretty, wearing a pale lilac suit with a short skirt that shows off her excellent legs.

'Lucy,' she says, and holds out her hand. 'How do you do?'

The other hand has a wedding ring on it and a big diamond engagement ring. Her voice isn't like her, but rich, low and dark. When we spoke on the phone that first time I wasn't sure for a moment if this was a woman or a man. I tell her it's very nice of her to agree to meet me like this and offer her a drink. She smiles, asks for white wine and studies the menu with the enthusiasm of someone fond of her food.

'Did you know our great-great-grandfather was a solicitor? He was called Samuel Henderson and it was his daughter married Henry Nanther.'

She nods. 'I know quite a bit about the family.'

'From your mother?'

'My mother never talked about her ancestors. What I know I got from Great-aunt Clara.'

For some reason I'm very surprised. Clara has had her own importance for me, deriving from that strange letter from her to Alexander which Sarah sent me, the one in which she calls her father 'Henry Nanther' and mentions the woman he kept in Primrose Hill. The fact that she was great-aunt to quite a few other people never seemed to have impinged on my consciousness. 'You knew her?'

'Not until a few years before she died.'

That explains it. When I found Lucy in David's tree I would have remembered if Clara had ever mentioned her. But I never saw Clara after Helena died and she became too infirm to continue living alone in that big house. She had gone off – of her own free will, my father would never have coerced her or even tried to persuade her – to live in sheltered housing, her small flat with its alarm that summoned the warden, its daily help and its aids to getting about the rooms and taking baths. I feel a twinge of conscience because I'd never asked after her that I can remember, and though she'd been kind to me – I recall the teas she gave us on those occasional Sunday afternoons – I'd never expressed a desire or a duty to visit her. But I was away at university, living as students live, and I didn't think of these things. Yet Lucy had gone to see her, must have got to know her quite well. Why?

Wine is poured and our order is taken. 'My mother used to visit her a bit,' Lucy says. 'You do know who my mother was, don't you? Diana Bell, born Craddock, the second daughter of Henry and Edith's second daughter. Jennifer and I were at boarding school but we did see Clara. I don't want to give the impression we often went, I don't suppose we did above, say, four or five times. Mum took us once in the school holidays. Then Jenny and I went a couple of times without her. Clara had been in that flat of hers for years by then, she was well into her nineties, but she could still more or less look after herself and she was absolutely compos mentis. Very bright, actually. Very clever.'

'Clara?'

She gives me a shrewd look. It's one of those looks feminists give men they think are making groundless assumptions about women. I'm not really, I'm not that sort of man, but I recognize the look. It sits oddly on her Marilyn Monroe face but accords with her voice when she says, 'Why not Clara? If she didn't become anything, if she didn't have a profession or make much of her life, that wasn't her fault. She didn't get the chance. She wanted to be a doctor. I don't suppose you knew that.'

'I did, as a matter of fact. It's in one of your grandmother's letters to her sister Elizabeth Kirkford.'

'Women could,' she says, 'but it was difficult, it would have been quite a battle. Too much for poor Clara, I'm sure.' She looks up as our first course comes. 'My sister's a doctor, she's a paediatrician.' That makes the second of Henry's descendants to enter the medical profession. 'The last time we saw Clara was the year before she died, in nineteen eight-nine. Jennifer must have been twenty-two or three and doing her training. Clara was so *pleased* that Jennifer was doing what she couldn't do.'

We've wandered a long way from the point and I have to get her back to it. I have to concentrate my mind on this pretty girl (a term she wouldn't like) and the food and adding information to my stock of Henry knowledge instead of what I'm doing, which is thinking about Jude in the clinic, having healthy embryos implanted. Two weeks after today we'll know. They'll do a pregnancy test and if it's positive . . . I'm about as far from the point myself as can be and Lucy's talking happily away, apparently oblivious of me, about her sister's brilliance at medical school, the accolades she's had from all sorts of people – just like Henry in fact. She's glad their mother lived long enough to see Jennifer's success.

So far, on the phone or here, haemophilia hasn't been mentioned. And now I'm face to face with her I'm shy about mentioning it. I suddenly think I haven't handled this very well. She's told me she's a carrier. 'Have you—' I begin hesitantly, 'have you any children?'

'Not yet.' She says it sharply and looks me in the eye. Suddenly her voice and her manner soften and she says, 'Look, can I call you Martin?'

'What else?' I say. I'm considerably taken aback.

'I don't know, only you're a lord, aren't you?'

Lords were two a penny where I used to be every day. I never get used to other people being overawed by a peer's title. 'You're my cousin. Please call me Martin.'

'OK, Martin. You asked if I had children because of the haemophilia, didn't you?'

I nod.

She takes a sip of her wine, rather more than a sip. 'I haven't. Not yet.'

'What made you have yourself tested? Did your mother tell you?'

She laughs at that. 'What, as part of the facts of life lesson? The home sex education? I don't remember our ever having any of that. Mum never said a word.'

'Did she know?'

'She said not. When I asked her, that is. Then she refused to believe it. She simply wouldn't have it discussed.'

I tell her that her aunt Patricia knew. She must have, in order to write that letter to Veronica.

'Ah, yes,' she says. 'But did she admit to herself she might be a carrier? I don't think so. There was a sort of wishful thinking going on. I don't know if you know there was a theory in the family that if one sister was a carrier the next one wouldn't be, though the third one might and so on.

379

Absolute rubbish, of course, but my grandmother Mary believed it. At least, according to Clara, she did.'

I begin to see the light. 'You found out from Clara?'

'That's right. Didn't I say? It wasn't far from us, where she lived, only Ealing, and we were in Chiswick. Teenage kids like talking to very old people, you know, they feel closer to them than to the generation above theirs. Clara had masses of photographs and a great fund of stories about living in that house in St John's Wood all that time ago. She remembered going to suffragette meetings and the fight to get votes for women and how angry her dad was when he found out. One day – I must have been eighteen or nineteen by then – she told me about the haemophilia. It wasn't done spitefully or in a sensational sort of way, she hesitated quite a bit before she did, she said she'd given it a lot of thought and it had been preying on her mind.'

'You mean she thought her sister Mary as likely to have been a carrier as her sister Elizabeth?'

'I shouldn't but I'd like another glass of wine, please.' I've been dilatory and I apologize. Just at that moment the waiter comes up and refills our glasses. I can see Lucy is finding this talk a bit of a strain. She plainly isn't going to finish her main course and she sets down her knife and fork. 'Clara said,' she goes on, 'that when she was a girl, while her father was alive and after his death, she tried to read some of his books. It's sad, really, very sad, this poor woman desperate for knowledge and having the means of getting it denied her all the time. Her mother was practically illiterate, you know. All she could do was paint bad pictures and take photographs. Mary was terribly churchy, always running around doing good works in the parish, and Helena – well, Helena sewed. Apparently, the house was crammed with stuff Helena had sewn, embroidery or whatever.' Lucy pauses, says, 'I'm sorry, I can't eat any more. My appetite always goes when I talk about it.'

'The haemophilia,' I say gently.

'Yes. She read her father's books, she was interested and she got to know quite a lot. She was only seventeen when her brother George died but she knew what was wrong with him, she knew it wasn't tuberculosis.'

'You mean George's mother didn't? His other sisters didn't?'

'Clara said no one ever talked about it. She'd seen George bleed when he hurt himself the way no one else she'd ever seen bleed. She'd seen him in bed for weeks on end just because he'd fallen over.'

I ask if she'd never tried to discuss it with other members of the family.

'She was scared of her dad. They all were – except George. If anyone said they wanted to know something but they daren't ask Father, George would laugh and say why not. Father was the sweetest kindest man, who'd never said a cross word to him. He was the best father in the world.'

I shake my head in astonishment. I'm reproaching myself for never talking to Clara, for never securing all this for myself.

'Clara did eventually ask her mother,' Lucy says. 'She said something like, George has haemophilia, hasn't he? Why do you all say it's consumption? That was the word they used, consumption. Edith just said – quite nicely apparently, she never lost her temper, raised her voice, got cross – she just said she didn't know what Clara was talking about. Women didn't understand these things. Her father knew best. In the end, a couple of weeks before George died, she did ask her father. It must have taken a lot of courage.'

'What did he say?'

'He was distraught over George. He hadn't long to live himself. She came to him in his study, knocked on the door of course. He asked her in and what she wanted. She told me all this, it was sort of printed on her memory. She asked him if she was right and George was a haemophiliac. Henry got to his feet, and said very coldly. "Never speak of this again." He pointed to the door and said, "Now go!"'

We're both silent for a moment, then Lucy says, 'George died two weeks afterwards. He was in the garden and he fell down some steps. Clara said he developed a huge sort of contusion on his head. His knee where he'd fallen was swollen like a balloon. That's how she put it, like a balloon. He seems to have died of some sort of stroke. Henry shut himself up in his study for three days. He didn't eat. He had a carafe of water in there. No one knew if he came out in the night or if he slept. He came out for the funeral and wept right through the service. Edith brought him home, made him go to bed and sent for the doctor. She could do anything with him, but no one else could.'

Poor Henry. Poor Henry, loving someone deeply at last. 'I'm taking it for granted Kenneth Kirkford, Elizabeth's son, had haemophilia.'

'So Clara said. He had it but it was diphtheria that he died of. That enabled Elizabeth to put it about that he *only* had diphtheria. But Clara knew, she'd seen his swollen joints and recognized them for what they were. She told Mary and Helena. Mary wasn't married then but she'd picked up this old wives' tale that a second sister couldn't carry it if a first one did. That's the way they thought it was in the royal family, though actually it wasn't.'

'Then who told Mary's daughter Patricia?'

Lucy smiles and puts up her eyebrows. 'I don't know everything, Martin. I don't know that. Maybe she got it from Clara too. Clara would only have been a bit over thirty when Patricia was born. She told me she'd had a couple of chances to marry but she hadn't because of the haemophilia. I don't think Helena even had the chances.'

I have to ask the awkward question. Lucy's sitting quietly, looking rather depressed. Her face was made for smiling, for happiness, and the sadness that's come over it ages her. She's suddenly much older in looks than Jude, the corners of her mouth drooping and lines furrowing her forehead. Neither of us can eat any more. We've ordered coffee. While we wait for it I have to ask the question.

'What made you think you might be a carrier?'

'Everything I've told you I told my sister. Not immediately. When she was nearly eighteen. I was about to take the Law Society's exams, she was at medical school. She asked me if I understood this might mean both of us were carriers or one of us was. Just because the gene had been hiding in there for a hundred years meant nothing.'

'If it was on the X chromosome,' I say, 'that Mary *didn't* pass on to her daughters it would have died out. But if it was on the one she did pass on . . .'

'Exactly. Jenny and I hadn't any idea of marriage then. Of course we hadn't, this was nineteen eighty-four, we were only young. Jenny hasn't now. She doesn't want marriage and she doesn't want kids and, ironically' – she gives me a rueful smile – 'she's not a carrier and I am. We were both tested as soon as it was possible. I told my husband when we were thinking of marrying. That made no difference, he said, and we went ahead. I'd made up my mind to give up the idea of children but now – well, they're just starting to do a sorting out of embryos and . . .'

'Preimplantation Genetic Diagnosis,' I say, interrupting her. 'My wife's having it. Today, as a matter of fact.'

'But she can't be a haemophilia carrier!'

'I suppose she could be but she's not. It's another faulty gene she carries.' To comfort her I say, 'It's worse in a way. She miscarries all the time and if our baby was born it would be – well, grossly disabled.'

'I'm sorry,' she says, and she really looks sorry.

'I have a son by my first marriage.' I don't know why I bother to say this, why I always say it. Probably, it's because of this ridiculous vanity I have that I don't seem to be able to suppress, this absurd pride in the fact that I *can* produce a healthy child. I'm as bad as Georgie Croft-Jones, so pleased with herself because she's almost uncontrollably fertile. I stop this nonsensical boasting and add, 'I carry it too.' Suddenly I long to know how Jude's getting on, what's happening, though nothing much can be, and no one will know anything more for another fortnight.

The coffee comes and Lucy tells me she and her husband have made one attempt to conceive a haemophilia-free child but it's failed and they're going to try again in a week's time. She wants to know if the gene's shown itself anywhere else in the family and I tell her about John Corrie. She seems strangely comforted by the fact that he's chosen not to have children and she, as she repeats, has refused to have anything but a 'designer baby'.

'There's still Caroline Agnew,' I say, 'Patricia's daughter. She's your first cousin. What's happened to her?'

Lucy says she's never met her. Or she may have met her when she was a baby but Caroline is ten years older and would be forty-seven by now. Jennifer had a letter from her when their mother Diana died – why Jennifer and not she, she doesn't know. She answered the letter but heard no more.

I ask if there was any information about her in the letter.

Lucy says rather dryly that if I mean, did she say whether or not she was a carrier of haemophilia, no she didn't. It was all about her having pleasant memories of Diana and about the last time she saw her being in Clara's flat.

'Did your mother ever mention this?'

'I don't remember it. But it may have been years ago while I was away at university. We're none of us great letter writers.'

For the past ten minutes I've been thinking of phoning the clinic as soon as I can get to a phone box but after I've said goodbye to Lucy and we've made one of those empty promises to keep in touch, I get in a taxi and go there instead.

There's nothing to be done now but wait. The Long Wait, they call it at the hospital, the fourteen days between replacing the embryos and taking a pregnancy test. In our case they extend between a date in March and a date in April. There are no measures Jude can take to improve the chances of the three tiny pinhead size embryos, no vitamins to help, no supplements, though she's supposed to avoid strenuous exercise and alcohol. She's so desperate for this to work I think she'd happily avoid *food* if it would assist success. I'm desperate for it to work in order to make her happy – or keep her happy.

She's not exactly happy now, though, for she hovers and trembles between laughter and tears, desperate sometimes for distractions from her all-absorbing ambition, then guilty because she's superstitiously afraid that if she stops thinking about it for a single moment her indifferent womb may go back on her and reject these foetuses through lack of her *wanting them enough*. It's all madness.

★

385

There are just eleven days to go now and she's fine. I think about hope again, that treacherous virtue, how it fills her body and soul, revitalizes her, makes her look ten years younger, puts a spring in her step and a light in her eyes. She's even apologizing to me for being so 'distant', so 'preoccupied'. She's not been much of a companion, not much of a wife, these past weeks, she says, but she'll make it up to me when she knows there's a healthy growing baby in there, and she pats her flat stomach. I'm not to worry about selling the house, we won't have to sell the house, she'll take a second job if she has to, be some popular millionaire author's private copy editor or, she adds vaguely, read manuscripts for someone. I reassure her and tell her I'm not worried, I know everything's going to be all right, but that's not the way I'm thinking. I'm thinking she doesn't know what it'll be like holding down one job with a baby at home, let alone taking on another. If by some wild stretch of the imagination I can believe it possible, I know I'll be at home with the child, able to do just enough work of some kind or other to pay a nanny. But, naturally, I don't say any of this. The days when we told each other our inmost thoughts are gone, when we were honest with each other, or as honest as people ever are. I'm even reluctant to tell her of the latest Henry developments. How can I tell a woman – my wife – who carries a faulty gene, about my discoveries of women who carry faulty genes? She knows I've met my cousin Lucy but she didn't want to know more, she didn't ask and I didn't tell her.

I haven't told her about Tenna and my belief that Barbla Maibach came from there. What's the point? Whether the PGD works or not I obviously can't go there. I understand she wants me with her. And I'll stay as long as that's what she wants. Damn Tenna. Bugger Tenna. I do tell David but he's not very interested. These genealogists don't seem to care much about personalities, birthplaces, historical oddities, only about names and dates.

Jude and I don't make love. She's afraid to disturb things. No one's told her to abstain but she's heard stories. And wishing for more with her than holding her in my arms, I'm reminded of something a woman once said to me about love. She was my girlfriend after my divorce and before I met Jude. One night she said to me that there ought to be something more for human beings who were in love, something *else*, not talk and being together which was friendship, nor lovemaking which was lust, but some quite other thing only discoverable when in that transcendent state. She seemed almost resentful that it didn't exist or she couldn't find it, she was angry – with what? God? Life? I didn't understand at all. What we had was quite good enough for me. But I wasn't in love. Not then. I've remembered what she said and I understand now, I want what she wanted and, like her, I can't find it.

30

It's fizzled out. Neither with a bang nor even a whimper. Jude had three embryos in there two weeks ago and now there's nothing. They've vanished in blood and not even much of that. The test simply showed negative, no blue line. Is she as unhappy, as shattered, as she's been on previous occasions? I don't know. I can't tell. For a whole day she was quiet and remote, a shadow of a woman, not staring or weeping or angry, but silently reading a manuscript she'd brought home with her. Unusually for her, she didn't comment on it, say a word about its worth or otherwise, and when she reached the final page, she closed it and laid it aside.

Of course she'll try again. When she broke her silence she said so. It was the first thing she said. I expected it, I'd have been astonished if she'd said anything else. Hope had come in, of course, hope had reared its ugly head and whispered to me that maybe she's had enough, she's resigned herself to being childless, she's realized there can be more, or other things, to life than having kids. She's had enough of lying on tables with her legs strung up, being poked at and probed. But the realist in me that counters hope told me to be my age, have a bit of sense. And when she said it I nodded and smiled and covered her hand with mine. I kissed her. I said I knew she'd succeed one day. I swear I didn't think about having to masturbate over that magazine again but I did think about the money. Another two and a half K up the spout, was what I thought. And then she said something wonderful, but not till next day, it was so sweet and so bloody *kind* I could have wept.

'Shall we go to Switzerland first?'

I just stare at her. Then I ask her how she knew I wanted to go.

'David told me. Oh, on the phone, before I wasn't pregnant any more. He said something about he supposed you'd be off to Switzerland in May when the snows were gone and would I ask you if you'd like him to go with you.'

'God forbid.'

'I'm sorry, I forgot to give you the message.'

'You've had other things on your mind,' I say.

So we're going, Jude and I. When we come back we'll do the egg and sperm thing again. The date we fix on is 5 May, a Friday, a flight to Zurich and from there the train to Chur. Jude says the alpine meadows will be in flower. She wants to see the precious stones collection in Chur Town Council Chamber. This is the first time for months I've seen her enthusiastic about anything, and although I know a lot of it is assumed for my sake, this makes me even more grateful. When Paul arrives unexpectedly in the evening we're sitting surrounded by maps – I've been down to Daunt's to buy them – and I'm consulting my Baedeker's *Switzerland*, descendant of the one Henry took with him on his alpine travels in the 1870s.

There's no reason, I suppose, why she shouldn't tell him. I'd just prefer her not to. He's such a glutton for disappointment, for failure, for striving that comes to nothing.

'How do they do it?' he says, meaning the mechanics of PGD.

I've started to ask why we have to go into that, a fatal remark that makes his lips twitch, but Jude answers him and, for once, he looks embarrassed. It's not the extraction of her eggs that does it but the idea of his father having to produce sperm. Like all his generation, he assumes we get treatment on the NHS, or if he doesn't he says nothing about the cost. Unlike them or many of them, he's uninterested in money, works for it if he needs it and never asks for a loan.

'Will you try again?'

'When we come back from Switzerland,' I tell him and he asks why we're going.

No one in his world ever goes to Switzerland. They go to Central Africa or Thailand or Cuba. I can't explain to him because I don't exactly know myself. To see the village my great-grandmother's great-grandmother came from seems an inadequate explanation, and anyway I don't know if it's the right one. Her genes have undergone a lot of dilution in nearly two hundred years. I suppose the truth is I'm expecting some world-shaking or biography-shaking revelation. I tell him vaguely it's for Henry research and he accepts this without demur. He's come for a drink before he meets a couple of friends at some club on Tottenham Court Road, though I'd have thought that whatever this club doesn't offer, unlimited drink will be available. While he's drinking a gin and tonic and Jude and I have wine, he says in that threatening manner he sometimes puts on that he may come to stay for his last few days before going back to Bristol after the Easter break. Jude and I say enthusiastically that we'd love that and he smiles in an enigmatic way.

Does any father have a happy, easy relationship with a son of his age?

Henry made no more diary entries after George died. If he wrote any letters none has survived. He seems to have seldom left the house. His second daughter Mary, already busy with her good works, teaching Sunday School, sewing for the church bazaar, wrote in July to her married sister Elizabeth Kirkford:

George's death has dreadfully affected poor Father. Mother is always so brave and strong, she has rallied, comes to matins regularly with me and has paid some calls and visits and is beginning to take up her photography again, but Father is as greatly felled by the blow as on the day it happened. We all know he has not always been the easiest of men. When I was younger I remember how I envied girls who had more affectionate, even indulgent, parents, and I know you did too, Lizzie, but if you were here now you could not but be moved by his wretchedness, his dreadful grief. Clara asked me the other day if I thought he would have been as cast down if it was one of us who had passed on. You know how awkward and tactless she is. Naturally, I told her she should not ask such a question, but I did ask it of myself privately. Father was seventy-two in February but he looks ten years more. Mother seems unperturbed. She looks after him as she always has but without, as far as I can tell, giving him any special attention . . .

Henry died in the following January. Only one more letter about his condition prior to his death remains but somehow I don't think he rallied or returned to his former pursuits. He was a few weeks short of his seventy-third birthday. Most people would choose to die in their beds if they had a choice, even if this means a husband or wife waking in the morning to find a dead body beside them. Henry, it seems, had stopped going to bed. Mary is writing in October:

I wasn't aware Mother and Father are no longer sharing a room until a noise from along the passage awakened me at three yesterday morning. It was the sound of some heavy object falling and it seemed to come from Father's study. As you know, I moved into your room after you married and that shares a wall with the study. Uncertain how best to act, I put on my dressing gown and went to investigate. Imagine my surprise to find Father there, neither fully dressed nor in his night clothes but wearing a smoking jacket I have never seen before over trousers and shirt. He was seated at his desk, staring at the inkwell which he must somehow have knocked on to the floor. You will remember the inkwell, it is the blue glass silver-mounted one University College Hospital gave him on some occasion, perhaps his sixtieth birthday. Fortunately, there was no ink in it, it had long run dry, testimony to Father's inability to work this past year and more. He asked me – quite gently for him! – what I was doing and I said I had heard a noise. Pick that up for me, will you? he said in the same quiet polite tone, And now go back to bed. Good night.

I said good night to him and in the morning I determined to ask Mother if he frequently spent nights in the study. For the past six months, she said in her cool unperturbed way. He can't sleep, he doesn't want to disturb me. How silent he must have been, all those nights, Lizzie, how still, so as not to have wakened *me* . . .

It was in the study that Edith found him dead on the morning of 21 January 1909. The time was nine-thirty a.m. She went to look for him when he hadn't appeared either in their room to dress himself or at the breakfast table. I owe all my knowledge of Henry's behaviour in the months prior to his death and that death itself to Mary's letters and once again I'm thankful for the sisters' hoarding instincts. Once her mother had told her and her sisters, Helena and Clara, Mary sent telegrams to Elizabeth in Yorkshire and to Alexander, at Harrow. Later that day she wrote to Elizabeth:

You will have heard by now that poor Father passed away last night or in the early hours of this morning. A massive heart attack was the cause, according to Dr Starkey. Well, Lizzie, a heart attack may have been the final blow but he died of grief. Perhaps Mother knows that too for she keeps saying over and over that it is a merciful release. She certainly cannot mean from bodily pain and illness, for though he had had heart trouble it had never seemed very serious.

Of course you won't attend the funeral. None of us females will and it would be specially unwise for you in your condition . . .

This may mean that Elizabeth is pregnant, maybe she was, but if so she must have miscarried because Kenneth, her first child, wasn't born till July 1910 and Henry died in January 1909. Kenneth would be Henry's second haemophilic descendant, his mother the first of the known carriers in her generation, and perhaps another feature of the merciful release was that Henry would never know. Did he suspect in those final grief-stricken weeks of his life while his daughter was apparently pregnant? He must have.

He had written nothing for ten years. Or, rather, the attempts he made at his definitive work, his *magnum opus*, came to grief or he destroyed what he had done. I incline to this view, for I've searched for it in those trunks just as I've searched for the notebook – the very possibly non-existent notebook – and found nothing. The end of his life was blighted by the sickness of his younger son. In the trunks are some of George's exercise books, which his father kept and obviously intended to be seen by a future generation. He was evidently a clever and gifted boy, accomplished at his lessons in a way no child would be today. I'll amend that and say instead he'd been taught things no present-day child would be taught at so young an age and had proved himself equal to them. Caesar's *Invasion of Britain*, which I remember struggling to make sense of at twelve, George read and understood when he was seven. A year before he died he was learning Greek. He seemed to have read all the plays of Shakespeare – in bowdlerized versions – *Paradise Lost* and a good deal of Browning and Tennyson. Two years before the Greek began he was learning algebra and evidently enjoying it.

Henry's love for his son must have been increased and enhanced by his intellectual brilliance. That enemy of mine, Hope, that ugly woman in the painting who sits on top of the world with a towel round her head, would have invaded Henry's dreams and made him believe that with the best care and watchfulness George stood a chance of growing up, of fulfilling his potential, of entering some demanding profession. It might even be that in the next few years a cure would be found. Not by him, alas, it was too late for that, but by some up-and-coming physician who had the advantages of modern science at his disposal. These were the kind of hopes the Tsarina had, Princess Beatrice had. They were doomed to the bitterest of all disappointments.

His mother's photographs show George as a good-looking boy too, if you let yourself see past the sickness and the suffering. He'd have grown up a handsomer man than Alexander. And how could a father not love a son who described him to his sisters as 'sweetest and kindest', as 'the best father in the world'?

Henry's funeral took place at St Mark's, Hamilton Terrace, and he was buried at Kensal Green beside George. Thinking of that makes me wonder once again who it is that puts flowers – now, still, when all his nearest are dead and gone – on the grave that holds the bones of father and son.

31

Everyone makes sneering remarks about cuckoo clocks and chocolate whenever Switzerland's mentioned. They forget, or don't know, what a beautiful country it is. Quite as beautiful, I'm sure, as Cuba or Thailand, and the cosy image is misplaced as well. How can a place be cosy when it has some of the grandest mountains in Europe?

Another truism is that all its trains run on time. So they do but that's hardly a fault, and they run at the same times on Saturdays and Sundays as on weekdays. Ours is a double-decker that travels along the southern shore of the Walensee. Thickly wooded hills, some crowned with castles, rise from the flat plain, and after the Bad Ragaz the high mountains begin. We arrive in Chur exactly when we're supposed to and have a taxi to our hotel in the centre of the town. They've given us a white bedroom with a polished wood floor, painted furniture and a four-poster bed hung with tie-on cream cotton curtains. Fat white duvets are piled on the bed, the window is wide open and it's all very fresh and bright and quiet.

There's a narrow street outside the window and a clothes shop opposite whose name makes Jude laugh. It's called La Donna Cinderella. We walk back to the station in the late afternoon sunshine and check on the train we'll take tomorrow and the bus which meets it. Dinner is at a big hotel, the Duc de Rohan, very elegant with eighteenth-century French furniture and good food. It starts to pour with rain and we have a taxi back to our hotel. We make love and it's good, in spite of the double foolproof protection, and afterwards Jude says, in the calmest most cheerful tone imaginable, would I have a vasectomy after we've got our baby?

At the moment I can't think of anything I'd like more. I wish I could have one *now*. But naturally I say none of this, only that of course I will, and she's happy. She puts her arms round me and says I do understand, don't I, but she'd never feel at ease if she thought she'd a chance of conceiving another – and there she pauses a bit before she goes on to say, 'one of those faulty ones, sick ones, I lost'.

I suppose I realize for the first time how she's felt about this. She's so beautiful, so physically nearly perfect, and yet her body makes disabled foetuses, maybe deformed foetuses. I understand now how she could turn against lovemaking, against the act that produces these abortions. She says she's ashamed of her own body and I tell her I love her body, I love her. I tell her with perfect truth that I've never loved her so much.

But I wake in the night, too hot under the huge puffy duvet, and as I throw half of it off me, I start thinking about Elizabeth Kirkford and Patricia Agnew and Diana Bell and Veronica and I wonder if they felt that way, if in each pregnancy they feared producing a son whose blood behaved with monstrous unnaturalness. When daughters came instead, did they fear they were only passing on to the next generation the burden of terror and anxiety they carried? And what of the women of Tenna, all these Ursulas and Annas and, indeed, Barblas? It's hard to say how much they knew, but in *A Treasury of Human Inheritance* a certain Dr Thormann, writing in 1837, refers to 'this great family of bleeders' in Tenna. Women must have seen their sisters, their cousins, their neighbours, give birth to children who suffered severe and often fatal haemorrhages and felt about their physical selves as Jude feels.

Keeping an eye on her, though she never wakes once she's in a deep sleep, I sit up, switch on the bedlamp and open the Bulloch and Fildes I've brought with me. I turn to page 255. 'The combination of a long day's sun and a dry atmosphere renders the village a healthy one,' Hoessli wrote, and at once I recognize the line. Where else have I read it? The Tenna population was on average 150. Poverty was unknown. Organic heart disease, scurvy and purpura were never seen, though inhabitants were prone to bronchitis, pneumonia and pleurisy. That's familiar too, from some other source.

Hoessli was by no means the first to research haemophilia in Tenna. Thormann published his findings as early as 1837. Another well-known compiler of haemophilia records was Grandidier who produced a monograph on Tenna in 1855 while a Dr Vieli, a physician at Rhazuns with an ancient family castle on the Rhine, contributed his observations to Grandidier's work. In their time many haemophiliac males remained in the area but when Hoessli arrived in 1877 all were dead. No one could say, of course, how many haemophilia *carriers* remained.

In the year of Henry's death, a man called Ludwig Pincus quoted a newspaper paragraph that the girls of the Graubünden area where Tenna is, had refused to marry on account of the disease. His investigations found that there was no truth in this statement, it was a fabrication, but a doctor in the hospital at Chur discovered two cases of abstentions from marriage for this reason. In Tenna itself there had been no cases of haemophilia for thirty years.

I've read all this before, of course, and struggled through the tables of inheritance and the lists of Tenna people who

397

had, or might have had or carried or died of, haemophilia. They are exhausting to decipher and somehow unmemorable except for the case histories which shock or dismay. 'Was called to Robert, aged one year and ten months, for epistaxis [nosebleeding]. Desired to plug the anterior and posterior nares [nostrils], but was resisted by the parents, who said the haemorrhage invariably lasted some days. Robert lay absolutely quiet, as if he recognized the danger of his condition. The blood slowly dropped from clots about his nares. The haemorrhage stopped spontaneously in five days. Robert is a bright strong boy, though spare. His skin is thin and transparent . . . Cuts or knocks are immediately followed by uncontrollable haemorrhage.' Was it like this for George Nanther? Did his parents have to witness this? The doctor goes on to tell what happened when Robert injured his throat with a stick. 'The blood was found issuing from the palate at no particular place. It was arrested but broke out again next day and continued all night. Blood was vomited . . .' Robert's ultimate fate isn't chronicled but after a long catalogue of haematomas, swellings, bleeding and pain, the doctor leaves him, aged ten, with one damaged leg permanently affected, and goes on to his next case history. He mentions, among many others, six sisters of whom four gave birth to haemophiliacs, a family of whom there were nine haemophiliacs in three generations and a boy who died at the age of five after bleeding for six weeks.

George Nanther, Kenneth Kirkford, John Corrie . . . I put out the light and lie wakeful in the dark thinking of Henry and Edith discovering, when he was perhaps nine or ten months old, that their younger son was a haemophiliac, and I wonder how they did. Perhaps his nappy pin scratched him. Or maybe he was older than that and walking and had his first fall. It doesn't matter how. Henry would have been scarcely able to believe his eyes, that he who had studied the bleeding disease all his life should be cursed with its appearance in his own family . . .

It's a cloudy brightish morning. There's snow on the mountains but perhaps there always is. Shreds of cloud drift across their lower slopes. The train takes us along the banks of the Walensee, then beside a wide rushing river, the Rabiusa, its water dove grey and its beaches grey sand. Lilies-of-the-valley are growing on the embankment, cow parsley and buttercups in the fields. Used to the kind of thing that happens at home, I can't believe a bus will be waiting at Versam to take us up the mountain, though we've been assured it will be there – and it is. It climbs up a road where every flower seems to be coming into bloom, violets and daisies and more lily-of-the-valley, then there are hairpin bends and we look down into a mist-filled valley with a river flowing through it on which people are canoeing, shooting the rapids. Orchards are in blossom and the fields are full of yellow daisies. I'd promised Jude flowers, so I'm happy to see plenty. She tells me their names, says they're wild orchids and geraniums, forget-me-nots and Solomon's seal.

I should have realized that if there's cloud on the mountains, once we get up there and penetrate it we'll find ourselves in thick mist. And that's what has happened. We're in the midst of it. The second bus, a small one, takes us to Tenna. And it's very cold up here. The mist is white and drifting and it puts a touch of ice on the skin. Luckily we've brought warm jackets. We're outside the village shop, a little supermarket of the kind you find all over Europe, and we go in and buy ourselves warming chocolate bars. The shopkeeper, who speaks quite good English, knows who we are and why we're here. Everyone in the village will know, of course. The historian we're to meet will be waiting for us, she says, and she points out her house, halfway up the next ridge of the mountain. I tell her we'd like to see the church first and, eating our chocolate, we make our way up there.

It's a pretty church, about as different from St Mark's, Hamilton Terrace, as you can imagine. All they have in common is that they both have spires. Tenna church is white, its tower and spire adjoining it but not standing at the end of the nave as ours would. Both are roofed in grey slate. We go in, where it's marginally warmer, and look at the fifteenth-century wall paintings, but it's the churchyard I'm more interested in and the graves. I'm rewarded and disappointed, both at the same time. Rewarded because many of the names recorded by the Vieli-Grandidier-Hoessli triumvirate are here, people called Gartmann and Joos and Buchli. Disappointed because these Tenna residents all died fairly recently, there's no one left from the nineteenth century. There's no Maibach at all but a couple of Barblas are here and this surprises me. I'd thought it was a diminutive of Barbara but it seems to be a name in its own right, a Safiental name.

Someone's waving to us from just down the hillside. It's the postman who's married to the shopkeeper and is also the keeper of the archives. I've already been told the archives are incomplete and that the period I'm interested in is missing. Someone borrowed the church books – we'd call them the parish registers – twenty years ago and they've never been returned. The postman doesn't speak much English but he's very happy to speak German to Jude. She translates and tells me the books that cover a great deal of the nineteenth century and quite a lot of the twentieth are missing. I can't understand how they came to let these documents out of their sight, let alone have them disappear, but I don't say so. Missing archives are noted in Bulloch and Fildes, so losing church books seems to have often gone on in Tenna. Jude interprets that the ones they have cover from 1666 to 1791. Are these any good to me?

'The trouble is,' I say, 'that I don't know.'

And I don't. A Magdalena Maibach is listed in Bulloch and Fildes, among the Hoessli findings, as being born in 1721. She had several sons, two of whom merit no further mention, and they are not even named, while the third is listed as dying at the age of six, *nachdem das Blut ihm alles ausgelofen, ist es in Gott entschlafen* (after all his blood had run from him, he went to sleep in God). So this Magdalena must have been a carrier. She may be a forebear of my Barbla. But when was Barbla born? David Croft-Jones doesn't know any more than he knows the birth date of her daughter Luise. I have to work this backwards. Edith Nanther was born in 1861 and her mother Louisa Henderson in 1837. So *her* mother Luise Quendon née Dornford may have been born any time between, say, 1800 and 1821, which makes it possible for *her* mother Barbla to have been born – when? If I had to guess I'd put her late in the eighteenth century or the first years of the nineteenth, and the archives for those years are missing.

The archivist unlocks the door of a wooden building rather like a typical village hall, but, because this is Switzerland, however remote, it's very trim and neat. The books have faded brown pages in ancient covers. Jude translates and tells me the population used to be double the present number in the nineteenth century, something which doesn't tally with Hoessli. The archivist goes into a complicated explanation of which books are missing but I can tell Jude's giving up the struggle to follow all this.

'Let's just have a look,' I say.

And we do. I have very little hope of finding anything and all we find is a Magdalena Maibach, daughter of Hans Maibach and Ursula Maibach, born Rüchli, being baptized in 1790, the year before the church book comes to an end. I ask myself if Hans Maibach was the son of that Magdalena Maibach mentioned by Hoessli who was born in 1721 and who gave birth to three sons, one of them the sad child who went to sleep in God when all his blood had run from him. I can't verify this because the relevant books are missing, but the dates work. Hans could be one of that child's brothers, a haemophiliac but, like Prince Leopold, still well enough to grow up, marry and have children. In Hans's case, he seems to have had just the one daughter, and not to have had any more. Perhaps he died. The archivist wants to show us much more, but I'm firm about this and say I've got as much as I want. Jude and I thank him and go down the hillside to the Hotel Alpenblick to see what they have for lunch.

Goulash. We don't have a choice. It arrives quite promptly, a rich brown stew with potatoes and peas and carrots, all served up together on our two plates. The dining room has a lot of carved wood, a wood floor and checked cloths on the tables. I tell Jude I'm so glad she came with me, I couldn't have managed without her. It's a strange thing that you can be married to someone for seven years, know they have a particular skill or knowledge you know nothing about, but never see or hear them demonstrate it. I'd never before heard Jude speak German, I just supposed she could because once or twice she had occasion to say so. It awakens in me a new admiration for her. And there in the cosy dining room of the Hotel Alpenblick I feel a strong surge of desire for her, a *different* kind of desire, and I ask myself rather uneasily if this is because her linguistic skill has made her into a slightly different person. She's smiling at me as if she's reading my mind, which I hope she isn't, and I say hastily that what we found back at the archives place was wonderful, was more than I'd hoped for.

'Could it be the same woman?'

'Why would you call yourself Barbla if your name was Magdalena?'

Jude doesn't know. 'The more I see of this village,' she says, 'so remote and isolated, the more I wonder how anyone living in it in those days could get to Versam, let alone London.'

I agree that that's a difficult one. It would be nothing today, it would be expected. A girl would have been study-ing English and come on a university exchange, or come over as an au pair or just on holiday. But no one left these villages in the early part of the nineteenth century. To get away you had to walk miles over the mountains, a trek that could only be managed in summer. There were no roads. This inaccessibility is what accounts for the concentration of haemophilia and why Tenna was such a rich fund for research by men like Thormann, Vieli and Grandidier. A woman married the neighbour who was there, irrespective of whether he bled profusely when he cut himself shaving or she had a brother from whom *das Blut ihm alles ausgelofen*.

I say that maybe the historian will have the answer to both questions. We have crème caramel for our pudding and then big cups of coffee. Jude has a look round and comes back to tell me that perhaps we ought to be staying here, on the spot. But when we emerge into the chilly white mist I'm glad we're not. If need be we can come back here on Monday. We walk up the hill and find the historian's house. It's quite a spacious chalet with chamois' antlers stuck up under the wide eaves and its name Rösslihaus done in what I suppose is pokerwork. She answers the door to us, a stout elderly woman in blouse and skirt, her iron-grey hair in a bun. It turns out that she's an amateur historian and she begins by showing us genealogical tables. Some of them go back to the start of the eighteenth century and a Hans Maibach is in one of them, as is his daughter Magdalena. As I thought, he died when she was a small child and his wife a few years afterwards. But this is no help to me as there's no Barbla Maibach in any of the tables. Plenty of other Barblas are though, and the historian agrees that it was a popular Graubünden name. Too popular for me, I wish there'd been only one.

About haemophilia she knows very little. After all, there hasn't been any here since about 1870. There was none in her family, the Engels, or her late husband's, the Walthers, and it's true that when I look at their family trees there's not a single name as far as I can remember that occurs in Bulloch and Fildes.

'How would anyone have got away from here in, say, 1810?'

Jude relays this to her in German and maybe she doesn't put it any more tactfully than I did, for Mrs Walther takes it as a slight on her beloved Tenna and replies that she's never wanted to get away. When she's been to Zurich, as she has a few times, to Berne and even, once, to Paris, she's been homesick and longed to get back.

Jude asks her how would you have left the village then if, for instance, you were obliged to. Mrs Walther says that the first time she went it was on her honeymoon (*Flitterwochen*) but I tell Jude to ask her for what reason a departure might have happened nearly two hundred years ago. She can't think of anything. People didn't leave.

404

'This one did,' I say.

I'm no more disappointed than I expected to be. Finding Barbla has loomed very large in my Henry-history but, after all, it's not that important. When I do the chapter on his forebears and his wife's I can write something like, 'Edith had a Swiss great-grandmother who brought the haemophilia into the Henderson family,' I don't have to say how she came to meet and marry Thomas Dornford. And yet I'll come back on Monday after I've had a day in which to think about it. I get Jude to ask Mrs Walther if Romansch is still spoken here. She says not, it never was spoken in the Safien Valley but only along the Rhine. I've been thinking about Henry – what else? – and since, I suspect, he only visited places where he could practise his Romansch, perhaps he never came here.

We're leaving when she says she's thought of something. Jude listens carefully to Mrs Walther and tells me there's a woman she knows living nearby who may help us. Mrs Walther refers to this Mrs Tauber in rather an awed tone, apparently because she lives in a castle. If we're coming back on Monday she'll do her best to get her here. We emerge into sunshine, the clouds all sinking behind the snow-capped ranges. From this steep hillside we have a magnificent view of mountains soaring into the blue sky, green and flowery meadows and the village lying there, its chalets red and black and the church tower pointing skywards like a silver knife. A ringing of cow bells comes from the cattle up on the slopes. Outside the *Gemeindehaus* the bus is waiting to take us back.

A day, Sunday, in which to think about it. It's a fine sunny one and we go for a long walk round the town, dropping in at a couple of churches to listen to the choirs and for Jude to hear the mass in German. All the shops are closed but cafés and bars are open. I consider the possibility of Barbla coming here to work in a hotel or inn and there meeting an English traveller called Thomas Dornford. Anyone might do that but I don't think a respectable girl would have done so in, say, 1808. Also it seems unlikely that someone able to travel in Europe would marry a girl who served him in an inn. Unless he spoke German they'd have had no means of communication.

We sit down at a table outside a café and order coffee. 'If she was born after 1791,' Jude says, 'you won't be able to find her. And she could have been. She could have been born in 1792 or 3 and still be Louisa Henderson's grandmother. She'd be about forty-five. It's quite possible to be a grandmother at forty-five and even more likely then.'

'Then whose daughter was she? Not Hans's. He only had the one child, Magdalena, and he died when she was two.'

'There was another brother, wasn't there?'

'Magdalena senior had three sons. One of them bled to death at the age of six. Hans grew up and married and fathered Magdalena junior but died young. Of haemophilia? We don't know. If he had it Magdalena would be bound to be a carrier. But it would be unusual for the three sons of a carrier all to have haemophilia, so it's likely Magdalena senior's third son didn't have it.'

It seems like a dead end. I try to dismiss it from my mind for the time being. We eat a big lunch and go back to the hotel to sleep, make love, sleep again. In the evening we wander about the town holding hands. Like young lovers, we stroll along the river bank, stop to kiss, then go into a bar and drink wine, finally we find somewhere to have dinner. By then it's quite late and we're going back to Tenna in the morning, but it can't be helped. It's a long time since I've seen Jude so happy and relaxed.

32

I'm tired but it takes me a long while to fall asleep. I suppose there are too many things going round and round in my head. Versam's been mentioned a lot since we arrived here, we've even been there en route to Tenna, and now at last I remember why it rings a bell with me. Or I think I do. Though I've brought Bulloch and Fildes with me, I could hardly bring the stacks of Henry correspondence, and I'm pretty sure it's in a letter Henry wrote to Couch or Fetter or someone that the name Versam occurs. The context, I think, is a long walk he made from there to a village in the Safiental. The figure of twenty miles is given, I think, though I can't be sure of this. But if it is, is the village Tenna? Even if Romansch was never spoken there? And I remember something else, or I think I do. That line from Hoessli about the climate of Tenna which Henry quotes directly in that same letter. 'The combination of a long day's sun and a dry atmosphere renders the village a healthy one . . .' Unfortunately, I can't be quite sure of any of this without seeing the letter and that's at home in its appropriate folder on my work table.

Of course, I'm now even more wide awake. I lie here thinking that the missed chance of speaking Romansch would weigh very little with Henry against the possibility of visiting the village made notorious among haematologists for its preponderance of 'bleeder families'. Even though Bulloch and Fildes wasn't to be published for another thirty years, he'd have read their sources, he'd read Hoessli, so they'd both have been well-known to him. Perhaps he was staying in Chur. It may even be that he didn't know how relatively near Tenna was until he was there, reading his Baedeker. Still, I can't check any of this until I get home. I can only speculate.

Life is so unexciting in Tenna that the arrival of the bus in the late morning is an event. It's even more of an event when strangers are expected on it. Several people are waiting outside the *Gemeindehaus* to welcome us. We're escorted into the shop and given coffee and cakes. The white mist that looks like cloud when you're lower down the mountain spreads its pall over Tenna and today it's wet, condensing on our hands and faces and making us shiver. We walk through it up to the Rösslihaus but when it's in sight I already have a pre-vision I'm going to be disappointed because there's no car a castle dweller is likely to drive outside it.

Hot chocolate and shortbread are provided to console us. Mrs Tauber couldn't come because one of her children is unwell and the new nanny hasn't yet arrived. I'm given her address and phone number and told she's a doctor, though she hasn't practised since she was married. But this leads me to think she may know something about the haemophilia and also won't get uptight about its existence in Tenna. It's when I've finished writing down the phone number from Jude's dictation that I look up and see the eggs. They must have been here on Saturday but I didn't notice them. They're all red or brown or dark green with a white pattern on them of flowers and leaves or a more abstract design. Mrs Walther – she must have a first name but no one uses it or tells us what it is – says, and Jude translates, that the white isn't painted on. What happens is that the whole egg

409

is painted dark red or some other colour and the white design is etched out of it with a sharp tool. That is, the white is the natural colour of the egg under the paint. Eggs. The symbol of continuing life, eggs holding the X chromosome, ready to pass on beauty or ugliness, health or sickness, long life or rapid death.

According to Jude, Mrs Walther is as disappointed as I am at her castle-dweller friend failing to turn up, but she has the added problem of feeling guilty about it. Jude reassures her, it's not her fault, these things happen. We may as well give it all up and go home, though the bus doesn't leave till four. Then Mrs Walther apparently has a brainwave and presents us with an egg each, compensatory eggs. She's decorated them herself, a ginger-brown one for Jude with a white lily on it, and a red one for me with a wreath of flowers. 'Typical Tenna,' she says, smiling, and even I can understand her. She packs the eggs into individual boxes because they're fragile and we have a long way to go.

The mist has lifted so after we've had lunch at the Alpen-blick – goulash again but different vegetables – we spend the afternoon going for a long walk along mountain paths and admiring the stupendous views. The bus comes on time, of course, and we go back to Versam and thence to Chur. The effect of all this has been to make me feel a bit of a fool and I ask myself what I really hoped for. Who now alive, after all, is going to know or care what happened to a young peasant woman born in the eighteenth century? If indeed she came from here. For all I know there may be Maibachs all over Switzerland, all over Germany and Austria for that matter. It would be a different story if, like Mrs Tauber, she'd lived in a castle, if she'd been well-born. I realize, as I'm getting out of the train at Chur station, that I've based my conviction about Barbla coming from here on the fact that, according to Bulloch and Fildes, a Maibach family lived here. But maybe they came from Nuremberg or Innsbruck, maybe Veronica has been right all along and they weren't Maibachs at all, but Maybacks from Manchester and my woman had the fairly common English christian name of Barbara.

If we get up very early tomorrow morning and take an early train to Zurich we could be flying to London before lunch, but we're booked on a five-thirty flight in the afternoon and we may as well stick with that. Besides, Jude likes it here. She wants to linger a while in the oldest town in Switzerland, eat in a good restaurant tonight and visit the Rhaetian Museum in the morning. She's a relentless museum visitor and no holiday is complete for her without 'doing' as many of them as she can find. We unpack the painted eggs and Jude says they must be a symbol of hope and of the child she's sure will be born next year. She knows what I think of hope but she doesn't say so.

The museum visit completed, we take a mid-morning train to Zurich and get there in time for lunch, but we still have two or three hours before we need to leave for the airport. The Bahnhofstrasse, according to Baedeker, is one of the finest shopping streets in Europe, but Jude doesn't want to go shopping, which is just as well considering the state of our finances. She wants to go to more museums.

I'm booking us into an hotel and Jude is beside me, as excited as I am and not at all perturbed at having to stay on another day. And, as we go up in the lift to our room, I'm reflecting on the operations of chance and contingency. We only had time for one, or at the most two, museums, and Zurich is full of them. She might so easily – for the choice was left to her – have chosen the Thomas Mann Archives

411

in the Schönberggasse, she nearly did, or the Johanna Spyri Foundation – she loved *Heidi* as a child – but she chose the Zunfthaus zur Meisen Ceramic Collection and the Baren-gasse Museum of Domestic Life. The ceramics were obvi-ous, she loves china, but why domestic life? Not specially to her taste, I'd have thought, she's never been an interiors woman, a 'her indoors'. But thank God she did.

We were looking at a very upper-class interior, a living room in a small castle on the Rhine called Schlössli Bene-diktus. The Rhine is a huge river and there was no reason for me to place it anywhere near Tenna. Nor did the photograph of the house, diminutive as castles go, turreted, steep-roofed, with soaring mountains behind, bring any revelations. Enlightenment came from a book which lay open on a small table between a harpsichord and a chaise longue. To me it meant nothing. I can't read Gothic and this book, which was obviously a diary, was handwritten in that curlicued, elaborate and now obsolete German script. Jude can, up to a point. She looked at the open pages, then at me, then at the left-hand page again.

'Martin, there's something . . .' She had gone rather pale.

'Are you all right?' I said.

'I'm fine.' She took hold of my hand and for a moment held it tightly. 'The name Magdalena Maibach is on that page. And a sentence later, "Barbla".'

'Can you read it?'

She sighed with exasperation. 'Not really. I could have once. I've forgotten how. I think it says something like, "give her a new name". It's definitely "*neue Name*", I'm sure of that.'

The date on the legend beside the diary was 1793 and the author of the diary given as Gertrude Tauber, a widow and owner of the castle since her husband's death four years before. All this was in English as well as German. A pity they didn't have a translation of the diary as well. It gave, the legend went on, a fascinating picture of upper-class domestic life in the eighteenth and early nineteenth centuries.

'If we asked the curator to let us have a closer look, always supposing he or she would, do you think you could read it then?'

'Darling, I know I couldn't,' Jude said.

'What do you think it means, this woman, this castle-dweller, re-naming a child called Magdalena, Barbla? Who was she to do that? What right had she?'

'I don't know. But listen, wasn't the woman Mrs Walther mentioned called Tauber? And, Martin – this is getting exciting – didn't she say she lived in a castle? This woman could be her ancestor. We have to know. And we've got a flight to catch in two hours' time.'

'Flights can be cancelled,' I said.

We had to have a hotel room before we could start making phone calls. Or Jude could. She's the one with the German and, blessedly for me, she seems quite to enjoy practising it. So we're in our room, a much more sophisticated and elegant place than the one in Chur, and Jude is making phone calls and I'm washing our underclothes in the bathroom sink. We thought Lorraine could have done them tomorrow but we won't be home tomorrow, we'll be – where?

'At Schlössli Benediktus, if we can find a way there,' says Jude.

She doesn't know yet. She's spoken to Mrs Walther who has confirmed we've got the right Tauber and that she's just heard 'Franziska's' child is better and she's given her the phone number.

I come out of the bathroom, my hands full of wet tights and underpants. 'Franziska being the present Mrs Tauber?'

'That's right, the one who was a doctor.'

'I'd like to see inside a little castle on the Rhine,' I say.

But that's not our destiny. The first time Jude phones the line is engaged and she waits impatiently, but after about ten minutes Franziska Tauber answers. Within seconds Jude's speaking English, saying she'll cancel our flight, we'll see Mrs Tauber tomorrow, her husband will be so grateful, she can't thank her enough, et cetera.

'In Chur. She'll meet us in Chur. She has to go there to meet someone. We could get the flight tomorrow or would Thursday be safer?'

Thursday, I tell her, you never know what we may have to follow up.

Franziska says gently, 'I believe you're trying to trace a woman called Magdalena Maibach.'

We're all drinking coffee at a table outside the Café Cuera which is on the banks of the river. Franziska – she's asked us to call her that – is about Jude's age, tall, thin, very fair. We've asked her to lunch with us but she can't. That's the purpose of her visit here, to lunch with someone else.

'I'm trying to trace a woman called *Barbla* Maibach.'

'Yes. One and the same, as I expect you guessed.'

'We didn't guess. My wife saw the names in a diary in a museum in Zurich.' I feel a great surge of excitement, which is ridiculous when I haven't yet got any proof.

'The Gothic script defeated me,' says Jude.

'Understandable. It defeats *me*. Barbla was adopted by my husband's ancestress, his great – multiplied by six or seven

– grandmother and taken away from Tenna. It's all in the journal she kept. Her name was Gertrude Tauber, born Wettach. She had one child of her own, a son, and then her husband died. After that she adopted two children.'

I hardly dare ask. 'Is there anything in the diary about haemophilia?' I ask.

'Lots, but it's mostly wrong.'

I ask her if she has copies of the diary but she hasn't. She's read it. She and her husband both read it before they gave it to the museum. Would I like her to tell us the story? I nod, I say yes, please. I want to know everything there is to be known.

'Magdalena Maibach,' Franziska begins, 'was born in Tenna in 1790. Her father was Hans Maibach and her mother Ursula Rüchli. You already know that? Right. Hans had haemophilia. While his father was a "foreigner" from Rhazuns, his mother was Magdalena Gartmann, *einer den Bluterfamilien*, and certainly a carrier, but he seemed not to be a bad case. He had various problems in youth, especially when a tooth was extracted, and apparently he was never without haematomas and purpuric spots.'

At this point Jude asks the waitress for more coffee for all of us. Franziska says no more coffee for her, she gets too hyped-up. She'll have orange juice.

'Hans grew up, married, fathered this one daughter and died when she was two. Another tooth had been lost, and bleeding from the socket lasted three days. The following week a horse pulling a cart he was travelling in bolted and threw him and he cut his head on a rock and bled to death. It's all in the journal. Gertrude was fascinated by haemophilia and went about the villages observing cases, though of course she was dreadfully ignorant of its causes and how it was passed on. But everyone was ignorant,

415

including the doctors. Quite a lot of them thought it and scurvy were the same disease.'

In the following couple of years his wife Ursula died of tuberculosis. 'Hoessli says there wasn't any in Tenna,' I say. Maybe I'm just trying to impress her.

'Hoessli says a lot of inaccurate things, but he wasn't alone in that. The child Magdalena was left to the care of her aunt, her mother's sister and a healthy woman, not a carrier as far as is known. She had three healthy sons. Whether the daughters were carriers isn't known. But there were seven children and, quite naturally, she didn't really want an eighth to care for.'

The coffee and orange juice come and rather wonderful Swiss cakes which Franziska refuses but we can't resist. The sun has come out and it's quite hot, light sparkling on the river. Franziska goes on to say that Gertrude Tauber had by this time adopted a little boy whose parents had also died and she offered to take Magdalena. She had theories of her own about the ways haemophilia was transmitted and because the sons of a haemophiliac can never themselves be haemophiliacs she assumed that their daughters couldn't be affected either. Where she had seen cases of the daughters of haemophiliacs giving birth to haemophiliac sons, she believed this had been passed on through those daughters' mothers. According to this theory, a haemophiliac demonstrated the disease which manifested itself in him in that generation but, with his death, came to an end in that family line. Therefore, she had no fears that in adopting Magdalena she was taking on a carrier of the bleeding sickness.

As soon as she had taken the child back to the castle with her she renamed her. She wrote in her journal that she had always disliked the name Magdalena and wondered at its popularity in Graubünden. Why name your daughter after a loose woman out of whom Our Lord cast seven devils? She called her Barbla instead, the name she would have given her own daughter if she'd ever had one.

'As you probably know,' Franziska said, 'adopting a child in those days was very different from what it would be now. Well, it was very different not only in the nineteenth century but pretty well up to the Second World War. You didn't have any authorities you had to satisfy with your credentials. No one did a – what do you call it? House study?'

'Home study, I think,' says Jude.

'Right. You just took on a child its parents didn't want or, more likely, couldn't afford because they'd already got seven others. And you didn't feel you were obliged to treat it exactly as if it were your own, give it the same status and privileges. Gertrude wasn't an aristocrat but she was certainly upper class. She was the lady of the manor and Hans Maibach was a cowherd. The little boy she'd adopted was some relative of her own, she doesn't say precisely what, but refers to him as "my kinsman's boy". So Magdalena, or Barbla as she's become, never lived on quite an equal footing in the household. By the way, I haven't asked you, what was she to you?'

'Barbla? My grandmother four times great.'

'Ah. I see why you want to know.'

She took her meals in the servants' hall but spent time with Gertrude, who taught her to read and write and, later, to speak French. She might play with the other adopted child but not think of him or refer to him as her brother. With Gertrude's own son, the heir, she was not allowed to play and had to address him as 'mein Herr'. It looks as if Gertrude intended her to become a governess or perhaps an upper servant and it's hard to see for what purpose she adopted her in the first place. Not to be a companion, certainly not a daughter, perhaps it was only done out of duty and charity.

There are long gaps in the journal, Franziska says, and many entries where the girl is never referred to. After that we only hear of her as accompanying Gertrude on a visit to Bern and another to Vienna, but in what capacity isn't clear. But if Barbla was originally destined for a lady's maid, this plan appears to have been dropped. Still, Gertrude is relieved when her son Sigmund departs for the University of Vienna. Though only fourteen Barbla is too good looking for them to associate any longer. But three years later Gertrude writes of Barbla as accompanying her to the opera in Salzburg, then to a ball in Rome. Apparently, she is very pretty, a blue-eyed, full-lipped blonde, and I'm reminded of her great-granddaughter Edith, Henry's wife. For I'm certain now that this is my ancestress.

They visit Paris and Amsterdam. Barbla is twenty. Gertrude, who is now immensely proud of her good looks and 'ladylike ways', is probably regretting she turned her into a bit of a Cinderella in her early youth but not regretting Sigmund's departure. He is now betrothed to a suitable girl of his own class. A young Englishman who has come to Amsterdam to buy diamonds sees Barbla at some function and comes to call. Gertrude calls him '*junge Herr Donfort*' and I don't think I'd be making too conjectural a leap to identify him as Thomas Dornford, the jeweller from Hatton Garden. The journal stops for a long while after that. The next entry – or the next extant entry – is six years later and all Gertrude wrote was, 'Barbla delivered of a son.' He would have been Luise Quendon's younger brother, I suppose.

'Did he have haemophilia?' I ask Franziska.

'I don't know. No one knows. Gertrude was sixty by

then and sixty was old in 1816. She gave up the journal a year later and died in 1820.'

That's it then. Everything I wanted to know and more. There's a lot to think about. I say a very heartfelt thanks to Franziska and she says it was a pleasure, it's always enjoyable imparting information. Jude compliments her on her English and she says, nothing to be proud of, her mother's English. Then she leaves, saying she has to meet her friend at twelve-thirty and will I send her a copy of my book when it comes out?

After she's gone we take a walk round Chur, looking at all the flowers that have come out since yesterday, that the sun has brought out. I'd like to see Tenna again. It's become part of my history, if not, thank God, part of my genes. I feel its green meadows and black conifers, alpine flowers and its red chalets, even its icy white mists, would look different to me now. The cradle of my great-great-great-great-grandmother. On a far less cosy level, the death source of George Nanther and Kenneth Kirkford. But it's a place in my origins no less than Godby and Hatton Garden, Bloomsbury and North London, and I say to Jude that maybe we'll come back here for a holiday, do a walking tour of Graubünden, because it has the glimmer of a feel of home.

'With luck,' she says, 'we won't be able to go anywhere on walking tours for the next few years.'

It's like a splash of cold water in my face. With luck . . . With luck we'll have a baby or two and the only holidays we'll be able to take will be to Disneyland. If we can afford them.

Returning to Zurich in the train this afternoon I think more about Franziska's account and what it means for me. I decide it's improbable any of those Quendons and Hendersons knew where their forebear came from. If they knew Thomas Dornford met his wife in Amsterdam they very likely thought she was Dutch. They wouldn't have wanted to know any more and if they had investigated and found she was a Swiss cowherd's daughter they'd have hushed it up. But in those days discovering it would have been next to impossible and why would they bother to hunt? It was Veronica who supplied me with Barbla Maibach's name, but she told me she knew nothing more about her. I notice now something that didn't strike me before. Gertrude Tauber allowed, or perhaps encouraged, Barbla to keep her own surname. No doubt, she'd have resisted her husband's distinguished family name passing to a peasant's child.

The really significant factor in all this is that the haemophilia's been traced back to its source: Hans Maibach, to whom it was transmitted by his mother, a Gartmann, one of the famous *Bluterfamilien* of Tenna, who passed it to his daughter Barbla. And she in her turn passed it on undiscernibly to her daughter Luise, Luise to Louisa, Louisa to Edith, Edith to Elizabeth and Mary, and those two, the gene still of course invisibly carried, to the present day.

33

The first thing I do when I get home is look up that letter Henry wrote in the spring of 1882. Not to Couch but to Lewis Fetter. But my memory wasn't otherwise much at fault. Tenna isn't mentioned by name but Versam is and the fact that it must have been Tenna is confirmed by Henry's almost quoting Hoessli word for word when he writes, 'Sunshine and a dry atmosphere render it a healthy place . . .' The letter is headed, Safiental, Graubünden.

Paul is twenty today. We sent him a card with a cheque inside. Anything we might buy him would be wrong. Inevitably, I spend a while staring out of the window, the Henry papers in a muddle on the table and thinking about when he was born and the months preceding his birth. It's a bit embarrassing now in retrospect to remember Sally and me telling people we were 'making a baby'. Especially, perhaps, as we weren't, but about to produce the result of an accident. Jude and I are making a baby now, that's an accurate way of putting it, for no baby was ever more deliberately and calculatingly manufactured. The deed has been re-done. And, of course, the second time is never so bad as the first. I hope I'm not going to have to talk about third and fourth times. They've implanted four embryos – our sperm and eggs never have a problem uniting – and now once more we wait and see.

The Government Chief Whip has just phoned and asked me to have lunch with him after the Whitsun break. As someone says in *The Taming of the Shrew*, I wonder what it bodes? It may be that he's been told I'm researching Henry's life and he has something relevant to tell me. Ubiquitous Henry. I've been re-reading the diaries, asking myself if he had any further comments to make on Tenna, though it seems not.

It's not clear how many of these walking tours he went on. Amelia Nanther kept all the letters her son wrote home from holiday and all appear to be extant. All, as far as I know, are on the table in front of me. I say 'as far as I know' but the only evidence for this is contained in a letter *she* wrote to her sister in which she says so. 'Henry writes such beautiful letters from these distant parts that I carefully keep every one of them.' In some he is precise as to his whereabouts. For instance, from Lake Thun he even specifies the name of the pension at which he is staying, and from 'Safiental, Graubünden' that he is at the home of people called Schiele. In others he merely gives the name of the Canton. But, in almost all cases, the letters are full of descriptions of named villages, mountains and lakes. Perhaps he thought this would be of particular interest to his mother, perhaps she liked to study geography. By the time she is dead and so is Hamilton (they died, of course, on the same day within four hours of each other) Henry has only Couch and Fetter to write to and the single letter he wrote to Fetter in 1882 from abroad, or the single surviving letter, seems positively cryptic compared to those he wrote home to Godby Hall.

Why doesn't he name the village? Perhaps because he knows Fetter will recognize it. Perhaps because Fetter *expects him to go there*. I don't know but, looking at the letter, I see something I didn't see before. After *sunshine and a dry atmosphere render it a healthy place*, he goes on, *except, according to V and G, as you know, in one respect.* When I first read it I thought V might be Dr Vickersley. I now see that V and G are Vieli and Grandidier, the medical men who first documented haemophilia in the district.

I feel a little disappointed. What was I hoping for? Something dramatic, I suppose. Of course, Henry in his position, would have read Vieli and Grandidier as well as Hoessli, for their work had appeared in 1855. There is no mystery, unless mystery is contained in Henry's secretive manner, using initials instead of names and omitting a precise address. But this was his way, his nature. It would have been odder if he hadn't been to Tenna, considering its importance in his particular field and the fact that he visited Switzerland many times.

I'm more inclined to ask, why didn't he go there before? Why wait till 1882? But maybe he didn't wait. Maybe he was only re-visiting Graubünden that year. He could have been there in the 1870s and simply not mentioned the name of the village to his mother, a woman who would have known nothing of haemophilia and cared less. Or he could even have been there while a student at the University of Vienna. Though he doesn't say so, he could have made a trip to south-eastern Switzerland with his friend, the Romansch speaker. This being left out of letters home is easily explained by the unwillingness of a son whose father is supporting him to let his parents know that not all the money which has come his way is being spent on studies. The more I think of it the less likely it seems that Henry would have neglected a visit to so significant a place.

The post comes very late but brings something worth waiting for. A letter from, of all people, my second cousin Caroline. It's handwritten. She includes her phone number, signs it 'Caroline' and there's no mention in it of whether she's still called Agnew, whether she's married or has children. It's not clear what Jennifer has told her, though she knows I'm writing our great-grandfather's life. There's something clipped and abrupt in her style, something ungracious. For instance, Jennifer's told her Lucy and I had lunch and she says she'd like to make it plain she doesn't want anything like that. She hates 'that sort of thing'. She doesn't know if the family knowledge she has is any use to me but she's willing to pass it on, only she'll come to me at home or I can go to her. Her home in Reading is only half an hour away on the train. She doesn't want this taken as a sign she'd like to meet other family members, so no one else present, please.

I don't want to go to Reading, but of course I will if there's no help for it. Re-reading the letter, I have the feeling inviting her for a meal or even a cup of tea would be a mistake, and it's with some trepidation that I pick up the phone. I expect an answering machine because I've made up my mind without the least evidence that she's single, living alone and with a full-time job. It's a small shock when she answers.

Her voice is low and rather harsh. I must be a snob, though I try not to be, but I notice at once her 'estuary English'. She speaks very differently from other members of my family. I must try hard not to let it grate on me, it's not good behaviour for someone who once nearly took the Labour whip. 'I'll come and see you if you want,' she says. 'Thursday about three?'

I'm not to be given a choice and I've a feeling if I don't agree I'll be told to take it or leave it. This Thursday is the last one in May and the last before the House of Lords gets up for Whitsun, but that doesn't affect me any more. I tell her it will be fine and how is she going to get here?

'I don't have a car,' she says. 'I'll come on the train to Paddington.'

How is it that I know instinctively taxis are not for her? I tell her to take the tube, Bakerloo Line to Baker Street and Jubilee to St John's Wood, and that I'm very grateful and look forward to seeing her. For some reason I expect more. I expect her to tell me why she's 'coming up to town' on this particular Thursday, for she evidently is. But all she says is, 'That's all right then,' and puts the phone down.

Fowler says we shouldn't use 'intrigue' in the sense of 'mystify, fascinate, interest' but choose one of those words instead, but none of them will quite do for me. I am *intrigued* by my cousin Caroline. I want to discover what makes her tick. Is she married? Has she ever been married? Her mother died a long time ago but what has become of her father? Of course it may be that no answers to these questions will be given me.

I get on to the Government Chief Whip's Office and say to his diary secretary that of the dates he's offered me I'd like Tuesday 6 June. I've chosen this day with care. It's the only one I was given that's *after* the date Jude will know if the implants have taken or not. By then I will know. In the unlikely event of the Chief Whip offering me some sort of job – what sort I can't imagine but it would bring in an income – I'll be in a better position to accept or decline it. If we have to fork out another £2,500 I'll have to accept it. And then I do what I've sworn to myself I never will. I start wondering how many attempts she'll make before she stops. Five? Ten? *Twenty?* Twenty would amount to fifty thousand pounds. But I must stop, it's useless going on like this . . .

★

Caroline Agnew is tall and big with it, a large heavy woman who must weigh fifteen stone, and looks every day, in fact more, of her forty-seven years. Her iron-grey hair is cut very short, but not fashionably, rather as if it's just been trimmed by a very conservative barber giving a short back and sides. No make-up, of course, nothing in the least feminine. Grey flannel trousers, a jumper, a cotton jacket and shoes in the Doc Martens mode.

I expect my offer of tea to be refused but she accepts, takes neither milk nor sugar but helps herself to a chocolate chip cookie. She hasn't asked me how I am, nor anything about myself, but after taking a sip of tea she looks round and says she supposes this was 'the old man's' house.

'Not the one your grandmother and my grandfather grew up in, no. That was sold and this one bought in the twenties.'

She doesn't ask questions, just makes statements. 'You live alone in this great place.'

'I'm married. I've got a son at university.'

She nods, plainly not interested. I ask her about Clara. She doesn't seem to have kept in touch with anyone else in the family, so why Clara?

'She was Mum's godmother,' she says, 'for what that's worth these days. Mum used to go to her place a lot, go to tea and all that with her and the other one.'

'Helena.'

'Right. I never did go, not then.'

'It was this place, the house I mean. They lived here.'

She nods indifferently. 'Mum died in a car crash. Dad was driving. He didn't die but he lost a leg. He's been living with me since then. I've got a flat, it's little but it's got two bedrooms. The woman next door keeps an eye on him while I'm not there. He's had a stroke.'

I take all this in. She's at least managed to tell me quite a lot. I ask, though prepared to be told it's not my business, if she works, if she has a job.

'I have to. I've no one to keep me.' She doesn't say what the job is.

We've come a long way from Clara. I ask when Caroline first went to see her and why, but I can already tell she's one of those people, unattractive, brusque, graceless, who are yet the salt of the earth, who can't be bothered with the Davids and Georginas of this world – nor come to that with the Martins and the Judes – but take for granted the need to visit and tend the aged and infirm. For them it's as much a necessary part of life as taking a bath or eating a meal.

'She was all alone,' she says. 'She was upset when Mum died. There was no one else but me.'

'Diana,' I say, 'Diana and her girls.'

'Diana never came near her until Lucy and Jennifer went away to some fancy boarding school.' Her tone doesn't change when she says this, she doesn't sound resentful. 'Then she started going and sometimes she brought the girls. I never saw them. Diana was OK, she hadn't any side to her. I wrote to Jennifer when her mum died. I don't know why Jennifer and not Lucy, she was the eldest, but I reckon I liked the sound of Jennifer better.'

'Did Clara talk about the family?'

'A bit. She'd nothing else to talk about really. Can I have another biscuit?'

'Of course.' I pour her a second cup of tea and one for myself and take a deep breath. Here it comes now. 'Did she talk to you about the haemophilia?'

I expect her to say, 'The what?' But she's unfazed, takes the question for granted. 'She did a bit. She wanted to know if I knew. But Mum had told me when I was still a kid.' For the first time she smiles. She laughs, a sound of repeated

427

exhalations without humour. 'She said I must tell my husband before I got married. I said I wouldn't get married. Of course I wouldn't. Who'd marry a person like me?'

How do you answer that? You don't. You can't. And I can't now ask her if that knowledge stopped her marrying. I might if I were a doctor or an analyst but I'm only a distant cousin and biographer. 'So you told Clara you already knew?'

She nods. It seems to be of no importance to her. She'd decided never to marry, no one would want her, so it hardly mattered. Born in 1953, she might have decided to have a child outside marriage but she evidently hadn't. I'm stuck now, I don't know what to ask, when she says, 'Some of Clara's stuff came to me when she died. Theo didn't want it, they said, so I took it.' She considers this. 'Was that your dad?'

I nod. 'Stuff?'

'A couple of suitcases and a box with her clothes and some medical books and a lot of old photos.'

So that's what a life comes to after it's been lived for nearly a hundred years, a few clothes and books and photographs.

'What sort of medical books?'

'Not her dad's. They were old but not that old. There was one about haemophilia and Queen Victoria and a medical dictionary. I don't remember the others. I gave them to the church sale. Yes, and there were a couple of notebooks with black covers.'

My heart jumps. It isn't possible, is it, that the missing notebook, the *other* one Henry wrote his essays in, the book that should naturally follow on from the one in my possession, that it should have turned up in these circumstances? I daren't quite ask. I hedge. 'They were Henry Nanther's? Our great-grandfather's?'

428

'I reckon. I never read them. The writing was too small.'

I go into the study and take the one I have off the dining table. She nods. 'I sent that one to Theo's widow.' It's my mother she means. My father had died soon after Clara. 'It was no use to me,' she says. 'I was going to send back the other one but it got mislaid and when I found it my dad was reading it. He had to use a magnifying glass but I let him get on with it. He doesn't have much to amuse him. Well, interest him, I suppose. He's eighty and he's not a well man.'

'It didn't come back to my mother.'

'No. I couldn't find it. Dad may have put it out for the recycling, this is only a few months ago. I'm sure it's not in the flat. Is it important?'

My jumping heart has sunk. I shrug. 'It could be. Too late now.'

She looks at her watch. 'I'd better go. My hospital appointment's at five and it's half-four now. I could forward you the photos if you like.'

Why am I convinced of something I certainly wasn't before, that Henry confided things to that notebook that he told no one and wrote down nowhere else? I find I'm shaking my head, which she takes as saying no to her offer. Why, I wonder, did Clara take the notebooks? Because medicine interested her so much while it meant nothing to the others? Or was there something in it she liked reading and re-reading because it reminded her of her father? But she hadn't much liked him, surely. I say in a rather pathetic feeble sort of voice, 'Do you think your father would remember what he read?'

'Not very likely. He's got very forgetful of late. I put flowers on the grave because he nagged me to do it, he

429

made my life a misery, and then when I said I had he'd forgotten he ever asked me.'

'Flowers on whose grave?'

'Great-grandfather Henry's.'

I'm finding this bizarre. 'Your father?' I say, bewildered. 'He couldn't have known Henry. He was only his – what? Grandson-in-law born after he was dead?'

'I know,' she says with her usual indifference. 'He said he felt sorry for him.'

'How did you know where it was?'

'My mum used to go there. She used to take flowers to Fulham for her mum and to Kensal Green for her grandma.'

After she's gone there comes into my head something an authority on pre-Columbian Mexico once told me. When they conquered the country the Spanish Conquistadores destroyed almost everything the Aztecs had written or painted so that only the occasional rare codex was saved. A short time later they came to regret what they'd done and did their best to replace the lost texts by recreating them from memory and much of those recollections is what survives today.

Maybe I'm going to have to rely on what a senile old man can remember. A strange old man who so pities another long-dead old man that he asks his daughter to put flowers on his grave. Did that pity come out of what he'd read in the lost notebook?

34

I've been invited to go back as a life peer. The call came yesterday, from a Downing Street aide. 'The Prime Minister has asked me to ask you if you will take the Government Whip in the House of Lords.'

I didn't expect it. It never crossed my mind. And, of course, as is the way with anything like this, you can't think, you can't appreciate what's been asked of you, you can't consider anything. The shock stops all that. I'm silent, trying to digest it and not succeeding.

'Perhaps you'd like a few days to think about it.'

'Yes,' I say, 'yes. Till the end of the week?'

The end of the week is only three days off and he agrees, obviously enjoying my stunned response. It must be a nice job, his, to be in the business of giving people delightful, or at least amazing, surprises. I put the receiver back and sit there, collecting my scattered feelings, attempting to recover from astonishment and finally, after staring out of the window for a long time and palpating in my hands the Tenna egg, ask myself, yes or no?

I miss the place, I want to go back. I like the freedom of not being there, having my evenings to myself and Jude and doing as I like. I'm flattered to be asked, yet I want to keep my liberty. It wouldn't be the cross-benches any more, no more independence, but a seat on the Government benches and obedience to a whip. How I miss the library, the beautiful dining room and even the horrible bread. And I miss too playing my small part in the government of my country. But I will have to join the Labour Party. They won't give the Government Whip to a non-party member. Yet wasn't I always thinking about taking the Government Whip before I was banished?

Jude comes home and I don't tell her. Not immediately. We have a drink, or I do. She's back on her alcohol-free regime and she's read somewhere that what a woman eats in the first few days of a pregnancy radically affects the unborn child for life. She's back in the land of hope and the hideous stress of waiting and not knowing, unable to keep to the neutrality of neither hoping nor fearing. As for me, I don't know what I want any longer, I only know how base I am. Because it's the cost I think of. That inner voice that says things to us we wouldn't tell a soul reminds me of the £5,000 so far expended, and I answer back in the other dreadful countering voice that at least if she's pregnant there'll be no more immediate outlay, while if not that's another two and a half grand gone to kingdom come. How mad we are to try to compensate for things we've only *thought* about someone. I 'make it up' to Jude by cooking the dinner while she puts her feet up and reads a manuscript.

We've eaten and I've drunk more wine than I should have. Why don't I want to tell her? Because I think she'll try and stop me, because she won't want me out late three nights a week? If that's so I must be seriously considering saying yes. Well, of course I am. Jude wouldn't try to make me do anything I didn't want to, I ought to know that. But I must tell her tonight because to wait till tomorrow would be unforgivable. I pour myself another glass of wine and tell her, abruptly. Her reaction's not at all what I might have expected.

She gets up and comes up to me, she puts her arms round me and says, 'Congratulations. What an honour!'

'So you think I should accept?'

'You're not thinking of refusing, surely?'

'I don't know,' I say.

Now that she knows she's quite excited and keeps on talking about it. She says it's well-deserved and she'll like coming back herself. Taking her seat below the bar with the other life peers' wives and husbands. That's why the Chief Whip's asked me to lunch on Tuesday week. Didn't I think of that? I know her so well that I see the change in her face when she talks of nine days hence. I hear the tiny faltering in her voice no one else would notice. By then, before then, she'll know if it's success or failure this time. Whether the blue line's there or not.

If it's not there now it surely will be next time or the next, another five grand later. That's what I think of when I wake up in the night and Inner Voice, nasty, insidious and coldly practical, tells me I've got to take this life peerage because *I need the money*. It's ten thousand a year expenses, twelve if I struggle, and it's tax-free. Never mind idealism, high-mindedness, working for what I believe in. Think of the money. And if the final stage of the House of Lords reform leads to elected peers who get a salary I'll have to stand for election. Because I need the money.

Georgie Croft-Jones is ill. She was perfectly fit all the time she was carrying Galahad, but this time she's sick every day and all day. A piteous phone call came from her this morning. Would we come over? She's so lonely and bored and low, she says. I'm not surprised she's feeling low, for the home help David has fetched in to look after her and him and Galahad is none other than his mother Veronica. Jude suggests this evening and says we'll eat before we come. We walk over to Lauderdale Road because it's a fine warm evening and these streets are pretty in the spring, the gardens bright with blue flowering shrubs Jude says are tea bushes.

Veronica is in the kitchen, still in her impossibly high-heeled shoes to do her chores but makes the concession of wearing an apron over her short skirt and black and white jumper. She makes it plain when we shake hands that she expects me to kiss her; apparently we know each other well enough for that now, so I brush her scented powdery cheek with my lips.

'Finished it yet?' she says.

I'm at a loss. 'Finished what?'

'The book you're writing about my grandfather of course.'

'I haven't even begun it,' I say and then I excuse myself to go and talk to Georgie, a pathetic sight in her large white four-poster, a bowl on the bedside cabinet and another on the floor. The room smells of vomit, though the window is open and the meadow-fresh air freshener spray in evidence. I've never seen Georgie so thin or, come to that, Galahad so fat. He's on the bed crawling all over her. The shape of things to come, I think to myself, and picture our inviolate bed invaded and plundered by a large vigorous baby.

Georgie knows all about the implants and exactly what stage Jude has reached. They're talking about it and Jude's being very frank about her hopes and fears, but I notice something new in Georgie, her marked lack of enthusiasm. Pregnancy isn't the merry fun-ride it was the first time round. David comes in, looking equally worn out, carrying a bottle of wine and two glasses. Jude, of course, won't have any and whatever Georgie drinks she sicks up. David and I have a glass each, nibble at small cheese biscuits which remind me of the ones they serve in the Peers' Guest Room, and then he takes his son off to bed. Galahad yells and screams and pounds David's head with his fists.

In his absence, as if a child of his age could understand, Georgie plunges into an account of her symptoms, the opinions of several doctors and various peculiarities of her reproductive organs. Jude seems fascinated. I creep away and find Veronica in the living room, now divested of her apron, drinking gin and reading the *Spectator*.

'That child needs a firm hand,' she says, for Galahad's screaming surely fills every corner of this not very large flat. 'Imagine two of them here. They'll have to get a house before the new one comes. You and your wife have the right idea.'

I eye her enquiringly.

'Not having children. Each generation seems more trouble and expense than the last.'

I've no comment to make. I decide to turn the couple of hours we're here to my advantage. 'I've recently met your cousin's daughter Caroline.'

She raises her eyebrows, says nothing.

'Her father is still alive. Did you ever know him?'

'Of course I did. I was a bridesmaid at their wedding – well, a matron of honour. I was married myself by then. Very good looking which is more than Patricia was, big gawky creature with a small head.'

'Her daughter's a bit like that.'

'I haven't seen her since she was six.' Veronica evidently has no interest in Caroline, what has become of her, where she lives. Malicious scandalmongering is more in her line. 'Tony,' she says, and I have to think whom she means – of course, Anthony Agnew, Caroline's father. 'Tony had been drinking when he crashed that car. I know that for a fact, though it never came out. He wasn't the one to get killed, oh no.'

'He lost a leg,' I say.

'Well, he was asking for it, wasn't he? Of course he was one of those who had a good war.' I've never actually *heard* anyone say that before, only read it. 'Major Agnew, which he never would have been otherwise. He was a car salesman but he lost his job after the accident.' She takes a big swig of her gin and I wonder if I should take to it. It seems to preserve people wonderfully. 'Patricia's father conducted the service at their wedding, and her mother was there too, my aunt Mary. My own mother was dead by then. Aunt Mary was a funny old bat, a religious maniac.' She preens herself, passing a red-nailed hand across her golden cap of hair. 'Women *aged* so quickly in those days. Bobbing and crossing herself at the wedding she was, on her knees when everyone else was up singing hymns.'

'I'm going to meet Anthony Agnew,' I say, though it's only this minute that I've thought of doing that. 'I'm going to have a talk with him.'

'Whatever for?' Veronica sounds quite annoyed.

'I think he may have something to tell me about Henry Nanther.'

'Why on earth? He died years before Tony was born.'

I am saved from answering by David's coming into the room with the wine bottle. Galahad is still crying. 'That's right, darling,' says Veronica. 'Shut the door on him and let him get on with it. It's the only way.'

It's extraordinary the smug satisfaction people like her derive from being unkind to babies. I ask her about her aunt Clara. Was she at that wedding?

'She may have been. I don't remember. She certainly wasn't asked to mine and nor was Helena. We'd quite enough family, Roger and I, without asking those two funny old things.'

'I gather Clara wanted to be a doctor.'

Veronica laughs. 'Then want must have been her master. Goodness me, women didn't do that in those days.'

'Do you know if she was particularly interested in her father's work? Maybe even in her father himself? Would she have taken away some of his — writings, after she was dead?'

'Are you asking me? I haven't the faintest idea. Would you get me another gin, David? It will help me to sleep if the child keeps up that racket.'

The racket is still going on when we leave. David says he's not sure if fetching his mother over was the best thing, but what was he to do? Jude promises to ask Lorraine if she will help out temporarily until Georgie gets better, something that everyone says will happen when the pregnancy's three months old.

Next morning I phone Caroline. She's there to answer, as I suppose she mostly is, but she doesn't sound pleased to hear from me. 'Meet my dad?' she says, and then, as if their home is in Tasmania or the Urals, 'You'd have to come all the way out here. He couldn't come to you.'

'When?'

She's taken aback by this simple direct question. 'I don't know.'

'Monday?'

'Monday's the spring bank holiday,' she says.

'Would that matter? Are you going out somewhere?'

'We don't go out unless it's to the doctor's or the hospital. I go to work mornings.'

Her father is old, she tells me again. He's had a stroke and he's only got one leg and he ought not to be upset. But at last she gives in and I make a date for Monday afternoon.

Jude has her own hospital appointment on Tuesday and of course I'll go with her. Meanwhile, now, today, I have to phone the aide and tell him – what? Yes or no? It's almost certainly yes, isn't it?

I really want more time, but of course I can't expect that. I said by the end of the week and it's Friday now. How much easier writing Henry's biography would be, how much *better* in every respect, if I had quiet and peace and leisure to do it in. If I could take time to find precisely the right word and phrase, the original metaphor, if I could stare at the page for long minutes, for half an hour, then get up and walk around the house, thinking. But I shan't be able to do these things if I say yes today, I shall restrict myself to three or at most four hours in the mornings, and if the House sits, not on Fridays at all. And the galloping of tiny feet and yells from tiny lungs may be around too . . .

But I need the money. I need the seventy odd pounds a day four or five times a week. It sounds pathetic, doesn't it, when you consider some people's salaries. I push all this out of my mind, it's still only eleven in the morning. I think about Tony Agnew, the ex-major who had a good war from which he came out intact, and a bad peace when he lost a leg. What sort of a man is this one-time soldier and vendor of cars who feels so sorry for a dead man he never knew that he gets his daughter to put flowers on that man's grave? And why do it then and not years before when he might have done it himself? I'd like to have some idea, some workable theory, before I get to Reading on Monday afternoon. But everything that presents itself to me is *not like Henry*. Confident Henry. Tyrannical Henry. Henry, who deserted one woman after another in order to marry a third he happened to like the look of, and when she died married her sister. Henry, who refused to discuss her brother's condition with his grown-up daughter and who would have been so adamant in his refusal to let her study medicine that she knew it would be useless to ask him. But, on the other hand, Henry whose wife was the only person who 'could do anything with him' and whose son described him as the kindest sweetest father in the world. Paradoxical Henry. Henry the enigma.

Jude's working at home today. She's in the living room with a manuscript she doesn't want to read but has to. I shall take her out somewhere for lunch and then, when we get back, I'll phone that aide. I'll tell him no. I'll refuse the offered peerage and then I can write my book in peace and hope that this one, for once, will sell. But while I'm thinking in this way, while I'm making up my mind, Jude comes in, flushed in the face, her eyes very bright, and says she's just done a pregnancy test. She shouldn't, they told her to wait till next week, but she's done it.

'It's positive,' she says. 'The blue line was dazzling.'

I kiss her and hold her. I tell her it's the most wonderful day of my life because this time I know things are going to be fine. This is a designer baby and, in spite of last time, that sort don't abort themselves. They've no defects, they're perfect, they live serenely inside there and when they come out they're – well, designer. They're the Versaces and the Diors of the baby world and they prove it by costing a lot more than your ordinary off-the-peg infant.

I pick up the phone and dial the magic number, the witching number, and when he comes on ask him to tell the Prime Minister I shall be happy to accept. I shall go back and be thankful.

35

He's a tall thin old man. If he's shrunk he must have been very tall indeed to start with but I don't think he's shrunk. He's very upright and the only evidence that he has an artificial leg is in a limp which isn't always noticeable. It's a funny thing but a man may be very good looking with a daughter who's exactly like him yet ugly. We have different standards of beauty for the sexes. Caroline's rugged face looks good on Tony Agnew, it *still* looks good, although he's eighty and can't have had an easy life. He has answered the door himself, perhaps to show me he's far from decrepit. Caroline's there, of course she is, and she's hovering, in attendance perhaps to see that I ask no questions too painful for her father to answer.

Why did she want to give me the impression he was a broken old man, scarcely in his right mind? Needing the neighbour to keep an eye on him. Needing *her*. To justify her existence perhaps. To show me she's given up her life to a worthy cause. 'Yes, all right,' she'd said at last when I'd asked her what time to come. 'Monday afternoon about three. He'll be awake by then. He'll have taken his second lot of tablets. There's a bus from the station passes this place.'

I didn't ask about cabs, I knew there'd be some. She'd been at the window when I got there, watching for me, noting the taxi. There's something disconcerting about meeting a watcher's eyes, that watcher known to you, your *cousin*, and see her turn away without a smile, let alone a wave. Now she wears a resigned expression. It's out of her hands and she's powerless to do anything about it. I wish she'd go away and leave us alone, I and this intelligent-looking old man in his tweed suit and waistcoat, but I know there's no hope of that. Not even when he asks her, very sweetly, if she'll make us a cup of tea, please, darling girl. She'll be back and soon.

Meanwhile, he's talking about his mother-in-law, Mary Craddock, born Nanther. She always called herself 'the Honourable', he recalls. Even in the parish magazine her name appeared as the Hon. Mrs Craddock. She was fanatical about her faith, went to church every day, she could always find Morning Service or Holy Communion somewhere, if not in her husband's parish. This devotion turned her daughter, his wife, against religion and their wedding was the last time she went to church. He speaks of his wife in a lower tone, almost with reverence. His voice is plummy, very much the army officer's and, probably, the twenties prep school, and it's quite different from Caroline's. She comes back with a tray on which china and spoons have been ungracefully piled, goes out again, returns with another on which are milk in a carton and biscuits in a packet. The sugar, however, is in a bowl but the kind that looks as if it's made for some other purpose, perhaps for mixing cake ingredients.

To my surprise she begins talking about her morning at work. The fact that it's a public holiday makes no difference to her because she's employed five mornings a week in an old people's home. The anecdote she tells is concerned with what someone said to someone else about a grave in a cemetery. It could be my cue to ask Tony Agnew about the flowers he wanted put on Henry's but I can't get a word in edgeways. It will have to wait. Tony – he asks me to call him this – laughs dutifully, though it was remarkably unfunny, and I take my chance to ask if we can talk about the notebook.

'The notebook?'

He's looking at me uncomprehendingly and for a split second I feel a kind of impatient rage. If he's forgotten its existence I may as well get out of here, go back to the station and home. But he hasn't, though I can see, as one sometimes notices in very old people, that it's just slipped out of his mind and he has to make an effort of will to find it and bring it back again. The struggle is made, he sighs and says, 'You mean Lord Nanther's book he wrote all those things in?'

'Yes.'

I take a biscuit. I'm suddenly very hungry, though the biscuits are the kind very young children like, crumbly sandwiches with red jam inside. Caroline is watching me, perhaps expecting praise for the morsel I've put in my mouth as if she'd made it herself. 'Very nice,' I mumble.

'He wants to know about it, Dad,' she says. 'That's why he's here.'

'What happened to it?' I ask.

Frustration and perplexity mingle in his expression. 'I don't know. I've been trying to remember but I can't. I don't know. I put it with some papers, newspapers. I mean I put it down on this table. On something.' He screws up his eyes in an effort to remember. I am beginning to see Caroline wasn't exaggerating. The first impression one gets of this old man is deceptive. He struggles hard to appear well, fit, in control, but after a time he fails. His voice has become fretful. 'On some magazines,' he says. 'That's where I put it. Then my – my daughter gave me the daily paper. I looked at it, I think, I put it down . . .'

442

'Dad, we've been through all this.' She isn't in the least impatient. 'You put it down *on* the book that was *on* the magazines and I put the lot out for the recycling. I never even saw the notebook, it was hidden by the paper.'

'If you say so, darling girl.'

'Papers are so thick these days, aren't they?' she says conversationally. 'There are so many bits to them.'

It's irretrievably lost, I know it is. I can picture it, see it in the recycling box, nestling there and concealed between section one of the *Daily Telegraph* – I am certain Tony, like Veronica, would be a *Telegraph* reader – and *Woman's Own*, with the sport section and Travel and Appointments all piled on top. And I see it standing on the forecourt of these flats and the dustmen, or whatever they call them these days, lifting it with a grunt at its weight, tipping the lot into one of those trucks they have with latticework sides. The notebook slides out and slips in among newspapers and magazines and biscuit packaging and cornflake packets and e-mail print-outs. It all goes off to recycling heaven where good papers go these days when they die. To be resurrected as dove-grey envelopes with 'Made from reconstituted paper' stamped on their flaps.

'Well, it's too late now,' I say.

Tony shakes his head sadly. 'I'm frightfully sorry. I'm not safe to be let out alone.'

He's not safe to be left *in* alone. Of course I don't say this. I make the best of things. I have no choice. It's not exactly Mill's housemaid putting the only manuscript of Carlyle's *French Revolution* in the fire, is it? Just an old man's jottings, only the key to a mysterious *volte-face* of character not otherwise to be resolved.

'You read it?' I say.

'Oh, yes.' Tony looks troubled. 'I rather wish I hadn't.

You'd think I could forget, wouldn't you, when I forget everything else?'

'Now, Dad,' says Caroline, 'you don't forget *everything*, you know you don't.'

'Thank goodness you're my memory, darling girl.'

I ask him what was in the book that's so unforgettable, so apparently painful. 'I know about remorse,' he says. 'I know all about it.' He's silent.

'He means Mum,' says Caroline as if I'm a particularly slow child. 'He means Mum and the accident. He blames himself, don't you, Dad?'

'Who else can I blame, my sweet? It was my fault. I killed her, as sure as if I'd put arsenic in her tea.'

She shrugs. She's been through all this before. Many times, probably. Maybe she agrees with him. She was twenty-two at the time, so it's unlikely she was with them in the car. But she knows the facts. There must have been an inquest, even a prosecution, in spite of what Veronica says. Perhaps he had been drinking or he fell asleep at the wheel. To my dismay I see a tear come into each of his eyes and begin a slow trickling progress down his cheeks. She gets up and wipes them away with a tissue she pulls out of a box on the table and says as if he's deaf or otherwise insensible, 'He cries. You don't want to take any notice. Old people do, I see it all the time in the home, especially the ones that have had strokes. I suppose it's what they mean by second childhood.'

She's one of the most insensitive people I've come across for a long time – no, Veronica is worse – but Tony doesn't seem to mind. He smiles waterily. He even thanks her. I'm so disconcerted by all this I wonder if I should go on, and if she'd stayed there, sitting between us, perhaps I wouldn't have. But something I hadn't anticipated and wouldn't have

444

dared hope for happens. The doorbell rings and Caroline goes to answer it. 'I won't be a minute,' she says, and this is true but not, as is often the case with this ambiguous remark, in the way she means. Whoever is at the door is invited in and because Tony and I are in occupation of the living room, taken elsewhere. The kitchen? Her bedroom? I don't know, but I hear doors shutting and I offer to pour Tony another cup of tea. Remorse, I'm thinking, why remorse? Whose remorse?

He accepts the tea, smiles again. 'Tell me about the notebook,' I say, trying not to let urgency sound in my voice. 'Tell me what you read.'

'They were sort of articles, pieces like you read in a – well, like in the paper. No, not quite like that.' He wrinkles his forehead, striving to find the words. 'Like a *confession*. But a confession he was making to himself. I felt bad reading them. I felt no one was meant to read them.'

'His daughter Clara read them. She got hold of the notebook after he was dead and kept it all those years.'

'Oh, yes, Clara,' he says, and he's deflected. Very willingly deflected, I think. 'I remember her. Nice old girl. Very clever too, used to be always reading highbrow stuff. *She* forgave me, not like some of that lot. Vindictive they were. *She* said no one ought to be blamed for what they didn't mean to do.'

I have to get him back to the notebook, tempting as it is to ask who was vindictive. Diana? Veronica? 'Did Henry Nanther blame himself for what he didn't mean to do?'

It's an inspired guess, for Tony wants to reply and with some vigour. 'He blamed himself all right, that was the point, that was all over those pieces, in practically every line, but he *did* mean to do it. That was the bad part, the awful part. He meant to do everything.'

'But do what?'

'I don't know.' He looks downcast. 'Maybe I'm just not bright enough. I never was all that bright, dear boy. Good soldier, says he modestly, but that's about it. There was a lot in those bits your great-grandfather wrote down I just didn't understand. Couldn't follow, if you get my meaning. What came through was – well, like I said, remorse. I can remember one bit he repeated a few times. It went something like this, "I blighted my posterity in advance." I remember it because I had to look up some of the words in the dictionary. Not that it made me understand what he was saying.'

At this point I start hearing voices from the next room and then someone crying. A door opens and closes, a tap is running in kitchen or bathroom. Tony says, 'That woman at the door Caroline let in, she lives next door, her husband beats her. She always comes here, telling Caroline her troubles but will she go to the police? Will she heck.'

Can it be the neighbour who sometimes looks after him? The crying continues and a radio is put on in the next room, presumably to deaden the sound of sobbing. I ask Tony what else he can remember. Of course the notebook has slipped from his mind and thinking I'm talking about the domestic violence next door, he launches into a rambling description of the damage done to his unfortunate neighbour. 'Henry Nanther's notebook,' I say to him.

'Oh, yes. Yes. He'd done something a long time ago. I don't know what. Caroline would have known, she's got her mother's brains, but she never had time to read it. He'd fixed something, done it on purpose, for medical reasons, he said. Well, what he said was, "for the future of medical science". I remember that phrase. It's stuck in my mind. But it wasn't that upset me so much. It was the poor

446

old chap's remorse and something he said about – well, above love.'

'Love?'

'My God, I wish I'd never put the damn thing down on those magazines, books, whatever they were. I've kicked myself a good many times for that. How did I know you'd turn up and be so keen on seeing what was in it?'

'Love,' I say. 'What did he say about love?'

He's going to cry again, but I can't help that. 'He said – he said he'd never known what real love was. He thought he had, he mentioned some chap, I can't recall the name, some chap who drowned, but that was nothing, he said, to what he felt now, what it was to love someone more than yourself, to wish you could die in their place. He'd never felt like that before, he said, not even over the drowned chap.' The tears are flowing and the old voice is breaking. 'And the bad thing was, the awful thing was, that it was *him* had made sure the one he loved would die while he would go on living . . . Oh, God, the poor chap, the poor chap . . .'

And now because the radio's been turned off the flat is full of the sound of weeping and sobbing, in here and in the other room. It's as if the whole world is in tears. I produce tissues for poor old Tony and mop up his face for him. There's no doubt I have to give up, I can't ask him any more, I can't subject him to cruel and unusual punishment. I feel like crying myself. What I do is find a bit of paper in the briefcase I've brought with me and make myself write down the things he's said, or the salient things. Gradually he stops crying, says he's a fool. What must I think of him? The sounds from the next room have stopped, the front door opens and closes and Caroline comes back.

'You've been upsetting him,' she says like a nanny to the

bully of the family. 'I knew that would happen once my back was turned.'

But Tony's no longer upset. He's probably forgotten what distressed him in the first place and wants to know what brought the neighbour to the door this time.

'He's blacked her eye. I wanted to call an ambulance but she'll never let me do anything. She says he really loves her and he's promised not to do it again. That's a really nasty eye she's got.'

I don't suppose I shall ever see either of them again. I'm sitting in the train, looking at the notes I made, but I already know the answers to everything. I know what Henry did and why he did it, I think I knew that as soon as Tony talked about blighting his posterity in advance.

Yet, although I know and have known for the past hour, the full impact of it is only now hitting me as I revert in my mind to the events and the people in his life I feel I now know so well: Richard Hamilton, 'the chap who drowned', his mother, the women, Jimmy, Olivia, Eleanor, Edith. Queen Victoria and the royal family, his triumphs, his discoveries, his children. The calculated wickedness. Switzerland and the artless innocent walking tours in the Alps. Blood, blood, all that blood.

The train comes into Paddington and I go to join the inevitable taxi queue, thinking of Henry. Monstrous Henry.

36

I returned to the House nearly two months ago, at the end of July before it rose for the summer recess. No one was invited to watch my entry as Lord Nanther of Lilestone. As a hereditary peer made a life peer I was permitted to take my seat without formal introduction, but Jude was there and, strangely enough, Paul. He asked to come, invited himself. Apparently, he doesn't object to appointed peers, only to hereditary ones, and he'd prefer what he calls 'elected lords' above all. He sat where I thought he'd never sit again, on the steps of the throne, and had quite abandoned that expression of supercilious boredom he wore when last there.

Lilestone because, as a life peer, I'm obliged to have a territory. Godby no longer belongs to the family, which wouldn't matter, but I don't like the idea of using it while other people live at Godby Hall. I thought of Alma. But the Battle of Alma, after which the square was named, was the first in the Crimean War, and Garter will only let you call yourself after a battle if you took part in it (like Montgomery of Alamein and Alexander of Tunis) or, better still for some sinister reason, sacked the place. So I've taken Lilestone, the manor of which St John's Wood was once a part and which remains only in the name of the estate in Lisson Grove. I've had my lunch with the Chief Whip, I've joined the Party and taken my place on the Government benches, in the second row from the back.

All this is pleasurable – I remind myself daily of my

nostalgia for the place during my banishment – and I've even better things to console me, yet life has its downside. What I've discovered about Henry hangs over me like a heavy cloud. I feel as I used to when I was younger and had read of some dreadful cruelty or seen some appalling photograph and it lingered in the back of my mind to return, somehow magnified and darkened, at times when I was alone in the day or wakeful at night. So it is now with Henry's act. I've so far told no one about it. Perhaps I feel – foolishly, no doubt – that it's unwise to tell such a terrible thing to a pregnant woman, that henceforward her life should be serene and untroubled. As I'm sure it is. As for me, it's wonderful to see her so happy, so full of joy now she's carrying two babies. And, strangely, after all my dread of renewed fatherhood, the twins' coming is also consoling. When I experience Henry's act of violence resurfacing before I sleep or in a dream, I remind myself of the two children I shall see grow up healthy and beautiful. Jude is nearly five months pregnant now, everything is fine, and all my dismay is gone. They will be born next January, and somehow I know they'll be born safely.

We can afford to stay in this house, we shall manage. I look back and ask myself how I dared complain, even in my heart, about the £5,000 the twins cost to conceive. Jude will go back to work after they're born, I shall have my expenses, stand for election if there's ever a question of election, we'll have a nanny and I shall try my hand at journalism while I'm baby-tending in the mornings. I'll do all the reviewing I can get hold of. For I've published my last biography and my life of Henry Nanther will never be written. I've known that for months now, faced it perhaps in the hope that abandoning his biography and trying to put all my research behind me will exorcise the images and the infamy. It hasn't happened that way.

Having told myself sparing Jude because she's pregnant is positively Victorian and something Henry might have done – hypocritical Henry – I've nevertheless considered telling it all to Paul first. If he'd listen, and I think he would. There were other possibilities: Lachlan, for instance, but I feel sensitive about anyone outside the family knowing; David, except that I don't think he'd much care, and I haven't the nerve to tell John Corrie, even in a letter, he's a bit too closely affected even if he is a scientist.

My relationship with my son has undergone many changes for the better in these past months. He says that as an only child himself, he wants a big family one day, but because he can't seriously begin that yet, two little sisters will do very well for a start. I could hardly believe my ears when he said that perhaps we'll let him baby-sit sometimes or look after them in the daytime. I never dreamed he had these aspirations. But perhaps I never bothered to find out. Anyway, we're moving towards a new closeness – Jude and he are already there – and I seriously thought of making him the recipient of – well, Henry's retrospective confidence.

He's in London this weekend and it's likely he'll look in. This evening perhaps. I'm half expecting him and waiting, not in our living room, but in my study where all the Henry memorabilia is spread or stacked on the dining table in front of me. And in the middle of it, on its stand, the red painted egg I was given when I went to Tenna. Jude has gone round to the Croft-Joneses, in the car because I don't care for her walking home after dark, even in these safe streets. Georgie is over her pregnancy sickness, and is as mountainous as she was last time. If it's a girl they've given up the idea of Yseult and intend to call her Brangaene, after Isolde's attendant in the opera.

I've also set a tray on the table with a bottle of whisky on it, a jug of water and two glasses, though I don't feel like drinking anything myself. Not for the first time since I talked to Tony Agnew I find myself holding the egg in my left hand, palpating it like worry beads, though I've no memory of how it got there. If I keep on with this, I'll wear all the red paint off.

Even if he does come perhaps I won't tell Paul. Perhaps I won't tell anyone, ever.

Control circumstances and do not let circumstances control you. That's what he thought he was doing, not understanding it's impossible. Thomas à Kempis didn't understand either and nor did all the people who remember Henry Nanther's words and think them so clever. Circumstances are bigger than you are. They are more powerful and that's all there is to it. He's a midget, cowering under their crushing hand.

Who can tell when the idea first came to him? Or why? It's possible, even likely, that he saw *himself* as the martyr. Wasn't it Jenner half a century earlier who injected himself with smallpox, having first been immunized, or so he hoped, with matter taken from cowpox lesions? Henry, supremely egocentric, may well have seen his actions in the same light. Experiments undertaken for the benefit of mankind, for the greater glory of science, but involving the sacrifice of the scientist. Or, at any rate, the sacrifice of the scientist's happiness.

It's probable he knew of Tenna's unique peculiarity from his time at the University of Vienna. There, with his developing interest in diseases of the blood, with his *fascin-*

ation for blood, he would have read the papers by Vieli and Grandidier published a few years earlier. Who knows but that his fondness for walking in the Alps sprang from these findings? It seems highly likely if not certain that his first visit to Tenna was made at that time. Believing, erroneously as it happens, that Romansch was spoken there, he may even have set about learning the language with further researches in mind.

Was he looking for a specific haemophiliac family in the early 1860s? I doubt it. Had he been he'd have found one and taken the steps he took twenty years later at that time. Perhaps it didn't occur to him. Or else it was only when he'd attained in almost anyone's eyes – except his own? – spectacular worldly success, when he was the leading expert in his own field, a royal doctor, a professor, that he came to ask himself what in fact he had actually achieved. He had pioneered nothing, made no new discoveries, unless you can call confirming other people's conclusions, such as the way haemophilia was carried and transmitted, a discovery. But suppose he had a haemophilia carrier in his own family? Suppose he had a haemophiliac of his own?

Did he at first dismiss the idea as monstrous? I'd like to think so, I'd like to think he had one redeeming feature. But I've no proof one way or the other. I've no proof of any of this except the knowledge that it has to be so, it's the only explanation. I'm pretty sure that once the possibility had come into his mind it stayed there and grew, he couldn't get rid of it even if he wanted to. He very likely told himself that if he lacked the courage to do it – for he saw only himself, only the great doctor, the Queen's favourite, at the centre of everything – if he lacked the courage to do it, he'd regret this omission for the rest of his life. Control circumstances, that's the answer.

The doorbell is ringing. Paul, of course, having once again forgotten his key. But it's not Paul, it's a man from the Maida Vale Society wanting my support in an effort to ban the two high towers they're proposing to build at Paddington Basin. He wants to come in, he wants to 'talk it through' with me, and it's in vain I protest that this is St John's Wood, at least a mile away.

'They'll be visible from this house,' he says, and as if this will clinch things. 'They'll be visible from Richmond!'

I haven't the heart to tell him that the huge trees at the end of this garden block out any view as well as most of the light and air at the back. Instead I promise to write to my MP, the Mayor of London and a few Westminster councillors for good measure. He's looking longingly at the whisky (or so I think) and suddenly I don't want him to go, he seems rather nice, and I need someone there to talk to me, talk to me about anything, even planning authority solecisms, to keep me from Henry. But when I offer him a drink he says he can't, he's driving, and I realize it wasn't the whisky he was eyeing but all my Henry stuff. He asks me what I'm writing.

'Someone's biography,' I say but I don't add, I *was*.

'That must be very rewarding,' he says rather wistfully.

'Sometimes.'

I think to myself, when he goes Paul will come, I won't have to be alone with these thoughts. As I let him out Paul will come and then Jude will come back. I'm a fool, aren't I? It's not my crime, my sin, my horror.

I go out on to the pavement with him and look tube station-wards down the square. There's no one but an old lady exercising a Yorkshire terrier, no Paul and, of course, no Jude yet. The Maida Vale man gets into his car and drives off to his next port of call. I go indoors. Dusk is coming fast and if I went back now to look for my son I wouldn't be able to see to the end of the street. What can Henry's thoughts have been like at dusk, in the dark? When he was old, when he regretted what he'd done?

The idea was there when he was young and when he was in young middle-age but something had to happen to trigger it off, make it no longer a wild dream but a reality. The trigger may have been Dr Anton Hoessli's publication of his Tenna conclusions in 1877 or it may have been Richard Hamilton's death. Henry loved Hamilton and if he had been able to marry Hamilton's sister – and so in a sense marry Hamilton in a way pleasing to society, binding himself to Hamilton for ever – the great idea might have remained what it was, the kind of horrible fantasy all of us have but never bring to fruition. The kind of fantasy I've had when I've hoped Jude would turn out to be irremediably barren or her child die. But Hamilton was killed in the Tay Bridge disaster. When that happened Henry may have thought that love and happiness were over for him and only ambition and acclaim for achievements mattered.

Two years later he was in love – or what passed for being in love for him – with Olivia Batho. At the same time he was conducting a typical Victorian gentleman's liaison with Jimmy Ashworth. Neither of these relationships could be permanent, they got in the way of his grand design. It was time to pursue his researches into the haemophilia-carrying families further.

The phone rings and it's Paul. A year ago he'd no more have phoned to say he was or wasn't coming over than he'd have embraced me, something that does occasionally happen these days. He's not coming but he'll drop in tomorrow if that's all right.

'How's Jude and my sisters?'

Did I say we now know for sure they're both girls? I tell him they're all fine. Jude's round at the Croft-Joneses and I'm about to have a whisky. Oddly enough, I do feel like a drink now and I pour myself a large one worthy of Lachlan Hamilton. What did those Victorian gentlemen drink? I've never bothered to find out. Madeira, probably, and pints of sherry. Brandy, as Samuel Johnson says, is the drink for heroes.

Henry went back to Safiental, walking the twenty miles from Versam to Tenna, and began asking serious questions of the villagers. Haemophilia no longer affected anyone living there but it lingered on in men and women's memories. This would have been in the spring of 1882. What he discovered was that a woman called Magdalena Maibach later called Barbla, had been taken from Tenna to Zurich and thence to Paris by her adoptive mother and benefactress. Barbla Maibach was worth pursuing. Her father was mentioned as a haemophiliac by Vieli and Grandidier and again by Hoessli, so therefore she must be herself a carrier. Henry believed the disease was in some mysterious way carried in the blood – what else? Perhaps, if his experiment succeeded, he'd find out just what that mysterious way amounted to.

I don't know how he discovered what had become of Barbla but with many European countries starting to keep birth, marriage and death records, it wouldn't have been too difficult. It would have taken time, that's all. In fact, it probably took him getting on for a year. He discovered that Barbla married a Thomas Dornford, a jeweller in Hatton Garden, and had several children. One of them married William Quendon and became the mother of a certain Louisa Quendon, now the wife of Samuel Henderson, a Bloomsbury solicitor.

Why go to all this trouble when part of his job was

treating haemophiliac patients? Surely he could have picked the daughter of one of them. Easily, except that secrecy was of the essence. Who would believe that a doctor who warned the daughters of haemophiliacs not to marry and haemophiliacs themselves not to marry, would, in full knowledge of what he was letting himself in for, marry a woman who had a fifty per cent chance of being a carrier?

His diary tells me that in the spring of 1883 he went on a walking tour of the Lake District. I don't believe it. He was more likely in Amsterdam, checking on the last stages of his hunt for Barbla and her descendants. His next step was to acquaint himself with the Henderson family. One way would have been to transfer his legal business to Samuel Henderson's firm. There were a good many reasons not to do this. It was an obscure little partnership of three attorneys, struggling, not doing very well. For a man like Sir Henry Nanther to consult them would have looked odd, even suspicious. Besides, he had his own lawyers, eminent giants in their profession, the Mishcon de Reya of their day. Later on, of course, he did transfer his business but by then he was secure of a Henderson daughter. But for the present, the idea of staging an attack and a rescue appealed to his sense of drama. In any case, it was an excellent plan, guaranteed to earn him as rescuer the gratitude of Samuel Henderson and the approval of the whole family, besides providing him with an excuse to pay frequent visits to the house in Keppel Street.

Of course he couldn't yet be sure that Hans Maibach's haemophilia had been carried down the female line by subsequent generations. But even at this stage he could make an intelligent guess. Perhaps Barbla's son had died young. Her daughter Luise had lost a young son, Louisa Henderson's brother. There again this offered no positive identification of Louisa herself as a carrier and later, when Henry had been warmly received into the bosom of the family, it must have dismayed him to see Lionel Henderson enjoying good health and clearly not suffering from a disease of the blood. By then too he would have ascertained from Louisa or her daughters by subtle enquiries that the latter had no dead small brothers.

Before this he had directed his drama in Gower Street and it succeeded even better than he expected. I was surely right when I concluded, much earlier on in my researches, that he employed Brewer to do the deed for a satisfactory payment and the promise of a wife, a house and a lump sum for his half-brother. Presumably, the little matter of Jimmy's pregnancy was glossed over. Henry was in, an honoured guest in Keppel Street and the recipient of confidences. The two girls were not so bad, not a patch on Olivia of course, but then Olivia didn't carry haemophilia. He dropped her and soon afterwards he dropped Jimmy.

Now he had to make his choice between the Henderson daughters. It's possible he preferred Edith from the first but made himself agreeable to both, trying to detect the signs, if any, of a haemophilia carrier. In his diary he writes that from early on he could tell that Princess Beatrice was a 'conductor' but this may have been no more than vanity on his part. No doubt he watched both girls carefully. At that time for a young girl to have mentioned menstruation in the presence of a man, even a doctor, would have been unthinkable. It was the height of indelicacy to speak of it in the presence of another woman, apart from one's mother, and then in the most veiled and euphemistic terms. Girls were supposed to pretend 'the curse of Eve' didn't exist. Yet something happened that summer to make Henry certain of his quarry and fix his interest on Eleanor. Can there be any doubt that this was the 'consultation' the girls' mother had with him in July 1883?

I'm guessing when I say Louisa Henderson wanted to ask him about Eleanor's periods, what we would call today her dysmenorrhoea. That and perhaps her tendency to bruise very easily. Would these disabilities mean she was a carrier? I don't know but I'm sure Henry thought he knew. *What is the answer, that is the question.* He had that answer. In the following month he proposed to Eleanor and was accepted. Now he was engaged to a woman who was a direct descendant of Hans Maibach of Tenna, a haemophiliac, whose daughter, granddaughter and great-granddaughter were very likely carriers, who was herself almost certainly a carrier.

Any ideas I or Jude may have had about Henry arranging her murder in the Great Western train disappear now, for Eleanor was the woman all his researches and records-tracing had led him to, the more certain of the two sisters to be a haemophilia carrier. Her death must have been as great a blow to him as if he'd been in love with her. He had no need to put on a pretence of grief. Real sorrow and bitter disappointment were what he felt. Now he'd have to start again, perhaps return to Tenna, find another haemophiliac whose female descendants, scattered across Europe, might or might not have, as he saw it, the fatal flaw in their blood.

Or was there instead someone nearer at hand? Eleanor had a sister, more attractive to look at than she. But how to be sure this sister was a carrier? If he had another consultation with Louisa Henderson there's nothing about it in the diaries but that doesn't mean it never took place. This time it was he who was asking the questions and Edith's mother supplying the answers. Henry may even have gone so far as to intimate to Mrs Henderson that he'd like to marry Edith but was worried about her health. Would she, for instance, be able to bear children? Did she too suffer from dysmenorrhoea?

For a prospective bridegroom to ask such things of his future mother-in-law seems to us a terrible instance of male pride in male domination, and the worst of bad taste. We revolt against it as the Victorians revolted against openness and calling a spade a spade. But taste changes, just as what it is acceptable to utter does. Besides, before we say any mother worthy of the name would have refused to discuss it, would have shown Henry the door, we must remember how dreadfully the Hendersons' hopes had been dashed by Eleanor's death. The good marriage, the big house in a fashionable suburb, the title, the famous eminent husband – all that went out of the window with Eleanor's body. But they had been given a second chance. His eye had lighted on their other daughter and everything Mrs Henderson could do to encourage the match must be done.

So what did she say to Henry? Something which she, surely, believed wouldn't have a discouraging effect. Perhaps that Edith's periods though heavy were regular. As to the bruising she may have acceded to this because it would have seemed harmless to her. She may even – I am stretching rather far out here – have said that Edith bled profusely when she cut herself, believing this to be a sign of health.

As to Edith herself, was Henry so cold-blooded that he could transfer what affections he had had for Eleanor straight on to her sister? They *were* sisters, they may have been very much alike. By all accounts Edith was a steady, calm and phlegmatic woman, the kind who wouldn't cause her husband any trouble. And Henry must have thought of the purpose of this marriage: to produce children. He wasn't getting any younger, he'd become forty-eight in the February of 1884. Was he to begin the weary work of finding a suitable bride and courting her all over again when here was one for the taking?

Control circumstances and do not let circumstances control you.

Jude has come in, full of news about the Croft-Joneses' new house which they move into next week. They have the biggest mortgage she has ever heard of anyone taking on because this 'town house' in Hampstead is costing them nearly a million pounds. I've kissed her when she first came in but now I take her in my arms and hold her, hug her so tightly that she struggles free and asks me what's wrong.

'Does something have to be wrong for me to hug you?'

'It does when it's desperate.'

She wants to know what 'this' is and when I tell her it's Henry she casts up her eyes and says, 'Bloody Henry.'

'He was, wasn't he? In more ways than one. If I wanted to be melodramatic I'd say he waded through blood all his life.'

She says I always want to be melodramatic and to tell her about it. So I do. I forget all that nonsense about treating a pregnant woman with great delicacy and I tell her. She takes the egg out of my hand and looks at it, at the place where my worrying it has begun to rub the red paint off.

'He was worse than even I thought,' she says.

We go into the living room and sit on the sofa, side by side. 'Go on,' she says.

'He married Edith, as you know, and got her pregnant at once. Their first child Elizabeth was born nine months later in August.'

'Do you think Henry looked at the baby and wondered if she was a carrier?'

'Probably. He'd have wondered the same thing about the next daughter and the next and the next. By the standards of the time he was becoming an old man. He might not live long enough to see his eldest married and discover if she was in fact a carrier.'

Jude has brought David's family tree with her and she's studying it. 'By the time Clara was born he was fifty-five.'

'Considered old then. Another thing, he still didn't know for sure if his wife was a carrier. Four years later she had a son.'

'Alexander,' says Jude. 'He still wouldn't have known because Alexander wasn't a haemophiliac.'

'He may not have been sure of that for several months. He got his peerage but he still hadn't achieved the ground-breaking discovery he aimed at, that which was to be the subject of his final definitive work.'

'But two years later Edith had George,' says Jude.

'Yes, George. When did he know? Did he carry out some test to see if he bled abnormally?'

'Don't.'

'I'm not going to. The boy seems to have been a severe case. I wonder if the parents discussed it much. We don't know how close they were, only that Edith was the only one who could "do anything" with Henry. I've never considered till now whether she and her mother and perhaps her sister knew about the haemophilia in the family. They may have had some idea. Henry's mother-in-law had seen her small brother die and may have been told what he died of. When Lord and Lady Nanther knew what was wrong with their younger son, her mother may have said something to Henry about her brother dying from a bleeding disorder and hearing that a similar thing had happened to an uncle.'

'Wouldn't she have said so before? Years before? After all, even though Victorian women were kept in the dark about what their husbands did, about most things really, she must have known what his speciality was. She must have known what his books were about.'

'Maybe she did say so before,' I say. 'Maybe she said what a coincidence it was that the very disease he specialized in was in her own family. It's likely though that knowing her own brother Lionel was healthy made her think she couldn't pass it on. And Henry would have encouraged this belief. It wasn't in his interest to have his wife think she might give birth to a "bleeder". She might have refused him sex.'

Jude asks if women could do that in the nineteenth century when that promise to obey a husband was taken very seriously, but I tell her we're talking about the last decade of that century when things were changing fast. Presumably, Henry wouldn't have raped her. Not even he would have done that. Besides, she may have refused him for a while and that accounts for the four-year gap between Clara and Alexander.

'But she came back to him,' Jude says. 'She must have regretted not keeping up her abstinence after Alexander was born.'

'If she did she wasn't alone. Henry regretted it too. "Regret" isn't the word. He felt the most bitter remorse.'

Jude's fists are clenched by now. She opens her left hand and I see she has crushed the Tenna egg into a crumpled mass. She looks at it as if she's had no idea what she was doing.

★

We're in bed and Jude's asleep. Her head is on my shoulder and her right arm round my chest. At the end of August she 'quickened', as Edith might have said, and as her swelling belly rests against my hip I feel the twins move, what was at first the merest tiny flutter increasing now to kicks and thrusts. Tears prick my eyes. Did Henry feel his children close against him as they shifted and settled in the womb and if he did, was he moved at all? A hundred years later Edith's embryos would have been removed and the haemophilia-free ones selected and George would never have been born.

It can't have been anything like this that Henry hoped to attain by his study of his son's disease. Designer babies would have been beyond his imagination. Did he intend experimenting on the child? Trying out various methods of stopping the bleeding? 'Don't,' Jude would say. If he did it's fairly certain he never carried them out. Because, almost from the first, he loved George. Late in life he learned what love was and it must have struck him with a kind of horror and terrible pain. Even his feeling for Richard Hamilton hadn't been like this.

Why he loved this sick child when he felt nothing much for his heir and his daughters no one can tell. He hadn't cared much for any woman and what he'd have called love would have been a powerful sexual attraction. It must have seemed to him a terrible irony that this boy he had spent years striving to bring into existence, this summit of all his hopes, was rendered quite useless for his purposes by so intangible and indefinable a thing as love. A mere emotion had destroyed all his aims and ambitions. But he was helpless against it. Circumstances had controlled him. Circumstances had won. He loved George with a passionate, consuming love so that he was unable to discipline him as he had his

464

other children, unable to utter a cross word to him, scarcely able to separate himself even for a few hours from this beloved child.

As to the *magnum opus*, that would never be written. While he saw his son suffer, his unstoppable bleeds, his swollen joints, his scarcely to be endured pain, his weakness, he could no longer even turn his thoughts to haemophilia except in respect of the boy. And he had caused all this! By his deliberate long-drawn out efforts, his calculation, he had brought this suffering and this no doubt early death on the sole creature he had ever cared for. And his life's work had become horrible to him, its details to be banished from his mind.

Remorse. This was what so cruelly upset Tony Agnew. I've not much doubt all of it appeared in the last essays in the vanished notebook, the outpourings of Henry Nanther's heart as he wrote down something very different from the great work he'd planned. Why did Clara abstract it? And from where? Not one of the trunks, surely. Perhaps she found it in one of those secret desk drawers so dear to the Victorian heart. Or even lying open on his desk, abandoned by him when he was taken suddenly ill with his fatal heart attack.

Henry had expelled her from his study when she dared to ask him if haemophilia was what was wrong with her brother. Did she keep it to gloat in later years over her father's remorse? Hardly. She wasn't like that. We don't know what was in the rest of the notebook. It may have contained confessions of his now regretted unkindness to the rest of his family, even a description of how he set about tracing and finding Edith, and Clara kept it to prove to herself that her father had been sorry for his treatment of her and her sisters in the end. But, no. She hated him for what he had done to her brother and perhaps to her sisters too. She kept it not for gloating but as evidence. For a future biographer? For me? She intended to tell Alexander, the heir, the 'head of the family'. She intended to tell him and perhaps to show him, but Alexander died first.

Henry watched George slowly dying and he knew that whatever self-congratulation he may have gone in for in the past, he was powerless to help him. Truly, he had murdered his posterity in advance. Would his daughters go through this when they had sons? He'd have done better, he must sometimes have thought, to have killed Edith and then himself on their wedding night. But he hadn't, he had carried out a monstrous pursuit in the name of science, more properly called self-glorification. And this was the result.

He didn't last long after George's death. His poor heart staggered on for a few months and then it finally broke. In agreement with Tony, I pity him too, I could weep for him. If I were a sentimentalist as well as melodramatic, I too would go over to Kensal Green and put flowers on his grave.

I gently shift my body from under Jude's and the bouncing twins. My arm is numb and I've got what feels like a frozen shoulder. I'll tell her in the morning what I've known to be true ever since I talked to Tony. I can't write Henry's life. Foolishly perhaps I can't face other people knowing what my great-grandfather did. I can't set it all down and have what I'd once have given a lot for, some Sunday newspaper offering to serialize the more sensational bits. The idea of people discussing it with me makes me shiver. Henry has jinxed me, I should never have begun on his biography.

Bloody Henry. Poor bloody Henry.